PRAISE FOR CAROLYN MILLER

"I have been waiting for TJ's story and am so glad it's here! It's perfect...This is truly a story about loving the unlovable and the blessings that come as a result." ~ *GOODREADS review*

"There is nothing like a wonderful redemption story where someone changes their life and becomes a better version of themselves. It is a good reminder to me that God offers incredible grace to all of us." ~ *GOODREADS review*

"Carolyn Miller keeps on turning out these beautifully written, tender hearted books!... There was humor and brilliant bantering conversations, heart stopping romance, as well as exciting descriptions (and sometimes dangerous passages of play) of hockey games. Well worth the late night/early morning read!" ~ *KAYE'S REVIEWS & NEWS*

"A sweet love story that continues the Original Six Hockey series by Carolyn Miller. The setting of Montreal with the Gardens and all the French woven throughout was delightful!" ~ *GOODREADS review*

"I am emerging out of my book hangover after reading *Checked Impressions* by Carolyn Miller....The romance, humor and themes of identity are so enjoyable and make for a great read!" ~ *BECKY'S BOOKSHELVES*

"A fun sports-themed contemporary romance, this makes for a great, quick read...perfect for those days that you want a story about trust and love and navigating the ups and downs of being with that special someone." ~ *GOODREADS review*

"Adrenaline, chemistry, romance, and lots of wooing!... You do not have to be a fan of sports or even knowledgeable in hockey and short track to appreciate *Love on Ice*." ~ *GOODREADS review*

"Carolyn Miller scores another win with *Love on Ice*, the second book in her Original Six Hockey series. I absolutely loved the faith thread in this story. It's message that success does not lie on what we do, but who we are is powerful." ~ *GOODREADS review*

"*The Breakup Project* is a fun, charming, and faith-filled contemporary romance with adorable characters set in the competitive North American ice hockey world. Highly recommended." ~ *NARELLE ATKINS, Author of Solo Tu & Her Tycoon Hero*

"Displaying a flair for comedy and witty dialog, Miller is clearly an author to watch...with clever, snappy repartee, creating an exciting and fast-paced read." ~ *LIBRARY JOURNAL*

BIG APPLE ATONEMENT

CAROLYN MILLER

Visit Carolyn Miller at www.carolynmillerauthor.com

Cover design by KT Design

Edited by Katie Donovan

Bible references are from the New International Version.

ALSO BY CAROLYN MILLER

<u>The Original Six hockey series</u>
The Breakup Project
Love on Ice
Checked Impressions
Hearts and Goals
Big Apple Atonement
Muskoka Blue

<u>The Independence Islands series</u>
Restoring Fairhaven
Regaining Mercy
Reclaiming Hope
Rebuilding Hearts
Refining Josie

Historical:

<u>Regency Wallflowers</u>
Dusk's Darkest Shores
Midnight's Budding Morrow
Dawn's Untrodden Green

<u>Regency Brides: Legacy of Grace</u>
The Elusive Miss Ellison
The Captivating Lady Charlotte
The Dishonorable Miss DeLancey

<u>Regency Brides: Promise of Hope</u>

Winning Miss Winthrop

Miss Serena's Secret

The Making of Mrs Hale

<u>Regency Brides: Daughters of Aynsley</u>

A Hero for Miss Hatherleigh

Underestimating Miss Cecilia

Misleading Miss Verity

'Heaven and Nature Sing' from the Joy to the World Christmas
novella collection

CHAPTER 1

October
Tarrytown, New York

He was, quite possibly, the ugliest man she had ever seen.

Margarita Anastacia Moritello stared at the muted television screen as the mid-game interview continued. Curly red-blond hair fanned away from under the hockey helmet—Ronald McDonald with a mullet. His nose was skewed, with enough bump to suggest a visit to a plastic surgeon might be in order. Bushy eyebrows menaced over eyes so blue and cold they could be mistaken for an ice-strewn Hudson River. But it was his beard, full and messy, like a lumberjack's, crawling over his face, that drew most attention. She could barely see his mouth, but he was talking, and from what could be seen, he was missing enough teeth she could almost drive her Volkswagen Beetle through them.

"A face only a mother could love, poor thing," Lacey Carruthers murmured from her chair near the big room's empty fireplace, sidling a look at her. "Don't you think, Emma?"

Emma—easier to say than Margarita Anastacia and sounding less like a certain kind of drink—sipped her tea and nodded.

"Hard to believe women find hockey players like him attractive."

"Really?" Emma almost choked on her tea. "Why?"

"I don't know. Maybe it's the glamor, maybe it's the money. I can't see it myself, but then, I don't need to." Emma's best friend smiled, stood, and moved up the creaking stairs to conduct the night rounds of the children's rooms. No. Lacey Carruthers certainly didn't need to worry about the handsomeness of other men. Not when she had her own handsome husband already.

"Do you think he's attractive?" Jacob Browne, Hopetoun's direct support worker, asked Emma.

Hadn't she just made her opinion clear? "No," she said firmly. Anyone of TJ Woletsky's character, let alone his looks, would never appeal.

Jacob studied her a moment longer, until she found herself wishing for Lacey to return from upstairs. Not that there was anything wrong with Jacob. It was just he had never tickled her fancy the way guys like Beau Nash or Dan Walton did. Not that she needed a guy to be handsome or play pro hockey, but it didn't hurt. And the fact that both men were unapologetic about their Christian faith, which translated into good works like running camps for disadvantaged kids—she'd seen Dan's amazing pictures on Instagram—meant they'd forever be a cut above the men she encountered in real life. Apart from her dad and brother, and Tim Carruthers, of course. And a million miles above the man whose history of fights was now being shown on TV.

"All asleep," Lacey reported, re-entering the common room and settling into the sofa next to Emma, cradling a cup of tea that smelled like peppermint. "They're still on Woletsky?" she said, studying the TV. "Poor guy."

"Poor?" Jacob snorted, pushing back his floppy blond hair. "How can you say that? Woletsky's just a highly paid goon."

"But don't you ever wonder why he acts that way?" Lacey continued. "Tim and I talked about this the other day. I know TJ's apologized for some of his hits before, like when he cracked Mike Vaughan's ribs a few years ago. I don't think he can be all bad."

Emma glanced behind her. "Don't let Leona hear you say that."

Lacey sighed. "She's still bitter, isn't she?"

"With every right," Emma said, her chest heating. "After what he did to Nick."

"Poor Nick." Lacey's face softened.

Nick Grenier, Leona Cherry's nephew, was really the man deserving sympathy here. Emma's heart panged as it did every time she thought about him. She really should see him again soon.

A noise at the door stole their attention to where Leona wandered in, her weariness evident in her slumped shoulders and lumbering step. Emma immediately rose. "Would you like a cup of tea?"

"Oh, yes, Margarita. Thank you, dear."

A glance at the TV showed the first intermission interview had—thankfully—cut to commentary for another game. Not New York's, though. As the others enquired about Leona's visit to Buffalo, Emma hastened to make her boss's chamomile tea, her heart soft with compassion.

Mrs. Leona Cherry, residence manager of Hopetoun Children's Home, had had a trying few years, caring for her terminally ill husband whose death last year seemed to have precipitated her own health battles, which had necessitated Emma stepping into the management role a few times. Then Leona's sister, Helen, had suffered a fatal heart attack in January, which was followed by TJ Woletsky's mammoth hit on her nephew Nick earlier this month—a hit that had seen Nick's team, Buffalo, fined by the league for questioning why Woletsky had only been assessed two minor penalties and a five thousand dollar fine for roughing, when all the commentators thought he deserved his fifth suspension at the very least. Hopefully Leona would feel too tired to insist on watching the rest of the game between Montreal and Woletsky's team, L.A.

Emma handed the tea to Leona, who thanked her wearily. "You're an angel."

"Saint Margarita," murmured Jacob, which provoked an exchange of rolled eyes between Lacey and Emma as Emma moved to resume her seat.

A scream punctuated the night. Emma held up a hand. "I'm up, so I'll go."

She hurried out of the spacious living room and up the stairs to the second floor, where the girls' rooms were located. Whimpers came from behind a pale pink door. She flicked on the light and moved to the bed where a small figure gasped, eyes shut, cowering under the bedclothes.

Emma gently rubbed the small form's back. "Shh, it's okay, Nessa. You're safe."

Lord, please heal Nessa's nightmares. Let her experience Your peace and sweet sleep.

She continued whispering prayers, stroking the curly dark hair until the whimpers eased. Nessa had experienced too much horror for one so young. She needed all the love and security that Hopetoun could provide.

Thank God that Karinda, a recent arrival to the group home, still slept. Nobody needed another night of broken sleep. Emma yawned, glanced around the girls' bedroom once more, then carefully closed the door.

She re-entered the big room and settled back into her seat. "Nessa. Poor sweetheart."

"What are we going to do with her?" Leona sighed.

"Pray."

"Yes, yes, apart from that."

Emma slid a look at her boss. Why did she always sound like dealing with Nessa was a hardship? Hopetoun existed to help children needing additional support after traumatic experiences, providing a safe, nurturing, family-like environment in a group home while children waited to be matched to a foster family. Nessa had seen counsellors and psychiatrists, and Emma had driven her to the doctor's just this afternoon. All of them said she would talk one day. The girl's trauma meant that finding an appropriate home with a foster family who could understand her complex needs was taking longer than anyone liked.

Leona offered an apologetic smile. "Sorry, Margarita. It's been a tough week."

Emma nodded. With the recent bout of chicken pox and the furnace threatening to give up the ghost, this past week had been tough on all the staff. The part-time staff and volunteers who came in each day, like Jacob and Lacey, had a slightly easier time of it—they at least could escape the insanity that sometimes overwhelmed Hopetoun. Emma picked up her tea—cold now, but she took a defiant sip.

"I don't know how you can drink cold tea," Lacey teased.

"I think I'm too tired to care," she admitted.

"I can make you another one," Jacob offered eagerly.

"I'm fine. Sit down. The game's about to start again," she said, waving at the screen.

The television flickered to show highlights of the other games being played tonight. Emma sat back and relaxed against the tattered cushions of the old sofa. Friday night. Hockey night. If she couldn't be at a game—like tonight, when New York were playing in Texas—then watching favorite players like Montreal goalie Beau Nash on TV was a nice way to escape the worries. And the loneliness. And the fear that here she was, thirty-one and not-been-kissed-in-ten-years, destined to spend the rest of her Friday nights with television and a cup of tea for company. Not that she minded. Too much.

Lacey's phone buzzed. "It's Tim."

Tim Carruthers, husband of her best friend Lacey, and New York's captain. "Tell him good luck tonight," Emma said.

Lacey grinned, texting back. "He doesn't need luck. He's playing so hot right now. But then, he is so hot, right?"

How to reply?

"That's nice, dear," Leona murmured.

Emma smothered a smile as coverage resumed of the second period of the Montreal-L.A. game. They'd switch over to the New York game soon, but any hockey was better than none. And if it meant a glimpse of Beau Nash, well, all the better.

The L.A. players streamed onto the ice, and already she could feel Leona's tension. It was there in her rigid shoulders, her fixed glare at the screen, as if she was gathering her hatred for the man who'd soon appear.

A hiss escaped Leona as TJ Woletsky skated back onto the ice. Emma exchanged glances with Lacey. Maybe it was time to change the station.

"Nash is playing well," Jacob observed. "Hasn't dropped a game since his move to Montreal."

"He must like it there," Emma said, glad for the shift in focus.

"I think he does," Lacey said, casting Emma a glance. "Did I mention he might have a girlfriend?"

"What?"

"I don't think it's a secret. Or maybe it is. Tim told me a little while ago, and I may have forgotten to share."

"Oh well." Emma gave an exaggerated sigh. "There go my dreams, crumbling into dust."

"You don't seriously like a guy like him, do you?" Jacob scoffed.

"Why not? He's tall"—like, really tall—"and is a Christian, and seems so sweet, and I *love* his accent—"

"Have you even met him?" he asked, one dark eyebrow raised.

Well, no. But, "I've met a few hockey players over the years"—thanks to her work here—"and I can tell who's a good one and who isn't," she insisted.

"Like him," Leona muttered, stabbing her manicured finger at the screen.

Woletsky skated toward the goal, shooting to Damon, who flicked it forward to Pavel, who struck it back to Macoretti. L.A.'s shots were quick and clean. Pavel shot at the goal, but Beau blocked it.

"Yes!" Emma clapped him on.

The puck slid back to Woletsky, who took his turn shooting at the net, but Beau caught it in his right glove, holding on as Woletsky got in his face.

"Woletsky's such a jerk," Jacob muttered.

No argument from anyone here.

A swift glance at Leona's narrowed eyes and tight expression showed it was definitely time to change the channel. But before Emma could pick up the remote control, Woletsky had charged into the net in a move that saw Beau stumble backward, his head striking the pipes before he slumped to the ground, ominously still.

Emma's heart hitched.

"Oh no!" Lacey cried.

Jacob swore softly, but for once Emma didn't reprimand him, her attention focused on Leona, who was breathing deeply, her brow furrowed, her hands clenched. "Leona? Are you okay?"

"No. No, I'm not okay," Leona cried, shaking her head with jerky movements. "How could they let him play again? This is exactly what happened with poor Nick!"

Well, not exactly. Nick had been slammed into the boards,

not a net, in a hit that the NHL had said was legal. Not that anyone here liked to admit that.

They watched as medics surrounded Beau and the camera moved to where the back-up goalie was limbering up.

"God, heal him," Lacey murmured.

"Amen." Emma watched as Beau was stretchered off, then quickly changed the channel for the New York game. She clutched Lacey's hand and gave a gentle squeeze. No wife wanted to see the reality of what could happen in a game like this. Not that anyone had ever died from playing hockey—that she knew of, anyway. But injuries happened and could be severe. Witness Nick's possibly career-ending hit ten days ago.

But even on this station, as the commentators gave a pre-game summary of New York's game, there was already discussion of the Montreal-L.A. game, the hit on poor Beau replayed again.

"Woletsky at it again," the balding former-NHL player said, shaking his head. "How long is it gonna take before L.A. gets rid of him?"

"He's a liability, that's for sure. I can't see any team wanting him after this," his graying co-anchor said. "Especially after what he did to poor Nick Grenier last week."

Leona inhaled sharply.

"That's right," the sports host said. "Grenier, and now Nash, who has always been known as one of the good guys in the game. I really can't see what Woletsky was hoping to achieve there."

"Apart from getting kicked out of the game?" his co-anchor said.

"Here's hoping," Jacob muttered.

"I can't wait to see what the league does with him this time," Lacey added.

But when the referee assessed the hit as requiring only a ten-minute game misconduct, Emma and her fellow employees of Hopetoun House were as stunned as the sports hosts.

"Are you kidding me?" Lacey shook her head. "No way is that fair."

"Montreal's not gonna be happy about this, I can assure you," the balding TV host said. "I think the league will be hearing from Tony Francois soon. Ten minutes for that kind of play?"

"Everyone knows you don't hit the goalie," his co-anchor said. "This is a big mistake from both Woletsky and the ref. Considering Woletsky's history, I would've expected a suspension at the very least. He's played for three teams in the last four years, and how many times has he been suspended now? Four? And for what many would consider lesser hits. I think there'll be plenty of people asking where's the justice."

Jacob muttered a less-than-glowing opinion of the referee's intellect while Leona pushed to her feet. "I can't stand this. I'm going to bed. I hate this game. I hate that man!" she cried, pointing at the television, where Woletsky sat in the penalty box, expressionless, mouth-guard hanging free as, around him, red-clad Montreal fans pounded out their anger on the glass screens.

"Leona," Emma called, but her boss waved her away, instead heading to her bedroom on the floor above.

Lacey grabbed Emma's hand and drew her back to the sofa. "Leave her. You know she'll only get further frustrated and upset the more sympathy she gets."

True. Emma sank back into her seat, her nerves as skittish as Mom's cat Twinky.

Hockey was amazing, the game so fast and requiring such skill, but at moments like this, she realized how brutal it could be too.

She gripped Lacey's hand, wishing she could impart assurance that Tim would be safe tonight. But she could barely watch New York's attempts to thwart Dallas's aggression, her mind and heart spinning with thoughts and prayers for what she'd seen tonight. Prayers for healing for Beau and Nick, for protection for Tim, for peace for their loved ones. And—as the sports commentators had pointed out—prayers that there would finally be justice for the thug who skated for L.A. Her skin crawled. Bile rose in her throat.

TJ Woletsky.

~

Los Angeles

"WOLETSKY, TAKE A SEAT."

TJ nodded his response and sat down across the desk from his arms-crossed coach and L.A.'s general manager. Uh oh. He'd seen that look before. It never boded well. He slid a look at Phil Mowbray, his stony-faced agent, and braced himself.

The GM looked at him, his expression hard. "I've just had Montreal's GM chewing off my ear. They're not happy."

No. He didn't imagine they would be.

"That hit on Nash was the final straw. Especially following the fight earlier."

"Yeah, but he started it—"

"Enough!" TJ jumped as his coach slammed his fist on the desk, setting things rattling. "Sooner or later you've got to admit to your bad attitude and take some responsibility."

"But Coach—"

"No. Don't sit there and try and make excuses. You've been making excuses for as long as we've known you. We thought taking a chance on you would bring energy to the team, but you've brought exactly the wrong kind of energy."

TJ had always thought his coach's motivational speeches, with their emphasis on energy and dynamics, a little too touchy-feely airy-fairy mumbo jumbo, like his previous girlfriend's fixation with Feng Shui. He also figured now was not the time to share that opinion.

Phil cleared his throat. "You brought my client here to do what he normally does, which is to use his skills for enforcing clean play."

Thanks, Phil. TJ settled more comfortably in his chair. That was exactly right. He'd always hated injustice and deceit. Maybe that was why he'd hated his childhood.

"But the problem is that he's not been."

Huh? Offense at being talked about instead of talked to spiked into protest. "Excuse me, Coach, but I have been. The league hasn't found my actions illegal. You saw the penalty I got for Nash. Ten minutes, and I barely touched the guy," he complained.

"The problem is that nobody else saw it that way," the GM growled.

When the GM growled, it was time to shut up.

"We knew we were taking a risk with you, with your reputation for hard hits. How many guys have you injured now? I seem to remember something about Mike Vaughan in Boston when you were playing for Florida."

"That was a clean hit, and Mike and I were friendly enough when we played together in Calgary. The guy invited me to his wedding, for Pete's sake."

Phil nodded. He'd been there too.

Why Mike had invited TJ to his wedding, and Thanksgiving the following year, TJ barely knew. But Mike had always been generous that way. Someone TJ'd almost dare count as a friend, if he had to count anyone. "Just because I play hard doesn't mean I play dirty."

"That's not how the fans see it."

The fans. TJ swallowed further protest. Fans meant dollars, which affected contracts. Like his. He folded his arms and glanced out the window, catching a glimpse of sparkling Pacific Ocean.

"I was really hoping this could be a turnaround," his coach said.

Well, yeah. TJ had kinda hoped that too. A new team, a fresh start, a chance to finally redeem himself, to prove the critics wrong—

"And there's still time," Phil said. "He's signed for this season."

"But ever since that hit on Grenier, we've had sponsors threatening to leave, and now, with Nash too, let's just say people's patience has worn thin."

Wait. TJ's gaze swiveled back to the GM. This wasn't sounding good.

"You're a liability, TJ."

He clamped his mouth shut. Exactly what he'd known all his life. The problem child. Skating on thin ice forever. Booted from team to team, as if getting drafted in the first round all those years ago had been forgotten.

"We can't afford liabilities."

"Sir, Coach, I can do better. I will do better," he assured, sitting straighter in his seat. "But you gotta know that I'm just trying to do the job you brought me here for. You wanted toughness, I bring toughness."

"You bring complaints," the GM muttered.

TJ cast a look at Phil, who had also now crossed his arms and seemed to be scowling at the GM's fancy fish tank, as if little Nemo might be responsible for the GM's bad mood. Uh oh. Looked like he wasn't gonna get any more help from his agent.

"I'm sorry, sir. If it makes anyone feel better, I apologized to Nash." Via text, but hey. The dude wasn't about to answer a call. They never did.

"Did you speak to Grenier like we asked?" the GM said.

Oh. That. "When I tried, he refused to pick up. I told you last time that I'd texted"—he hurried on, not liking the look the GM shot him—"and that I'd visit him next time I was on the east coast."

"So you haven't."

Well, er, "No," he owned.

The GM sighed. Ah, the sound of disappointment. TJ knew it well.

"I think you'd have to agree that whole incident was very unfortunate," Phil said. "TJ can't be blamed for what was essentially Grenier not properly watching the play. The league seemed to understand that, which is why he wasn't fined more."

Judging from the scowl being shot Phil's way, TJ didn't think his agent was helping any.

"Blaming the victim for what he didn't do is not what we do here. Not when we're talking about what *you* didn't do." Now the GM's scowl was being levelled TJ's way. "Woletsky, we're trading you."

"What?"

His question was echoed a second later by Phil. The tension ratcheted up more. Why hadn't Phil done more to save him? What kind of useless agent was he?

"For a seventh round pick."

TJ blinked. "Are you serious?" How insulting. Humiliation prickled his skin, made his gut clench. He gripped the chair's wooden arms to force himself to not escape.

"Where?" Phil asked.

"New York."

New York? Why would an Original Six team want him? Maybe he could swallow the indignity—

"Apparently their farm team thinks you'd be a fit."

"Hartford?" Phil asked.

TJ's coach—well, his former coach—nodded.

TJ coughed. He couldn't be serious. "This is a joke, right?"

"No joke," his coach said.

"I'm gonna go play in the AHL?" Talk about a demotion.

"If they'll have you."

What? There were questions about whether he'd even play in the minors?

He shot a panicked look at Phil, who'd sunk his head in his hand, and knew there was no hope for him there.

No. He'd give anything to not go back to playing in hockey's minor league. Goodbye, dream apartment with beach view. Goodbye, great climate. Goodbye, great life. Hello, the dynamics of professional sports. He swallowed a stupid desire to laugh—maybe his coach did know something about energies and dynamics after all—and forced himself to shrug, then stand. Not for anything would he let them see how much this cut him. He'd play the flippant card until the end. "Okay."

CHAPTER 2

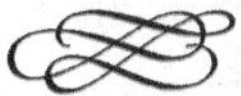

The hospital room was dim, shadows stretching across the floor. Emma waited in the doorway for the nurse to finish talking to Leona, but from what she could hear, it seemed to consist of "no change," "no improvement," and "no news."

Sadness crossed Emma's chest as the slump in Leona's shoulders grew more pronounced. Poor lady. Poor Nick. She prayed for both as she stood waiting, offering the nurse a small smile on her exit from the room.

"Keep an eye on her," the nurse murmured, inclining her head to Leona. "She looks really tired."

"Of course," Emma said. Leona was exhausted. Emma's workload reflected that, picking up the pieces Leona kept missing. Concern for her boss had led to Emma's offer to chauffeur Leona here on Emma's day off.

She stole into the room where Nick lay, his form motionless under the blanket save for the faint movement of his chest. Her eyes filled, and she blinked tears back as she placed a gentle hand on Leona's back. "Have a seat," she whispered, pointing to the nearby chair.

Leona wilted into it, and Emma shifted to the other side as Leona grasped Nick's hand. "She said there's been no change."

Emma nodded as if she hadn't already heard.

The past two weeks had proved to be a rollercoaster of emotions, trying to buoy Leona's spirits while dealing with the Home's issues as well as concerns of her own. But at least Nick was out of the coma, even though his concussion and other injuries would keep him off the ice for months, if not forever. Poor Nick. How long would he remain here? He'd need a haircut soon—his dark hair was getting longer—and judging from the scruff on his chin, he still refused to be shaved. A twinge crossed her chest.

The room was silent save for Leona's rasping breath and Nick's soft exhalations. Sorrow arrowed through Emma at the waste of life he represented. How could a game he loved bring him so undone? But even though Leona's hatred was fixed and forceful, Emma knew it was unfair to lay the whole blame at Woletsky's feet. Accidents happened. Even if it would've gone a long way for him to offer Nick an apology.

Her gaze trailed to Leona, to the dark shadows under her eyes that testified to too many late nights due to her fears. Too many late nights pleading with Hopetoun's board of trustees, begging for more money. Winter was soon approaching, and the furnace needed replacing. As assistant residence manager, Emma did what she could to support, but Leona was growing increasingly brittle. She really needed a break. Emma had hoped today's visit would bring a change in her demeanor, but no joy. God bless Lacey for deputizing at the Home today.

Leona released a heavy sigh, sparking fresh concern. "What is it?" Emma asked gently.

"I don't know what to do," Leona said. "Should I keep him here? It's so expensive."

It was. But the compensation awarded by the NHL's player fund dealt with most of the astronomical medical costs. Besides, what was the alternative? Leona could scarcely look after him at Hopetoun. "It's a good thing he has insurance."

Leona shuddered. "I can't imagine what would happen otherwise."

"And it's a good thing you're able to be here to visit, and that this didn't happen in Vancouver or someplace far away."

"I suppose you're right, but oh, it's hard to be positive sometimes."

True.

Nick stirred, long dark-lashed blinks finally shuddering to awareness. "Oh, Nicholas," Leona cried. "It's so good to see you."

He blinked and drew back, as if uncertain he thought the same.

Emma shoved the uncharitable thought down and ventured a small wave. "Hi, Nick."

He shifted as if moving to face her, but the agonizingly long time he took made her scamper to join Leona on the other side of the bed. Here, with her back to the door, he'd avoid sunlight in his eyes.

"Hi." His voice was flat, and there was no animation in his gaze.

"How are you feeling today?" Leona asked.

His attention shifted to Emma, and she recognized the weary resignation of being asked that same question every time his aunt came. Sorrow dug deep. How could Emma help him when his aunt—her boss—barely knew what to do?

"Have you had any visitors?" Emma asked, dreading to know the answer.

He squinted, as if questioning her intelligence.

"I'll take it that's a no, then."

His top lip curled in a sneer. "Can you see anyone wanting to visit me?"

She pressed her lips together, but her eyebrows rose of their own accord as her head tilted to his aunt.

He exhaled. "Apart from you two, of course."

Leona sighed heavily. "I wish people would understand how hard this is."

"Yeah, it's pretty hard for you," he said sarcastically.

Emma coughed. "Leona, do you think Nick might like a snack?"

Nick rolled his eyes at Emma, at her code for "distract Leona," but he played along. "That'd be great. The food here isn't wonderful."

"Oh, but it's costing so much," Leona complained.

He shot Emma another look as if to say *look what you've done.*

She shrugged, keeping her gaze narrowed on him until he turned away.

"Margarita, dear, will you be okay if I leave you for a few moments?"

"I'll manage," she promised.

After checking what Nick wanted to eat, then worrying aloud if it might make him gain weight before admitting that perhaps that might be a good thing after all, Leona finally left.

"Whew," Emma said, wiping at her brow.

Nick's lips flickered into what could almost be a smile. "Thanks for making me fat."

"You're welcome."

Okay, so that was definitely a smile, small though it was. She shifted closer, grasped his hand. "So, what have you been doing?" she asked. "How is therapy going?"

He shot her a look as filled with skepticism as the look he'd shot his aunt before.

"So it's going well, then?"

"You're real funny," he mumbled.

"I know."

She squeezed his hand, glad to see that today, at least, he'd found something of the sense of humor she remembered from high school. Nick had been good at hockey even then, spending so much time playing that she'd tutored him in math. They'd lost contact when he moved away and only reconnected a few years ago when she took the job at Hopetoun. She'd been pleasantly surprised to find her new boss's nephew was someone she knew from over a decade ago. Not that they'd had much to do with each other. Until the hit from TJ Woletsky, which had seen Nick in a coma for days and stuck motionless in bed for what would likely prove weeks. And despite the efforts of the staff and all the encouragement she and Leona could offer, his spirits seemed little better than when he'd first wakened.

"What's going on in your world?" he asked slowly.

She glanced at him in surprise. This was the first time he'd asked about her in a long time. Their conversations in recent years had been swift and mostly focused on hockey. She swallowed, thinking Nick wouldn't like to know about hockey or the latest incident involving the man who'd inflicted damage on another. So instead, she told him about her brother and sister, Marc and Rose, and their jobs in the city at the FDNY and the Rockettes.

"Rockettes, huh?"

"Yeah. Marc surprised us all."

This did score a small chuckle, something she'd count as a win.

She squeezed his hand again. "Rose has worked so hard. It's wonderful to see her scoring such a gig." Even if she was only the swing dancer at this stage. "She and Marc are sharing this tiny apartment, which apparently works well when he's on shift. He likes to come back home to Mom and Dad's when he's not on call, so they're making it work."

"Proud big sister, huh?"

"Yes." And sometimes envious big sister, too. But she was doing her dream job, so she couldn't complain. And it wasn't like she had skills or interest in dancing or dealing with fires. "I'm hoping to catch up with them sometime soon."

He nodded. "And you?"

She shrugged. "Same old, same old. Kids are doing well, although Nessa—you met her before—she still has her night-mares, and Brandon is still struggling along." Poor little man. "It's Halloween soon, so we'll probably do a party of some sort. We're supposed to do some pumpkin carving soon, too."

Something she still *really* needed to organize. In past years these kinds of events had seen visits from various groups—including Tim and his teammates—happy to splash a little joy, something which the children had always responded to well. Who didn't love a nice surprise, something that proved a point of difference in their day? It was a little like Nick's own ordeal, stuck here in a hospital room, seeing the same faces day by day. Anything that could bring brightness or cheer was welcome, and part of Emma's role was to provide a steady diet of enter-tainment and distraction, which meant coordinating the occa-sional outing squeezed around medical and counselling visits. It was often easier for people to come to the Home, which saw volunteers with music expertise, art therapy, gardening, and more. But with all of her extra duties, Emma hadn't been as organized as she preferred to be.

"You should come," she said. "I'm sure the kids would love to see you."

"Me?" This time Nick's laughter held mockery as he slid his hand from hers. "Nobody wants to see me, Emma. Didn't you get the memo?"

"But the children—"

"Especially the children," he muttered. "You really want them seeing someone like me? 'Hey, look, kids, this is what you have to look forward to. You'll be a has-been at thirty.' Yeah, thanks but no thanks."

She pressed her lips together and bowed her head.

"You should go," he said roughly.

"But Leona—"

"Comes here because she feels guilty or has some stupid sense of family duty that makes her come. She doesn't care for me."

"You're wrong," she countered. "You're always on her mind. She cares for you deeply. What do you think she's doing, up here as often as she is?"

"She comes because you make her."

She swiped her hair behind her ear. Well, yes, that might be true, but also, "She loves you, Nick."

"I don't know why."

She stifled a sigh. When he grew morose like this, she felt renewed appreciation for Leona's patience. "You know we care about you," she said softly, looking into his eyes, willing him to believe her.

His gaze held hers for a long time, then his lips flattened and he turned away. But this time, when she placed her hand upon his, he didn't shrug it off. So she squeezed his hand and bowed her head and prayed. Prayed for Nick. For Leona. For the kids. For health, a sense of purpose, and God's direction. And that one day they might be able to forgive the man who had brought them to this place.

TJ HALTED outside the opened door, the room revealing a woman beside Nick Grenier's bed. The woman's wavy dark hair flowed halfway down her back and held reddish glints, and the sight of her holding Nick's hand did something strange to TJ's heart. Okay, so he had an intellectual understanding of what happened when a guy got injured and the consequences for his family and friends. But TJ himself had never experienced major injury, and having little in the way of either family or friends meant he'd never really thought through the ramifications. Hospitals. Tears. Broken dreams. He knew about that last one, at least. But that moment of intensity passing between Nick and the woman before—for all his cluelessness, he wasn't that stupid, at least—hit him harder than a puck to the face, slamming guilt through his chest.

He gritted his teeth. He hated feeling like he was desperately in the wrong when he was here trying to make things right. Hated standing here filled with indecision, wondering whether he should stay or leave. He tied his hair back, then tugged his plaid shirtsleeves over his forearms, covering the ink, glad he'd taken his agent's advice for once and trimmed his logger-like beard. He had no desire to put people more offside than his usual sparkling personality did. But everything about today had already proved a challenge, his trip through this part of upstate New York everything he remembered from ten years ago: dirty, run down, and depressing. No wonder people thought he was a perfect fit.

A shuffle beside him drew his attention to a nurse. "Can I help you?" she asked softly.

"I, uh, I'm just waiting," he muttered, gesturing inside the room.

"You're not family, are you?"

He shook his head no.

"A friend?"

Nope, not that either. Nick and the woman there would probably count him an enemy. He shrugged.

She glanced inside and nodded. "I'm still new here, but from what I've been told, he doesn't have much family—an aunt, or something. I think that one is his girlfriend."

He hadn't known Nick had a girlfriend. He felt even worse. "I, um, might come back later," he muttered.

It wasn't like he hadn't tried. He'd already sent the dude an apology message, like he usually did. He'd never actually visited any of them before. Of course, none of them had ever been in the hospital for this long before. But hey, he'd done all he could.

"You can go in," she encouraged.

Go in and spark new nightmares for the man in the bed and his girlfriend? He shouldn't have come. This was a bad idea. He chewed his bottom lip.

"Go on. It'll do him good to see a fresh face."

Yeah, probably not this face.

But before he had a chance to slip away, she'd entered the room, her fingers firmly grasping his sleeve and propelling his feet, still reluctant to move.

"Look! You have a visitor," she said brightly.

Nick's eyes widened, and the woman beside him gasped. Gut clenching, TJ glanced at her, got a glimpse of an open mouth and blue eyes behind glasses before his gaze swung back to Nick, whose scowl said TJ should've gone with his first, second, third, and fourth instincts and gone directly to the city instead of side-tracking here. "Hey," he offered with a lift of his hand.

"You."

"Me."

Nick's sneered look suggested he didn't think TJ amusing. "What are you doing here?"

"I was in the neighborhood."

Nick released a soft curse, which scored tight lips from the girlfriend.

"Came to see how you are. Say I'm sorry." Again.

"You've seen, now you can leave." Nick glanced away.

Come on. "You know it was an accident, right?" He glanced at the woman, now shooting him her own narrowed stare. "It wasn't intentional."

Her eyebrows lifted, sparking his defensiveness.

"Stuff happens," he insisted.

"Stuff always happens around you," Nick muttered.

Yep. It did. Had done so all his life. Witness his mom and dad's stellar blame game as they pinned their issues on him. Sure, he hadn't made it easy on them, but he'd realized long ago that the bombshell his mom dropped on him before releasing the hand grenade that had blown up his world hadn't been his fault. Was it any wonder people thought him such a screwup, with that lurking in his past?

"Believe it or not, I *am* sorry." TJ bit back the desire to point out that if Nick hadn't been looking away he'd likely be okay. How not to apologize, that.

"You seriously expect me to believe you?"

"That's on you." He shrugged. "Take it or leave it."

"Wow. That's your idea of an apology?" Nick scoffed.

Okay, so that hadn't been much better. But apologizing wasn't something he'd practiced much. Apparently he had some work to do.

The woman placed her hand on Nick's, which seemed to calm him down. Would that TJ had his own personal peacemaker.

"Okay, then. See you around."

Hope not—he could almost hear the words not said aloud. With a nod to the woman, who still eyed him askance, he pivoted and left the room. Only to encounter an older woman in the hall, whose mouth swung open as the candy bars she was holding spilled to the ground.

Great. A fan. Or non-fan, as the case seemed to be. "Here, let me get those for you," he said, reaching to collect the spilled candy.

"You're TJ Woletsky, aren't you?"

"Yeah."

"Don't!" she cried, shooing him away. "Don't you dare touch this!"

Yep, definitely a non-fan. He backed away.

"How dare you come here?" she said, her graying hair escaping a plastic clip dangling past her ears.

He backed farther away, hands held palms up. "Just came to offer my regrets."

"Regrets?" she screeched. "I'll give you regrets!"

With a speed he'd never have anticipated, she flew at him and slapped his face, her nails catching his cheek above his beard. As she shrieked about Nick and illness and money, he gently wrestled her hands away, conscious that she was older and frail-looking and that there were nursing staff hurrying from the other end of the hall.

Nick's girlfriend raced from the room. "Leona, leave him," she commanded, tugging the old woman away.

Huh. So the girlfriend did speak.

The nurse from before panted, catching her breath as she asked what was going on.

"That man!" The Leona woman pointed to TJ. "He's the one who put my nephew in a coma."

The nurse blinked. "I thought you were a friend."

"Friend? He's evil," Leona hissed with old-lady crazy eyes.

Well, he'd never been a saint, but—"That's going a bit far."

A slight movement drew his attention to the girlfriend, whose twitch of the lips vanished as she pointed to her left cheek. "You've got some blood."

He swiped a finger and examined his fingertip. So he did.

"Come on, Leona," she said, wrapping an arm around the woman and ushering her away with placatory words.

"It's probably best you leave now," the nurse from earlier said sternly. "And don't plan to return."

"No problem."

He strode out the hall to where he'd parked his bike, then shrugged on his jacket and tugged on the helmet. He'd done what L.A. had asked, gone above and beyond, and had no intention of returning. Or seeing either Nick or his crazy aunt again.

CHAPTER 3

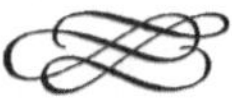

"Now, Brandon, can you please find me the yellow triangle?"

Brandon Smith, one of Hopetoun's kids awaiting placement, slowly lifted his head.

Emma offered a smile she hoped looked encouraging, digging deep for patience as he took his time before finally pointing to the pyramid-shaped piece. "Very good!"

He smiled his gap-toothed smile, and her heart knew another twist. Poor Brandon wasn't ever going to be high on the placement lists for wished-for kids, not with his intellectual delay and teeth that would forever need expensive correction. It was just another example of how shallow this world could be, that those children deemed to have sweet smiles could zoom ahead in life while the plain and challenging ones forever lagged, their sweet natures quite overlooked. Not that looks automatically secured a golden future. She knew that only too well.

"Read?" he asked, pointing to the book waiting on the side of the table.

She nodded. "As soon as we put the rest of the puzzle pieces away."

"Puzzle."

"That's right." She encouraged him to find the pieces, waiting as he took his time.

"You're so patient," said Lacey a few minutes later, the story now read and Brandon having joined the others watching TV. "I don't know how I'll ever be patient enough to be a mom."

Emma grabbed her arm. "Is there something you're not telling me?"

"No! No." The amusement filling Lacey's face faded. "I'm starting a new round of IVF, so here's hoping." She crossed her fingers.

"I'll be praying," Emma promised.

"Thanks."

It seemed an odd thing that just as some deserving kids could not find homes, neither could some deserving couples gain a family. And while there might seem to be an automatic answer connecting the two, it wasn't always that easy. And who could blame Lacey and Tim for wanting a family of their own rather than taking on someone else's child? Some people's parenting skills made her question God's wisdom in allowing them such a privilege—witness many of the children here—while denying other worthy candidates such a joy. Emma's former college roommate had been married to Tim for five years now, and just as back then, Lacey had never shied away from sharing her private thoughts. Not that Lacey was privy to all of Emma's secrets.

The Home's phone rang, and Emma scurried to Leona's office to answer it. Leona's absence today—unsurprising after her stressful encounter with Woletsky yesterday—had drawn new pressures, some of which were thankfully alleviated by Lacey's staunch assistance. God bless her friend and her willingness to step in and help again.

"Phone's ringing!" called Lily.

Emma gave the small blonde girl a quick pat on the shoulder as she hurried past her before snatching up the insistent machine. "Hello? This is Emma at Hopetoun."

"Ah, Emma, this is Richard." Mr. DeVries, the president of Hopetoun's board of trustees. "I wonder, is Leona available?"

"I'm afraid not," she said.

"Oh."

He sounded so nonplussed that she explained. "I'm afraid she had a trying day yesterday and was unable to come into work today."

"I see."

Richard DeVries was a compassionate but business-savvy man, perfect for the role he undertook for no recompense or glory.

"Is there something I can help you with?" she asked.

He sighed, and she knew a disconcerting twist within. "John, the accounts clerk, mentioned something, but it's probably nothing. Nothing to worry about at the moment, anyway," he added. "Perhaps you can let her know I'm eager to speak to her when she returns."

"I'll pass it on," she promised. Although, whether the same could be said about Leona's desire to speak to him remained to be seen. Sometimes she got the feeling Leona didn't like Richard overly and avoided him. And John.

She said goodbye and replaced the phone, her gaze falling on the calendar. With only another week until Halloween, she really should've planned the pumpkin carving and party by now. A sigh of her own escaped.

"Sounds serious," Lacey said from the door.

"I'm just kicking myself for not being as organized as I would normally like."

"What's wrong?"

"Can you believe I haven't done anything about the pumpkin

carving? I usually have this sorted, but this year I feel like I'm forever behind."

"You've had a lot on your plate, covering for Leona as much as you've done." Lacey eyed her. "You deserve a pay raise."

"Yeah, I get the impression from what Leona says that there's not enough in the budget for that."

"Maybe you deserve her job."

Emma shrugged. Maybe she did. But she wouldn't put her hand up for it. Not when it seemed to be the one thing keeping Leona going. Between Leona's concern for Nick and finances and her own health battles, Emma would do whatever she could to help her feel a sense of ease. And if that meant taking on some of Leona's duties for no extra pay, well, that was okay. It was what God would want her to do, anyway.

"So what will you do?" Lacey asked.

"About what? Oh, the pumpkin carving?" Emma shrugged. "I've got no idea. I don't suppose Tim has anyone he can spare?"

Lacey laughed. "I can ask. There's always a few newbies willing to do whatever."

"Thanks. You know I hate to ask."

"Sure you do," Lacey teased. "Any chance to have a hot guy make an appearance, right?"

"Can I help it if it comes with the territory?"

But Emma knew that part of professional hockey's culture was to give back to the community, and one of the ways they did that was through partnering with various charitable organizations. Whenever Tim or his team members had visited the Home, they'd always been very well regarded, and Emma liked to think that they enjoyed their time here too. It probably helped that the Home was situated not too far from the Rangers' practice facility, so it wasn't too far out of most players' way to be asked to attend something here.

Theirs was a funny town—less than an hour from Times Square, depending on the traffic, yet a world away in pace and noise. She loved living here. Loved that she had a job in her hometown. Loved that her parents lived nearby. Loved that she could be passionate about a sport and sometimes see the players downtown at the local store. Some of the players had houses around here, given that the training facility was nearby and most of them preferred to live close to their practice location rather than try to deal with the sky-high rents in the city. The team used the local airport for their trips to play away rather than deal with JFK, so it made sense to live close. The fact that Lacey and Tim lived in the next town over made things even better.

"So you'll ask him then?"

"Absolutely. You'll have some people here. What day?"

"Whatever day works best for them. I should've gotten this arranged weeks ago, so I know their schedule will be tight, but honestly, I'll take whoever he can give, whenever they can make it."

"I'll mention it to him now," Lacey said, dragging out her phone.

"You're a star."

"Yes, I am," Lacey said, quickly tapping a message on her phone. "There. All sent."

"Thanks so much."

"We'll have someone here. Who knows? Maybe he'll prove to be your man of destiny."

Emma rolled her eyes. "Please."

"Well, it doesn't seem to be Jacob."

She coughed. "Sure isn't."

Lacey laughed again. "He just tries a little too hard, doesn't he?"

"And is a little too young."

"A year or two shouldn't matter, Em."

"He's twenty-four."

"Oh."

"Exactly."

"Yeah, okay, well, let's not worry about him, then." Lacey hooked her arm through Emma's as they made their way back to where the children were finishing watching the Wiggles DVD. "We'll trust God will bring along Mr. Right soon."

"Sure," she agreed, like she hadn't been praying that these past ten years. Ever since the man she'd thought so right had proved to be so very wrong. She swallowed, pushed her glasses higher. "Okay, kids, who's ready for break time?"

TJ GLANCED AROUND THE ROOM. More than a few players looked less than thrilled to see him. More than a few had been on the receiving end of his fists. Still, this was hardly his choice. The captain, Tim Carruthers, gave the usual guff about being glad he was joining the team, but TJ could tell it was only half-hearted. This morning's meeting with the coaching staff had just reinforced just how thin the ice was here.

The GM had been blunt. "Nobody wants you here, Woletsky. Your attitude and penalty time mean you're a liability. We're only taking you to get one of L.A.'s picks, so don't think you're doing us any favors."

Ouch. Who needed a punch to the head with comments like that?

"This is your last chance, Woletsky, or it's back to the minors for you. You're gonna have to show us you're willing to change, or I will be packing you off to Connecticut before you can say tomorrow."

TJ looked around the locker room again. Each time he glanced at someone, their gaze would drop or they'd turn to the person next to them, avoiding eye contact with him like they'd catch the plague. Only Tim stared back, his head tilted to one side.

TJ lifted his chin. The captain set the tone for the room, and the fact that Carruthers hadn't backed down drew a small measure of respect. He'd encountered too many people who said one thing to his face then another behind his back, and had no time for them. He'd had enough of that growing up.

Carruthers glanced at his phone, and TJ exhaled and resumed taping his stick. He knew he was lucky to have not been sent to the minors. Phil seemed to have done his job right for once and had convinced someone somewhere that it was a waste of TJ's salary and his skills to be playing there. But the GM hadn't been too impressed, telling TJ he had one shot to prove himself.

"You're lucky McDermott got shingles and is out for a few weeks. We'll see how you go in the next game, whether you can fit with the team and prove you're worthy of being here or else it's goodbye. Comprende?"

TJ had nodded, thanked him, and promised to do whatever it took to win their trust. And he meant it.

Carruthers stood and drew near, unsmiling. "Nick Grenier is a family friend. I hope you're sorry for what you did to him."

Sorrier than he'd ever know. "Despite what everyone thinks, it wasn't my intention to injure him."

"No?" Carruthers raised an eyebrow. "Just rough him up a little? Send him into a coma for a week or two?"

The room had grown silent. He didn't need to look at the faces to feel their enmity. The cold air in the room was sucking all life away. "I'm very sorry for that."

His voice sounded too flat. From the death stares still coming his way, it didn't seem like anyone believed him. He swallowed. "Really, I am."

Carruthers studied him a moment longer before nodding slightly, as if partly satisfied. "In that case, welcome to the team." He held out a hand, and TJ grasped it in a long power struggle that revealed to each other the years of strengthening exercises. Better let Tim win.

He joined the procession out to the ice, knowing this practice session would be another test. The guys who had something to prove didn't mind giving him the occasional shoulder barge. Others were too scared to do more than the courtesy tap. He tried to rein in his temper, but one of the unfriendly taps soon tipped him over the edge, sending his mouth into action. He knew most of these guys. Knew what would get their goat. For some it was a crude comment about their girlfriend or wife. For others he might question their sexuality. Most tried to ignore him, but after enough, even the saints snapped eventually.

Tim skated near, breathing hard. "This is how you prove you can play in a team?"

This was how he survived. "It's just talk."

Tim pointed to the corner, barking at the others to continue shooting. TJ supposed it was fortunate the coaches were huddled on the side, probably trying to figure out how best to use him. If they used him at all. McDermott might be out, but they could call up a guy from Hartford. TJ might be lucky to get on the fourth line.

"I don't think you really understand the situation," Tim said.

"That I'm on probation?" TJ asked.

"That they don't want you here. That nobody wants you here."

"Actually, the GM already said that."

Tim's eyebrows rose. "And you don't think they're looking for a way to get rid of you?"

TJ shrugged. "The way I see it, I might as well retire."

"Wow."

"Wow what?"

"I really didn't expect you to be a quitter."

Quitter? "Look, you've just told me nobody wants me here. Looks like they just want me to go to Connecticut, which is next door to playing in the ECHL. I might as well go play in Slovakia."

Tim eyed him for a long moment, brow lowered, arms crossed. "You were drafted the same season as me, weren't you? You went the first round, though."

TJ shrugged. "So?"

"I was drafted in the third round, and ever since then I've had to prove myself, prove to every team I played for that they should've picked me first. Do you know how hard I've worked?"

Nope. And he didn't care.

"Have you just coasted all these years? Traded whatever skills those scouts saw in you for a big mouth and bigger chip on your shoulder?"

"No."

"Then how do you get away with having such a bad attitude? I don't understand it at all."

"Nobody says you have to."

But something about Tim's words stung. Okay, maybe he did have a little bit more self-respect than that. Those scouts all those years ago had offered him a lifeline out of small-town Loserville and all the associated fun of being the pastor's kid when that pastor's world had imploded. There was a reason he'd never gone back, and his skating and puck handling skills had everything to do with it. No way did he want to prove those critics right. "What do you want from me?"

"I want you to prove them wrong. Show them the first round pick you were, that you still could be. Show them you're more than just an enforcer, that you have skills they need." Tim looked over his shoulder. "I probably shouldn't say this, but the fourth line lacks the energy you could bring. But only if you're prepared to pull your finger out and contribute. And not just the hits and talking smack, but the goals, the passing—that's what that line needs."

He nodded. He'd wondered the same, having watched a few

replays of New York's games, but why was Carruthers telling him this? "Why do you care?"

Tim shrugged. "I don't," he called, skating off, which provoked a huff of amusement.

Clearly the man had his own reasons for saying what he did, but it had triggered something inside. So for the rest of their practice, TJ kept his head down, staying focused, attending to whatever the coaches said, doing his best to keep his nose clean. Keeping his mouth shut was a strange sensation, especially as he'd relied more on that than on his passing ability in recent years. But there was something kind of fun in rediscovering the skills that had seen Ohio draft him as the thirteenth pick all those years ago.

He joined the others skating off the ice, until Coach Koder beckoned him near. "Thirteen." A small concession to his usual number. Unlucky for some, lucky for him. Sometimes. "You'll be skating with Jenner and Desi."

Fourth line. TJ nodded.

"I don't want to see any of your usual tricks tomorrow, understood?"

"Yes, sir."

Koder raised an eyebrow at that, like the *sir* came as a surprise. "I don't know why you're here, but I suggest you make the most of it. McDermott won't be back for a while, and there's plenty of men hustling for your place. You're just lucky you're here right now."

Lucky? Maybe he was. He knew his dad didn't believe in luck, believed such circumstances were proof of God's ways being higher than man's own. But TJ's luck had never been anything he could count on, so he knew it was only a matter of time before he'd be booted on. He nodded to the coach anyway and trudged up the tunnel to the locker room.

He tugged off his helmet. Sat in his stall. Wondered if he'd be here long enough for the suspicious glances being thrown his way to change. Jenner and Desi hardly acknowledged him, and he wondered if he should make an effort to convince his line-mates that he was a nice guy.

Except he knew he wasn't. And trying to win people's approval had never been his style. And while he hoped to prove the GM and all his critics wrong and play well tomorrow, he also hoped that his line-mates would be professional enough to let private differences lie.

"Woletsky." He glanced up. Carruthers jerked his chin. "You're coming with me."

"Why?"

"Don't argue."

Okay. He stuffed his protest down. "Where, then?"

"You'll see."

Great. So he had a captain who liked to play mind games. A minute later they were in a different room, and he was meeting another team employee whose pretty face and honey-blonde hair was just his style. But judging from the way she eyed him, like she was here under protest and he was slime, now wasn't the time to point that out.

"Tim wants me to talk to you about some of the community organizations we're involved with." She shot a look at Tim as if questioning his sanity before her gaze returned to TJ. "We're always getting requests from different groups wanting to partner with us or to have someone from the team make an appearance. I have been advised"—she shot Tim another glare —"that you would be someone who would be very willing to participate in such events."

"I don't know where you got your intel, but—" TJ stopped, his own glance at Tim revealing the captain shaking his head. Right. "—but you're absolutely right. Anything you want, I'll be your man."

She cringed, like she thought he was making a pass. Which he wouldn't mind owning if he thought he could get away with it. But judging from her expression, he definitely couldn't. "Your community service man, I mean. Nothing else. Promise."

"Thank you for clearing that up," she said stiffly.

"You're welcome," he said as meekly as he knew how. See? He could do nice guy. Maybe.

She started spouting a list of activities and organizations, including kids' safety talks at city firehouses, serving Thanksgiving dinner, visiting a kids' home.

"Sign me up to everything," he said. They wanted him to fail? He'd show 'em.

She checked about police checks and clearances for such things, like she thought his reputation for brawling on the ice naturally lent itself to a jail term as well.

His chest heated. "Listen, sweetheart, I don't know what you've heard, but I'm as clean as Timmy here." He jerked a thumb at his captain, whose look of amusement had faded. Okay, so that might've been pushing it. He needed the guy on his side. One guy on his side would make a nice change. "I would've thought L.A.'s front office had sent that stuff across already," he added in a far more conciliatory-sounding tone.

"We'll need you to sign forms for the state of New York as well," she said.

"Sure." He watched as she moved to collect a clipboard with a bunch of papers on it. "What, now?"

"No time like the present," Tim said. "You didn't have other plans for today, did you?"

Apart from figuring out someplace to live? Or was all this way too soon to think long-term? Maybe he should stick it out in the hotel a little longer. "Nope."

"Good."

TJ scrawled his name on a bunch of forms, most of which he barely read, trusting the girl not to be lying when she said what they were for. He finished the last one, dating it with a flourish. "There."

"Thank you," she said, not looking at him, like she thought her eyeballs might catch a fungal disease.

"Good," Tim said, clapping him on the back.

"Hey, I want you to know that I'm happy to do whatever it takes."

"Whatever it takes?" Tim asked, a slight smile on his face.

TJ shrugged. "Sure."

He'd do whatever it took to prove New York needed him here. And not that maybe he needed them more.

CHAPTER 4

*E*mma stared at her best friend. "What did you just say?"

Lacey gestured outside the office window to the front porch, where a pile of pumpkins waited forlornly. "If you want the pumpkin carving done, it can be done today. This afternoon."

"When?"

"Like"—Lacey glanced at her watch—"any minute now."

"But we're not ready for guests. I need to check the schedule, and—"

"Looks clear enough to me."

Emma stood and examined the timetable on the whiteboard, which listed the varying medical appointments and activities listed for today. Huh. As luck would have it, Beth, another support worker, was scheduled to take Nessa to a behavior intervention specialist appointment, but apart from that they were free. But that didn't mean she couldn't protest. "But the kids need to be prepared and the pumpkins washed and—"

"Tim said it was the only time available." Lacey arched a perfectly plucked brow. "Do you want the pumpkin carving done or not?"

"Yes."

"Am I telling Tim to turn around or to come here?"

"He can come," Emma said, mock-sighing.

"And you don't mind who he brings?"

Another huff of breath. "No. It'll be fine." She hoped.

"Beggars can't be choosers," Lacey reminded her. "And Tim said he had a willing taker from the team who can come today."

"Did he say who?"

"Nope. Just said it was best to strike while the iron was hot." Her mouth twisted into a half-smile that seemed edged with wryness.

"Huh. Well, as long as the guy has filled out the appropriate forms and stuff, then that should be okay. We can make it work."

"I knew you'd think so. Look, we can get Jacob and Elle to set up the tables and prep the pumpkins while we deal with the kids. It won't hurt for them to have a surprise like this."

"No." Probably not. Although some kids like Brandon and Nessa didn't like surprises. They needed structure, order, a sense of security to alleviate the pain-filled chaos of their first few years of life.

"Then let's go!"

The next twenty minutes saw a mad scramble of busy little bodies—and bigger ones, too—clearing up the big room, washing hands, straightening ponytails and clothes. Lacey was right. The kids seemed to enjoy the excitement of this break from routine, their cooperation high as they worked as a little team. It was moments like this Emma wished the trustees could see how efficient she could be, that they'd consider her worthy of a pay rise for all that could be done when Leona wasn't here. Not that she wished the woman ill, but it would be good to feel valued a little more.

A hasty explanation to Jacob and Elle, another worker, had seen the table prepped, the pumpkins gleaming, and the implements they'd need readied. She knew another moment's regret that this wouldn't be more widely known, for events like this in the past had often seen media attendance, which boosted not only Hopetoun's profile and potential funding but that of the pro sports team as well. But still, beggars and all that…

"Oh no!"

"What?" Lacey asked.

"We can't have guests without serving food."

Lacey bit her lip. "Tim won't mind, but whoever he brings should probably feel welcomed. Should I go to the store?"

"I think there's something in the fridge."

Jacob, Elle, and Lacey kept watch of the children while Emma raced to the kitchen. In the deep freezer she found a Tupperware container of mini blueberry muffins. She pried open the lid, then threw them on a tray and into the oven to slowly warm. Better than nothing. And with a few packets of the nice cookies they used for when the trustees visited, maybe they could get away with things so it didn't look too last minute.

She spent a moment arranging plates, her mind ticking at a million beats an hour. Would their guests want tea? Coffee? Something cold? It wasn't like they had that much in the way of things to offer. Maybe Tim could be a doll and take the guys somewhere later for a nice coffee. Rosie's in the center of the village did a nice coffee and cannoli.

Thank God for Tim and whoever was coming to help them out like this, even if it was last minute. This certainly wasn't his usual style, to spring things on them so suddenly, but neither was it like Emma to forget these basic things. Who was he bringing? Was Lacey's reference to *hot* some form of code about the guy's attractiveness? Her heart fluttered with anticipation. Maybe it was. Maybe this mystery guy was hot.

"Ouch!" Her fingers sizzled against the hot oven—yet another thing they'd need to replace as soon as they could afford it. But seeing as the kitchen wasn't a space used by children, Leona had deemed kitchen renovations unimportant. One day. Soon. After the temperamental furnace was replaced. Emma hoped.

She ran her fingers under the tap, her heart pulsing with anticipation. Who would be coming? Did she have time to run upstairs and brush her hair, maybe refresh her lipstick? She didn't usually wear much makeup, but a chance to meet one of Tim's friends wasn't a time to be too complacent. Her movement upstairs was halted by the sight of Tim's Wrangler driving up the street, the tinted windows not revealing who was with him. A man on a Harley followed close behind.

"Emma!" Lacey called.

Emma wiped her hands on her jeans and hurried through to the big room, where she joined the excited children who were waiting patiently for the men to exit.

She smiled at Jacob, who beamed back. She instantly dimmed her smile back to zero. No. She didn't have time to raise his hopes in this dance around asking her out, like he'd hinted at way too many times before. Not when everything inside of her screamed to know who the hot guy with Tim was.

She heard Lacey's gasp outside and smiled at her overly dramatic friend.

"Miss Emma?" Brandon tugged her shirt.

"What is it?"

"I don't feel good."

Oh no. Brandon and excitement never mixed well. She gently stroked his cheek. "Would you like to sit down over there?" She pointed to his corner, where a bunch of beanbags and books made for a basic chill-out zone for the kids.

"Yes."

"Come on." She held his hand and walked him over, settling him on an over-large beanbag with tigers printed on the fabric cover. "Pick a book, and I'll be back to read it in a moment."

Judging from the wave of excitement rippling through the

room, Tim was walking up the steps. Which meant the hot guy would be too.

"I'll be back in a moment, okay?"

Brandon nodded. She stroked his cheek again and joined the others as Tim said a big hello to the kids before turning to gesture forward his teammate at the base of the steps, who was also wearing the same famous blue-red-and-white jersey.

Her mouth dried. Then fell open. No. Oh no. The hot guy was nothing of the sort. Instead, he was just the opposite. For Tim's teammate was none other than TJ Woletsky.

THE "FREEWHEEL BURNING" soundtrack to his ride died as TJ braced himself for whatever lay ahead. His trip following Tim's Wrangler from the city through the burbs had opened his eyes to several things. One: renewed appreciation for what being part of this storied NHL club could mean if management decided to keep him around. Two: the wish to actually be someone team management decided to keep around. Three: that for all his Yoda-captaincy "play by the rules," Tim Carruthers didn't mind speeding. TJ filed that information away, somewhat amused that someone who was a poster boy for the team and talked about safety and responsibility was not opposed to bending certain rules.

TJ had also grown aware that the huge houses in this neck of the woods scarcely looked like they'd appreciate a wannabe biker, and he'd appreciated the relative anonymity the Harley gave him, even if only for the helmet that obscured his face. Whatever this place was they were going to—Tim was hardly a goldmine of information—it was planted in an expensive-looking neighborhood where the homes were bigger, older, and grander, with the trees and big lots he wasn't used to. Money had lived here once upon a time. Maybe it still did.

This place—the fancy-scripted sign out the front said Hopetoun House—was three stories of stone and timber with a utilitarian garden and some huge oaks and other trees he hadn't seen too much of in the past couple of years. He'd propped the bike on its stand, secured his helmet and shrugged off his leather jacket, and now reluctantly followed Tim up the brick steps. Who lived here?

"Hey, kids, I want you to meet a new friend of mine. Kids, this is TJ Woletsky."

TJ caught a glimpse of wide eyes and fallen jaws, as if they'd never seen a full beard before. Or red hair. And that was just the four adults.

His gaze snagged on the brunette with glasses, whose face looked a little familiar.

"Kids." Tim's voice pivoted TJ's attention back to the kids. "Can you say *hello, Mr. Woletsky?*"

A chorus of exactly that followed in the tradition of all young schoolchildren, their own versions of the adults' double-takes not exactly warming the cockles of TJ's heart. But it wasn't like this was the first time he'd had to work to win people over.

"Hey, guys," TJ said, lifting a hand.

"Is your beard real?" one of the girls asked, her blonde hair tied up in a ponytail.

"Yep."

"You look like Santa Claus," one of the boys said before giggling.

"Don't be silly," the first girl said. "Santa's beard is white and longer."

TJ nodded, kinda glad he'd trimmed it from the wizard length of L.A., and shot a look at Tim, who was beckoning forward the adults.

"TJ, I want you to meet my wife." Tim shrugged an arm around the curvy blonde, whose green eyes were wide with something between fear and fascination. Yeah, he'd seen that look plenty of times before. "Lacey, look who's joined our team."

She shot Tim a look that made TJ bite back a smile, sure Tim would be getting an earful at home. But the woman pasted on a smile and politely shook his hand.

"Pleased to meet you," TJ offered. He'd bet his Harley that he'd not see an invitation to the Carruthers' house any time soon, but it wouldn't hurt to pretend that her lack of warmth didn't sting a little.

"Jacob," a weedy guy said, with a lifted chin and narrowed gaze and general air of hostility that said TJ wasn't his cup of tea.

Feeling was mutual. "TJ," he said, gripping the kid's hand a little harder than necessary before releasing it. He bit back another smile as the kid flexed and straightened his fingers before his gaze shifted back to the brunette, who still stared at TJ with narrowed gaze.

As if noticing, Tim beckoned her near, and she drew closer with reluctant steps. "And this is the assistant residence manager of Hopetoun House, Emma Moritello." Tim's gaze was soft. "I'm real sorry for the short notice," he added, as if for her ears alone.

Unluckily for him, TJ had always had the hearing of a bat. "Hey, if it makes you feel any better, I sure as heck wasn't expecting to end up here today."

He tried to smile, but it was an effort. Her blue gaze, partly hidden behind glasses, narrowed on him like he was a piece of dirt under the toenail of a big hairy scary baboon that she had no intention of getting near. Which said more about her prejudice than it did him, he knew, his chest tensing with resentment. What kind of person judged others before getting to know them?

"TJ Woletsky," he said. "It's a real pleasure to meet you," he added, goading her as he stuck out his hand.

She looked at it before offering the limpest, quickest hand-shake in handshake history.

"Don't worry, sweetheart, I've had my flea shot."

She raised her eyebrows, just like his mean third-grade teacher Miss Simpkins used to. She was even dressed the same. Makeup-free, dressed in her shapeless off-white sweater and long brown skirt, her hair in a fat braid down her back. He still got chills thinking about school.

"I beg your pardon?"

Her voice tugged at his memories—someone he'd spoken to not so long ago. *Had* he seen her before?

Tim laughed nervously. "TJ is going to be one of your most regular regulars. He can't wait, can you, bud?"

TJ winced at the slap on the back. "Yep, can't wait."

The eyebrow queen raised hers even higher. "And why is that?"

He looked around the room, the sloe-eyed faces shining with anticipation. Why was he going to help? He shrugged. "I like kids."

She narrowed her eyes and took a step forward. "Yes, but these are special kids, Mr. Woletsky, or didn't Timothy tell you that?"

She shot his teammate a look that would've frozen most men, but obviously "Timothy" had been on the receiving end before, because he laughed. "I didn't have much of a chance to tell him anything," he confessed.

Her eyes narrowed again, and she bit her lip. He could just imagine what was going through her mind. None of it pleasant.

"Excuse me," she said, dragging Tim back a few paces, where she placed her hands on her hips as Tim's wife hovered nervously nearby. Jacob had his arms crossed, eyeing TJ like he was responsible for deliberately spreading Ebola. He nodded to a thin woman who looked to be in her forties. Her gaze fell. Swell.

"I really don't think this is a good idea," the brunette murmured. "What happens when Leona finds out?"

TJ frowned. Who was Leona? Why did that name ring a bell?

"Honey, this is a mistake," Tim's wife said, placing a hand on her husband's arm. "I know you wanted to help, but this will not end well."

"I can leave if you want," TJ called.

Three heads spun to face him, their faces creased with what he hoped was shame.

A hand tugged on his shirt. "Are you here to help with the pumpkin carving?" the little blonde girl asked.

Pumpkin carving? How long since he'd done that? "Um, sure." If Ms. Eyebrows let him. "Can't wait."

"Can you help me with my pumpkin?" she asked.

"I'd love to," he said, shooting his own raised-brow look at Tim and co.

The woman—Emma, was it?—sighed, her shoulders deflating as she joined the others in drawing closer. "Lily, please wait a moment while Mr. Tim and I speak to Mr. Woletsky."

"TJ," the little girl said.

Emma's lips flattened as she nodded before Lacey ushered the girl away.

"Mr. Woletsky—"

"TJ." He echoed the little girl with a smirk.

Emma inhaled then exhaled slowly. "Have you signed the appropriate documents? We don't just let anyone come and visit here."

TJ held up his hands. "I signed everything they asked me too, and hey, it's not like I've never done kids' visits before. I used to do them all the time in Calgary and L.A."

One of her eyebrows shot up skeptically, dragging up further defensiveness.

"And the only reason I'm here is because Timothy dragged

me along. I had no idea what I was getting into, but if you don't want me here, then hey, no biggie, I'll leave."

She pursed her lips as if considering his offer, and suddenly he found himself wanting to fight to stay. He bet these kids knew rejection as well as he did, people's perceptions and pre-judgments pigeonholing them to other people's narrow-minded expectations.

Finally, she sighed. "Very well." She cast Tim another scowl that made TJ bite back another spurt of amusement. Looked like Timmy was gonna be getting it from all angles. "We're doing pumpkin carving for Halloween."

"So that's what the big pile of pumpkins is about?" he mocked.

She shot him a death stare, and he grinned, pleased to see her look away. "Well, in that case, you'd better make yourself useful."

The next few minutes passed in a whirl of instructions, and TJ soon found himself wielding a large knife and seated between two kids—the blonde girl and a kid called Ben—who were arguing about whether the eyes they'd drawn on their respective pumpkins were scary enough or not. "What do you think, TJ?" Lily asked.

"I think it's the mouth and teeth that really make it look scary. See?" He used a Sharpie to quickly draw some misshapen teeth, not unlike what his own looked like without his plate.

"Yeah, that's good!" Ben said.

"Make mine look scarier," Lily said.

"Please," murmured Emma from behind him, which triggered a "please" from Lily.

TJ quickly glanced up at Emma, but she looked away before shifting to the corner where a small boy sat alone. "Who's that?" he asked Ben, nodding to the kid in the corner.

"That's Brandon," Lily said. "He doesn't like noise."

"Fair enough."

He eyed the kid, who was shaking his head at something Emma was saying, until Lily nudged his arm. "TJ, I want my teeth to look scary!"

TJ arched a brow.

"Please?" she asked.

He smiled, nodded, and helped guide the drawing until she finally pronounced herself satisfied. Then they began the carving, the knives that they used seeming a little too big and sharp for small kids. Kinda weird that the authorities-that-be had concerns about safety, given the huge size of these knives. Still, it was fun to plunge the knife into the pumpkin to carve eyes, to make a nose, to get those teeth done until a little girl was satisfied.

"Do we do the top now?" TJ asked, pointing to the stalk.

"Yeah! Cut him up," she cried, clapping her hands—a little too bloodthirstily, it seemed.

The top removed, it was then time to scoop out the fleshy center and seeds, before Lily then decided she wanted a back face carved in as well. "See?" she said, pointing to Tim's creation. "I want my pumpkin head to look happy on this side, like that one."

TJ exchanged glances with Tim, whose smirk said that he'd heard, so, stifling a sigh, TJ obeyed her wishes. But he didn't mind. This was actually kinda fun and not something he'd ever done much of growing up. His parents had always been too conservative and strict, Halloween one of those forbidden rituals he'd watched other kids do while he'd been forced to spend his time in church. Or been too busy playing hockey, when he'd been able to tag along with some of the other kids— because his mom and dad were too busy with their congregation. He kinda knew just how that kid Brandon might feel.

Half an hour later, he lined up the three pumpkins he'd helped carve out on the front porch, above the front steps. "Ours are the best," Lily said, clapping her hands.

"The others look good, too," TJ said. "But yeah, we make a good team, huh? Solid effort," he said, giving her a gentle fist bump before offering Ben the same.

A noise made him glance up in time to catch Emma look away, her gaze on the pumpkins.

"We did great, huh, Miss Emma?" Ben said.

"They look very good," she said, her gaze finally catching TJ's. "But there's three."

TJ shrugged. "I made an extra, for Brandon if he wants it."

Her face softened. "That was kind, thank you."

He nodded, her praise eliciting a tight feeling in his chest, and was relieved when Lacey clapped her hands and called the kids inside to wash up for an afternoon snack.

Emma stayed on the porch as if unsure whether to go back in, which made him wonder if she had something more to say to him. "It's looking more like Halloween now," he offered, pointing to the pumpkins lining the steps.

She nodded absently, bending to adjust one so the lantern face would be more clearly seen.

He shrugged, not knowing whether to stay or go, a decision taken from him when Lily demanded to know where her friend TJ was. His heart softened a little. So maybe today hadn't been a complete fail.

"Emma?" Lacey called before coming onto the porch. "Oh, here you are. And you too, TJ." The smile she gave him seemed more genuine than before. "There's something for you to eat inside. I'm afraid it doesn't mean good coffee," Lacey apologized. "I keep telling Emma that she should insist on installing an espresso machine, but she seems to think a new furnace is a higher priority."

"Weird," he said, stealing a glance at Emma, who followed him.

"Right?" Lacey said. "You'd think coming from an Italian

family she'd have her priorities straight, but she sometimes takes a while to come around to things."

"Like certain hockey players showing up uninvited?" he said, his glance drifting back to Emma.

Emma's lips pressed together, then she heaved out a sigh. "I'm sorry if I didn't exactly come across as your biggest cheerleader."

Try any cheerleader. Not that he was looking for cheers.

"You did well with the kids."

"I beg your pardon?" he asked, daring to tease. "Was that a compliment?"

Her gaze flashed to him, the corners of her mouth twitching up, then flattening as if she was trying to suppress a smile. "Please do not get carried away, Mr. Woletsky."

"It's TJ, sweetheart."

"And it's Emma, or Miss Moritello, Mr. Woletsky," she countered swiftly.

Huh. So she had sass. He bit back an appreciative smirk, conscious that Lacey was studying them. "So, point me to the Kool-Aid."

CHAPTER 5

"I can't believe you did that," Emma said, smacking Tim on the arm. "Why didn't you tell us he'd joined the team?"

"Hey, it's only just happened."

"Why does the team think they should have him?" Jacob asked, arms crossed. "He's a loser."

Tim shrugged. "I'm only the captain, not the one who makes trades."

"But you were the one who brought him here today," Emma persisted. "In what universe did you think Woletsky coming here was a good idea? Especially knowing the situation with Leona."

"Look, what can I say but sorry?" He slid a look at Lacey. "When Lace messaged me to say you needed people here, well, TJ was available, and hey, it got the job done, didn't it? Pumpkins got carved, nobody got hurt. I really don't think you need to worry anymore."

"TJ did really well," Lacey said. "Did you see him go to read with Brandon? Oh, my heart might've melted a little then."

Emma shot Lacey a frown, but yes, the man had surprised

her with his quiet exit from the mayhem of the kids' mid-afternoon snack time. Much to her shame, she'd only realized Brandon was missing when she went to find him and discovered TJ awkwardly plonked on a kiddie-sized beanbag, reading a book aloud to Brandon. Her initial protest about a male visitor being alone with a child died as she saw the way Brandon looked up at him and, as if by magic, smiled. And yes, okay, her own heart might've melted a little in that moment. She hadn't seen Brandon smile in weeks. And then TJ had looked across, caught her gaze, and winked. She'd wanted to turn away, her skin heating with warmth she couldn't put down to the faulty furnace, but forced herself to move toward them and remind Brandon he could come have something to eat.

"Not hungry," Brandon had murmured.

"Mr. Woletsky?" she forced herself to say. "Would you like another muffin?"

"Nah, I'm good." His lips curved to one side. "Well, not good, as you no doubt know, but let's just say I don't need to eat."

She'd nodded stiffly, Jacob calling her attention to something else, and next she knew, Brandon was by her side as TJ spoke quietly to Tim, then made his goodbyes.

Now he and his motorcycle had left, and she was here with this feeling of unease, like something had shifted and she wasn't sure what. Coupled with this was the prickling sense that he hadn't acknowledged recognizing her from the other day, a fact which left her nonplussed, then wondering why she cared. There had been times when she'd looked up to catch his brow-pleated gaze, only to instantly avert her eyes. Which was stupid, to be so self-conscious around someone she didn't care for except to make him very aware of all his many faults regarding Nick. Which still didn't explain her feeling of pique.

"I don't trust him," Jacob said, arms crossed. "Woletsky is a bully and a motormouth."

"But he was great with the kids," Lacey insisted. "I don't think you should write him off."

"What about Leona?" Emma felt the need to point out. "What if she'd been here?"

"But she wasn't," said Lacey. "And even if she had been, then it might do her some good."

"How?"

"Like help her learn to forgive," Lacey said softly.

Tim nodded. "And I figured it might be good for him too. He's trying to make a fresh start. I think you should give him a second chance."

"A second chance? How can we give someone who did what he did to Nick a second chance?"

"Well, you're gonna have to find some way, because he's going to be around for a while."

"What do you mean?"

Tim shrugged. "I get the impression that he really wants to prove himself, to help put a positive light on the organization and not get booted to the minors."

"Where he belongs," Jacob muttered.

"You know, he's actually a good player."

"If you count fighting as a plus," Jacob countered.

"He was a first round selection," Tim continued. "I wasn't."

"But it's one thing to be selected first round, quite another to prove yourself over many years," Lacey said, squeezing her husband's arm.

"And that's exactly it," Tim said softly. "He wants to prove himself now."

Emma's eyebrows shot up. She'd been raising them a lot today. Hopefully it wouldn't increase the wrinkles she knew were waiting to deepen on her forehead. "So that's why he came? It's not because he likes kids." She shook her head. "What were you thinking?"

"I was thinking he needs a second chance, Em," Tim said. "Like we all do."

Guilt gnawed as a memory flashed of Brandon looking up at Woletsky as if fascinated by his ugly beard. Brandon had always managed to get under her professional skin, and if this man could make him look like that, then yeah, maybe he was worth giving a chance. Not that she'd make this easy on him. "Well, I'm still not too happy about it."

"Real-ly?" Tim crossed his arms. "Well, Em, you can't always get what you want"—he half sang the words—"but sometimes, you might just get what you need."

"You know they're not the right lyrics, don't you?"

"Still true, though."

She rolled her eyes. "Don't go getting all Rolling Stones on me." A smile slipped out anyway. How many times had they played that silly music trivia game? The number of nights she and Lacey had laughed themselves silly before Tim had entered the scene and proved to be something of an expert in sixties and seventies rock.

"Just give him a chance, Em," Tim pleaded. "He needs one."

She sighed. "I still don't know how we're going to explain any of this to Leona, but okay. He gets one chance." She raised her eyebrows at a suddenly grinning Tim as she lifted her finger. "One."

And God help her try to explain any of this to Leona.

"IT'S LOOKING QUITE WONDERFUL," Leona said the next day, glancing around the big room that now boasted vases of orange and red leaves from the trees outside and would soon host strings of drawings from the kids' activities today. "Those pumpkins outside look lovely. You've quite transformed the place."

"It needed to be done," Emma said softly, glancing around with satisfaction. The dark timber beams lining the ceiling of this old house might look impressive but never made for a sense of ease—certainly nothing like some of the modern places she'd worked in prior to coming here. But decorating with garlands and fall colors had certainly softened some of the oppressive feel.

"You must've had some help," Leona said.

"Santa man," Lily called out from her position at the end of the long central table.

Uh oh.

"I'm afraid you must be getting your holidays mixed up, dear," Leona said, smiling at the little girl. "Santa comes at Christmas, not Halloween."

"Santa man," Lily insisted, her forehead puckered as she continued coloring her picture of a fall leaf with an array of warm-toned crayons.

Leona shot Emma a bemused *she's not all there* look accompanied by raised eyebrows. Here went nothing.

"Tim, Lacey's husband, called in yesterday with one of his teammates."

"Oh, that was nice of him."

"Yes," Emma said. Should she explain now? Last night they —*they* meaning the others but not Emma—had decided that Emma needed to be the one to admit to Woletsky's presence. But she'd try to avoid mentioning his name for as long as possible.

"Tee Jay," Brandon said slowly from next to Lily. He hadn't touched his crayons at all.

"I beg your pardon?" Leona said, smiling at the boy.

"Tee Jay," he repeated.

"I'm afraid I don't understand," Leona said, sending Emma a look of enquiry.

"He was here," Lily said. "The Santa Claus man. He carved my pumpkin, Mrs. Cherry. Don't you think it's the best?"

"It's lovely, darling," Leona said absently, her gaze fixed on Emma. "I'm afraid I still don't understand," she said softly. "It sounds like they're trying to say deejay. Have you organized another dance party for Halloween? Is that it?"

"What a good idea!" And a great chance to change the subject. "What do you think, Lily? Should we have a dance party for Halloween?"

"Yeah!" Lily clapped her hands. "I loves dancing."

"You're a very good dancer, too," Emma said.

"Can TJ come? He could dance with me."

Emma coughed, the image of TJ dancing to the Wiggles at a little kids' party spurting amusement through her chest.

Leona blinked. "Emma, tell me who exactly came with Tim yesterday."

Any hopes of getting away with not telling Leona swiftly died. "Now, you don't need to worry. Everything went well, the kids had fun, and—"

"Wo-lets-ky," Lily said slowly.

"What did you say?" Leona said, paling.

Bek, another direct support worker, whose idea of working often seemed limited to supervising art play, looked up from the table where the kids were coloring in.

"Come on, Leona. Let's talk in your office." Emma nodded to Bek and Matt, leaving them to supervise while she encouraged Leona to sit in the comfortable chair usually reserved for visitors.

"Tim brought his new teammate, so TJ Woletsky was here," Emma finally admitted, perching herself carefully on Leona's cluttered desk. "He's been traded to New York, and Tim thought it was a good opportunity for him to start contributing positively and being seen to mend his ways."

"Tim thought this? The man is insane!"

Emma shrugged. Tim might be her friend, but she had no qualms about throwing the man under the bus, especially when he'd not dared to tell them his plans and just dumped TJ on their doorstep yesterday.

"I cannot believe it. I cannot—"

"Leona," Emma cautioned. "You don't want to get upset. Remember what the doctor said."

"It's Tim who's upset me, and that stupid man TJ. What kind of name is that, anyway? Oh my stars, I don't feel well," she said, fanning herself. "I think I need to have a lie down."

Emma's lips pressed together. With all those who might normally deputize having scheduled days off, she'd been counting on Leona to pull her weight today, but with her heart condition, it seemed that was not to be. Bek and Matt were both too new to be much help. But with the way Leona was carrying on, it seemed they'd have little choice.

"Leona, how about I make you a nice cup of tea."

"I don't want a nice cup of tea. I want that evil man to stay away from us here."

Emma repressed a sigh. "He was actually quite good with the children," she admitted. "Brandon and Lily especially seemed to warm to him."

"I don't know how you can stand there and make excuses for him," Leona snapped, her nostrils flaring. "He's bad news, and I want nothing more to do with him. I cannot believe you allowed him here! I'm so disappointed in you, Emma."

Her chest grew tight, awash with the injustice and humiliation of knowing she couldn't defend herself. Oh, why had Tim put her in this position? It was all well and good to say Leona needed to learn to forgive, but trying to be the Holy Spirit's little helper and then leaving Emma to deal with the fallout certainly didn't seem fair. But the reminder prompted her to pray, softening her heart.

"I'm sorry you feel that way, Leona," she said gently. "Now, sit and relax, and I'll make a cup of tea."

She moved past, and Leona grasped her hand. "I shouldn't take it out on you. I know you loathe the man as much as I do. I can't stand for Nick to know that man was here."

"He need not know if you don't tell him," Emma said softly. "There was no media here, nobody took photos with him, and those of us who were here decided to keep it to ourselves."

"But you can't expect it to stay a secret forever," Leona complained. "People will talk. They always do."

"Well, let's hope Nick doesn't hear about it anytime soon." She patted Leona's hand. "Now, let me get your tea."

But that night, at dinner with her family, she learned her hopes of keeping TJ's visit quiet were in vain.

"I can't believe New York signed TJ," Rose declared. Emma's sister—here for a flying visit—glanced up as Emma placed the salad bowl down on the dining table. "Can you?"

"Who signed who?" Mom asked, setting down the plates of pasta carbonara, then smacking Rose's hand as she lifted her fork. "Your father's gotta pray."

Dad said grace, then grabbed two pieces of garlic bread from the plate in the middle of the table. "New York traded for TJ Woletsky—you know, the one who took out the Grenier kid?"

"Oh, you mean Nick?" Mom asked Emma.

She nodded. "Leona's not happy."

"Well, it's not as if she's going to have to see 'im," Dad said before his gaze snagged Emma's. "What is it, Em?"

She shook her head, concentrating on forking in a piece of creamy pasta.

"Don't you do that thing," her sister warned.

"What thing?"

"When you pretend you're too good to spill the tea. You know stuff, don't you?" Rose said, eyes gleaming as they always did when she thought Emma might have juicy hockey news courtesy of Lacey.

"I know lots of things," Emma said mildly.

Rose rolled her eyes. "Quit playing Saint Margarita. What do you know about Woletsky? Is he moving here?"

"What? No." He'd better not be.

"Then what is it?" her sister demanded.

"He visited Hopetoun yesterday," she admitted.

"What?" Rose cried.

"Ya kidding me?" Dad said.

For some reason, the fact they all seemed so shocked dug protectiveness on TJ's behalf. "Tim asked him to come—"

"Are you for real?" Rose asked.

"—and he came and carved pumpkins with the kids, then read Brandon a story." She shrugged, not wanting to admit just how much that scene had touched her. "It was kind of sweet."

"Sweet?" Rose's eyes narrowed. "I thought Nick was your friend."

"What was Tim's excuse?" Dad asked. "I woulda thought a man like that'd have more sense."

"He thinks it could be good for Woletsky, giving him a second chance."

"Everyone deserves a second chance," Mom said complacently. "It's what we all want."

"Just wait until I tell the girls this," Rose said, digging into her salad, her expression of glee probably more to do with the fact she'd extracted information from Emma than her love of lettuce and tomato.

"Rose—"

"Is he nice?" her sister continued, ignoring Emma's attempt to protest. "Some of the girls were talking about him today. Have you seen his tattoos?"

"Yeah, he was showing them off to all the kids yesterday."

"He was?" her sister asked, her sarcasm radar on mute as always.

"No, Rose. He wasn't."

"I wouldn't mind seeing 'em. Apparently they're all over his body. Some of the girls think he's *fine*."

Please. Emma exchanged glances with her mom. They'd heard Rose talk like this before. Emma had tried to talk to her little sister about men, about how they weren't always trustworthy, even those you thought you knew well. Her stomach clenched, and she exhaled.

"Well? Is he?"

"Is who what?" Emma asked, forking in a bigger serving of pasta as if that could bury the guilt from long ago.

"TJ Woletsky," Rose said. "Some of the girls have said all kinds of things about him that would make your hair stand up..." Rose's voice trailed away, as if she was suddenly conscious both parents were looking at her funny. "Never mind."

"I don't think we shall. TJ might be Tim's teammate, but there's no reason to think we'll ever have anything to do with him. Am I right, Emma?" her father demanded.

She nodded, conscious of a queasy feeling in her stomach that had nothing to do with the richness of tonight's meal. They might wish to have nothing further to do with TJ, but wishes had a funny way of never coming true. At least, that had been her experience, anyway. And between his connections to Tim, and Tim's relationship to Lacey—and thus to Emma—she had an unwelcome feeling that they'd be seeing a lot more of the man Leona loved to hate.

THE SMELL of New Jersey's arena filled TJ's nostrils, a spray of ice arcing across the rink as he pivoted and turned. Today, his first game since being traded, had seen the usual niggles as he tried to gel with his new line. Just as expected, Desi and Jenner were wary, not passing to him too much, which made his job all the harder. But he was trying to keep his cool, trying to prove he wasn't just a mouth and a pair of fists on skates.

"Here!" he called, but once again Jenner ignored him, passing to Desi, which got intercepted and forced TJ to skate back up the ice. Sure enough, New Jersey shot and scored, the arena filling with horn and crowd noise.

A few minutes later the first period ended, and they moved to the locker room where, after removing equipment and grabbing drinks, Coach Koder tore into Jenner. "You had Woletsky free and clear, and did you pass? What's wrong with you?"

His center shot TJ a scathing glance, then shrugged.

Yeah, the dude didn't need to talk to make his feelings plain.

The atmosphere grew tense until Tim talked strategy about the next period before a little reminder about the need for teamwork—with emphasis on the *team*. TJ was glad when they finally trooped back onto the ice.

"Pass to him," Tim warned Jenner. But the look Jenner shot TJ didn't suggest he'd obey.

Apart from the tension with his line-mates, the game passed as many of his did, even though he'd toned down the chirping and insults and worked to show his skills, not his hot-headedness. The opposition seemed aware of this, and he felt the welcome mat of rock-hard checks, hits, and thumps into the boards. It seemed his line-mates weren't the only ones not thrilled he no longer played on the west coast.

The puck bounced his way, and he scooped it up, holding it close to his stick as he skated around New Jersey's defensemen and shot at the goal. The puck thudded against the pipes, to the cheers of the crowd. A curse fell from his mouth as he skated to catch the play, and before he knew it his line was off and Tim's was back on, and he was back on the bench, sucking down Gatorade.

He watched the play, then skated back onto the ice when Coach Koder called for his line to return to the ice. This time the Devils were waiting, one of the forwards stirring TJ up as the crowd goaded them on. He felt the pressure inside rise and muttered curse words to himself, wishing he could keep it together. The guy shoved him, making TJ stumble. He put out a hand to push him away, stuck out a stick for balance. He didn't need to get a penalty on his first outing for New York. But the dude kept yammering and yammering and—

The whistle blew, stopping play, and Smithson, the ref, signaled for TJ to hit the penalty box. "Slashing."

"What? I didn't touch him," he said. "He fell over me."

Smithson eyed him like he was a snake. "Two minutes, or you wanna make it five?"

TJ gritted his teeth as he skated to the box, ignoring the crowd around him belting the plexiglass with their fists. It wasn't the first time he'd been so quick to make friends.

A glance across the ice revealed Koder, hands on hips, staring at him. The surge of adrenaline faded as he realized what this meant. This might only be a minor penalty, but he might've just blown his chance at redemption faster than his efforts at keeping his cool, on a play that he hadn't even intended. Goodbye, Original Six; hello, the minors. Good thing he hadn't done anything about looking for a house.

Regret kneaded his chest. What a stupid call. What a stupid play. What a stupid way to end things, and just when he'd glimpsed sight of how things could be. Call him crazy, but Tim's efforts with him had seemed way more genuine than most, even daring him to think that one day it could maybe amount to friendship. Then there'd been that surprising ease he'd felt yesterday at the kids' home, giving back to kids he wasn't all that different from. He'd gone to sleep hoping it might be a sign of things to come, but it seemed New York was all out of second chances. He should've known it was too much to hope for.

He watched New York's penalty kill, doing their best to make up for his mistake. He ground his teeth as the puck slid into New York's defensive zone before sliding past Backstrom and into the net. Awesome.

The plexiglass door swung open, and TJ skated back onto the ice, drawing the full glare of his team as he neared the bench. "Thanks," Jenner said.

He shrugged. "Wasn't intentional."

"It never is, is it?" Andrei Novak, a defenseman, swore.

"Smithson has it in for me," TJ muttered. Always had, ever since Ohio had traded him to Florida all those years ago and he'd gotten a little too mouthy with the ref, who apparently still felt he had something to prove.

Tim glanced at him, expression tight, but said nothing. This wasn't how his first game was supposed to go.

When TJ's next shift was on, he skated down the ice, the burden to prove himself steeling his legs. He'd show them they should keep him. New Jersey had the puck and were circling around. He checked the winger, scrabbling to get the black disk from his opponent's stick. He had to be careful, or else Smithson would throw the book at him, but neither would he let up on physicality. Not when he might have a chance to redeem his earlier play and hopefully save his spot on the team.

He worked the puck free and pivoted away, skating hard and fast around the Devils' defense as he looked for someone to pass to. But Desi was nowhere to be seen, which meant he'd need to take this chance himself. He lined up to shoot and—

Whack!

He fell to the ice, his face slamming against the cold ground, his nose exploding in a rush of red. Around him, skates stilled, voices called, as sticky blood caught his eyelashes, making each blink harder to see. He carefully wiped a hand over his face—

felt his nose move, then his guts churn. He coughed, blood spraying onto the ice as Tim crouched to ask him if he was okay —well, no, genius—before yelling for a medic.

A trainer appeared with a white towel, which TJ held over his face as he gingerly got to his feet. His head swam, and he blinked the sensation away. No way was he going out for concussion. He skated carefully off the ice, conscious to not give any appearance of the wooziness clutching his head as his teammates encouraged him by banging their sticks against the ice. He followed the trainer down the tunnel to the medic station, determination gripping his chest akin to the pain flaring around his nose. No way was a stupid stick to the face gonna stop his chance to play for an Original Six team.

CHAPTER 6

The slap of her sneakers on asphalt filled the early morning chill. Emma huffed out a hot breath as she dragged cold air into her lungs. Even though the temperatures were cool, she loved this early morning routine. It wasn't any wonder that so many of the rich and powerful had chosen this part of New York to build their mansions and estates. The Hudson River seemed impossibly wide at this section, the hills and bluffs on the other side almost fortress-like in size. She drew up at a viewpoint, dragging in long breaths, stretching her hands above her and bending from one side to the other as she closed her eyes and listened to the wash of water on the shore.

Past her heart's fast pumping, she sensed God and took a few moments to breathe in His presence. To still. To listen. To be. In the crazy clatter of her life there were few moments where she could pinpoint peace. But these times away from people and away from responsibility, these times were precious—increasingly so, as winter would soon be here, and snow and ice would make such times much harder, if not impossible.

Another exhalation. She opened her gloved hands. Kept her focus on God. "Have Your way."

Slowly, the chaos in her mind ebbed away. Here, she could listen. Here, she could hear. And she wanted to hear, because sometimes she wondered if this was all there was to be for her life. She'd known ever since she was a girl that she wanted to help people and ever since she was a teen that she wanted to help kids specifically. Then she'd known ever since she was twenty-one that she didn't deserve to hope for anything more. How could she hope for more when she'd done what she had?

God was good, and she'd long ago determined to prove He was right to not give up on her and that His grace would not be wasted. Which meant reconciling herself to the fact that service to God meant denial of other things, contentment—or was it resignation?—something she'd more or less managed a few years ago. Even if she still wondered sometimes if this was all there was to be.

"I'm not discontented," she said, opening her eyes. Heaven forbid a fellow exercise enthusiast come across the crazy lady talking to herself. A glance to either side said she was safe. "But God, lately it just kind of feels like I'm not really living in sync." Like she was out of step, like when she tried to take Reddy for a run. It made her steps smaller than she was comfortable with. That's what her life felt like—a little hobbled, sometimes.

"Please use me for Your purposes," she prayed aloud.

Images flickered to mind. The children. Helping Leona. Friendships. Family. There *was* value in her life. She was making a difference in the lives of others; her life wasn't being wasted. God was sure to be pleased with her efforts, and this feeling of discontent would ease one day, right?

A niggling sense that she was supposed to be doing more listening to than talking at God with her thoughts made her slow her breathing, focus hard on what God might want to say to her. But trying to shut off her brain was so hard, her thoughts like running water, unable to be captured and paused.

"Have Your way," she prayed again, her breath forming white

cloud puffs in the cool air. *Your way, God, not mine. Whatever You want, I'll do.*

Another image wafted to mind. She blinked, willing it to dissipate. No. This was supposed to be part of her quiet time, God time, not thinking-about-hockey time.

Why she was still thinking about last night's hockey game she didn't know. She thought she'd dealt with it all with her sleep last night. Okay, so maybe TJ had impressed her a little bit. Almost as much as he'd obviously impressed the commentators, who couldn't stop mentioning the way he'd returned in the third period, his face still bloodied, stitches on his forehead, his nose askew, only to score a goal. The commentators—even Lacey, with whom Emma had watched the game on TV—had all said how much grit he'd shown. And yes, it was the mark of a tough player. She didn't hate him so much she couldn't admit he'd shown courage. "I don't hate him, God," she clarified aloud.

But the burr in her chest suggested otherwise.

Okay, so maybe she didn't *hate* him, but neither could she like him unreservedly. What he'd done to Nick and Beau refused outright admiration. His reputation, his long legacy of fighting and poor attitude, meant he'd forever be someone she wanted to keep at arm's length. But she couldn't forget the way he'd considered Brandon, the way Brandon had looked up to him, that Brandon seemed to have a sixth sense with people and could discern those who had good hearts from those without, as unsettling as that was.

Maybe this discomfort in her chest suggested God wanted her to do some forgiving.

Her eyes opened. This was impossible. And she had a big day, so she didn't have time to corral every stray thought. She must be really tired to have so many of them.

She resumed her jog, veering from the waterfront into the historical center of town, the part tourists liked to visit for selfies before checking out Sleepy Hollow. The town was starting to wake up, but not too much, seeing it was Sunday, after all. She jogged past the restaurants and cafés, the clothing stores and places selling tourist things, where every second item was logoed with a headless horseman. How funny that a tale written by a man two hundred years ago had captured the imagination of so many. Not that those owning the tourist stores minded.

Another few streets, then it was back to her house. Back to the place she'd known all her life: her parents' house.

Some might call the fact she still technically lived with her parents at the age of thirty-one a little concerning, but given that her shifts meant she often stayed overnight at Hopetoun during the week, the chance to be amongst adults and few responsibilities and no rent definitely made staying at her folks' worthwhile. And it sure didn't hurt for her to feel the love. She jogged up the drive and, puffing, opened the front door to be greeted by the ecstatic yapping and slobbering kisses of Reddy.

"Shh!" She knelt and hugged him, willing him to quiet before her parents woke. She was used to early hours, and they loved their weekend sleep-ins, and the fact that Reddy preferred to lie around indolently and refused to join Emma's morning runs had proved a bone of contention. "Don't wake up Dad."

"Too late," a voice called from down the hall.

Emma sighed and rubbed Reddy between the ears. "You scruffy muffy, you."

He barked, rubbing himself against her legs, forcing her to quieten him again. "Why can't you be like Twinky?"

Twinky slunk in, eyed Emma with her superior gaze of condescension, and then slunk away to her parents' bedroom. Mom's cat really only liked Mom, which her mother said was a true sign of discernment. For some reason, that made her think of Brandon, which led to other troubling thoughts. Maybe a shower would wash them away.

Three hours later, she was exiting the church pew with Lacey and Tim, her heart more at ease. Her parents preferred a more traditional church, but Emma had found the services here spoke more to people her own age. Even if the pastor was inclined to think that because she worked with children during the week, she would want to spend her weekends teaching Sunday school too, and could never really understand why she resisted.

"Excuse me, Tim?"

While Tim was held up talking to a fan, Emma waited with Lacey in the auditorium's aisle as the musicians finished singing a song Emma often listened to when running.

"Gosh, I love that song," Lacey said. "Some songs just really speak to you, right?"

Emma nodded. "It's that Heartsong Collective song, right?"

"That Sarah girl wrote it, I think. She always wrote the best ones. It's such a shame she left the group."

"Did she?" Emma asked.

"Didn't you know? She got engaged, became a teacher—"

"I don't follow social media like you."

"Oh, you should, because then you'd know! So, then there was this awful accident, and he was killed—"

"Who was?"

"The guy she was engaged to."

"Who was engaged to?"

"The girl who wrote this song. It's so sad."

God, comfort her. "Poor thing."

"Can you imagine how awful that would be?"

"God help her."

"Amen," Lacey said, shuddering. "Anyway, that's not what I wanted to say. I wanted to know if you can come for lunch today."

"What day is it, Lace?"

"Sunday."

"And what do I do every Sunday?"

"Look, I know your parents love you, but it's not like they need you *every* Sunday. Not like I need you," she added quickly as Tim drew near.

"Rose and Marc are coming for lunch, so thanks for the invitation, but I can't today."

"You'll miss quality time with someone, then," Tim teased.

Lacey sighed. "Tim's decided to be a good Samaritan and has invited TJ to join us."

He had? "What a shame I can't come," Emma said, her smile broadening. Phew.

"Real shame," Lacey grumbled. "I wanted someone else to be there to take the pressure off."

"I don't even know if he'll show," Tim said. "After that hit last night, I think he'll be doing well to be at the doctor's in time, let alone make it out here."

"But didn't you say something about him wanting to look for a house?" Lacey asked.

"Is he going to stay?" Emma asked, her heart sinking. Not that she wished the guy ill, but it would certainly make life easier if she didn't have to consider Leona's emotions every time they watched New York play.

"You saw the game, right?" Tim asked. "From what I was hearing from everyone, they were impressed with his grit and commitment, so yeah, I think he'll be hanging around."

"Great."

Lacey laughed. "Come on. Didn't you just hear that sermon? About loving the unlovely?"

"Please. I'm not about to love him."

"No one's saying that. But you've gotta admit it was impressive."

"It was impressive," she echoed robotically.

Lacey laughed. "Look, just be nice to him. If I have to, then you can too."

"Are you making her be nice to him?" Emma demanded of Tim.

He palmsed-up her. "Just trying to practice what gets preached. But yeah, I gotta admit I feel a little sorry for him. I don't think he's a bad guy."

"He can't be a bad guy," Lacey insisted. "Not if Brandon likes him."

Emma bit her lip. "I'm willing to be nice, but don't expect too nice, okay?"

"Just be nice enough." Lacey eyed her, then tucked her arm through Emma's as Tim was called to speak to someone else. "And while I know you have this thing about not caring about finding Mr. Right, it doesn't hurt to make an effort to be nice to guys. You can use it as practice until Mr. Right finally comes along."

Emma's lips flattened. In all that she'd shared with Lacey, she'd never admitted to what happened when she was twenty-one. It was best to forget it and pretend that she was happy to be like the apostle Paul and remain single forever rather than let her emotions get caught up with her hormones and fail again. "I hope you're not trying to say that I should be trying to appeal to TJ Woletsky."

"Not at all! But with the Halloween party on Friday night, you might want to think about what you're going to wear."

"What's wrong with wearing the usual?" Emma protested.

"Nothing. You make an excellent Little Bo-Peep. But Tim said that some of the other guys will be there, so it's a chance to dress up in something other than your multipurpose crinoline."

"But I like my sheep."

"I know," Lacey said, patting her hand. "But you can't trot around with a stuffed sheep forever."

"You're so mean," she grumbled.

"I know. But I love you." Lacey grinned. "You sure you can't come to lunch? Please? Pretty please?"

"I'd never hear the end of it if I didn't show. But hey, you have fun."

Lacey sighed. "I'm praying for God to give me the strength to like the guy, because I don't mind admitting that I'm still struggling. But Tim thinks there's something worthwhile there, so I'm willing to give it a shot."

Emma nodded, hugged her, and said goodbye.

Good for Lacey, Emma thought, walking to her Beetle. Lacey hadn't known Nick except as Leona's nephew, so her history and interactions were limited, and she wasn't as emotionally invested as Emma. And yes, she'd heard the sermon about the Good Samaritan and knew the pastor didn't preach without wanting his words to stick. But letting a man off from his faults seemed so reckless, seemed to display such a shocking disregard for the feelings of Nick and Leona, that it was a struggle to even contemplate, let alone do.

But on the drive home, the questions wouldn't cease, and knowing she'd get no peace when she walked inside her parents' house, she pulled up outside the cute home she'd one day like to own. Like when her parents decided she was too old to live at home. Her lips tweaked. As if that would ever happen. Her parents loved family so much, insisting on these regular Sunday lunches and family meals together whenever possible. Which was great and all—she loved her parents, and her siblings too— but it didn't stop her wondering what it would be like to live elsewhere. And if she could pick anywhere, she'd pick here. The cute cottage held so much charm with its shuttered windows and cross-paned glass, its yellow paint the perfect complement to the pretty flower garden lining the path out the front, purpled with the last of the lavender for the season. She'd long considered it the prettiest cottage for miles, which said a lot, considering the gorgeous heritage homes in this part of the state.

"God." She exhaled. Tried to still her thoughts. "Okay, being honest here, I don't hate him, but I really don't like that man. I get that You somehow love him, and I know that You want us to love others, so please help me. Change my heart so I can love others too. And"—she gritted her teeth—"bless him. Amen."

Weight lifted. Some of the soul grime the morning's service hadn't cleared seemed to fade. Okay, she'd need some more Holy Spirit intervention, but she'd do her part and not hate on the guy anymore. And yes, she might need to grit her teeth, but she'd play nice.

She pulled up outside her parents' to see her brother's truck in the drive. Rose was probably here too, as they tended to travel from the city together. And sure enough, when she opened the door to Reddy's enthusiastic yelps, there they were, Marc sitting next to Dad, watching the pre-hockey game show on TV, while Rose was helping Mom in the kitchen, from which delicious smells wafted. Twinky eyed Emma, then stuck her little pink nose in the air and walked off.

"Hey, Marc."

"Sis." He stood, gave her a hug. "How you doing?"

"Good. You?"

He sank back into the suede sofa, eyes back on the screen. "Doin' okay."

"How's work been?"

He shrugged. "Much the same."

"Seen one fire, seen them all?" she teased.

He shot her a squinty-eyed glare. "Not quite."

"I might leave you to it, then. That game sure looks more interesting than me."

He threw a cushion at her, which she caught and hurled back, laughing as it struck him in the face.

"Hey," Dad protested. "I wanna watch the game."

"I didn't think you cared too much about Detroit or Pittsburgh," she said.

"Detroit's playing really hot right now," Marc said.

"Karlsson? He's going for a streak."

"Did someone say Brent Karlsson is gonna streak?" Rose said, fanning her face as she sat on the arm of the suede sofa. "Now this I've gotta see."

"I think they meant he's scoring well," Emma explained.

"Oh. Well, if he's playing, I don't mind watching. That man is hot!"

"And married." This much she did know.

"But hot," Rose said.

"And his wife is expecting a baby soon."

"How do you know that? Oh, let me guess. Lacey."

Emma nodded. "Apparently it got mentioned at one of the online Bible studies Tim goes to." A skater chick, Lacey had said. An Aussie who'd won gold in Vancouver last year.

"Oh. I forgot." Rose sighed. "He's just a bit too hot to be a Christian."

"What's that supposed to mean?"

Rose's gaze trickled down Emma's church attire. "Just most Christians I know seem to think makeup the work of the devil."

"I don't think that."

"No?" Her sister arched an eyebrow.

"I don't. Amongst other things, I just don't see any point in dressing up when I'm working with kids all the time."

"Were you working with kids today?"

"No. But there's nobody at church I'm wanting to impress."

"But what if there was?"

"I don't need a boyfriend."

"Have you told Mom this?" Rose murmured, rising to drag Emma partway down the hall. "You know she wants us all to get married. It's all about the grandbabies for her."

That might be so, but thank heavens Emma seemed to have the only Italian mother who hadn't pushed for her eldest daughter to marry and settle down. And Emma wasn't about to switch things up just to find the validation from a man that

Rose seemed to think so necessary. Anyway, God had her future sorted, so she wasn't going to ask for more.

"Em," Rose said, clutching her arm. "I just remember when we were teens you used to go all out to look pretty. Then you went off to college and changed. I don't know what happened—"

Because Emma had never couraged up to tell her.

"—why you think you don't need a man—"

"Do you really think a woman is incomplete without a man?" Emma interrupted.

"No. But a man can certainly give you a good time, if you know what I mean." Rose winked.

Her mouth soured. Yes, she knew exactly what Rose meant. "I don't want cheap love."

"Are you saying I do?" Her sister's eyes flashed, and she tossed her dark hair, so like Emma's own, over her shoulder. "I was just trying to be nice."

"And I don't want to see you hurt." Not like Emma had been. "I want you to be happy, to find Mr. Right and settle down instead of hoping you'll find him in clubs and parties." And whatever else went on after too much alcohol. Guilt stung her chest.

"Hmm. Well, anytime you want a makeover, you know who to ask."

"Wow." Emma blinked as heated indignation roiled through her. Who cared about loving the unlovely? Right now she was struggling to even like her own flesh and blood.

"You're welcome," her sister said, oblivious to Emma's humiliation.

"You people ready for lunch or what? Come on, switch that off," Mom said, moving to the TV and blocking the screen from view. "I want to see people at the table pronto. That is, if you expect to eat."

Mom's threat worked, as it always did—Marc had apparently

never forgotten the time when Mom fed his meal to the dog for being too slow—and they said grace and tackled the lasagna and salad with gusto.

Talk veered from work, to Marc and Rose's apartment, to sports, which led back to hockey. "Did you watch New York's game last night? Woletsky, wow," Marc said, shaking his head.

"Gotta hand it to a man who breaks his nose then gets back on the ice to score a goal." Dad took a drink of beer. "Woletsky seems to want to stick around."

"Ugh. I saw a picture of him. He's really ugly, isn't he?" Rose said.

"Maybe he's a Christian," Emma murmured.

"Why would you say that?" Mom asked.

"Rose seems to think all Christians are ugly," she said snidely.

"Rose?" Mom said, disapproval lining her forehead.

"That's not what I said." Rose shot Emma a withering look. "It's just like they don't care."

"Not everyone can be as pretty as you," Marc said to Rose.

Hurt cramped inside. Yes, her brother was a doofus who lacked tact. And yes, she could probably do with making more of an effort. But she'd seen what happened when she tried to attract a man based on her looks rather than her personality and character, and the realization of the utter ridiculousness of wanting such a superficial man had set her on this course ten years ago. But that still didn't mean she wanted her brother to say Rose was prettier. Even if it was true. She sipped her lemonade and glanced away.

"You think he'll stay around?" Dad asked Marc, as if Emma wasn't best friends with the wife of the Rangers' captain.

"Tim seems to think he'll be sticking around," Emma offered.

"Huh. I wonder if we'll see him around here."

She shrugged, her vow earlier to be kind halting her from saying those things she might wish to say. Like *I hope not.*

"There's a few of them who live nearby, aren't there, Em?" Marc said.

She nodded, taking care to fork the meat in to avoid answering anymore. Her family seemed to have the special sauce that tipped her tongue into saying things she really wished she'd withheld. It was a miracle they'd never questioned what had happened ten years ago.

"Well, I don't think we need to worry. It's not like we need to see him, is it?" Rose said.

But Emma might, she knew. And from the way Tim and Lacey had talked earlier, it might not take too long.

TJ STUDIED himself in the hotel's bathroom mirror. Winced. Yeah, there was a reason he'd said no to Tim's invitation today. Two black eyes, eight stitches, and a nasal splint did not a pretty picture make. Neither did it allow for a motorcycle helmet. Maybe Tim shoulda thought that one through before inviting him to lunch an hour away.

Still, at least he'd not lost any teeth. He'd been part of teams before where their media units would ask players what they'd prefer: a broken nose or to lose a tooth. He was an expert in this, having broken his nose three times now and having lost eight teeth. Well, six if you counted the yoyo in front that kept needing replacing and finally made him agree to a plate. At least a broken nose could be dealt with once rather than the tinkering mouth surgeries that wasted so much time.

But he hoped he'd done enough last night to prove that the team should have him stay. Tim seemed to think so, anyway, which was something, at least. That man better be careful. TJ might actually start liking the guy.

But today, a day off, felt like there was too much time, a bit like when he was stuck in the box while his penalty minutes counted down. He was itching to be doing something—anything—to contribute, to prove himself. Maybe he should contact the PR person to see if there was another way he could show his willingness to help.

He sent a message to her and was surprised to get an answer back immediately. Clearly the woman didn't do the church thing like Tim.

He studied the text. The team was engaging in a fire safety thing with a hero theme. *Sign me up*, he texted back. As long as his face wouldn't scare little kids.

That thought triggered a landslide of regrets, and he moved to the window, looking out on this part of the city. Noise, pollution, people. He'd never liked his small town growing up, but after living in L.A., he could now appreciate something of a small town's peace. There seemed a degree less stress, and he bet living in one of the world's biggest cities would hardly be easy, let alone affordable.

He placed his hands on the glass, looking down at the tiny figures far below. So many people, so much noise, so much dirt. Maybe if his contract was to get locked in he should investigate purchasing something out of town. And maybe if Tim asked him again to visit that kids' home he might say yes. He'd liked the town. He'd liked feeling like he made a difference, even if it was only for a kid or two. But who knew? Buying a house there sure had to be a heck of a lot cheaper than here, and it would likely prove a good investment and better economy than paying rent. So maybe if Tim asked him, he might visit and see if there was anything available in his price range. That was, if New York appreciated his laying down his body for the team and was prepared to keep him on.

CHAPTER 7

"How's Nick?" Emma asked Leona.

Leona jumped and closed her laptop screen. "Oh, my dear! I didn't see you there."

"Is everything okay?" Emma asked, leaning against the dark wood framing Leona's office door, gesturing to the computer.

"Oh, yes. Well, no. I'm just trying to figure out how I should pay for Nick's treatment."

"He's coming out of the hospital? That's good news."

"He's being released, but they don't want him to go home just yet. Not that I know where home should be for him. Ever since Helen died it's like he's lost and doesn't know where home should be."

"I thought he had an apartment in Buffalo."

"Once upon a time," Leona said sadly. "He sold it—at a loss, I believe, or so poor Helen said."

"He is an adult, though, and is being looked after by the club and the player's fund, or so I understood."

"It's not as simple as that," Leona objected. "There's so much paperwork to fill out and interviews and reports that need to be filed before funds are released. Truly, I'm finding this overwhelming."

"Would you like me to help?" Emma asked, feeling the pinch of obligation.

"Would you? Oh, my dear Emma, you'd be such a lifesaver."

She nodded. "Happy to help." Well, she would be. "Tell me what you need done."

But when Leona passed over a thick file in a manila folder, Emma understood why Leona had been so quick to hand this over. A brief scan of the contents showed just how complicated this process was, something that would not be fixed within an hour. She sighed.

That night, she visited Lacey in her grand farmhouse home in the next town across. The acreage might not count as a real farm, but it gave enough space for Lacey's dogs and horses and the other animals Tim had promised when a child came their way or when he retired. The restored farmhouse had featured in several magazines and showcased Lacey's impeccable Hamptons-flavored style.

Lacey's invitation to visit while Tim was playing away on a short trip to Florida had given Emma the chance to escape the Home for a few hours. Not that Emma didn't love the kids, but sometimes she needed a break and a reminder that the world was larger than damaged lives, sore throats, and missing toys.

"Here you go," Lacey said, handing her a large cup of home-made tomato soup. "Have a sip and tell me it tastes divine."

Emma obeyed. "It's really good."

"I know! I made the stock myself and everything, " Lacey said proudly. "Now, sit back, relax, and tell me everything about your day."

Sharing about the Home's troubles didn't exactly make for relaxation, but it was good to clear some of the spiky clutter from her heart, to get it heard by someone else who wouldn't judge her but understood on both a professional and a personal level.

"So you agreed to Leona's request for help with Nick's paperwork why?" Lacey asked.

Emma shrugged. "It's complicated."

"You can't feel responsible for Leona's family or for Nick. He's an adult. He has an agent. I would've thought someone from the team should be helping him with this."

"I thought so too, but Leona seemed unsure. Leona's just been so stressed lately," Emma felt the need to explain. "And she's started snapping at the kids, so anything I can do to ease the situation has to be better than nothing."

"But that still doesn't make it your responsibility," Lacey said gently. "Why do you feel the need to help all the time?"

Emma shrugged. "I want to help people."

"And you do."

How to explain that it never felt enough? That she'd never *be* enough? She clasped her hands around the large white cup and sipped her soup instead.

"Emma, I feel like you need to be careful. Sometimes it seems like you're the one heading for Leona's burnout. You need to add some fun to your life."

"What do you think I'm doing here?" Emma protested.

"Apart from me, because, as we both know, I bring the fun factor wherever I am. So go on, tell me. Fun. You. What have you done lately?"

"I have fun," she said stubbornly. When Lacey's eyebrows rose, she insisted, "I do!"

"Go on, then. Tell me the last thing you did for fun."

"I had lunch with my family."

"Erk. Wrong answer."

"I went for a run this morning."

"Double erk. We're not talking exercise. Did you laugh? Did you get all giddy smiles?"

"I don't do giddy smiles, Lace."

"You used to. Back when I first knew you."

"That was a long time ago."

Lacey eyed her, head tilted on one side.

"What's with the twenty questions?" Emma asked. "Don't you like my company?"

"When was the last date you went on?" Lacey asked.

"What does that have to do with anything?"

Lacey studied her, no trace of a smile now.

"What? Why has everyone decided I need to date? I don't need to date. I'm perfectly happy being by myself. It doesn't mean there's anything wrong with me."

"Who else has said you need to date?"

"Rose."

Lacey rolled her eyes. "She's always been boy-crazy, hasn't she?"

Emma nodded. "Which is why I get a little worried about her."

"She's smart. She's a Moritello."

"We're not all smart," Emma muttered. Witness the girl who'd thought she was, until she'd realized she could be as stupid as her little sister. "I guess I worry about her."

"She knows karate, though."

A smile poked out. "She's tougher than those costumes make her seem."

"So stop worrying about her. I think it's time to stop worrying about Leona as well. It's not a sin to focus on you."

But it was. Too much focus on what she'd wanted had steered her onto this path, into this life. "I don't know what you mean."

"It's not a sin to love yourself. Jesus wants us to love our neighbors as ourselves, so it helps if we practice a little self-care occasionally."

"I don't have time or inclination"—or a whole lot of extra cash—"to be going to day spas all the time."

"Nobody is saying day spas, but to care for others you have to have your own well replenished sometime, and relaxing, taking time off to rest, is important. Must be, because God did it."

"I'm not God."

"Exactly. Which is why you need to be careful not to burn out." Lacey sipped her water, her expression sober. "Emma, can you talk straight with me?"

"When do I not?" she mumbled.

Lacey's grin flitted then vanished. "Is working at Hopetoun all you want in life?"

Emma looked away from Lacey's green eyes, round in their concern. To have this question posed to her by two people in three days, both of whom knew her so well, was almost too much. "I don't know."

"Honey, you're thirty-one. Now, I know it's not a crime to not want to marry or have kids, and if you truly are happy and satisfied doing what you're doing, well, I'll say no more. But if there's the tiniest shred of doubt, then I wish you'd say something."

Emma bit her lip to stop an unaccustomed quaver. She blinked hard.

"You do want more, don't you?" Lacey said softly.

"I don't want to talk about it," Emma said.

"Emma, you're my best friend, and I hate that you don't want to share something with me that obviously troubles you."

"Pile the guilt on, why don't you?" Emma tried to smile.

"It's only guilt if I'm speaking the truth." Lacey grasped her hands. "What happened, Emma? Why don't you want to date or ever talk about finding Mr. Right? I feel like I've been really selfish these many years because I haven't asked you and I've focused on my relationship with Tim, then our struggles to get pregnant. I'm sorry for being such a bad friend."

"You're not a bad friend," Emma whispered. "Not at all."

"Then why don't you tell me?" Lacey looked close to tears herself. "I promise I won't tell Tim. Not unless I absolutely have to because it would force me to tell a lie. But if there's something I can help you with, you know it's good to share what's burdening your heart."

Emma placed her cup down, propped her head in her hands, and leaned over the table. She knew Lacey was trustworthy and wouldn't go blabbing her secrets to all and sundry. And she knew secrets had a way of poisoning things, reframing perceptions and beliefs. Maybe it was time to share a little of the past. *Lord?*

But before she could speak, her phone buzzed. A glance at the screen revealed it was Jacob. Jacob, who had taken her shift at the Home tonight, no questions asked, and whom she had told to call her if there was an emergency. Her pulse spiked. "I'd better take this."

Lacey nodded as Emma answered the call. "Jacob?"

"Emma, you need to come straightaway."

"What's happened?" She pushed back her chair.

"It's Leona."

"What about her?"

"She's—hey, wait, you can't go in there!"

"What's going on? Jacob?" Her chest knotted.

A pause. "Mr. DeVries is here along with two cops. You need to come right now." He hung up.

"Em?" Lacey stood too. "What's happening?"

She sucked in an unsteady breath. "It's Leona. Apparently there are police at the Home."

"Want me to come?"

"Please." Emma shoved the notes into the folder, grabbed her bag, and headed out to the Volkswagen. Ten prayer-filled minutes later, she was pulling up outside the Home. The drive held Mr. DeVries's silver SUV and two police cars, fortunately with their lights not flashing. She raced inside only to have a policeman command her to stop.

"My name is Emma Moritello. I work here, and—"

"Emma Moritello?" He glanced at the sheet of paper in his hand. "I'm afraid we don't have you on our list. There's a Margarita Moritello, but no Emma."

"That's me. I'm Margarita. More often known as Emma. Jacob Browne called me. He said something about Leona."

"Ah, you're the assistant residence manager?"

"Yes," she said impatiently.

"Then you're the one they're waiting for." He nodded to Leona's office. "In there."

She glanced at Lacey, who was now being interrogated in much the same way. But there was no time to waste. She could see little people at the top of the stairs—little people who should by now be in bed. Where was Beth? "Excuse me."

Ignoring the policeman's call for her to stop, she placed the file on the hall table and hurried up the stairs, smiling at the children to hide her fears and hopefully lessen theirs. Some of them had experienced trauma being separated from families at the hands of police, so their visit here tonight could prove unsettling. "Now, Lily, can you tell me why you're out of bed?"

"We wanted to know why the police cars were here."

How to explain when she didn't know the answer herself? Redirect. "Now, there's nothing for you to worry about. You're all safe here." Emma glanced at little Nessa. "You're safe here, Nessa, okay?"

The girl's huge dark eyes watched Emma, and she hugged her toy bunny close—a gift she'd received as part of the Dignity Backpack all children received when they came to the Home, as so many arrived with their meager belongings stowed in a trash bag.

Lord, heal her. Emma gently stroked Nessa's braids before turning to Lily, whose own family history—passed from one drugged-out family member to the next—and forthrightness meant she was often the spokesperson for the little band of children housed here. "Where is Beth?"

"She's with Brandon. He's sick again."

A retching sound came from the boys' bathroom, up the next half-flight of stairs. Poor Beth. "Okay, well, I want everyone to hop back into bed now."

"Can we hop, *please*, Miss Emma? I likes hopping," Lily said.

"If you can hop quietly, like *tiny* little bunnies, then yes. I'm going to count to ten, and whoever is not in bed by ten will not be getting a story read to them tonight." By Lacey. Or whoever else was first released from the inquisition downstairs. "One, two, three..."

With a sound more like dinosaurs than quiet bunnies, the children scampered to bed, and Emma took another precious few moments to tuck them in and make them promise to stay in bed until their story reader came. "I have to go downstairs, but I'll be back to check on you soon. Now, who promises to behave?"

The chorus of "me" would hopefully buy a little more time. She hurried back down the stairs, grabbed the file, and met Jacob, who was listening as Mr. DeVries spoke to the police.

"...do not understand how this could have happened."

Emma nodded to Pete Pilova, the older policeman with whom she'd had dealings when some children had come into their care in the back of his police vehicle. "What's happened?"

Lacey came to clutch Emma's hand. "It's Leona. She's missing. The police are saying she's stolen funds."

"What?"

"Miss Moritello, I need you to come down to the police station with me. This is a very serious crime."

"I don't understand. She was here today. She gave me these

files to look at." Emma handed them to Mr. DeVries, who glanced at them before placing them in the officer's outstretched hand.

"We'll need to see that," Pete said. "Now, Mr. DeVries, you and Miss Moritello and this young man here," he said, gesturing to Jacob, "will all need to come to the station with us now."

"But why? We really don't know anything," Emma said.

"We need all the information we can gather. And it seems you three were the ones who had the most contact with Leona, which is why we want to find out all we can now."

"Now?" Richard said. "Can't this wait until morning?"

"I'm afraid not. Not if we're going to find her in time."

"You'll probably wish to speak to John, our accounts clerk, as well."

"Very likely," Pete said. "Have you got his number?"

As Richard gave that to him, Lacey glanced at Emma, her brow creased. "I'm calling Tim."

Emma nodded. *Stay calm. Think.* "Can you stay here to watch the children?"

"Of course. Someone needs to." Lacey shot the police a mutinous look. "Tim will know a good lawyer."

"Your friends are not under arrest, Mrs. Carruthers," Pete said kindly.

"Then why are you insisting they go to the station in the middle of the night, like you think they're criminals?"

"No one is accusing anyone of any crime."

"Except Leona," Emma said softly.

Poor Leona. What had made her so desperate that she'd done such a thing?

~

"Are you serious?"

TJ glanced up from tying his skates to where Tim was

frowning on his phone. The noise level in the locker room dropped as other players seemed to tune into whatever was bugging their captain. TJ glanced at Tim's stick. *With me*, Tim had written over the tape, next to a crudely drawn cross.

"Wow."

Yeah, this was a wow. Granted, they hadn't played too many games together, but TJ had come to learn that Tim never answered calls before a game. Whoever this was, whatever had happened, it had to be serious.

Tim hung up, his forehead pleated.

"What's happened?"

"Lacey said Emma's been taken to the police station," Tim said quietly.

"She's been arrested?"

"Right? Crazy stuff. Lacey calls her a saint, because she's never put a foot wrong in her life."

TJ straightened, conscious of an insane desire to laugh. "So what'd she do? Jaywalk?" For all his faults, he'd never gone to jail. Who'd have thought the perfect do-gooder whose look of contempt could shrivel stones would have it in her?

"They think she stole money from the kids' home."

TJ felt his eyes widen. "No way. Emma did that?"

Tim shook his head. "Not Emma. Leona, the home's residence manager."

He whistled. It'd taken skill to learn considering his missing teeth. "So why is Emma at the police station?"

"Apparently Leona is missing, and they're trying to find her. Lacey is really stressed. I don't know what to do."

"You know a lawyer?"

Tim nodded.

"You've got a job to do tonight. You need to focus on that and get your lawyer to help your wife. And Emma."

Tim nodded and made another call, and TJ could almost see his brain ticking as he then tried to mentally focus on the game.

"Relax, man," TJ said. "It's gonna be okay."

"Yeah?"

TJ pointed to Tim's stick with its scrawled words. "Is that true or not?"

Tim glanced down, heaved out a breath, then looked up, studying TJ with a look he couldn't decipher.

"What?"

"You're the first person to have ever said anything about that."

"Maybe I'm the first pastor's kid you've had the honor to sit next to."

"Are you serious?"

"Yeah, don't tell anyone. It's not good for my rep."

Tim cracked a smile. "Okay. I'm gonna make a call. Then we've got a game to win."

THE GAME PASSED QUICKLY, Florida throwing everything at them. It hadn't been too many years since TJ had been playing here, when he'd accidentally rammed Mike Vaughan into the boards and been labeled a thug ever since. Mike might've forgiven him, but he knew some of Mike's friends hated his guts, even though they called themselves Christians and were supposed to be all about love. Over the years, Brent Karlsson from Detroit had made no secret of his loathing, his hits always a little harder than they needed to be. Of course, turnabout was fair play, so TJ made sure to get his own back, which probably hadn't endeared him any. He knew Mike had a few other friends, like Beau, who TJ had accidentally hit in Montreal. Now, that certainly hadn't been intended, but did it stop others from hating on him? Maybe he should stop reading social media, where nobody ever had anything good to say.

But despite his best efforts to prove his worth and stay

focused on the game, to do his best to ignore the chirping from players he used to call teammates once upon a time, thoughts of what was happening thirteen hundred miles north refused to go away. He hoped Emma was okay, that the kids—especially Brandon—weren't too worried. He forced himself not to ask Tim in the breaks, not wanting the dude to lose his captaincy mojo, but each minute that passed amped up his curiosity. He didn't dare pray—God wouldn't listen anyway—but he sure hoped things were okay. Did hoping for something even work? Prayers, he knew, sure didn't.

The game finished, and TJ was glad when Tim broke the deadlock in overtime. This night was stretching on way too long.

Later, after media interviews and pumping out the lactic acid by riding stationary bikes, he was finally able to ask Tim when he caught him studying his phone.

"Any news?"

"Lacey left a message. Emma's back at the Home, but they haven't found Leona yet."

TJ knew a ping of relief. Not that he liked the woman or anything—she'd made her feelings very plain about him—but he didn't like to think of someone who was trying to help kids being put into such a situation. "That's good, isn't it?"

"Yeah." Tim's gaze lifted, and he stared at TJ funny.

"What?"

"You know Leona is the aunt of Nick Grenier."

"What?" The man he'd put into a coma? "No way."

Tim's brows shot up. "You never met her?"

"I've only been to the kids' home once."

"I thought you said you'd been to see him in the hospital."

TJ's mind spun back to that time when he'd been at the hospital near Buffalo. Vague recollections of a graying woman with talon nails clawing at him were immediately followed by those of a dark-haired woman who—

He swore.

"What?"

"Emma."

"What about her?"

Guilt strummed his stomach. "I don't know why I didn't realize it before."

"Huh?"

TJ shook his head, conscious of a tight feeling of unease followed by a twinge of disappointment. No wonder she'd viewed him with contempt. He couldn't blame her for hating him. How could he have not realized that Emma was Nick Grenier's girlfriend?

CHAPTER 8

"I'm so sorry this has happened, Emma," Richard DeVries said, leaning back in Leona's office chair. "You should never have been put in such a position."

Emma nodded, pressing her lips together to avoid saying something she might regret. She glanced around Leona's office, still a shambles from the past days of police investigation—days which had meant trying to fulfil her duties while also answering questions from dozens of people she still didn't have any answers for.

"I'm sure it was simply the fact that, as you've assisted Leona in various financial matters over many years, they assumed you would know more."

"Obviously I didn't," she gritted out. What a fool she'd been. How had she missed the fact Leona had been drawing off the budget for years?

"The board has voted unanimously for you to continue as interim residence manager while we get to the bottom of this."

Another nod, tighter lips, in case the wildness inside escaped. Her car troubles this morning in the rain should have clued her in to the kind of day this would be.

"I can assure you, whatever Leona has done will not reflect on you."

"I don't know how you can offer that assurance," she said stiffly. "Everyone is now aware of what's happened, and I can't help but feel that Hopetoun will forever be under a cloud."

"Now, now. You can't think like that. Things will improve, I'm sure."

How he could possibly sit there and be sure, she didn't know, but she nodded all the same. "How are we fixed for funds? We're currently understaffed, and we desperately need a new furnace, and—"

"I'm afraid John and the accountants are going to have to look at that. Oh, and that reminds me. It seems we're to expect a visit soon from the health and building inspectors—"

"What?"

He sighed. "Did Leona not mention this either?"

"No." No way were their premises up to code. "Richard, surely you can see the importance of getting the furnace sorted as quickly as possible. You've seen the cracks in the walls"—she pointed to the ceiling—"and I'm sure such things will be red flags as far as any inspections are concerned."

Another sigh. "I'm going to ask the board to investigate some state grants and see if we can access funds another way. It is problematic, being so small and such a unique facility as we are. I'm not sure we can count on the state prioritizing support for us over larger facilities."

Her stomach clenched. "What are you saying? Is there a chance they might close us down?"

"No, no." But the wrinkled brow he wore didn't fill her with certainty. "One day at a time. In the meantime, perhaps we'll need to consider fundraising some more as well. I'm not sure what your baking skills are like..." he added, offering a small smile, like he thought this was a joke.

Baking skills? Was he serious? "But sir, we're heading into winter, and if the furnace doesn't work—"

"Please, don't worry," he said, patting her on the arm like the grandfather he was. "I'm sure things will all work out."

How nice for him to sit in his comfortable waterside home and be so sure. Meanwhile, those who lived here and dealt with the children every day...

"Now, if there's anything I can do, please let me know."

Reminding him of the urgency of getting a furnace didn't seem to have worked. "Sure. Thank you, sir."

She walked him through the small vestibule to the front door, lifting a hand as he said goodbye then hurried to his car through the rain, all the while working to hide the shakiness inside. How could she do this? A broken-down old home filled with broken lives, and all this new responsibility weighing her down. Was it truly possible that the home may be forced to close?

And today was Halloween, and judging from the weather, there'd be none of the candy hunt outside in the garden that she'd envisaged for the children as their alternative to trick or treating. What could she do?

Her phone buzzed and she drew it from her pocket. *Sorry, Emma. Can't make it today. I'm sick. Beth.*

She gritted her teeth. Great. Understaffed had just become chronically understaffed. If someone from the state licensing authority visited now they'd be right to shut them down. This was wrong. *Lord, please help!* She spent the next ten minutes on the phone until she secured another worker who promised to be there within the hour. An hour? It was better than nothing, she supposed.

Tension rippled under her skin, and she took a moment to breathe, to try and relax. It would do no one any good to continue to let the pressure build inside in case it spilled out on the kids. That was the last thing anyone needed.

She moved back to Leona's office, stood in the doorway, and sighed. Surely the police had visited enough this week that she could finally start cleaning up. There was no way she could do any work when it looked this chaotic. Drawing up her spine, she entered the room and began straightening the desk and what files remained as best she could. It didn't seem likely that Leona would return, so perhaps she should look at rearranging things more comprehensively so the office space would work more efficiently, in the way that Emma had always envisaged. But after that burst of energy, her strength was fading, her emotions as battered as the flimsy porch outside—one false step and she might crumple.

A vase of dead flowers taunted her. That was something the police wouldn't worry about, surely. A toss in the trash later, and soon the cleared surfaces began to look more promising. Perhaps it wasn't that surprising that Leona had felt so overwhelmed. There was a lot to be said for people keeping things neat and organized, if only to provide the illusion that things were under control. She knew all about illusions.

The phone rang, and she snatched it up. But it wasn't Lacey's number—Lacey, who was supposed to be coming with Tim for this afternoon's party and whom Emma longed to see. Instead, it was an unknown number. "Hello? This is Emma at Hopetoun House."

"Emma, you were Leona's assistant, correct?" a female voice said. "Oh, it's just terrible what that woman did."

No argument there. "Can I help you?"

A sigh. "You could ensure that we're paid on time. My name is Elina Beutsch, and my company supplies bulk foods for organizations such as yours. Beutsch Foods—I'm sure you've seen us around."

Emma nodded. "I've seen your delivery vans, yes." They were the ones responsible for the large trays sitting in the kitchen's chest freezer, the pre-prepared meals that required time in an oven and consisted mostly of large generic pasta bakes, the likes of which would cause Emma's mother to die of horror if she knew. But while unappetizing and carbohydrate-heavy, they got through a lot of these types of meals, which proved easy on weekends and the days when their cook didn't come in.

"Look, I know this isn't your fault, but this is my business, and Leona owes us for at least two months' worth of food."

Two months' worth? Emma's head sank into her hand.

"I'm being instructed by my partners to not send any more deliveries until we receive payment for what has been delivered already."

"I'm sorry this has occurred, and I can understand your concern, Elina, but you must know that these circumstances are out of my control right now," Emma explained.

"Oh, I know this must be a very trying time for you, but I'm sure you can also appreciate our concern when we, in good faith, have distributed food that has put us in the red."

Emma sucked in a deep breath, breathed out slowly, steadily. She'd studied some basic accountancy as part of her social work degree, and this did not make sense. Why any business would be demanding money from a charitable organization and sailing so close to the red in needing their payment was beyond her. Perhaps something else was at play. Like a business wanting to sever all connections with an organization they now considered fraudulent, in case it reflected badly on them.

"Emma? Are you there?"

"Yes, sorry." Why was she apologizing? "I was just thinking."

"Well?"

The woman's snappish tone drew defensiveness. Emma swallowed it, working to speak calmly. "I will speak to the trustees and see if we can get that payment sorted as soon as possible, but as I said, things are so chaotic right now that it would be really helpful to not have to worry about interruptions to our food services. Especially considering the children for whom this food is needed," she added, reminding her of the real victims of Leona's crime.

"And I'm sure you can understand that we don't need to be wasting good food on bad clients."

Emma clenched her fingers. Prayed her voice would stay steady. "The children here should not be disadvantaged just because of an unscrupulous person. It's not fair on them."

"Of course it isn't, and it's because of that we have delayed this as long as we could. But I'm afraid we will not be making our next delivery."

"Which was due when?" Emma asked, dreading to know the answer.

"Tomorrow."

She closed her eyes. "You do understand we are a charity? For children?" *Disadvantaged, discarded, and neglected poor children*, she could've added, but didn't.

"And we have supported Hopetoun for many years, never raising our prices even when it meant we were barely making a profit ourselves."

"But the children—"

"Beutsch Foods is not a charity, Emma."

"But what are we to feed the children?" she asked, panicking.

"That is not my concern. Prompt payment today, please, or else I'll be sending in the debt collectors."

"But—"

But nothing, as dial tone played in her ear.

She replaced the receiver, her fingers shaky. "Lord? What do I do?"

Mr. DeVries's offer of *anything I can do* floated to mind. Oh, there were certainly some things he could do. But when she called his number it went straight to voicemail, and with her thoughts tumbling faster than the Home's aged laundry dryer, she could only leave a basic message asking him to call her as soon as possible.

What to do? What to do? What to do?

Okay. First things first. Check the freezer. Figure out how much food remained. What supplies they had. It wasn't like they were in a remote, poverty-stricken African village miles from a store. They'd find a way.

She moved to the kitchen storeroom where the chest freezer was kept and lifted the lid. Inside, about halfway down, lay ice-encrusted boxes of food labeled with the Beutsch emblem of a grinning mask. Maybe a week's worth of food.

She closed the lid and braced her hands on either side of the freezer. Think. She had to think. But a yawning despair about the complete inadequacy of this Home and its structural and organizational problems loomed so very large. How had she ever thought this was a good place to work?

It *was* a good place to work, she told herself fiercely. It was about the kids. It was never supposed to be about the inefficiencies of the management.

"Emma!" Jacob's voice, holding its own version of panic.

Her eyes closed again as she braced for whatever new crisis was lying in wait. She could do this. God would give her strength. Wouldn't He? She moved to the base of the stairs.

"Emma! Come quick!"

A pounding of feet and two flights of stairs later, and she was dodging a seemingly possessed shower hose in the boys' showers, which spun and twirled as it sprayed the white-tiled walls. "What happened?"

Just then, the shower nozzle twisted to spray water at her. She gasped, shrieking as water hit her chest. "Turn it off!"

"I can't!" Jacob yelled, desperately twisting the faucets. "There's something wrong."

"No joke." Except this felt like a giant joke. A giant, cosmic-sized joke. All she needed now was for Lacey and Tim to show up with Tim's teammates.

"Miss Emma?"

At the sight of Brandon's, Trey's, and Ben's anxious faces peering through the doorway, Emma grabbed the nearest towel and covered herself as best she could. "Boys, I need you to go get changed with Elle. We're having a water crisis here."

"Bad shower," Trey said, pointing at the water.

Emma firmly removed them from the room. "I need to go to the basement and turn off the water. Now, please go hop into your animal onesies, and I'll be back to help you soon."

She shut the door, sure the water soaking the bathroom floor would soon escape to leak down the hall and stairs. She grabbed two extra towels and placed them in the hallway, where the door was half an inch above the floor. Jacob would have to fend for himself.

"Miss Emma," Lily called, Rasheel hovering behind her. "My fairy wing is torn."

Of course it was. This day must have been designed in hell. "Ask Elle if she can help you. If not, I'll do my best to mend it soon. Now, off you go."

She raced down the stairs and down to the basement, where the watermain was, and broke two nails as she did her best to twist it closed. Who knew if this was the best technique for dealing with this type of situation? Maybe her dad would know.

But when she looked at her phone, it held the bubble moisture dampness and nothing on the screen. "No, no, no!" The shower blast must've killed her phone.

Tears sparked to her eyes, and she bit back a sob. "God, help!"

"Miss Emma?" Karinda's voice wafted from above.

She took off her fogged-up glasses and scrubbed a hand over her face, pushing at the headache pounding beneath her brow. The kids didn't need to hear her panic, didn't need to see her fall apart. Hopetoun House was meant to be a respite from drama and strife, not adding to the children's trauma. She dragged in another breath, wiping at her smeared glasses. She could call Dad from the office phone. He'd help, if he was back from work.

But when she ascended the basement stairs to the main hallway and pushed back her still-sopping hair, it was not to see Lily with her broken fairy wing. Nor was Brandon standing there dressed in his giraffe onesie.

Instead, she saw Lacey and Tim, looking as if they were struggling not to laugh. And with them stood two others, one of whom was none other than TJ Woletsky.

THE AMUSEMENT FILLING his chest at the sight of the bedraggled woman with brown streaks on her face quickly faded as TJ realized she was struggling not to cry.

"Emma? What's happened?" exclaimed Lacey. "Why are you all wet?"

Emma glanced down, and the towel covering her top half fell, revealing a wet T-shirt that would do any number of Spring Breakers proud. TJ shrugged from his jacket and moved to hand it to her. She stared at it, as if unsure what to do.

"Put it on," he said roughly.

"Emma." Lacey snatched it from him and wrapped her friend in his jacket. "What's wrong? Why do you have dirt on your face?"

"What?" Emma rushed to the mirror by the door, pulled off her glasses, and frantically rubbed at the dirty marks that gave her a raccoon-like look. "I was downstairs, it was dirty, and— oh, it's not coming off!"

TJ spied a pack of wet wipes sitting on the shelf of a nearby cupboard and handed them to her.

"Thanks," she murmured, swiping at her face.

He nodded and again had the impression she was struggling to hold it together. Averting his gaze, he glanced around at the wilting streamers, the shrunken balloons, the strings of cray-oned leaves pinned to the dark, heavy beams that said this place was old. He shoved his hands in his back pockets, shifting his weight as his gaze returned to the women.

"What were you doing downstairs?" Lacey asked. "I thought we were having a party."

"We were—we are. Well, I don't know anymore." She glanced up, her gaze touching TJ's before veering to her friend. "We have a shower issue, and I had to turn off the water."

"Leaky faucet?" Andrei said from next to TJ.

Emma's blue eyes focused on Andrei. "Someone broke the shower hose, and the water wouldn't stop. Jacob is still up there, I think. If he hasn't drowned."

"I'll go," Tim said, and Andrei followed. Leaving TJ standing awkwardly as Lacey consoled her friend.

"It's okay," Lacey soothed. "Just relax. We're here now. Let's find something else to put on. Where's Beth? She's rostered on, isn't she?"

Emma's lips quavered into a smile. "She's rostered on, but she's sick."

"Oh. So the kids aren't ready?"

"Kids aren't ready, food isn't ready, decorations aren't finished. I've been on the phone for half the day dealing with people: the media, the trustees—oh, and people like the food services who are demanding to be paid."

Lacey drew her to the lounge area. "Come on. Sit down for a moment and breathe."

Emma slumped into a chair, shaking her head as she wiped her glasses. "I was on the phone to one of the food delivery groups we deal with, who are now saying they won't deliver any more food because Leona didn't pay."

"What?" TJ asked.

Her gaze shifted to him, then back to Lacey, who looked as gob-smacked as he felt. "They can't do that," Lacey said.

"I've been told debt collectors are on their way." Emma's chin wobbled.

"What? That's ridiculous. The kids need to eat. What has Richard said?"

Who was Richard?

"He's not answering his phone either. Not that I can call him anyway. Not with my phone getting a soaking too."

"Doesn't it work?" TJ asked.

She shook her head.

"Do you have rice?"

She blinked. "What?"

"Do you have rice?" he asked again.

"I think so. But—"

"Give me your phone." After a moment, she stretched it out hesitantly to him, and he glanced at it, wincing at the moisture lining the screen. "Where's the kitchen?"

Lacey directed him, and he moved down the hall and veered right. The kitchen, like every other part of this place that he'd seen, was old, the cupboards outdated with a few doors hanging askew like they had broken hinges, looking as beat up as the ancient VW Beetle parked outside. How this building had passed fire and health regulations he did not know, but he knew this was definitely not the time to ask about that. He opened a timber door and, like he'd hoped, found it was a pantry. A quick scan of containers and he found one of rice, which he lugged back to the counter. He scooped out a couple of handfuls of rice and stuck them in a bowl before placing her phone within the rice.

He took the bowl back to where the women sat. "Here. It should help a little. The rice draws out the moisture."

"Thanks." Emma's gaze touched his again, and she offered a tentative smile.

"Let's go see how those kids are doing," Lacey said. "You

should get dry and into your outfit, and we'll give the kids the party they need. That *you* need."

"I can't pretend to have fun. I'm so tired and so stressed, and I haven't done anything—"

"What can we do?" TJ asked.

"What?" Emma blinked, as if she'd forgotten he was here. "What do you mean?"

He shrugged. "Is this supposed to be a party? Is there food? More balloons? I don't know. What were you planning to do?"

"I haven't had time to plan anything," she said. "I thought we could do a candy hunt for the kids, but the rain put paid to that."

"No trick or treating?"

"Given the nature of the types of kids we have here, it's not considered appropriate," Lacey explained.

"Of course." Should've realized. "Get changed and we'll come up with something. Do you have snacks somewhere?"

"In the kitchen," Emma said.

"Okay. We'll sort it." His cheeks pushed up in a smile he wished she'd believe, and she nodded and hurried up the stairs.

"Poor thing," Lacey murmured. "She works so hard, just to have this dumped on her like this."

Guilt gnawed, as it had ever since he'd realized just why things were so bad. If it wasn't for his hit on Nick, then Leona would never have stressed about the money and devised a way to steal what she thought she needed. Really, all of Emma's stress—her tears—could be traced back to TJ. He winced.

"How about I deal with the snacks while you help with the kids?" he suggested.

"Good idea." Lacey moved up two steps, then turned. "Thanks, TJ. You're really thoughtful."

Yeah. His thoughtfulness had gotten Emma into this mess.

He returned to the kitchen, quickly finding the bags of sugar-free candy bars and salt-reduced chips that had been put to one side. Obviously, trying to eat healthy was a priority for someone here. After tipping them into bowls, he wondered what else he could do. Checked out the contents of the fridge. Okay, scratch the healthy memo. The big bowls of what looked like cheese and macaroni were hardly going to satisfy three NHL players' appetites. Maybe they'd be better off ordering pizza as well. Kids liked pizza, didn't they? He sure did. Not that this afternoon was about him. Even if his morning had kind of felt like it was.

His lips curved as the memories from this morning resurfaced. The team wanted him. Okay, maybe *wanted* was a little generous, but the coach had told him after practice that McDermott had been officially ruled out for the season, and seeing TJ was playing so well, they wanted him to stay, with all that that would mean.

Relief had consumed him, so much that he could only hope Coach hadn't seen. "I'll do my best," he'd promised.

"I have a feeling you will." Coach Koder had even found a gruff smile. "Guess you're gonna have to move out of your hotel."

That was no loss.

Conversation with Tim had led to an invite to coffee downtown, where he'd learned that a number of his new teammates had homes in the area.

"It makes it easier to get to training and the airport," Tim had said, following with an invitation to join Andrei and him at the Halloween party at Hopetoun that night.

The conversation had made him linger in town a little longer, checking the listings of realtors. There seemed little point in wasting rent on a place when he could afford to buy, and this area was only going to increase in value. So, much to his shock, he bought a house. His first house, after living in apartments and rentals all these years. It wasn't new and it definitely wasn't big—which was why he could afford it—but it was his. A place he could call home after spending so many years feeling lost, if not precisely homeless. He'd been in a celebratory mood when they arrived at Hopetoun only to be greeted by Emma's despair. And now he had a gnawing sense that perhaps he'd been too hasty in purchasing a house when his money could've gone to a far more worthy cause.

Guilt strummed his chest as he wandered back to the big room. Nobody was there, so he ventured up the stairs, where a clanking noise suggested the bathroom was being fixed. Or trying to be fixed, at least.

He poked his head in. "How's it going?"

"You any good with pipes?" Tim asked.

"I've fixed a few," he admitted. Sometimes fixing things himself was a heck of a lot easier than waiting on a building superintendent's pleasure. One of the surprising legacies of summer mission trips to underprivileged places when he was young.

"What are we doing wrong?"

He took the wrench from Andrei and made a few quick adjustments. "Try that."

"The water is turned off," the wet worker—Jacob, maybe? —said.

"Then turn it back on," TJ said.

He was pretty sure whatever the guy muttered was not something kids should hear. "He might need to wash his mouth out," he said to Tim. "Pretty sure Miss Emma wouldn't like those words being spouted about here."

Andrei laughed, and amusement creased Tim's face. "Jacob is trying."

"That's for sure," TJ muttered, which earned another chuckle from the defenseman.

"Come on. Not everyone has your particular brand of charm," Tim said.

True, that.

Jacob returned, his appearance prompting a turn of the

faucet and a ping of relief within TJ's chest that his actions seemed to have sorted whatever the issue was. "Looks like it had a screw loose."

"Not the only one, huh?" Andrei said.

TJ shot him a look he hoped did his third-grade teacher proud.

"How'd you get so good at plumbing?" Tim asked TJ.

"I've done my share of renovations."

"Hey," Lacey called from the door. "Is it fixed?"

"Is now," Tim said. "Thanks to TJ."

"I thought you were doing the food."

"Did that." TJ shrugged. "But I gotta go where my skills are needed."

She grinned. "So, I guess we know the answer now."

"The answer to what?"

"How many NHL players does it take to change a broken shower?"

"That was bad, babe," Tim said, wiping his hands on his jeans before swooping in to kiss her.

"But there were no lightbulbs, so…"

TJ cut a look at Andrei as Tim's and Lacey's voices faded as they moved downstairs. He followed Andrei outside to the hall and down one flight of stairs, only to almost bump into Emma, who was dressed up in some fancy old-fashioned costume. "Hi," he blurted.

"Hi." Her gaze dropped, then returned to him. "Is the shower fixed?"

"Is now."

She nodded. "Thanks. And, um, thanks for before. I'm not normally so emotional, and I don't usually get so frazzled, but there's been a lot going on, and I…" The huge white puffy sleeves of her dress bobbed up and down as she shrugged helplessly.

"It's okay. The kids will be okay."

"I hope so."

"It *will* be okay," he tried to assure her.

She sighed. "I can't believe Leona was so selfish that she didn't see how this would impact them."

Regret made his stomach queasy. "I don't think many of us take the time to consider the consequences of what we do." He knew that only too well.

"Well, thanks for your help."

Her hesitant smile drew his own. His gaze trickled down to what she held under her arm. "Um, why are you holding a sheep?"

She glanced at the stuffed toy. "I'm supposed to be Little Bo-Peep, but I kind of need a sheep, otherwise the kids just think I'm dressed like Cinderella."

"Appropriate."

Her lips lifted on one side. "Because I wear sooty clothes and work all hours?"

"Because you're caring, like a shepherd who goes after the lost sheep." Whoa. Where had that thought come from? Maybe Dad's sermons had burrowed deeper than he'd thought. Judging from her look of shock, she was just as surprised as him, something which drew discomfort and made him rush to speak. "I just meant that your kind of job means you care, and that you should be concentrating on the kids and their emotional well-being, not on the practical concerns others can deal with."

She blinked behind her glasses, and he had an awful feeling she was about to cry again. What had he said this time?

He stepped toward her, feeling helpless except wondering if maybe she needed a hug.

"What are you doing?" she asked, flinching and stepping back.

He blinked. Yeah. What *was* he doing? He'd never been the type to make moves on another man's girl. People might think him wild, but he had standards. But something about the way she'd maintained eye contact, the way he'd finally managed to win her smile, had made him forget the legacy of his family's dysfunction and want to offer what little comfort he could.

"Emma, are you coming or not?" Jacob called from the top of the stairs.

TJ tensed. How long had he been standing there?

He didn't care what the man thought. But he couldn't deny he was starting to hope that Miss Emma might finally see TJ in a good light. And that one day she might be able to forgive him for all the trouble he'd brought to her. And to Nick. He frowned.

CHAPTER 9

"Nope. It's gotta have some boogie to it, hear the song? When you get to the chorus part, you've gotta boogie on down."

Emma suppressed a smile as she watched TJ demonstrate to Lily and the others who were trying to copy his moves as he shimmied and did a version of the twist she bet wouldn't be Rose-approved. But it definitely had the kids shrieking with laughter. Another knot of tension released.

"See Andrei there? He's got the moves. Must be his Russian genes. They're well known for their boogying ability."

Jacob snorted, TJ glanced up, and she quickly looked away. No way was she going to admit she found TJ's efforts tonight a little impressive. But she couldn't deny that the day that had proved so challenging might actually work out okay after all. Well, not the many questions that still loomed over the future of the Home. But maybe, for one night at least, she could do as everyone else here tonight seemed intent on doing and forget her troubles and focus on giving the kids a good time.

"What do you think, TJ? Am I dancing good enough?"

"Mmm." TJ paused, knuckling his chin as he eyed Lily seriously, although Emma was pretty sure he was struggling not to laugh at her improbable ballet moves. "Yeah, okay. You've definitely earned yourself a candy bar. Come pick your poison."

"Poison?"

"Oh. My bad. It's not poison. Not to cute little girls on Halloween," he said, giving a uncomfortably good impression of an evil laugh as he rubbed his hands together.

Lily shrieked with excitement, and TJ glanced over at Emma again. She forced herself to meet his gaze, not wanting him to know just how disconcerting she found him. That moment in the hallway upstairs when she'd thought he was moving in to hug her and she'd snapped like the fishwife she wasn't. He perplexed her, this man who could blithely injure others but who could then almost quote a Bible verse and play the fool to win a little girl's laugh. She liked this man. Well, she could if he hadn't proved what lurked below the surface. He was complicated. Way too complicated.

"Are you finished?" Lacey asked, collecting paper plates.

Emma nodded, the crusts of her pizza, which the men had ordered in to supplement their pasta, lying soggy on the plate. She handed it to Lacey and moved to help her.

"No, don't get up. Sit down, relax for a moment."

Well, okay then. She didn't need a second invitation.

"He's kind of fun," Lacey said, pausing to watch the dance show.

TJ and Andrei had decided that, given the weather's lack of cooperation, the kids could earn their treats by dancing. "It's a good way to burn off the sugar," TJ had said.

And it had been. And had proved laugh-out-loud funny as the professional sportsmen tried to outdo each other with their crazy moves.

Lacey had ended up filming part of it, promising Emma to keep the kids out of it. Some of them were here because of the courts and were not meant to have their photos published. But

Tim and his teammates were all good sports, and she couldn't help but feel grateful for their efforts tonight.

She exhaled. What a crazy night.

Her skin flushed as she remembered how bad she'd looked when they arrived. Who needed to dress up in disguise when she looked exactly like poor Cinders, only wetter?

That reminded her. She needed to get TJ's jacket from her room upstairs.

"I'll be back in a moment," she murmured to no one in particular, then stole to the stairs.

"Miss Emma?" Lily called.

"I'm coming back," she promised, her glance lifting from the small blonde girl to connect with TJ's blue gaze. He smiled, and her chest pinged, and she hurried upstairs accompanied by an unwanted feeling of fluster. What was that?

She wasn't one to find someone like him attractive. He wasn't attractive. Everything about him should—had, *did* —repel her.

Except he'd shown himself to have a gentle, thoughtful side, which her battered heart had responded to and couldn't deny. Obviously she was really tired and really needed sleep.

She stole into her bedroom, where her wet clothes from earlier lay in a huddled heap on the floor. She winced, hoping her wet T-shirt hadn't been too revealing. She'd never been overly prudish until she'd realized what could happen. And she bet no woman on the planet wanted to look her worst when meeting three handsome NHL players. Well, two handsome ones, anyway. And one whose face still wore stitches and bruises from a recent busted nose.

A noise at the door made her turn and jump. "Jacob! What are you doing up here?"

They had strict protocols about where men and women were allowed to be. The men were not supposed to go to the girls' bedrooms and vice versa.

"I came to check on you," he said. "Are you okay?"

"Oh. Thanks, I'm doing better. It's been a pretty big day, hasn't it?"

"I can't stand watching Woletsky downstairs with a stupid grin on his face like he doesn't realize this is all his fault."

"He didn't make Leona take the money," she said gently.

"She only took it to help out Nick."

Well, that was true. "Regardless, he is trying to make an effort, and you have to admit that if it wasn't for him, the party would've been a massive fail."

Words looked to be bubbling in his mouth, which hastened her to say, "Anyway, I just came to get his jacket to give back to him."

She snagged it from the bedpost and moved past Jacob, the space between them small. "Are you okay?" she asked him, frowning. It wasn't like Jacob to be in her space.

"Don't get deceived by him. He's not a nice guy."

"I beg your pardon?"

"You know what he's capable of."

"I don't mean that," she said. "What exactly makes you think I'm going to be deceived?"

"He smiles at you, and you smile back."

"No, I don't."

He crossed his arms, his raised eyebrows telling her that apparently her face wasn't as well behaved as she'd thought. Whoa. Was that why TJ had thought to lean closer before as if to hug her? Maybe she should find a mask that she could wear whenever he was around. This was not good at all.

"You're being ridiculous. Now, I need to get back to the kids."

"But, Emma—"

She moved her arm away from his grasping hand. "Please, don't touch me," she said. "I really can't deal with this on top of everything else that's happened today."

She hurried away, breathing unsteadily. Jacob was a little too familiar sometimes and seemed to think she was interested when she had no interest in any man, nor would ever be likely to. But the way TJ's gaze searched her as she returned to the room, the frown he wore as Jacob returned a few seconds later, made her chest tight.

"Are you okay?" Lacey asked.

"I'm fine." She nodded, tried to paste on a smile. Except this tension she wore said otherwise.

IT WAS MUCH LATER, when the kids were all in bed, that they were able to gather downstairs. Emma felt ready to collapse, but given the help of Lacey, Tim, and Tim's teammates, she couldn't trundle off to bed just yet. Not when they'd given up whatever fun plans they could've had for a night spent dancing with little kids.

"What a night," Lacey said as Tim held her hand. "I can't imagine how you feel, Emma."

"I'm pretty tired," she admitted. "But thank you, everyone, for all you've done. I really didn't expect you all to step up like you did. I know the kids had lots of fun."

"Come on, admit it. You had fun too," Tim teased.

"I might have. It was nice to forget all the stress for a little while, at least."

Lacey sighed. "So, what's next? What did Richard say when he finally called you back?"

Ah, Richard. "In his defense, he apparently did try and call me on my cell. And when I didn't reply, he didn't think it was urgent. He said the board is going to have an emergency meeting tomorrow to discuss what we can do about the finances."

"Do you have to go?"

Emma nodded. "I think so."

"Do you know what they'll be asking?" TJ asked.

"I suspect they're going to be looking at the future of the Home. I know there are some board members who think that what we do is unnecessary, especially considering there are other state-run facilities nearby who do similar things. But none of them have the family atmosphere that we provide here at Hopetoun, so I don't see that as an option for these children."

"It's gotta ultimately be about what's best for them," TJ said.

"That's right." She studied him, unnerved by his insight and compassion. "Have you had experience with other homes like this at your other teams?"

"A bit." His gaze fell, and he plucked at the corner of his sweater.

"You were really good with them, TJ," Lacey said. "I think Lily might be in love."

He chuckled and shook his head. "She's a cute kid. But they all are."

They were.

Tim reached to grab a Hershey's Kiss from the bowl centering the table. "I think I earned this."

Lacey snatched it from his hand. "Thank you." She unwrapped it and swallowed it down.

He laughed and picked up the bowl, pitching the silver-wrapped candies to his teammates and Jacob before ceremoniously handing the bowl to Emma. "I think you earned this most of all," he said, pilfering one from the dozen that remained.

She smiled, loosening her hair from the too-tight braid, finger-combing her hair to ease the taut strands. She'd kill to wash her hair and get rid of the last of the grime she could still feel from her misadventure downstairs, but no way would she leave these wonderful guests after all they'd done for her. They'd earned the chance to relax and eat chocolate, just as she had done.

The silver paper she scrunched into a ball, then she popped a candy in her mouth, savoring the way it melted on her tongue.

A lift of her eyes and she saw TJ glance away, the sight causing another tight feeling in her chest. Why did he keep looking at her?

"So, what do you think will happen?" Lacey asked. "At the board meeting tomorrow."

Emma's spirits dived again. "It's hard to know," she said. "I got the impression from what Richard said earlier that we're going to have to prove to them that we can contribute. There are some board members who don't want to feel like they're just always handing over the cash."

"Who's Richard?" TJ asked.

"Richard DeVries is the trustee president," Lacey said. "He's a local businessman and has been on the board of trustees for years. I think his father was, too, if I'm not mistaken."

Emma nodded. "The DeVries family have long been involved in philanthropic causes, and Hopetoun House has long benefited from their support." She pushed up on the comfortable sofa. "This house used to belong to a family called Hopetoun, who donated it to the town for the use of children requiring emergency and longer-term accommodation while they're assessed for fostering arrangements. We're one of the few private facilities that caters to children with special needs." Her gaze met Andrei and TJ. "I know it must appear a little old and rundown, and we're only too aware of its faults and the need for things like a new furnace, but it's the best we've got, and we do what we can with the resources we have."

"It's a good cause," Andrei said.

"I think so." She unwrapped another Hershey's Kiss. "Which is why we're glad you can lend a higher profile to what we do here."

"You need to raise money?" TJ asked.

"I'm pretty sure that's what the board will be saying tomorrow."

"Well, we'll have to think about what we can do," Lacey said. "But raising the profile shouldn't be too hard, especially when I post videos from tonight online."

Andrei and TJ groaned. "Do you have to?" TJ asked.

"What happened to a good cause?" Lacey teased.

Tim reached over to clap TJ on the back. "Speaking of raising the profile, some of us might be able to contribute a little more very soon."

"What do you mean?" Jacob asked.

Tim grinned. "TJ? Want to tell them?"

TJ stretched out his legs. "I got told by Coach this morning I'm on the team."

Emma's smile felt wavery, uncertainty rushing through her, but she knew she had to say what was expected. "Congratulations."

TJ's mouth ticked up. "Thanks."

"You're on the roster?" Jacob asked, his tone disgruntled.

"Yeah." TJ studied him before his blue eyes turned to Emma. "Guess that means you'll be seeing a little more of me."

She nodded, wondering about the swooping feeling in her stomach. Why were her emotions so volatile today? Bed was looking increasingly inviting.

"So, will you be staying nearby?" Lacey asked.

Emma was relieved by the question. It didn't look like Lacey had known this and not told her. Imagine if he were to stay in the neighborhood…

"Tim mentioned that a number of the players live nearby, that it makes it easier to get to practice." His glance strayed to Emma again. "Gotta admit I wasn't loving staying in a hotel."

She nodded again, pretending interest in a stain on the couch. The sofa might be comfortable, but it bore the wear of use over many years.

"So I decided I might look around here."

Her stomach tensed. Uh oh.

"You will?" Tim said. "That's good. I can advise you on some good neighborhoods, if you like."

"Thanks, but I should be okay."

"You sure?" Tim asked.

TJ nodded. "Yeah, I found something I like that suited my budget."

"Already?"

"I might've been a bit excited," he admitted, looking a little embarrassed.

"I'll say," Lacey said.

He shrugged. "I've hated renting. It just seems like dead money, so when I had a look this afternoon, turns out I was the first to see it, as it just came on the market, and they agreed."

"You bought a house?" Tim asked.

"Like I said, I hate renting, and I figured it might be time to prove I'm willing to settle down."

Lacey gasped. "I didn't know you had a girlfriend."

He coughed, studied his shoes. "I don't."

"Yet," she said pertly.

"I can't see any girls wanting to get with me," he said quietly.

The room filled with incredulous silence before Jacob laughed. "Aren't you supposed to be some kind of chick magnet? I thought you had girlfriends coming out of your ears."

"Maybe once upon a time." He shrugged. "But I don't want to be that guy any more. I'll do whatever it takes to prove to management that they're right to keep me around. Besides, I really like the thought of finally having a home."

The way he said that drew a tug of compassion inside Emma. She knew of his volatile career, that he'd rarely stayed with any team for very long. Perhaps this would help ground him and settle him and help him find what he was searching for.

"So, where's this new house?" Tim asked. "You gonna have a housewarming party?"

He shrugged. "Maybe, when it finally closes, but they accepted the offer, so I'm hoping it'll be really soon."

"Is it near?"

He nodded. "It's just a little cottage, three bedrooms, but that's enough for me. It's on Grove Street here in town."

Oh no. Emma's mouth dried. "Is it yellow?"

"You've seen it?" he asked. "It's kind of cute, with these shutters and nice glazed windows. Not really my usual thing, but the price was right, the owners eager to sell. It needs some work inside."

No. *No, no, no.* "I…I didn't know it was for sale."

He shrugged. "They have a sick daughter in California who they want to be near, so I guess it's just good timing, huh?"

He grinned, but she felt sick. This man whom she'd just felt sorry for had gone and bought her dream house.

THE ELATION FILLING his chest died a quick and sudden death when TJ glanced back and saw Emma was staring at him, her eyes wide and mouth sagging, as if in horror.

"Emma? Are you okay?" Lacey asked. "You look pale."

She looked like he'd suddenly morphed into a toad.

"What?" he asked her.

She pressed her lips together, and he knew a disconcerting twist in his guts. Was she that upset about him moving to the neighborhood?

"I'm tired," she said.

He hoped that was all she was. She looked pretty ticked off with him, too.

"We should go," Lacey said, tugging Tim upright. "Especially given all that's happened today and the fact it sounds like you're going to have another big day tomorrow."

Emma nodded, her tight expression easing as she hugged Lacey and thanked her and Tim and Andrei. "I don't know how I would've managed if you guys hadn't come when you did."

"It's our pleasure," Tim said. "I wouldn't have missed TJ's awesome dance skills for anything."

"Yeah, if anyone deserves praise it should be TJ. Between the food and the shower and the dance moves, wow." Lacey said. "I didn't know that about you," she said to him.

He shrugged. "It kept them amused."

And he thought he'd caught a glimmer of a smile on Emma's face as well. He wished he knew what he'd done to change her opinion once again.

"And buying the pizza," Andrei said. "It was good."

Emma nodded, her gaze not quite meeting TJ's. "There are some good places to eat in town."

"Good to know, huh?" Tim said, clapping TJ on the shoulder.

"Yeah," he said automatically. It was good to know, but it would be even better to know he had someone to eat there with him.

"Pizza is great for one night," Jacob said, arms folded, "but we can't rely on donations all the time."

Emma shot her colleague a frown, which wrinkled into concern. "We are going to have to think about the food situation. I forgot about that."

"Maybe they'll come up with some options in your discussion with the trustees tomorrow," TJ offered.

"Maybe." Her head lowered, like she didn't want to see him.

TJ exhaled. Women. So unpredictable. You thought you were doing okay, then they proved to have misunderstood you all this time.

He joined the others in saying goodbye, and overheard Lacey ask Emma if she'd heard anything from Nick.

Emma's glance at TJ suggested she didn't want him to over-hear. He didn't let that stop him. He wasn't a gentleman. He pretended to be listening to Andrei talk about his weekend plans. "No," she murmured. "I tried. He didn't pick up."

Huh. Not the way he'd treat his girlfriend.

"He's probably as shocked as the rest of us," Lacey said.

"Yeah."

"Do you plan to go up there to see him?"

"When I get the chance to get away, but with everything so crazy now..."

"Hey, it'll be okay."

Emma bit her lip, nodded.

A strange feeling, almost like disappointment, swept through his chest. Why she cared for a guy who seemed to have little care for her, he didn't know. And why he cared about this at all, he didn't want to explore. He had to force a smile, force himself to meet her eyes. "Thanks for a good night."

She met his gaze for a swift second, then it fell. "Thank you for all your help."

"Sure thing. Anytime." He bit back the *sweetheart*, knowing he sounded a little sarcastic, but disappointment tugged at the bridle on his tongue.

He joined the others getting into cars and kicked his chopper into gear. It was late, and he'd have to ride back to the city to catch some z's before catching a flight to Toronto tomor-row. Maybe the ride would be enough to settle his heart into normality.

CHAPTER 10

A week of meetings and frustration and disappointment and more frustration culminated in a Friday afternoon train trip to the city with Lacey. Emma swallowed the last of her chicken cassoulet, knowing it would be hours until they met Tim for dinner after the game late that night. Thank God for Lacey. Thank God for the chance for mindless escape. She needed a chance to recalibrate her heart and escape the endless turmoil of her week. Her car had decided to act up again—a faulty motor, Dad thought, which considering its vintage status, could only mean an expensive repair that she'd put off as long as she could. But that was nothing compared to the nausea-inducing situation created by Leona's actions. She'd been discovered boarding a plane in Seattle, trying to get to some Pacific island hideaway, and she had been remanded in custody while police sought extradition to New York.

The whole Leona scenario and what it meant for the Home was so embarrassing that Emma felt like she couldn't go down the street without people whispering about her or speculating about what really might've been happening at Hopetoun House. Maybe it was ridiculous, as her parents pointed out during last

Sunday's lunch, but Emma didn't think so, judging from the comments she'd seen on Facebook. Lacey's footage of several dancing hockey players had been posted with the intent to promote the Home, but scattered among the laughing emojis in the comments that suggested plenty of people were as surprised as she was by TJ were those comments that questioned the financial integrity of those who ran the Home. How could anyone tar them all like that?

At least here in the city she didn't need to wonder if people thought about her like that. Here, people were just focused on themselves and getting where they needed to go, and she didn't have to wonder about anything except the immediate goal: finishing their meal at this bar and meeting up with Rose and Marc to watch the game with Lacey at Madison Square Garden.

Lacey—wonderful friend that she was—had insisted on Emma accompanying her to a favorite hair salon for a surprise booking, where the girl who tended Emma's hair did something amazing with the cut that made her feel rather better about herself. Maybe there was something about trying to look good that actually did make one feel better.

"Because it's one thing to say you're fine," Lacey said. "It's quite another to have that sparkle in your eye that says confidence."

"And girl, with hair this color, you should be on top of the world," the stylist said, fanning Emma's hair through her fingers before calling over another stylist to examine the color and softness. "It's natural?"

"Yes," Emma admitted.

"I'm so jealous."

"Honey, there are women in the city who would kill for hair as good as this," the other stylist said. "If ever you want to cut it off, you can get a lot of money."

"For what?" Emma asked.

"Wigs."

"Uh huh," the first stylist said. "You better not go swishing that fine mane over the back of any chairs, just in case you're missing a big chunk the next day."

Emma laughed. "You're not serious."

"Honey, we've seen it all."

"Mm-hmm," the other woman said, nodding. "There are some crazy people in this town."

Apparently so.

As ridiculous and heart-lightening as that seemed, it had at least distracted her from the seemingly hopeless situation that was Hopetoun. At least, until her thoughts had tracked back to the Home's troubles an hour north.

"What's that look for?" Lacey asked.

"I just can't help worrying about what's going to happen."

"With the kids?" Lacey guessed.

Emma nodded.

"Look, I know things are tough, but there are positives too. Didn't Rasheel, Nessa, and Trey get placed this week?"

"Yes." A bit of a miracle, but it helped with their staff-to-client number protocols.

"So focus on the positives. Now, do you think an appletini will help?"

"I don't really know how much an appletini will help the future of the Home."

"Emma, Emma, Emma. Come on. Let it go," Lacey chided. "You've been stressed all week, and there are plenty of people trying to solve things. You don't have to feel like you're doing this by yourself."

Except she did feel like she was in this by herself. Lacey, good friend that she was, didn't live with the kids almost full time. Her heart wasn't entwined with them like Emma's was. Neither did the board of trustees really understand all that was going on. Even trying to explain it to her parents seemed impossible. They didn't understand why Emma carried this so close to her heart. Emma barely understood it herself. Only that if she failed, it would feel like she'd failed not only the kids but also God. How to put all that in a pithy sentence so that Lacey would be sure to understand?

"Come on. Let's see that confidence again," Lacey begged.

Emma pasted on a smile—the lipstick shade brighter than she was used to—and swung back her new hairdo. "The jeans are nice."

"Right? I told you they looked good on you."

After the haircut, they'd detoured via a quick trip to Bloomingdales, where Lacey's last name seemed to open doors Emma knew would never open for her.

"So, does the fawning thing happen everywhere you go?" Emma asked, taking a sip of water.

"What?"

"Those sales assistants at Bloomingdales who wouldn't leave you alone."

"I don't go there often enough to notice." But the tweak to her mouth suggested maybe she did. "Look, I figure it's the perk of what Tim does. If his contract means he has to play away a lot and risk injury that could be permanent, then I'm not above seeking perks people are only too keen to offer. It's not like it hurts anybody, is it? I get a discount, they get a mention on social media. You could be more high-minded than me, but most of the girls I know feel much the same."

"Because most of the other girls you know live in this exact same world."

Lacey held out her hands. "The way I see it is that it's my husband who's a public commodity, so I'm a little bit like one of those wives married to a famous actor. Except my husband can lose his teeth."

Emma laughed.

"It's not funny," Lacey said. "It's a very real thing."

"Tim has lost a tooth or two, hasn't he?"

"Yes, but the team dentist got it straight back in. He's certainly not as hard core as TJ is."

TJ. Her spirits sank. The man who'd stolen her house.

"There it is again. What *is* it with you and that man? I thought you appreciated what he did last week."

"I did," she said, her flat tone not even convincing herself.

"Then what? Are you still blaming him for what Leona did? Sooner or later people need to understand that Leona is responsible for her own actions. And as hard as this might be to hear, even Nick was not completely blameless. I've looked at the footage again, and Tim is right. TJ played tough but fair, and Nick should've been aware of what was going on."

"I don't blame him for that anymore."

"Well, hallelujah. So what *do* you blame TJ for?"

The issue of the stolen house sounded so silly, so petty and juvenile, she couldn't say it aloud. "Just put it down to a big week and the fact that I'm still not completely comfortable around him. Is that okay?"

"That's okay. But fair warning: if it continues, I'm going to have to ask you if you've forgiven him yet."

"Thank you, Pastor Lacey."

"I could be a pastor, couldn't I? I've got this compassion thing down, right?"

"Totally down," Emma said, rolling her eyes.

"You're so mean."

"I know."

Lacey laughed and finished her cocktail with a slurp. "Okay, it's party time. Where are we meeting your sister and hot fireman brother?"

Twenty minutes later they had bypassed the queues, Lacey's status as wife of the team captain affording her gold-star treatment, people stopping to chat to her like she was a celebrity and had the inside scoop on the game tonight. Emma glanced around, glad that she'd taken the trouble to dress up more than she normally would. This crowd saw a lot of suits and tended to be a little more sophisticated than some of the fans the TV showed around the league. The wives and girlfriends section where they were headed was no exception. Lacey was normal, with a normal job, but even she tended to dress up, not wearing a sweater as some girls did but a stylish blue jacket and red shirt combo. The more fancy dress code wasn't surprising, given some of the players were married to popstars and actresses. Emma had visited on one occasion and been introduced to a very famous English soccer star and his fashionista wife. She wondered who they might see today.

Her phone vibrated, and she glanced at the screen. Marc wanted to know where she was, so she messaged him back, arranging to meet him and Rose in the bar.

Unlike Lacey, Emma didn't have any obligation to schmooze, so when she explained to Lacey where she was going to go, Lacey nodded and continued her conversation. Emma took the stairs to the bar and grill where Marc was waiting. Hugs and kissed-cheeks later, she took a stool while he asked what she wanted to drink.

"I'm good."

"Saint Margarita. I'll get you an appropriate beverage."

He bought a beer for himself and her namesake cocktail for her, which she protested when it arrived. "I've already had a drink with Lacey."

"Are you driving home?"

"No. We came on the train, and we're meeting Tim after for a meal and he's driving us back."

"Then don't complain. Games are always more fun when alcohol is involved, and after the week Mom said you've had, you need some more relaxing."

"I'm not going to argue with you there." They clinked bottle neck and sugared glass rim and exchanged details about their past few days.

"So, what's gonna happen to her?"

"Leona?" At his nod, she shrugged. "I haven't been told anything official, but I've been led to believe that there may be some leniency, given the situation."

"Yeah, I don't know. The way I see it, it's all Woletsky's fault."

Lacey's words from earlier rang through her ears which, combined with a little voice she suspected might be God's, made her say, "She was still responsible for what she did."

"Yeah, but—"

"I told her, many times, that there was help available, but she didn't want to listen. And considering she was heading to Hawaii, not using that money for Nick, I think it's hard to see how TJ can be held responsible for that."

He took another swig and eyed her. "That's the first time I've heard you defend him."

She shrugged. "You don't need to worry, brother dear."

His gaze unnerved her. "You sure? I've been hearing things about him, that he's visited the Home a few times. I saw the pictures Lacey posted on Facebook."

"He was only there because it's part of his job. He's got to convince the powers that be and be seen to be community-minded so they let him stay."

"As long as he's not trying to schmooze you."

"Please. Can you imagine?"

"Em, you're not a princess like Rose, but you're a catch."

"Sure." She eyed him over the rim of her glass.

"Don't believe me, then," he said, waving a hand. "I'm trying to be supportive."

"Yeah, I'm pretty sure you can be confident that he's the last man on earth I'd ever want to be with. He's not a Christian, and you know that's important to me. So never fear, brother dear. I shall not be seeing that man any more than absolutely necessary."

"Okay then." His skeptical glance almost pushed another

protest from her, but knowing he'd be quick to accuse her of Shakespearean levels of denial, she refrained.

"I wonder what happened to that sister of ours?"

Emma glanced at her phone only to find that there was indeed a message from Rose. "Something came up."

"Something always does," he said. "Nice of her to tell us she's not coming."

"She's always been good that way."

"So I guess I get to sit by myself. Awesome fun."

"Haven't you got a friend you can call?"

"The game starts in ten minutes."

"Call them now and they could be here for the second period." She paused. "I could ask Lacey if you can come and sit with us, at least for the first period."

"And see how the better halves live?" He finished his drink and stood. "Call her and let's go."

Ten minutes later they were watching the players skate onto the ice, Marc's appearance in the special box reserved for the players' families and guests not drawing too much surprise. He'd thanked Lacey, his hands filled with the complementary hotdogs provided, offering running commentary on the skaters as they were introduced.

"How did Woletsky get on Tim's line?" he asked Lacey.

"He's been playing well, and Coach Koder thought to mix things up with Montreal tonight."

Montreal meant Beau Nash was playing. Emma watched as Beau moved to the Montreal goal and couldn't repress a small sigh.

"Sorry, Em, but he's got a girlfriend."

"For real?"

"Uh huh. You really should follow some social media," Lacey admonished Emma. "He was in a photo with some other Montreal players for Halloween and had his arm around a woman."

"Oh well. C'est la vie."

"You might need to try a little closer to home," Marc said.

"Like who?" Lacey said. "Our girl is a little fussy."

"I don't need a man to feel content, thank you very much," Emma retorted.

"I told her she'd better not go getting any ideas about Woletsky," Marc said, leaning in front of her before taking a huge bite of his hotdog.

"I told you that you're insane, right?" Emma pushed him from her line of vision. "He's not a Christian, and even if he was —that would take a miracle—I don't think he's attractive at all." Apart from his eyes that seemed to hold a magnetic quality. She swallowed. "I hate his beard."

Lacey laughed and pointed at the screen. "Well, maybe God can do a miracle."

"What?"

She eyed the Jumbotron, where a cleanshaven face appeared next to the number thirteen. "He shaved?"

"They all did," Lacey said, smirking. "Apparently it's for men's testicular cancer awareness, called Movember. They have a bet to see who's going to have the most scruff by the end of the month." She shuddered. "I told Tim it's a good thing he's got so many away games this month, because I don't like kissing him when he's got a beard. It's not like it's playoffs."

Emma nodded and ducked her head. That moment of seeing TJ had been unsettling. He didn't seem nearly as pirate-like without a beard. And the fact this disconcerted her was disconcerting too. Because she didn't want to find the man attractive in any way. No. Uh uh. No way. God would help her stay sane. For as much as she believed God could do anything, she didn't think God would do something as astounding as save TJ.

~

THE PUCK FLEW past his visor, and TJ sucked in a breath. He'd been hit in the face before with a puck, his beard the legacy of hiding the mark left by one that hit his mouth and destroyed his smile, leaving a scar two inches long crawling up from his mouth to balance the new one that now scored his brow. Pretty, he had never been. But what was that compared to the Movember challenge? As much as he'd hated to shave the beard, it was for a good cause. Not just to raise money for something he believed in—he'd lost former teammates to cancer before— but if it helped convince team management they'd made the right choice in keeping him, then that was fine.

TJ pivoted, chasing the puck, shooting it across to Tim, and together they attacked the net guarded by the huge body that was Beau Nash. TJ gritted his teeth, doing his best not to respond as Montreal's defensemen roughed him over. Yeah, it was no surprise they didn't like him after what had happened last month. But it had been an accident, and these things happened.

Beau gloved the puck, eyes narrowed as he waited for TJ to get back into his zone, then passed the puck behind the net, where Montreal's defense moved it out from the blue line.

The game passed with heat, most of which was directed at TJ. Every pore screamed to defend himself, but he knew if he reacted then he'd be booted from the first line. And this was such an honor that he'd put up with a whole lot of crap before losing this chance again. Why Koder had even thought this was a good idea he still didn't really know, but he wasn't going to question the coaching staff's decisions. Maybe Tim had had a say.

The puck slid to his stick, and he scooped it up and passed to Tim, who shot it back, then TJ took another swing.

Beau reached, but the puck went over his shoulder, the lights flashing and siren blaring as the Garden filled with cheers. Nice. Nothing like a little validation with a home goal.

He skated toward the bench, following Tim's glance up to where the wives and girlfriends sat, only to see, seated next to Lacey, Emma. And next to Emma, a man.

His heart stuttered, and he almost missed the pats on the helmet and thumps on the back as he took his spot. Who was that? Didn't Emma have a boyfriend? What was the deal with Nick?

The period soon ended, and as he trudged to the locker room, he knew he had to refocus his thoughts, get his head back into gear. This was how he'd used to play, mind games with others to throw them off. Now that it was happening to him it wasn't so funny. And the worst thing? He was doing it all to himself.

The next period wasn't as smooth, as again he took the brunt of Montreal's offense. They hadn't liked what TJ had done to Nash, and they hadn't liked his goal either.

One of Nash's defensemen slammed TJ into the boards, then Sekkonen, Montreal's winger, started swearing at him, getting up into his face, agitating for a fight. Fire rose, and TJ fought it and fought it and—

Snapped. He threw off his gloves and grabbed the guy's jersey as he swung until his fist found face. He felt a corresponding thud in his side and started to wheeze before someone grabbed him from behind. He moved to throw him off, then realized it was Tim, the black-and-white referee uniforms not far behind. A word his father hated escaped.

Tim shoved him to one side. "Shut up."

"I couldn't help it," he protested, skating to the penalty box.

Still, the record of nearly two weeks without a fight had to be worth something, right?

He sat in the sin bin, his glance straying to where Emma sat as he ground his teeth, wincing at how stupid he must've looked. Why would she even look at him, meathead that he was? Especially when she had someone like that dude sitting next to her. His fingers clenched. Agitation rose. But what about Nick?

Another cuss word leaked. He'd failed. He wouldn't stay on the top line. He'd never win. All he was good for was throwing punches and losing teeth and getting stitches. He'd never be good enough to win, let alone win the girl.

~

"Woletsky."

TJ turned, the tunnel dim enough he hoped no one would see the effect Koder's chewing out had had on him. Then startled at who was wanting to speak to him. "Nash."

"Lucky goal."

The dude was teasing him? He'd bluster all the same. "You and I both know it was all skill."

Beau's mouth twitched. "Yeah, you need skills to get past me."

"Watch me." He moved to walk away.

"Wait. We need to talk."

TJ sighed. He'd done so much talking already tonight. Apologizing to the coach. To Tim. "Look, I'm sorry about that hit."

"Yeah, that's what I wanted to talk about."

"Everything okay?" Tim asked, arriving on the scene. "Hey, Beau. Good to see you, man."

"Tim." Beau grasped his hand, then leaned in for a quick man hug.

Huh? Oh, that's right. They were both part of some Christian group. He'd seen Tim doing these video message things with some of the other do-gooders who loved to hate on sinners like him.

Beau finished catching up with Tim, then turned to TJ. "Look, I know it wasn't you."

Wait, what?

"We're staying in town tonight, since we play New Jersey tomorrow. I'd really like the chance to explain a few things." Beau scratched the back of his head, his trademark long hair cut off after TJ's run-in with him last month. Beau nodded to Tim. "You can come too, if you like."

"How long will it take?" Tim said. "I've got my wife here, and I planned to have dinner with her."

"You can bring her too, but what I have to say is really for TJ here."

That didn't sound good.

TJ sucked it up and agreed to meet in a hotel restaurant not far away.

"You know what that's about?" Tim asked when Beau had left.

"Doesn't sound good," TJ muttered.

"You never know. God can work all things out for good."

TJ tossed him a choice swear word, which drew Tim's smirk.

"Yeah, maybe keep that to yourself until you hear Beau out."

AN HOUR LATER, TJ was sitting in a leather chair in an expensive restaurant, opposite Beau, as Tim sat next to him. Lacey had opted to meet them later, saying she and Emma were happy to wait. There was no mention of Emma-the-two-timer's dude, and he wasn't about to ask. Not when Beau was sprawled back, arm stretched along the back of the next chair, eyeing him with furrowed brow.

"So, you want me to apologize again?" TJ asked. "Your teammates seem to think I need to."

"Yeah. That." Beau heaved out a breath and leaned forward to put his elbows on the table. TJ's mom would've had a fit. "Look, I need to say something to you, and I'd really prefer it not to get around."

"Anything you say dies with me."

Beau slid a look at Tim, which drew a similar response.

"Okay, here's the thing. I know everyone thinks you hit me and I hurt my head and got knocked unconscious, but you and I both know it wasn't exactly that."

"Huh?" Tim said.

Beau exhaled. "You know I went to the hospital, and yeah, I had a concussion, but it wasn't really caused by the hit."

"So what was it?" TJ asked.

Beau's lips pursed. He glanced at Tim, then back at TJ. "My girlfriend told me I should tell you. That it was only fair considering how much abuse you get."

"Tell me what?"

"Man, I love that woman, but I hate having to admit this." Beau sighed.

TJ glanced at Tim as the pop of a nearby champagne cork filled the air and they waited for Beau to speak.

Beau winced, then shook his head. "Okay, here's the truth. I fainted."

TJ blinked. "You what?"

"Fainted. Had what they call a neuro-cardio event. The docs weren't super sure why it happened. They reckoned it might've been an adrenaline spike when you rushed the net, but hey, it happened, and I'm telling you because you need to know the truth. Or at least my girlfriend seems to think you do."

Huh. TJ downed half his beer, his mind chugging down this information. "Why exactly are you telling me this? Your teammates don't know, do they?"

"No. And to be honest, I'd really rather they didn't. If they start getting worried I can't do my job, then who knows what they'll do?"

"But you keeping this quiet means I'll always be the fall guy."

"Yeah, pretty sure everyone thinks I'm the guy who fell." Beau's lips twisted. "Besides, I didn't think you'd care too much about what others thought. But yeah, I'll tell the team not to take it out on you so bad."

"You gonna tell the guys?" Tim asked. "You know Brent and Dan blame TJ."

"Only Brent and Dan?" Karlsson and Walton. TJ knew they played for Detroit and Toronto. "I thought they all hated me."

"You know Mike?"

"Vaughan?"

Beau nodded. "He seems to think you're not too bad."

"Big of him." But he did the man a disservice. Mike had proved genuine—one of the more lives-what-he-believes Christians he'd come across.

"You should call him sometime." Beau glanced at Tim. "Or have a conversation with this man here."

"About what?"

Beau finished his own drink, then set down the glass and studied TJ evenly. "About a little thing called grace."

CHAPTER 11

The definition of awkwardness? Sitting in a hotel restaurant with her best friend and her best friend's husband, next to a man whom others might assume was her boyfriend but who in actual fact had refused to look at or speak to her since he and an apologetic Tim had appeared thirty minutes ago.

Emma glanced at Lacey, who gave her a shrug as if to say she had no idea what was going on either. All Tim had said in postponing the post-game dinner was that Beau Nash wanted a quick word with him and TJ and could they stick around a little longer. And as much as Emma would've preferred to have gone home rather than be forced to endure a silence that felt this sticky, she couldn't deny curiosity about what had happened. Clearly something had happened. TJ's tension was palpable, his knee jerking under the table like he was a ticking time bomb. She understood from what Lacey had said that Beau was one of Tim's good friends, but why he would want to meet with TJ she did not understand. Maybe it had something to do with TJ's hit on Beau last month.

"The steak is good," Tim said. "How's yours, TJ?"

"Okay."

Hardly a resounding endorsement of something that cost the equivalent of a couple of dinners for all of Hopetoun's hungry mouths. She so should have gone home. Maybe she still could. What time was the last train?

"Good game," Lacey offered, obviously at as much of a loss for conversation as Emma was. "Even if it wasn't a win."

"Yeah, we tried," Tim said tiredly.

Lacey squeezed his arm, offering him a sympathetic smile, then turned to TJ. "You seemed to be getting it from Montreal tonight."

TJ slid a look at Tim, and Emma wondered what was being left unsaid. Was he upset about the fight? From where she'd been sitting, it'd looked like the Montreal player had been the one stirring up trouble.

"Your goal was good," Emma felt she needed to contribute.

This at least scored her a glance and a grunt that might have been meant to express appreciation. She didn't know. She barely cared. The man was an oaf. She was tired. It had been a big day to finish a huge week. She exhaled. Turned to Lacey. "So, when do you plan to go? Maybe I should see if the train is leaving soon."

"Oh!" Lacey shot Tim a look that Emma couldn't quite decipher. "Um, soon?"

"Yeah, if soon isn't in the next half hour, then I'm going to have to go catch that train. It leaves in"—she checked her phone—"twenty minutes."

"Sorry we took longer than expected," Tim apologized again.

"It's okay. I know stuff happens. But I need to get back soon. I've got another big day tomorrow."

"We'll take you," Tim promised.

She relaxed. That had been the arrangement. And while she wasn't opposed to late night train travel, she'd feel safer without.

"So, what are you doing tomorrow?" Tim asked.

"I'm doing some cooking with my mom."

"Wow. Big day," TJ muttered, sarcasm dripping with every word.

Her chest heated. *Ignore him.* She faced the others instead. "With everything that's been happening and all of the uncertainty around the Home's meal arrangements, I thought some home-cooked meals could be helpful in the short-term."

"Great idea," said Tim.

Lacey nodded. "Ooh, maybe some others could donate a meal, like what happens in church when people are sick or in hospital or have a new baby."

"That's a good idea. We'd just need to make sure that everything is done without certain ingredients and allergens that might affect the kids, so we'd have to be careful about how it's done," Emma cautioned. "I'm pretty sure we're supposed to have commercial grade quality kitchens for the food preparation."

Another grunt from the man beside her.

"What?" she asked, placing her fork on her plate.

"How does the kitchen at Hopetoun pass muster?"

"I beg your pardon?"

"It's as crappy as that beat-up car that's always parked outside."

Indignation heated her chest. That beat-up car held a lot of sentimental value, sentiment being something the man beside her was probably allergic to. She gripped her water glass with shaky fingers, willing herself to calm.

Lacey shot TJ a narrow-eyed look before offering Emma a sympathetic smile. "I suppose meal donations mean there are no measures to assess who's cooking what and how it's done."

She nodded, appreciating her friend's reversion to the previous topic. "It's a shame, but it means we can't just accept any offering, as well-intended as it might be."

"So you're going to do it at home? I didn't know you had a commercial kitchen," Tim said.

"We don't. But Mom has begged the use of the commercial kitchen at the community center near where she works, so while we wait for permission to do that, we're just going to stick with baking cookies."

"Cookies don't require a permit?" TJ asked, forking in the last of his potato bake.

"Apparently not." Not that she'd enquired too closely. There was fine line between compliance and expedience sometimes.

"So, there's still no word about how long it takes before you know what's going to happen with the Home?" Tim asked.

She shook her head, toying with her water glass. "It could take months to unravel the mess. Apparently Leona isn't talking, and now there are questions over her mental fitness for a trial. Meanwhile, I've been told there's going to be a building inspector's visit soon, and I'm pretty sure they're going to find a lot of things to fail. That was also part of what Leona was supposed to do, but it's obvious she wasn't on top of that either. I have to admit it was nice to come here tonight and just forget Leona and the Home's troubles for a little while."

A glance up saw TJ look away. Tension still hung around him like a thick woolen cloak. Honestly. Was he trying to channel a glowery Mr. Darcy? It sure wasn't working.

Lacey's phone buzzed, and she started tapping out a message on her screen.

Tim sighed. "You think you know someone."

TJ swigged his beer. "Yeah. People can be so fake." He glanced at Emma, his gaze scorching.

"Leona obviously has a lot to work through," Tim said.

"She's not the only one," TJ said, his gaze narrow, fixing on Emma. "People who say one thing, do another. I hate that."

"You hate hypocrites," she said.

"And liars. And two-timers." Again, that one-eyed, narrowed glance at her.

Wait. Did he think she was fake? She didn't think of herself as insecure, but she knew she couldn't leave his comment alone. "Is there something you're trying to say?"

He stabbed his steak. Funny that a man with a reputation as a motormouth would shy away from speaking openly.

"You know," Lacey said, her head popping up as if she'd been oblivious to the previous conversation, "I think we could turn this into a fundraising event."

"I beg your pardon?" Emma asked.

"You cooking with your mom. People love to help, and if you're worried about ingredients, maybe you could ask people to donate supplies. Or some of the local businesses to contribute meals. I bet there are a few places in town that would love to help."

Lacey's enthusiasm kindled Emma's own, the embers of which had almost been snuffed out by TJ's critical mood. "That's a great idea."

"Right? And I bet there's a few people we know who would just *love* to help out by cooking in the kitchen." Lacey batted her eyelashes at her husband.

Tim laughed. "Hon, you know I can barely boil water."

"All the more reason for you to learn."

"And we've got a pretty full schedule this month."

"Come on, honey. I know you'll have at least one weekend free. Don't you care about the kids?"

"Sure I care."

Lacey smiled and tucked her head on Tim's shoulder. "How about you, TJ? Can you cook?"

"A bit," he muttered.

"Well, in that case you should definitely join us. Especially if Emma's mom is in charge. She's an awesome cook. Her Thanksgiving meals are legendary."

He grunted while Emma threw her friend a frown. Was that a hint? No way was she ever going to invite this grumpy man to Thanksgiving.

Lacey only grinned. "Emma's mom is Italian, and she makes these divine desserts." She sighed. "I really wish we could be there this year, but it's Tim's mom's turn this year. We'll be travelling to Duluth, Minnesota."

"It's nice to have a couple of days off," Tim said. He turned to TJ. "You got plans?"

Emma's jaw sagged. Surely Tim wasn't going to be all Christian charity and insist TJ visit Emma's family or something crazy like that? She subtly shook her head at him.

"Nah."

"No family?" Lacey asked.

His lips tightened, and despite her misgivings, Emma couldn't help but feel a little sorry for him. She still didn't know too much about his background, but from what she'd previously gathered, and what she could see now, his family life had not been easy.

"If you're not doing anything, the team is always looking for volunteers to help with the soup kitchen here in the city," Tim said.

Emma exhaled. Great idea. Stay away. The more miles the better.

"Or you could volunteer with serving the meal at the Home with the kids," Lacey said. "It's nice for them to have visitors on a special day."

TJ's lips tightened. Emma could see a pulse ticking in his jaw.

Lacey rolled her eyes and glanced at Emma, the frustration lining her face morphing into tease. "Maybe you could charm Emma and ask to be invited to her house after."

What?

Another lift of hooded lids and a flicked glance. "No, thanks."

Emma blinked. Wow. Distress at her friend's outrageous comment quickly settled into pique. Was he serious?

"It was a joke, TJ," Lacey said kindly.

"I don't care what it was. I have no interest in spending time with someone who can't be trusted."

Emma's mouth swung open. "Excuse me?"

"I don't know what planet you're from, but Emma is one of the most trustworthy people I know," Lacey said, her eyes flashing. "She's Saint Margarita, for goodness' sake."

"A saint, huh?" TJ said, pale eyes drilling into Emma. "If people only knew."

Breath caught. For a moment she thought he knew something of what had happened with Dwayne. But how could he? She exhaled unsteadily, felt her own eyes taper. The best defense was attack, after all. "Do you mean to sound so rude, or are you so rude because you're so mean?"

"Huh?"

Emma placed her napkin beside her plate and pushed to her feet, clasping her hands together to avoid the others seeing them shake. "As charming as the company is, I think I'm going to wait in the lobby. I'll meet you there, okay?" she said to Lacey and Tim, ignoring TJ.

"Hey, I didn't mean—"

"I don't care." She swished her hair over one shoulder. She'd never thought of herself as a drama queen, but she was going to own this awesome hair and new lipstick and jeans. She moved to leave, then paused, her eyes settling on TJ. "I don't know what your deal is, but you are acting like a jerk. And the kids at Hopetoun don't need any more adults in their world who can't act like one. So don't bother coming back until you can prove you're not a jerk."

And with a high-heeled turn she was immensely proud of, she strode past the open-mouthed diners and exited the room.

Wow.

The chaos in TJ's chest eased in reluctant admiration of Emma's boss-lady move. Most women he knew were too eager to please, too quick to capitulate, and never called him out for being a jerk even when he knew was being one. And yeah. He knew he was being one. He deserved her scorn.

But he'd never had time for secrets and had never liked the two-timing that went on in sports, where some guys with wives and families had a secret girlfriend on the side. Or—his chest knotted—mothers with children who had a secret boyfriend. He downed the rest of his drink, placing the glass on the table with a little more force than necessary. Those people were weak. Cheats. Hypocrites. That was why he never invested in relationships and made sure the girls he met were as single and looking for no-strings fun as he was.

But for weeks now this woman had gotten under his skin, his admiration kindled by the way she cared about the kids while not seeming to care too much about her appearance, let alone about impressing him. It had made him want to work harder for her to notice him, to think about him, which made him sick at himself, as he knew she was committed to Nick. At least, he'd thought she was. Until he'd seen her with that guy tonight.

He gritted his teeth. And then she'd shown up here with amazing hair and tight jeans and red lips that made him so tense he couldn't look at her in case he said or did something he'd really regret.

Like kiss her.

Man, he was a screwup. Talk about a hypocrite. He hated himself. And all these conflicted feelings were writhing below the bombshell of Beau's revelation tonight.

"Are you not feeling well?" Lacey asked him, her gaze as

arctic as Emma's had been. An impressive effort, as she had green eyes.

"Leave it, honey," Tim cautioned.

"No, I will not leave it. How can you be so rude to Emma when she wouldn't harm a fly?"

TJ tilted his chin.

"You really can be a jerk sometimes. You know that, don't you?"

"Sure do."

She heaved out a breath, her gaze holding frustration and disappointment before it cut to Tim. "I'm going to wait out there too. I hope whatever it was you were talking about earlier was worth it."

Worth it? No.

TJ slumped in his seat as she left, and Tim turned to eye him, his expression troubled. "You're not doing yourself any favors."

And didn't he know it. "I didn't mean it."

"Yeah, from where I was sitting, it kind of sounded pretty pointed."

How to explain this irrational jealousy? He couldn't own up to it. He'd be seen as a bigger hypocrite than anyone else to admit to liking the girlfriend of another man. Another man whose injuries he'd caused.

Tension rippled within, and he clenched and unclenched his hands. He needed to get better at hiding his anger, hiding his pain, not letting people goad him.

"Is it what Beau said before?"

An outlet. He exhaled and tossed out a few choice words. "I can't believe he's been willing to let everyone think his injuries were my fault. What kind of guy does that? A weak one, that's who."

"Hmm. Well, what kind of guy takes his frustration out on a woman and tries to make her think it's her fault?" Tim countered, his eyes narrowed.

A weak one, that's who.

TJ closed his eyes, placed his hands over his face, and slowly exhaled. "I didn't mean to make her angry."

"No. You seem to have a special way of just drawing it out. Dude." TJ looked at him. "I don't know what's going on with you, but I feel like we've been getting on okay, and Lace and I have been letting you into our lives."

He shrugged. But yeah, he had valued it. It had been a long time since anyone without an agenda had taken as much time with him as Tim had. "Look, I appreciate it, but—"

"Do you?" Tim's gaze nailed him. "I'm going out there in a minute to two very upset women, and I think everyone's gonna want to be hearing more than some lame appreciation."

He glanced at the restaurant window, looking out into darkness. "Tell them what Beau said."

"Really? You're gonna sacrifice Beau for your own sake? You don't care that he asked you not to tell others? What happened to secrets dying with you? Are you the liar you say you hate?"

"He didn't care about me."

Tim crossed his arms.

Yeah, okay. He was acting like a spoiled brat. He'd give his own hide a whipping if he could. "I just don't understand how someone like Beau can call himself a Christian, have the nerve to let me bear the blame, then have the nerve to talk about grace."

Tim frowned, then his expression cleared. "So that's what this is about."

"What?"

"It's the God stuff, isn't it?"

"I don't need a sermon. I heard enough growing up."

"You can listen without really hearing."

TJ rolled his eyes.

"I know I don't have the whole picture, but I'm guessing from what you've said in the past that something happened that turned you off God, something that made you the angry person everyone sees."

TJ crossed his own arms and looked away.

"I'm gonna take a stab in the dark and say you think your parents or the church or whatever let you down, and now you're blaming God for their mistakes."

"Listen to the shrink," he jeered.

"Yeah, you listen." Tim leaned forward. "You've been given chance after chance with the club, with people, and you seem hell-bent on destroying it all. Beau was right. You need to learn that nobody is perfect, that we all make mistakes. And if you can't see that, then you're a bigger fool than you like others to think. You want to talk about hypocrites? Want to talk about liars? You're lying to yourself, man. You think the world owes you when really it's time you showed others a little bit of the grace you've been shown time and time again. And if you can't see it, then Emma is right, and you've got no right trying to help little kids who have a better understanding of relationships than you."

"Don't hold back now."

Tim—perfect Christian that he was—let loose a curse word TJ had rarely heard him use.

"Perfect Christian, huh?"

Tim tapped his chest. "Not perfect. But forgiven. By grace. As you can be, too."

TJ's fingers clenched, and he watched his captain leave without another word. Great. Leave him with the check to pay.

Tim veered to talk to the waitstaff near the door. Jerked his head to where TJ sat alone. Waved a black credit card. Huh.

But no. Despite Tim paying, TJ wasn't gonna let him off the hook. Not when his words had pierced TJ utterly and completely. He drained his glass, motioned for a waiter to draw near. "'Nother drink."

"I'm afraid the bar is closed, sir."

"I said I want another drink."

"Sir, I'm afraid the restaurant is closing soon."

"Don't you know who I am?"

"Oh, we do, Mr. Woletsky. Which is why the bar is closed."

TJ spat a word worse than Tim's at the man and staggered to his feet. He needed to get out of here. Go someplace where the demons couldn't find him.

He *was* a jerk. A brat. A failure. He needed his insides scooped out and replaced with something milder. He hated this anger. Hated this constant sense of disappointment. Hated this tension, like any second he'd lose control. He'd lost it in the game tonight. Nearly lost it in the bar with Beau. Had definitely lost all chance of winning Emma's friendship tonight.

He reached the door. Tim and Co. were nowhere to be seen.

An ache that felt like loneliness swept over him.

He should leave too. Should go find his hotel. Or maybe stay here. Book a room. Book a girl? No ties, no care, no responsibility.

The pain pounding his heart and his head hurt too much. He was so tired of fighting this. He should let the demons inside win.

CHAPTER 12

The scent of cinnamon and melting chocolate teased, the warmth inside Emma's mother's kitchen a stark contrast to the gray skies outside. There was a forecast of rain in an hour, and Emma planned to get her run in, seeing as she'd slept past her alarm this morning from the late hour last night. This kitchen held so many memories of laughter, family, and friends, of her grandmother and her legendary failures to cook American food. Her grandmother's overuse of herbs and spices might have inspired Emma's mother to learn to cook well, but her smile at the family's tease had prompted Emma's desire to emulate her, to laugh at trials. Even if that proved too much of a struggle now.

"Add more sugar, Emma."

Emma obeyed, sprinkling the powdered sugar over the dough.

"Don't be stingy. We need more. Whoever wanted to eat a cookie that didn't taste sweet, huh? Not those poor kids. That's for sure. Now, be generous."

Emma nodded and followed her mother's instructions, even as her last word triggered an ache in her chest.

On the drive home last night, Tim had listened to both Emma's and Lacey's complaints—well, it was mainly Lacey's—before urging them both to be patient with TJ. "He's dealing with stuff, so we have to be generous and kind with him."

"He'll be dealing with me if he ever speaks to Emma like that again." Lacey had flashed Emma a smile from the front seat. "Although, you were fierce, girl. So proud of you."

"Thanks."

But she knew she hadn't been kind or generous in that moment. She'd wanted TJ to own his mistakes. To rub his face in them until he begged for mercy.

"I just don't know how he can accuse you of double standards when everybody knows he's got so many issues of his own."

"Maybe that's part of it," Tim had said thoughtfully. "He feels like he's being honest with his sins, and others like to hide theirs. Not that you're bad at all, Emma," he added, glancing at her in the rear vision mirror.

She'd smiled, but she'd known it wasn't true. Some people might call her Saint Margarita, but she knew who she really was. And that sinner struggled with being both kind and generous toward someone who took potshots at others in an attempt to feel better about himself.

"Are you okay, Em?" her mom asked now, hands on her hips. "You're not acting like your usual self."

"Sorry," she apologized. "Just tired. Last night went later than I thought."

"Hmm. Hockey has a lot to answer for, huh?"

"Tim got caught up with talking to some others."

"He's a nice boy, that one."

Tim was. His teammate sure wasn't.

For a moment she dared wonder what her mom would make of TJ. Her mother had never shied away from telling her children what she thought about the friends in their lives. She was a fan of Lacey, liked Tim, didn't mind Nick, had disliked Dwayne. Emma's stomach tensed. She bet her mother wouldn't like TJ. So it was just as well there was zero chance of them meeting. Which was good, because Emma had no clue how she would've managed to negotiate the land mines of conversation.

She finished shaping the balls of dough, then flattened them on the large cooking trays, adding the chocolate chunks in the shape of faces. The kids always liked to see who'd get the grumpy ones.

Her mind flicked back to last night and that strange feeling that skirted under her offence. There had been that moment when she'd felt sorry for TJ, when the comment about Thanksgiving and his family had made her wonder. Perhaps there was more going on than he revealed, so maybe it was worth heeding what Tim had said and giving the man another chance. Not that she wanted to. But wasn't that what grace was all about?

She exhaled. Tried to cover it with a smile as her mother glanced at her. "You sure you're okay, honey?"

"I need to go for my run before it rains."

"Running, running, running. What does it do besides give you sore knees and bad ankles?"

"It helps clear my head, Mom. And helps me when I eat these." She motioned to the cookies awaiting the oven.

"Who says any of these are for you?" her mother protested.

"You know it's important that they get tested."

"Hmm. I know your father thinks that's his job."

"And as he's at work, I guess you're stuck with me being your taste tester today." She backed away. "But I really need to run."

"Okay, okay. There might be a spare one when you return. Or there might not be."

"Thanks, Mom."

Two minutes later she was turning the corner of the street, breathing in the sharp air as she forced her sluggish limbs to work. The wind held a trace of rain, and she knew she wouldn't have enough time to run the riverside path today. A block or two would have to do unless she wanted to return home soaked. She took Oaks and jogged past the townhouses that had been built recently for some of the commuters who worked in the city. Everyone had been amazed that they'd been passed, their modern style so out of place, given the historic nature of the rest of the village. They had nothing on the cute cottage she'd once dreamed about owning. Her chest stabbed. The cottage now owned by TJ.

She didn't want to turn up Grove Street, but it was like her feet wouldn't listen to her brain. Maybe he hadn't moved in yet, and she could have one more look before she'd need to avoid it forever.

A glance around saw no vehicles out on this wild day, so she tugged her woolen cap down and moved to the opposite side of the street, then paused next to a tree, clasping hold of the trunk as she pretended to stretch.

The cottage sat silent, its lights off, like nobody was home. Maybe nobody was home. Maybe the previous owners had left. Or maybe TJ was in there, fast asleep, recovering from a hangover. Indignation creased her chest. It still seemed so unfair that he'd snapped up the one thing she wanted. Why did good people always come last? It wasn't fair. *Just lucky,* he'd said. Yeah, well, lucky for him meant unlucky for her. Didn't God want her to be blessed?

She'd need to leave in case he woke. Or in case one of the neighbors here thought she was a stalker or something like that. She'd stalk the house, but never the man. *Never* the man.

With another glance at the sad flowers that she just knew were going to die under the new owner's care, she turned to go away. Only to jump.

"TJ! What are you doing here?"

He gestured to his attire: sweats, long-sleeve T-shirt, gray knit cap. "Running. Same as you."

His glance trickled down her sweatshirt to the sports leggings she wore on cold days like this, then back up. She fought the instinct to cross her arms.

"Good place to stretch, huh?"

"How long were you watching me?"

"How long were you watching for me?" he countered.

"I've never been watching you."

"Just my house?"

"Yes, if you must know," she snapped. "I've always liked it, until you moved in."

His lips flattened, and she could see the scar near his mouth more clearly than the dim light of the restaurant had allowed last night. "I didn't know."

"Why would you?" She moved to go.

"Emma."

She paused, facing away.

"I'm, uh, real sorry about what I said last night."

Something in his voice seemed to break something inside. Her offence, maybe. Or her defenses. She kept herself ruthlessly still.

"I really am sorry." He moved around to face her. "I was upset about something, and I took it out on you, and I shouldn't have."

She chewed her bottom lip, dared to meet his shadowed eyes. The blue eyes held unhappiness, something she recognized only too well. Her heart softened.

"Say something."

Emma pushed a loose strand of hair off her face. "Why don't you think I'm trustworthy?"

He studied her for such a long time that she had to look away.

"Well?" She rubbed her arms. "You seemed to have a lot to say last night. I don't understand what I've done to make you think that."

"It doesn't matter."

"It does. You sat there and accused me of something bad you apparently think I've done. I want—I deserve—an explanation." She met his gaze again.

"I…" He clasped his head. Gritted his teeth. Glanced away.

All at once she could see his agitation again. Agitation. Unhappiness. Stress. Whatever his problem, she suddenly realized there was far more at play than whatever imaginary issue he had with her.

"Forget it. I'm gonna go. It's cold, and I think it's gonna rain."

"Who was the guy you sat next to last night?"

"What?" Her voice had pitched so high she could scare dogs. "At the game?'

His chin jerked, and for a second she wondered if he was jealous.

"You mean my brother?"

He blinked. "Your brother?"

"Yes, my brother. He's a firefighter in the city, and sometimes we attend games together."

"Huh." He dragged his hands down his face and groaned.

"What now?"

"Nothing." He dropped his hands. "Like I said, I'm really sorry."

She didn't know whether it was the pleading note in his voice or the entreaty in his eyes, but she found herself believing him. This was a remorseful man. She couldn't hold his sins against him. "Fine. I forgive you. But I've got to say, I don't understand you at all."

"Join the club." His smirk didn't animate his eyes.

She studied him, unsure what it was that propelled words to her mouth. "You seem to have this great connection with kids like Brandon and Lily, and they're not stupid about people, not at all. But then you can be like you were last night and make people hate you."

A beat. Two. "Do you hate me?"

The rasp in his voice made it seem like he really cared about her answer. And no. She didn't hate him. Apart from God commanding his followers to love and not hate, there was something about the man she could be drawn to. In a strictly platonic way.

"You do, then." He backed away. "I get it. I don't blame you."

"No." She swallowed. "I don't hate you."

"But you don't like me."

"Not all the time, no," she admitted honestly.

"Some of the time?" he asked.

"I don't know why you care, but"—she shrugged—"maybe. A very little amount." She spaced her fingers apart a quarter inch. "And only a very little amount of the time."

The left side of his mouth pulled up, his scrutiny almost overwhelming, like he was asking for something she didn't know how to give.

"What?"

"Thanks," he muttered.

"Don't thank me. You should thank Tim, who seemed to think you needed defending for some reason."

"Did he?"

"He's obviously not feeling very well."

The other side of his mouth pulled up. "I didn't figure you for more sass."

"You don't even know me."

"Apparently not." He considered her a moment longer, then stuck out his hand. "Hi. I'm TJ Woletsky. My friends call me Tyler."

She glanced at him, then at his arm, lingering in the space between them. Somehow this moment seemed weighty with cause. She sighed and gently touched his palm with hers. "Margarita Moritello. My friends call me Emma."

He clasped her fingers. "Em. A. What's the A stand for?"

"Anastacia."

"Margarita Anastacia. Wow."

She raised an eyebrow. "Wow what?"

"Would you please quit doing the eyebrow raising thing? You remind me of my third-grade teacher, and she was scary."

"Are you saying that I scare you?"

Yes. The unspoken word seemed to hover between them, although how she could possibly scare him she had no clue.

He sighed. "I can understand why you'd prefer Emma. Margarita Anastacia—that's a mouthful." His gaze flickered to her lips then back again. "Nice to meet you, Emma."

"You too." Tyler. *No.* She tugged her hand away. "Gotta go."

"Your mom's making cookies, right?"

"Yep." And no. They might be at a truce, but no way was she was going to invite him over. "See you around."

"Except if I see you first, right?"

She smirked. "Right."

He laughed, and she quickly jogged away, only casting a glance back as she turned the corner to see he'd been watching and now lifted a hand and waved.

No. This was stupid. She was overtired. She needed more sleep. She couldn't think of him as a friend. But neither could she think of him anymore as an enemy.

THE TENSION that had abated in that brief exchange with Emma outside TJ's house quickly ramped up again the next day. One question might've been answered—she wasn't a two-timer, after all—but so many others remained. Questions about his family. Questions about God, about TJ's purpose on the planet, about grace.

Emma had shown him grace in forgiving him when he knew he really didn't deserve it. What kind of twisted fool had the nerve to ask a woman if she was two-timing? Only the kind who despised those who had affairs, the kind who couldn't keep his mind from chasing her. Tim was right. TJ was so weak, but he couldn't help the surge of greedy pleasure in that moment when he'd grasped her hand, and he'd nearly admitted the truth that yes, she scared the crap out of him. But that moment had slid from apology to tease to something that had felt almost like flirting. Which soon made him hate himself again. How could he think like this about her?

He'd needed an extra-long run through the rain to finally knock sense into his brain. But the knowledge of her forgiveness made him really glad he'd left New York when he had that night, without seeking further entertainment, even if the ride here had been cold and slow and made him wonder if he should investigate getting a car. At least he hadn't met any cops and been told to walk a straight line he probably wouldn't have made.

THAT DAY off was followed by a road trip to the west coast, which saw four games in six days. Every minute filled with flights and travel and practice and games, every moment bringing the consciousness he needed to prove himself. Every second of every game he had to guard himself against allowing the arrows of opponents' taunts to get beneath his shield, knowing they'd be looking for any excuse to break him. It was exhausting. Trying to keep a lid on simmering emotions made him snappish with his teammates and led Tim to pull him into his room on the Friday night after their game in L.A.

"Another fight again tonight. That makes three this week. What is wrong with you?"

What was right about him? He shrugged.

"I'm busting a gut out there, trying to convince people that you should be playing on something other than the fourth line, but you gotta give me something to work with. You're so angry, dude. It makes people want to avoid you."

"What's new?"

Tim exhaled loudly, studying him, like he was counting to ten. "Did you apologize to Emma?"

"Yeah."

His eyebrows rose. "How was she?"

"Better than you about it all."

"Lacey calls her Saint Margarita."

"Yeah, well, that saint didn't mind telling me she doesn't like me much."

"Good for her. She speaks straight. That's one thing you have in common, anyway."

He didn't want to think about what they had in common. Not when there were so many things that showed they'd need to stay apart. He dug his fingers into his scalp.

"So, if things are okay with her, then it must still be the God thing, huh?"

"There is no God thing."

"Please. There's a God thing. There's always a God thing, even if people deny it."

"Careful. You're starting to sound like your friend Beau."

"Is that what it is then? The grace thing."

TJ clenched his hands. Tim could really learn a thing or two from Emma about speaking straight. "What are you actually trying to say, Tim? I don't have all day. We're supposed to be asleep, remember?"

"Very well." Tim crossed his arms. "You once told me that your dad was a pastor. You know Bible verses. If I was a betting man, I'd bet you made a commitment to following Jesus when you were a child."

"Which didn't stick. Obviously."

"If it had, do you think you'd be this angry now?"

TJ ground his teeth, fighting the desire to punch something. He forced himself to breathe deeper.

"TJ, people are concerned about you. If you're angry all the time, then you can't play your best. You use up a lot of emotional energy that would be better used in your game. I think that's why Beau is so good at what he does—because he's so relaxed."

"So relaxed he feels like he can drop a sermon on a stranger about grace. What the heck did he mean, trying to get me to talk about grace? I don't need to talk about it. I know what it is. It doesn't mean it's real or applicable to me."

"Why not? What makes you so special that God can't forgive you?"

"What makes you think I need forgiveness?" he challenged.

Tim raised an eyebrow.

"What if I don't want to be forgiven?"

Tim shot him another *are you serious?* look.

"You want to talk about my dad the great pastor? He used to talk about grace all the time on Sundays, but he never showed me any. He and my mom…" His voice faltered, and he hitched it up again. "…used to argue all the time. Then she ran off with another man. Do you seriously think I would want to have anything to do with a God who allowed that?"

"I'm sorry."

TJ glanced away, unwilling for anyone else to peer inside his soul. Emma's peek inside the other day outside his house had been disconcerting enough.

"But you're blaming God for people's bad choices."

"See?" He pivoted back to face Tim. "That's the thing. Everybody likes to think God cares enough to intervene in our lives, but I've never seen that. If I had, then I wouldn't be like this."

"Like what?" Tim probed gently.

Broken. Angry. A mess. A screwup. And desperate for

nobody to know. He went on the attack. "Christians are all the same."

"The same as what?"

"Judging people, pretending they have it all together when really they're the biggest screwups of them all. You gotta be delusional to think otherwise."

Tim chewed his lip.

"What?"

"I'm trying to decide if I should be offended by you thinking me a screwup and calling me delusional, or whether the delusional screwup is actually you."

"Yeah? Join the club."

"See? I don't think you're either. You've shown yourself kind and loyal—when we were at the kids' home that last time, you were thoughtful and generous. That's not the sign of a screwup to me."

"That was an accident."

"That was a sign that you've been making progress. You're not as angry as before."

"Because I've wanted to keep my job. I've got a freakin' mortgage now."

"And you got that mortgage because you want to prove you're different."

"But what's the point?" TJ swore. "Even when I try, I fail."

"And that's exactly the point. None of us are ever going to be good enough. Our best will never measure up. That's the point of grace."

Grace. Undeserved favor. He'd always thought it more like under-served favor, where God's favor meant little to him, with it never proving to be quite enough.

"Aren't you tired of being angry? What have you got to lose by giving your life to God again? By accepting the grace he's got for you?"

TJ paced back. "I ain't having a come-to-Jesus moment here with you."

"I don't care where you have it. You know you need it. And you need it soon. Otherwise, man, you think your life sucks now? Just wait for the explosion."

"Thanks, coach. Great pep talk. Catch ya later."

"I'll be praying for you," Tim called.

TJ slammed the door and jogged down the fire stairs, unwilling for the coaching staff to see him exit the hotel. With a game tomorrow, he shouldn't be out, but he didn't care. He needed to escape, to drown the ceaseless questions as he'd learned to over many years. And there was no better place than where he'd honed his skills, here in L.A.

L.A. The city of angels. The city stalked by his demons.

Twenty minutes later, he was in a club, having found a former L.A. teammate more than happy to blow off tonight's loss with reminiscing in the way they used to. Loud music. Strong drinks. Pavel may have been using, but things were permitted in this state that TJ had never really gotten into. Blame the narrow-minded upbringing which still saw some sober tentacles stretching from the past. Besides, who needed drugs when he always could drink like a fish?

He downed another drink. Two short-skirted blondes sashayed up to where they were sitting, one of them thrusting her ample assets in his face.

"Well, if it isn't TJ. I've missed you, baby."

What was her name? Didn't matter. He didn't care. She only wanted the drinks he'd supply and whatever else he'd offer. He clicked his fingers, ordered another round.

She sat on his lap, stroking his face with neon nails. The other convinced Pavel to dance. "Wanna dance, TJ?" his blonde asked.

"Nah." He only wanted to drown his sorrows.

"Wanna do something else?" she asked slyly.

He shook his head. Their drinks arrived, and he started on his third, vaguely noticed she held a pale green drink with a slice of lime decorating the side. A margarita. His guts wrenched.

Margarita. Anastacia. Em. A.

No!

"What is it, baby?" she said, putting her drink down then shifting to place her hands behind his neck. "You look really tense."

He studied her, his gaze trickling down her face, down her throat to where a silver name necklace lay. Lily.

"Like what you see?" she asked provocatively, shimmying a little more.

He grabbed her arms, shifted her off. No.

"What's wrong?"

"I can't do this," he muttered. She was someone's daughter, someone whose innocence might've long gone, who was definitely not white as snow, but was even more lost and anchorless than that poor little mite back in New York.

Which meant he was just as lost as her too.

No. He didn't want to think like this!

"Why not?" She stroked his face, his chin, her hand sliding under his shirt. "You know I think you're hot." She murmured into his ear. "I love your scars and your tattoos. *All* of your tattoos."

His guts heaved. "I gotta go."

"Why?"

He straightened, grabbing her hands and keeping them away from him. "Because you share the same name as a sweet girl in New York, and I don't want to do something with you that I'm gonna regret."

"Haven't you always said we should live like there's no such thing as regrets?"

But there was. He knew that now. His life was jam-packed with them.

"Then let's just dance." She swayed her hips, lifted her hands above her head so her shirt rode high. "We can still have a good time," she purred.

His head felt like it might explode. Nope. He had to leave. Had to get away.

"Come on." She grabbed his hand. "Dance with me."

"No." He staggered away. "To be honest, I'd rather dance with her than dance with you."

"What? Have you got a girlfriend?" she screeched.

Would that shut her up? "Yeah."

She slapped his face, yelling something about his paternity that his dad would object to for lots of reasons. He was vaguely aware of cameras and stares and had an uneasy feeling this was not going to go down well if the team found out. He needed to get out of here now.

He didn't bother trying to find Pavel among the mass of dancing bodies as he left. Pavel made his own choices. He found an Uber whose objections to his smell of beer and sweat were finally overcome by a tip fat enough to buy his silence.

An hour later, he was lying on his hotel bed, clutching his head, thankful this trip meant he didn't have a roommate. How to explain sneaking in during the small hours? How to explain his retching in the bathroom? This team was way more straight-laced than he was used to. What would they say if they found out?

But the questions pounding in his head beat as loud as the DJ's songs tonight.

Who was he? Was this what his life had become? He was nearly thirty-three and still trying to live like a dude ten years younger. What special kind of pathetic did that make him?

His stomach heaved, and he rolled off the bed and crawled back to the toilet, releasing the contents of his stomach, his head whirling with the effects of cheap booze. Was that what happened when he tried to clean up his act? He couldn't hold his liquor anymore?

He couldn't do this. He was going insane. His world was falling apart. Yet again.

But what was the alternative? He'd tried the God thing, he'd prayed the prayer, back when he was ten. And look how that'd turned out. No way. Maybe he'd been a little too naïve and young, but he wasn't so stupid as to trust God again. Not after He'd let TJ down and destroyed his family, his life, and all he'd known. No way was he going to step into that void and believe God might help him.

Another heave of nausea made him clutch the porcelain bowl, then wipe his mouth and slump to the cold tiled floor. He groaned, then hoped it hadn't been loud enough for anyone else to hear. Sunglasses and meds might hide a hangover tomorrow, but there was no hiding his pathetic state here.

He closed his eyes, tonight's slapped cheek pressed against the icy coolness, wishing it could cool the whirling thoughts within. *Cool heads win games*, his coaches had always said. Cool heads, not hotheads like him.

Cool heads. Cool hearts. Not hot heads. Not hot hearts. Too fiery. Too wild. Too angry. People disliked him. Tim didn't like him. Emma didn't like him. A failure. A loser. Pathetic. A hypocrite.

Snatches of conversations from past weeks and days pecked through his alcohol-hazed stupor. He *was* weak. A hypocrite. As false as those he'd scorned for so many years. How could he point the finger at someone's splinters when he had logs hanging out of his eyes?

Another groan. Too much God stuff. It felt heavy on his chest. Beau's comments about grace. No, no, no. He didn't deserve it. He'd never earn it. What was the point of forgiveness that made him feel worse?

Except…

His mind flashed back a week. To a woman whose touch had scorched his skin. He looked at his hand. Remembered her hand in his. Her forgiveness brought ease, her words like a balm over the pointy bits of his heart. He hadn't deserved it. But he'd liked it. Saint Margarita.

He dragged his fingers down his face. No! He had to stop thinking about her. This was wrong. How pathetic was he? Why did people bother with him? He hadn't deserved Tim's friendship nor the care extended by Tim and Lacey. Why did they bother with him?

Water. He needed water. He pushed himself upright enough to get to the sink, turning on the faucet and scooping it into his hands as he lapped like a dog.

Another memory flashed. A sermon. Old Testament. Soldiers, scooping water like dogs, upright, on guard. Men God could use.

No, no, no. Why did everything keep coming back to God?

He stared at his reflection in the mirror, a sight that needed a few blinks before he realized it was actually him. He looked so old. Decrepit. Where was the athlete he'd once been? He'd never been good-looking, but the shadows and scars were enough to make his own stomach queasy. Things had to be bad if he scared even himself.

But deep within, a little voice insisted the man he faced in the mirror wasn't all of who he was. There *was* more. He just couldn't see it now, not when he was in the shadows. He flicked on the overhead light. Flicked it off again so the light didn't sear his eyeballs.

He splashed water over his face, scrubbing at his eyes, then opening them again. His vision blurred—two of him, then only one. He needed ibuprofen now. Two pills later he stared at his reflection, the ugly scars on his forehead and near his mouth that his beard no longer hid. Ugly. No wonder people disliked him. He didn't like himself either.

The pounding in his heart refused to leave, so he popped two more, wondering how long before they'd take effect.

His gut burned. His vision blurred again. He needed sleep.

He stumbled from the room, pausing to draw the curtains against the city lights. This city that looked so pretty held a dark side people didn't always see. Nobody ever saw the entire picture. People got things wrong. Like he had with Emma.

New regret churned across his chest. Imagine if she saw him now. What would she say? What would she think? Oh, he *despised* himself for still thinking about her.

Emma. He'd been wrong about her. He closed his eyes, thoughts of his mistaken idea about her circling back to his conversation with Tim. Was he wrong about God? Maybe he wasn't seeing the full picture there either. Could he trust God?

Tremors roiled through his body, his skin crawling in a kind of shivery sickness. What could he do? Talk to Tim? Not this time. He'd used up all his chances, and he had no wish to let his captain know just what he'd been up to tonight. Tim would feel duty bound to tell the coach, then TJ would be kicked off the team. Who then? Who'd be up and able to talk sense at this time of night?

A name pierced the darkness. With shaking fingers he retrieved his phone, found a name, tapped to call. It was probably too late. Of course it would be too late. But maybe—

"Hello?"

"Mike?" TJ's voice sounded scratchy.

"Tyler? Is that you?" A yawn. "Do you know what time it is?"

He shouldn't have called. He should hang up. "Sorry." He pressed end.

Five seconds later his phone rang. "Tyler? It's Mike. What's going on? Where are you?"

"L.A. hotel. I…" His voice shook. "I don't feel too good."

"Where's Tim?"

"Hotel." The walls were tilting. His head was spinning. Pain was inching up his throat. "Don't care."

"What do you want?" TJ heard a baby's cry. "I'm up on baby duty, so don't hang up. What is it?"

He stifled a groan. He really didn't feel good. He closed his eyes and swallowed, then forced himself to speak. "I think I really need to talk to you about God."

CHAPTER 13

The church kitchen buzzed with laughter and industry and the scents of melting cheese and cooking meat. The church had proved the perfect backup when the community center's kitchen had been fully booked, and Lacey had proved the perfect organizer as the donations of meals and ingredients from local businesses poured in this past week until the only place they could be stored safely was in the church's commercial kitchen. Why Emma hadn't thought of this as an option before, she didn't know. But it didn't matter now. All that mattered was the sense of community, of working together, of feeling like their efforts could really make a difference. So far, nearly a dozen slabs of lasagna had been made, and several pots of pasta waited to be scooped into foil trays. There was so much food that Emma knew Hopetoun House couldn't store it all, so the plan was to donate to other nearby refuges and community organizations as well.

"Looking good, ladies," Emma's mom said, peering into the pots. She nodded to Emma, who was sprinkling shredded mozzarella on top of the creamy sauce of one of the pasta bakes. "Not too much sage," she said with a wink.

Emma smiled. Her grandmother had been legendary for adding sage to everything, rendering even the mildest of cream sauces unpalatable. There had been many a meal where they'd had to unobtrusively spit food into paper napkins and stop by burger joints on the way home. Gran might've laughed good-naturedly with them about her lack of cooking skills, but the comment about sage had entered family folklore.

"Now, who's ready for a break?" Lacey called. "This morning's break is proudly brought to us by Rosie's Sweet Treats on Main. God bless them for their service. We've got chocolate cake, chocolate cookies, and oh, look, it's another cake, which is—"

"Chocolate!" the women in the room called.

"Good thing we like chocolate, huh?" Emma murmured to her mother.

"It would be a crime against humanity not to." Her mother paused as, around them, people surged to the table for their coffee and cake. She drew a hand over Emma's hair, tucked up in a ponytail. "It's good to see you looking happier."

"I am happy," she insisted.

"Yes. I can see that."

She hoped her mom wouldn't ask her why. She didn't really know why, especially with the confirmation that Hopetoun House would be inspected on Monday next week for building and safety violations. That had precipitated her call to Richard, who had organized a mini working bee today to deal with some of the more obvious cracks in the walls, promising to see the plaster repaired and painted over before Monday's visit. She'd tried to stay, but he'd insisted on taking care of things, which made for a nice change, especially as she'd already committed to today's cooking fest with Lacey.

Lacey had once again proved to be thinking ahead, filming part of today's proceedings to be posted online as part of a fundraising campaign. The laughter today had been an effective distraction against the worries of the Home, boosting Emma's spirits in a similar way to the strange conversation she'd had with TJ a week ago and knocking some of the clutter from her heart. Not that she cared what he thought of her. She couldn't care less about a man whose fights in three games proved he still had as many agitator qualities as ever. But somehow, it was nice that he didn't think her untrustworthy.

"It's good to see things are finally starting to get sorted with Leona," her mom continued.

Emma nodded, relieved that her mom attributed her good mood to this rather than anything else. "I can't believe it's taken this long," Emma admitted. "It's not like she's some mastermind criminal. But I don't know if putting her in under psychiatric evaluation is going to be helpful long-term."

"What does this mean for Nick?"

"It doesn't change things. He's moved out of the hospital into his own apartment, and when he finally picked up the phone the other day he couldn't talk for long because apparently he has some nurses who come and help him each day."

"Poor boy."

"He didn't seem to be in a good way." She sighed. Another visit upstate might be on the cards soon.

"Well, just remember, Em, you're not responsible for him," Mom said. "Now, come and have a coffee and put those thoughts to one side. You must be pleased with the turnout today."

She allowed herself to be taken to the table and selected a chocolate cookie to go with her coffee. "It's wonderful to see the community coming together. Lacey's done a wonderful job." She glanced across at Lacey, who grinned before pulling out her phone with its Britney Spears ringtone.

"Tim!"

Emma smiled at her friend's obvious excitement. The poor thing had been missing her husband so much she'd volunteered for some extra shifts at the Home. Seeing as the kids loved Lacey, Emma had reveled in the chance to spend more time with her friend as they planned and plotted how this day's cooking-fest would run.

But her smile faded as Lacey's jaw dropped. "No."

What had happened? Emma eased past chattering women and moved toward her.

Lacey beckoned her near, and they withdrew to the church auditorium, away from prying ears, Lacey's ear planted firmly to the phone. "Is he going to be okay?"

"Is it Tim?" Emma murmured.

Lacey pointed to the phone. "He's on the phone," she mouthed.

She exhaled. But what had happened?

"So they think it was deliberate?"

Her heart pricked. Now she really wanted to know. Was what deliberate? Had someone been hurt? Apart from TJ's fight, she couldn't remember anything out of the ordinary during last night's game. Were they referring to the game? What had happened? And to whom?

"No."

Lacey's falling features drew a new throb of concern. "What is it?" Emma asked.

"It's TJ," Lacey whispered.

Her heart prickled. Why that name should concern her so, she couldn't explain, but she began to pray for him and whatever challenge he was facing.

"Are you doing okay?" Lacey asked her husband.

His reply drew her to place a hand on her mouth and to nod. Emma drew closer, wrapped an arm around her.

"We'll be praying," Lacey said. "I love you."

Emma faintly heard his reply of the same, then the call ended. She drew Lacey to a chair and encouraged her to sit. "What's happened to TJ?"

"He...he..." Lacey blinked, and a tear spilled onto her cheek.

"What is it? Is he injured?" Her chest froze. Was he dead?

Lacey shook her head, and the tight band around Emma eased. "He's in the hospital."

"What?"

"Oh my gosh," Lacey murmured. "I can't believe it. It doesn't seem real."

"What's happened?" Emma asked urgently.

"He overdosed."

"What?"

"From what Tim said, it seems he was at a club, drank too much, went home, and took some pills."

No. *Dear God, no.* "How awful," Emma whispered. "I didn't think he did drugs."

"No, they were just painkillers, but he had too many, and mixed with the alcohol..." Lacey's breath caught. "I don't know why I'm so upset about this, but it's such a shock."

"Is he going to be okay?" Emma asked, gently rubbing Lacey's back.

"Tim said it's still only very early, but they think he'll need to be in hospital for a few days. He's going to have to stay there until the doctors release him. Tim's head is a real mess, but he has a game to play tonight."

"I can understand Tim would be upset, but he can't blame himself."

"He does, though," Lacey said. "He said he argued with TJ after last night's game, and it was straight after that that TJ left the hotel and went to the club."

She winced. Poor Tim.

"The only good thing is that TJ had been on the phone to Mike Vaughan, one of the Bible study guys—"

"While he was at the club?"

"No, afterward. Apparently TJ wanted to talk to him about— get this—God."

Emma blinked. "What?"

"Yeah, I know."

"Wow."

"Right?" Lacey sighed. "So anyway, Mike was on the phone to him when TJ suddenly stopped answering. Mike then got on the phone to Tim and asked him to check on TJ as TJ had been complaining about not feeling well. So it was Tim who found TJ and called nine-one-one."

"Poor Tim," Emma murmured.

"Poor TJ."

"Do they think it was deliberate?"

"They don't know. It's such a mess. The team isn't happy, mostly because he broke curfew and was drinking way too much. From what Tim was saying, it looks like TJ will end up being bumped down to the minors, if he ever returns to pro hockey again."

"Oh no."

"It's awful."

"Poor TJ."

Lacey looked at her with wet eyes. "Can we—do you mind if we pray for him? I'm a little scared. I don't know why. It's not like he's that nice of a human, but it feels like if he's having conversations about God, then maybe the devil is trying to stop him."

Emotion coiled in Emma's throat. Why had she never seen it quite that way before? Of course that was what was going on. The battle for people's lives was not just one that could be seen in the physical realm. There was a spiritual war being waged as well.

"Of course we'll pray."

The next few minutes they spent holding hands, murmuring prayers for protection, for wisdom for the doctors, for God to penetrate TJ's heart once and for all. They prayed for Tim, for his teammates, for the coaches and management that held TJ's future in their hands. They prayed for peace to surround TJ's family and friends, which reminded Emma of something he had once said. He didn't have much in the way of family. Would they even be aware of what had happened to him?

"Thanks," Lacey said, wiping under her eyes, smearing mascara.

"Emma?" her mom called, moving into the church sanctuary. "Oh, Lacey, what's happened? I've got everyone back working, but what's happened here? Is Tim okay?"

Lacey gestured for Emma to explain, which she managed, but with a quavering voice. Why this had hit her so hard she didn't know, but she knew TJ would continue to be firmly in her thoughts. And her prayers.

THE BLEEP of machines drew him awake, revealing the concerned eyes of Tim and the team's coach. TJ blinked, but his head felt like it was layered under several feet of snow. His skin felt prickly, his throat raw, and there was a burning sensation in his guts.

"What happened?" he rasped.

Tim shifted forward on his chair. "You're in the hospital. You got sick two nights ago, and we brought you in."

"I got sick?"

"You drank too much at the club," Coach Koder said. "Then apparently tried to chase it with a few too many pills."

"I don't do drugs," he protested. He didn't. Did he?

"Only over the counter."

Memories flashed. Music. Blinding lights. Shots. Beer. Mirror. Pills.

"How'd you know I was at the club?"

"Pretty hard not to when your face is plastered all over social media."

Was that why Coach looked mad? Probably time to change the subject. "Where'd you find me?"

"Mike Vaughan called me," Tim said. "You were talking to him when you passed out. He called me, I called the team doc, and now we're here."

"Another game?"

"It's Sunday. You spent most of yesterday throwing up, or so the nurses say. They've said you can be released, but only if you go into care."

"What, like rehab?"

Coach Koder sighed. "That might be best, but Carruthers here thinks you might do better under his watchful eye."

Huh? "Why?" TJ asked Tim. "You don't even like me."

"That's not true."

"I don't think it's worth it," Koder said to Tim. "Not if he can't be bothered trying."

"He might when he understands what's at stake."

"What's at stake?" TJ asked.

"You. Your position on the team," Koder said. "I'm under immense pressure to kick you off, and the only person standing in the way is Tim here. For some reason he seems to think you're worth fighting for and has assured me that after a little bit of down time getting your head together, you'll be ready to play like the man we first saw last month. I'm not so convinced."

Tim leaned forward, elbows on knees, his hands clasped. "If you say no to coming home with me, then you're saying yes to rehab and yes to the farm team."

"But—"

"You don't get to argue here," Koder said. "The choice is simple. Go to Tim's and get yourself straightened out, or get kicked off the team. I don't need to tell you how disappointed everybody is."

No. It was written all over the coach's face.

"So I need to stay with you and Lacey for a while?" TJ asked Tim.

"Until the team doc decides you're fit enough to return to play, yes."

Coach Koder stood. "Our flight leaves in three hours. If you're on it, then I'm assuming you've decided to make some changes in your life. Number one should be no more self-harm."

"I didn't try to top myself—"

"I'd like to think you're not as stupid as others believe, but everyone knows you don't do drugs after drinking as much alcohol as you had."

"I wasn't thinking clearly."

"No. I suspect you haven't for quite some time." The coach nodded to Tim. "See if you can make him see sense, otherwise, good luck and goodbye."

He left, and TJ turned to Tim. "He doesn't want me on the team."

"He doesn't want a loose cannon. You had a lot of people worried."

"Like who?"

"The guys. Last night's game was incredibly hard. They thought you'd tried to kill yourself," Tim said. "There were a lot of rumors flying around. Man." He shoved his hands through his hair. "When I got the call from Mike to say you'd stopped talking, and then I rushed to your room and found you slumped on the floor, I thought you were dead, man. I thought you were dead."

"I really didn't mean—"

"You drank too much, like an idiot freshman at a kegger. There are pics on Facebook, which the team has tried to take down, but they show you with some girl, and there was a fight, and...man." Tim shook his head.

"It wasn't like that," he insisted. Although, he was barely sure of what it *was* like. But he was sure it wasn't that. "Ask Pavel. He was there."

"I have a feeling Pavel is getting a lecture from his team too. What were you thinking?"

He shrugged, inching his way up the bed, plucking at the blue hospital gown.

"Was it what I said?"

"Huh?"

"Mike said you'd been asking about God. It made me wonder." Tim shrugged. "Look, I'm sorry if something I said triggered you, but not sorry if it means it's gonna finally make you think."

TJ struggled to push past the dullness in his brain for something about what he'd talked about with Mike. But, nada. "What else did he say?"

"Just that you were asking questions, that you felt like a fake." Tim's mouth creased into faint amusement. "Nothing new there."

"Thanks."

"Look, much as I'd love to stay and talk more about God, you need to make a decision about what you're gonna do. Are you gonna come and stay with me and Lacey? Or are you gonna take your chances with rehab and maybe lose your career?"

Rock, meet hard place. What choice did he have? "I'll go with you and Lacey," he muttered.

"Good. Then get up and get changed so we can get out of here." Tim pressed a call button. "The team's expedited things, so all you need to do is sign some papers and we can be on our way."

So he could continue his walk of shame.

A few hours later he was hiding behind sunglasses, dodging questions from concerned teammates, his movements shaky, his emotions raw. He slipped in and out of sleep on the plane as memories of the past forty-eight hours surged and fell like the waves on the shore.

Music. Headache. Margarita. Lily. Failure. Mirror. Mike. Mike's words.

They propelled back into clarity like a gunshot.

"You say you want honesty, so I'm telling it to you straight. God loves you. No bull. He loves you. Despite you."

No one could love this mess he was. His birth mom hadn't wanted him. His adoptive mom hadn't loved him enough to hang around. His dad loved the church more than him.

He'd tried to explain some of this last statement, but Mike wasn't having it. "Are you always going to judge God because you see him through the prism of your father's imperfection? He made mistakes. So do you. So do I. None of us can say we've got our lives right, because if we do, that's just pretend. You say you're a pastor's son and that you've heard all the sermons. What about the Bible verses? What about the one about the heart being deceitful above all things? You're fooling yourself if you think life has been working for you."

"Don't hold back," TJ had muttered.

"You want honesty? Go talk to God about just what Jesus's death means for you."

"But He wouldn't want to hear from me."

"Try Him," Mike challenged.

"I can't. I walked away. I'm too screwed up."

"You're broken, and He's the only one who can fix you. Tyler, God wants you to accept His grace."

No. He didn't deserve it. Undeserved favor. So undeserved.

"Believe it or not. That's on you." Mike's words had dug deep. "But don't you dare pretend to yourself that God hasn't cared. Don't you dare tell me that Jesus's death on the cross didn't mean everything could change for the better."

Could his life change for the better? Really?

"What do you have to lose?" Mike had said.

What *did* he have to lose? Maybe doing things differently would mean he could lose some of the shame. A quick glance at Facebook had him shutting his phone, switching it off. He couldn't be that man anymore. He needed to change. God help him, he actually *wanted* to change. But what if this time didn't take either?

Still, anything had to be better than where he was now, slumped in his seat, pretending his stomach and brain weren't lurching all over the place, knowing if he complained there'd be too much fussing, when really he knew he had no one else to blame. Had his teammates really thought he'd tried to hurt himself? He hadn't. Well, he didn't think he'd intended it. Regardless, he knew a bone-deep sense of shame that once again he'd been responsible for causing so much pain.

Somehow he made it off the plane, managed to apologize to and thank his teammates for their support. Managed to collect his bag and pretend he wasn't swaying like an old drunk until he got into Tim's Wrangler. He closed his eyes, leaned his head against the window, prayed he'd keep his guts together and not soil the pristine interior of Tim's car. Tim didn't speak except to call his wife and tell her they'd be there in fifteen.

A quarter hour later he was being hugged, seeing tears in Lacey's eyes as she whispered, "I'm so glad you're alive. You've got no idea how much we've been praying."

"We?"

"Me. Mike. The other Bible study guys," Tim said.

"Really?"

"And me," Lacey added. "And Emma."

He swallowed, blinked back emotion, pressed his lips together, looked away.

And then, helpless against the weighty emotions, he cried.

CHAPTER 14

"Miss Moritello, you can see by the long list here that Hopetoun House is facing a number of violations." Gordon Francis, the official charged with inspecting the building, handed her a three-page document filled with checked boxes where the building did not comply. "In order to continue operations you will need to ensure these are completed by December twenty-fourth, or else we will be forced to ensure the Home is closed."

Emma blinked. "Close Hopetoun House by Christmas? You can't be serious."

"I understand there are challenges in completing this in time, but we hope it need not come to that."

Challenges? Oh, like no money to pay for the recommended repairs and alterations? She bit back a hysterical laugh, wishing for the millionth time that Richard had managed to escape his other meeting to attend this one with her today. God bless the man for the patch-and-paint job he'd orchestrated on the weekend, but repairing the porch and installing a kitchen that met health regulations wasn't going to take a weekend and a few hundred dollars. Try more like a few hundred thousand dollars. Breath hitched, she felt her look of ease waver and instantly pinned her smile back on.

"Well, thank you for your time today," she managed. "You can be sure we will complete everything listed here and be ready for your visit on Christmas Eve. Do we book that in now?"

"I really don't think that's something we'd be pressing for the day before Christmas."

"And I really don't think you'd want to be leaving a number of special needs children in the lurch and trying to source alternative accommodation during the holiday period, would you?" she said as smoothly as she could. "We will be ready at nine a.m. for your visit so there's enough time for you to complete the paperwork and determine that we can remain open. Does that sound reasonable?"

Gordon studied her, and she wondered whether he could see the panic inside. *Please, God, give us grace. Soften his heart to us.*

"Fair enough," he finally said. "But if it's not acceptable, then you'll need to find other accommodation for the children here," he warned.

"It will be acceptable," she promised. *God, help us!* "Now, shall I walk you to the car?"

"It's fine," Gordon said, and she wondered if he thought she was trying to hurry him off the premises to avoid seeing anything else that might construe a violation.

"Miss Moritello," he said, pausing in the vestibule, "I am not against you. You understand that, don't you?"

"I know you're doing your job," she said, hating how her voice had a wobble. She sucked in a breath to smooth it out. "I also know that I'm responsible for these children, and I can assure you we are doing our utmost to help them here."

"I wish you all the best," Gordon said before exiting.

Her fingers shook, and she took a moment to compose herself before re-entering the facility. Deep breathing. Big prayers. More phone calls, the first of which would be to Richard, then to see what they could do about getting quotes to do the work. So much for any Thanksgiving preparations today. She had a mile-long list of things to do on top of her new responsibilities. God would need to help her.

With shaking fingers, she called Richard. This time he answered.

"That was today?" he said when she explained the situation. "I'm really sorry."

Not as sorry as she was. "So we now have a long list of alterations we need to make before Christmas."

"By Christmas?"

Panic flared again. She breathed deep to tamp it down. "We'll need quotes that will have to be approved as soon as possible so the work can commence and be finished in six weeks."

"Six weeks? I'm sorry, Emma, but I really don't think the board will be able to work that quickly."

"What about what you did last week? That was finished without fuss."

"There's a world of difference between a volunteer paint job and a kitchen," he said patiently, as if he thought she was a child. "And when there are huge expenses to pay for, then of course the board needs a judicious process to ensure it can happen in a cost-effective and timely manner."

"But that's the thing, Richard. We don't have time. We need this done urgently."

"I understand, but…"

She kind of got the feeling he would never truly understand. Perhaps a more direct approach would be necessary. "We need the furnace fixed."

He sighed. "Again?"

"Or replaced. It's an old house, and the furnace was always going to give up the ghost at some point."

"Has it given up the ghost?" he demanded.

"Well, no. But it isn't heating consistently, and the last time a repairman came he said it needed replacing."

"We will discuss it at the board meeting next week," Richard said. "In the meantime, you'll need to be extremely frugal with any spending."

"But it'll soon be winter," she protested. "We can't let the children freeze."

"No one is saying anything about the children freezing—"

Well, she was, she thought indignantly.

"—we just need to be seen to be wise."

"Surely it's wise to consider the health of the children," she countered.

"Yes, but I think the important consideration is whether the future of the Home can be sustained, especially given the long list of repairs that are required to keep it up to code."

She blinked. "Are you saying you think we'll be closed down?"

"No, no. Not at all."

"Then what are you saying?" she said slowly.

"I'm saying, one never knows what the future holds. And what has been a proven strategy in the past is not necessarily going to prove successful in the future. Once upon a time, large-scale orphanages were considered necessary. These days there is a lot more emphasis on getting children into appropriate families. Smaller, independent operations such as ours may find their skills better utilized by working in closer partnerships with bigger groups of greater resources."

Coldness slid across her chest. "You're not exactly convincing me that you're not closing us down."

"Look, Emma, you must know that what has happened with

Leona has really turned a spotlight on what we do here. And while the premises are under the guardianship of the trustees, we will be exploring every avenue to ensure the legacy of Hopetoun can continue. But it would be remiss of me to not let you know that one day, down the track, hopefully many years from now, things may look a little different from what you see now."

His words scarcely reassured, and his request to keep this to herself meant she had nobody to talk to. But wasn't avoiding fixing the furnace proof that Hopetoun would cease to be far sooner than Richard had said?

"And what about the repairs to get up to code?" she asked shakily.

"We'll discuss it at the next board meeting."

Which would never allow enough time for the work to be carried out by Christmas. "You are aware that if the building isn't approved by then, we'll be needing to rehome all of the children on Christmas Eve. Is that something the board would be happy to do?"

Another sigh. "I will communicate that too. But Emma, whenever large sums of money are involved, the board has a duty of care to ensure it is handled responsibly. I know John has been most concerned about the lack of funds coming in."

"I understand that," she gritted out. "Can I at least source some quotes so we can start this process as quickly as possible?"

"You can, but I'm afraid unless the board releases the money, there will be nothing to pay them with. If people were willing to donate their time, that would be one thing, but we're talking brand new kitchens and new furnaces and the like."

It seemed hopeless, her pleas falling on deaf ears. But something stubborn within said it wasn't hopeless. That God could still do miracles. Couldn't He?

~

"HEY, TYLER. HOW'S EVERYTHING GOING?" Tim said, dropping his bag from the recent road trip at the door.

"Good." He motioned to the kitchen. "She's in there."

Tim nodded and moved, and soon there came a cry of "You're back!" and something which sounded an awful lot like a kiss. Tyler slouched a little deeper in the sofa, not wanting to observe the passion with which Tim embraced his wife. He'd found himself in the way on more than a few occasions these past few days.

Staying with Tim had given him new insight into his captain's private life, which was something he was pretty sure Tim hadn't counted on when he'd first insisted Tyler stay with them. But it was kinda nice to see a relationship still had sparks, even after a few years of marriage.

He'd tried to not make it too hard on them, having no desire to be in the way more than he already was, but his emotions still felt too fragile for much beyond the safe harbor this place had proved.

His tears that first night had led to the most surreal moment of his life: Tim leading Tyler to his study, praying for him aloud, as Tyler shuddered out each grief-soaked breath and prayed the sinner's prayer he'd first prayed over twenty years ago. With nothing to lose and everything to gain, he'd confessed his many, many sins and felt the weirdest sense of peace rush over him.

Tyler knew now he was loved. That God didn't need his attempts at goodness, let alone perfection. And after being so tired, tired, *tired* of running, he was glad to stop and feel like he'd finally been found. God loved him. That fact still amazed him. But he *knew* God did, he felt God's love, and he had this deep, deep sense that this time it was true.

And now, four days later, he still felt like the road grime of life had mostly been cleaned, but that he was also in this strange space of feeling fragile, feeling vulnerable, like he didn't know who he was anymore. Hiding out here, reading the Bible, praying, talking things through with Tim, with Mike, even Beau, had helped a lot. But he knew there was so much farther to go. There'd been barely any time to consider what all of this might mean for his hockey career. That was the least of his concerns. Instead, he felt like this was his time to finally get things right.

Tim reappeared, a beaming Lacey under his arm. "So, Lace tells me you've been behaving yourself."

"I've tried."

"Cooked a few meals too, I hear."

"They were delicious," Lacey said kindly.

Delicious was over-selling things, but he'd take it. "It's the least I can do."

He wondered how much longer they'd insist on having him stay. He liked the security of this place, knew the house in town would prove harder to keep media away from. Probably something he should've thought about before he bought it.

"So, what have you been doing?"

He explained a little of how he'd spent his time—reading, praying, helping Lacey with chores. It felt so ordinary, but inside he felt so different.

"Tyler's been great with helping with the horses and the dogs," Lacey said, ruffling her golden retriever's ears. "Bilbo loves him, doesn't he?"

"I haven't had a dog in years," Tyler admitted. Decades, even. His career had never allowed for it, and the one dog his parents had agreed to when he was ten had run away within a year.

"So you're feeling a little better."

"Yeah. A lot better, actually."

Tim nodded. "Some of the guys were asking after you. Andrei said to tell you he hoped you might be pulling out some more dance moves soon."

"That might take a while."

"Been anywhere yet?" Tim asked.

Tyler shook his head. How to explain he didn't want to see anyone, couldn't bear their questions or speculation.

"I think he should come with me to Hopetoun tomorrow," Lacey said.

Tyler looked quickly at her. And see Emma? "I don't think that's a good idea."

"Why?" Lacey smiled. "The kids like you, and there's always something to be done. I hate to say it to Emma, but the place is falling apart. I honestly think it's just a matter of time before they close it down."

"What?" Tyler asked. "They can't do that."

"I get the impression that some of the trustees think they should," Lacey said.

But those kids needed a place like that. He knew, better than most, that kids deserved to feel safe and secure, which was what Emma and Hopetoun House provided.

"I've got a day off tomorrow," Tim said. "We could go over there, see if there's anything we can do."

"But I don't know if anyone"—like Emma—"would want to see me," Tyler muttered. "Nobody needs a headline drawing attention to a place like that."

"Come on. It's not that bad. Not everybody's focused on you," Lacey teased.

"Might do you good, get you focused on others," Tim said. "And you know the kids like you."

Because he could relate to their brokenness and rejection.

"And I think Emma will be as pleased as we are to see you're making some positive changes in your life," Lacey encouraged.

"What do you say?" Tim asked.

What could he say to these kind and generous friends who had offered up their lives and home and encouraged him to find Life? "Okay?"

~

THE PUMPKINS of a few weeks ago had been replaced with decorative gourds, the yellow and orange plastic vegetation adding a bright spot of color to Hopetoun's big room. The kids had enjoyed the last chance to dig outside in the vegetable garden with Jacob and Beth before the ice-laden winds had chased them inside. Now, hands washed, stencils out, they were doing some coloring while the TV blared something about Dorothy the Dinosaur and the smell of baked cookies lingered in the air.

"Miss Emma, come see my drawing," Lily demanded.

"I'll be there in a moment," Emma said, continuing to help Brandon hold his pencil. "See? That makes it much easier, doesn't it?"

His little shoulders slumped, his fat yellow pencil falling to the table with a clatter. "Don't wanna color."

She pressed her lips together. A phone call an hour ago had brought the news that Brandon would likely soon be moved on to another residential program. His withdrawal had concerned the child psychologist, who believed it was best for him to find foster parents as quickly as possible. Emma had protested, but she couldn't deny that she was concerned about the young boy too. For weeks now he had moped around the facility, barely interacting with the other children or answering when she tried to talk to him. She didn't know what was wrong with him—had prayed about it and had tried to discuss it with Jacob and Lorraine, the weekend supervisor, but neither of them had any answers.

She gently stroked his head. "What would you like to do?"

"I don't know."

Lord, please show me how to reach his heart. Comfort him, help him know Your peace.

"Look at my bunny," Karinda said, holding up her picture.

"Could we have a bunny?" Lily asked.

"Yeah, a bunny!" Karinda clapped her hands.

"I loves bunnies. They're so soft," Lily continued. "And they have little pink noses that wiggle like this." She demonstrated.

"And they like to hop like this," Karinda said, bouncing in a move more like a kangaroo, complete with paws up.

"They don't hop like that," Ben said. "They hop like this."

Brandon watched Ben as he demonstrated a move more like a frog than a rabbit, then slowly copied it.

Emma's heart lit. Oh, if only he could continue to engage with others.

"And what do bunnies like to eat?" she asked.

"They likes carrots," Lily said.

"And lettuce," Karinda said.

"Do you think they'd like ice cream?" she asked.

"No-o-o!" the children chorused.

"That's silly," Lily said.

"Maybe they'd prefer hot dogs," she suggested.

"No-o-o!"

This continued for a while longer, adding some lightness to what had been a hard few days. No way was she going to communicate her concerns about the Home's future to the kids. At least Lacey's shift was due to start soon. She'd missed Lacey's company but knew her best friend's presence had been required elsewhere. Another prayer floated heavenward for all that was going on at the Carruthers' house.

Jacob looked up from where he was fiddling with the thermostat. "I think the furnace is on the blink again."

"Really?" The levity of moments earlier fled as she got up to join him. "We had the repairman out not long ago."

Not that they could afford it. Richard's comment from two days ago that they needed to be extra careful with their finances had sunk deep. She'd talked it over with her dad, who knew a contractor who might be able to call in and offer a quote for the kitchen this weekend, but given the holiday period—Thanksgiving was just over a week away—how could anyone expect to get this work done in time? Let alone at a rate that would prove affordable?

"Emma?"

She startled and returned her attention to Jacob. "Sorry. I was just thinking."

"About?"

She shook her head. Her friendship with Jacob would never extend as deep as he appeared to wish.

"You planning on watching New York's next game?" he persisted.

"When is it?"

"Tomorrow. New York against Columbus."

"Oh. No." For some reason hockey had held little interest lately. "I was just thinking about the furnace and what we'll do."

"D'you want me to go have a look downstairs?"

"Uh, okay, sure. Thanks." She appreciated his enthusiasm, but sometimes she had her doubts about Jacob's ability. He wasn't always the most practical-minded of people. Witness the shower hose debacle of several weeks ago.

Her thoughts tracked back to the man who had fixed that, and she wondered if he knew anything about furnaces. She closed her eyes. How ridiculous. Almost as ridiculous as not caring about watching the hockey, simply because she knew someone wouldn't be playing.

Lights from a car turning into the drive flashed through the windows, and a knot of tension eased. Finally. She moved to the door, opening it as Lacey hurried up the steps, then drawing her into a big hug. "How are you?"

"Oh, Em. I've missed you."

"You okay?" she asked, pulling back to study her friend.

"Yeah," Lacey said after a moment. "It's been an interesting few days."

But judging from the heightened noise from the big room, this wasn't the time to find out more.

"Come on. Let's stop the riot." Emma moved back to the room and clapped her hands three times. "Hey, kids, look who's here!"

"Miss Lacey!" Lily called. "Come see my drawing."

"That's beautiful, darling." Lacey squatted beside her, asking about various things Lily had drawn.

Emma bit her lip. Lacey looked drained. The past few days of emotional turmoil had left its toll in her shadowed eyes. Emma had barely dared to call her, knowing she and Tim were caring for TJ. She hadn't known it would leave her looking like this.

Jacob's return from the furnace fixing—unsurprisingly, it remained unfixed—was soon followed by his offer to read a story, which Emma jumped at, explaining she and Lacey would prepare the afternoon snack in the kitchen. And finally catch up.

"How are you doing?" Emma asked, slicing up apples for the fruit tray. "Is TJ behaving?"

"Yes. Of course he is. He's been really quiet, and I've heard him have a few really long talks with Tim." Lacey unpackaged a box of cookies and laid them on the white plastic tray. "Tim hasn't told me too much, but it seems like TJ—I mean, Tyler—is really wanting to change."

"Tyler?"

"We're trying to call him Tyler. Apparently that's his real name, and Tim thinks it will help him believe we want to be his friend."

She nodded, her thoughts tracking back to when he'd introduced himself. He'd called himself Tyler then too, like he'd wanted her to be his friend. Her stomach tensed. "It's good he wants to change."

"Call me crazy," Lacey whispered, "but I think he's had a God-encounter."

"Really?" Her heart kicked.

Her best friend nodded. "Yeah, I think he's been on this journey for a while now," Lacey confided. "But this was the kick up the backside he really needed."

"Wow. That's amazing."

"Isn't it? I'm still not one hundred percent sure, so don't say anything. But God can do miracles, right?"

"Right." TJ—Tyler—was seeking God?

"So keep praying for him, okay?"

"Sure."

But there was something about praying for someone that softened her heart and drew it a little closer to his. She didn't want to admit it, but he was often in her thoughts. She wondered how he must feel, watching Tim go off to practice and games knowing he had to stay behind. From what she'd seen posted by the club, Tyler was on leave—on injured reserve, which was code for unable to be played. It must be tough, seeing someone else called up to take the place he'd been fighting for. But just when she began to feel sorry for him, she'd remember the other posts about his drunken antics at a club in L.A., reminding her that thinking too much about a man who was not even a professing Christian was a recipe for disaster. She didn't want to be that girl again. She wouldn't let her emotions get the better of her brain. And so yes, she would pray for him, but she would keep her heart out of it, which would mean praying that God would protect her as well.

"How's the food supply situation going?" Lacey asked, pulling her back to the here and now.

"Things seem to be improving. We've had some donations from local businesses for Thanksgiving next week, which is great. The trustees have paid the outstanding debt, but we've decided not to use that company again. The money we're saving is going toward preparing our own meals again. So yeah, the food situation is okay."

"But other situations?"

Emma collected plastic cups and retrieved a container of milk from the fridge, then studied her friend. "Richard tells me we need at least two hundred thousand dollars to pay for the repairs to get the building up to code and another fifty grand to clear Leona's debts."

Lacey's mouth fell open, and she sank onto a stool. "A quarter of a million?"

"By Christmas," she said.

"But, Em, that's only five weeks away."

Put like that, Emma felt a surge of hysteria again. "God can do miracles, right?"

"Oh my goodness." Lacey put her chin in her hands as she eyed Emma. "What's the board going to do?"

She didn't think it was a secret. "I don't know. There's a chance they may have to close us down."

"What? They can't do that. The kids here need what we do."

"I know." Her voice broke. "But a quarter of a million dollars, Lace. How am I going to find that?"

"It's not just you," Lacey assured her. "It's the board. They're the ones ultimately responsible. You just need to stay focused on the here and now."

"I'm trying," she murmured. "But it's really hard to not think about the consequences for the kids if we fail. We have to fix a million things to meet the code for what we do here, and Richard says there's no money, and I don't know what to do." She gulped. "I've been praying, asking God for a solution, and nothing."

Lacey moved around to give her a hug. "One day at a time, Em. Trust God for this moment, then the next."

She breathed in Lacey's perfume, felt her heart ease as the panic ebbed away. "Thanks, Lace."

Another flash of lights—the afternoon sky was darkening by the minute—carved a path across the ancient kitchen cupboards. Who else was here? After the past few days, all she wanted was to hide away, preferably with chocolate, a good movie, and an endless cup of tea.

"Actually, hold that thought," Lacey said. "You wanted a solution? I think one might've just driven in."

CHAPTER 15

Tyler didn't want to get out of Tim's Wrangler. Getting out meant showing himself to a world he was sure would hate him, would judge him quicker than a man could swat a fly. Man. Who'd have thought he'd have turned so quickly into a wuss? He got out, glancing at the rust-bucket of a car beside them. It looked as sorry as he felt, advertising its wear and tear for all to see. He shook his head, exhaled slowly in the cold afternoon air. This wasn't about him, he needed to remember. This was about the kids.

"Coming?" Tim asked.

"Yep." The kids. He'd stay focused on the kids. Or at least on whatever task Tim and Lacey would find for him to do. As for Emma, he'd be real glad to avoid her. After their last few encounters, everything felt strange, a no-man's land of almost-friends where he still wished he could be more but feared all she'd offer was her pity.

He tucked his hands in his pockets and followed Tim up the steps, waiting on the rickety porch as Tim knocked on the door. A moment later it was opened by the weedy guy who hated Tyler's guts.

"Tim! Oh, and you." The scowl didn't scream friendliness. "Can I help you?"

"Actually…" Tim cast Tyler a look, then turned back. "We're here to help you."

"I'm sorry?"

"You don't need to be," Tim said. "Lacey and Emma know."

"Know what?" the man persisted, arms folded.

"Dude," Tyler muttered. Who did he think he was? Bruce Willis? Emma's bodyguard? Who else had such a nerve as to stop Tim Carruthers from going in?

"I'll need to check—oh, Emma."

Tyler's gaze snapped back to the door, noting Emma's wide-eyed glance instantly shift away as she welcomed them inside, insisting that it was too cold to be outside today.

But being here, near her, in her space, made him feel too warm. It was best for all concerned if he stayed away from her. Didn't look at her. Wasn't dragged into the ocean that was her eyes.

"I'm so glad you're here," Lacey said, beckoning them to follow her to the kitchen.

As they passed the big room, Tyler glanced across to where the kids were watching TV. Brandon looked up, his features creasing into a smile. "TJ!"

Tyler lifted a hand, but a wave apparently wasn't enough, as Brandon hopped up and ran toward him. Tyler crouched, his arms wide as Brandon ran into them. "TJ," Brandon said, pressed hard against Tyler's sweater.

"Hey, bud. I missed you." Tyler closed his eyes. If only everyone could accept him with the ease this kid did.

"Brandon, that's enough now," the weedy worker dude said. "Go sit back down with the others."

"I want TJ," he said, clinging to Tyler's hand.

"Dude, I'll be around. Be a good boy and I'll see you soon, okay?"

Brandon studied him seriously. "Promise?"

"Promise," Tyler said.

"Come on," Lacey insisted. "Emma has something important to say."

Tyler patted Brandon on the shoulder, gently encouraging him to return to the others, as his heart toyed with what could be so important for Emma to share. Another glance at her revealed shadows under her eyes, like she hadn't slept well for days. His stomach tensed as her gaze dropped.

"What's happened?" Tim said once they'd reached the relative privacy of the kitchen. A couple of platters of browning cut fruit were on the table.

At Lacey's gesture for Emma to speak, Emma sighed. "We need to raise a lot of money and get work done before Christmas or else we might be shut down."

"Are you kidding?" Tim asked.

Judging from the broken look in Emma's eyes, she'd never been more serious.

"I'm sorry," Tyler murmured.

Emma studied the table. "I don't even know if I'm supposed to be mentioning this, it still feels so raw and new. But I don't know how we can manage to keep things a secret." She pushed her head into her hands. "It feels so huge and impossible. I mean, I know God can do impossible things"—she slid a look at Tyler that made him wonder what else Lacey might have said —"but we have to raise money, get quotes, and get the work done in five weeks. It feels overwhelming."

"What has the board said?" Tim asked.

"They're not even meeting until this weekend," Emma said, her voice breaking.

"What needs to be done?" Tyler asked.

She spouted a long list of things, concluding with the fact the furnace still wasn't working as it ought. "It's working now, but sometimes it just switches off, and Richard seems to think it's not worth fixing, not if we're not going to be here in the new year."

"Has he said that?" Lacey asked, her eyes wide.

"Not in so many words, but how can we remain open if we can't get the work done?"

Tyler's heart twisted with compassion, for the kids as much as for poor Emma.

God?

He was still rusty with this praying thing, but surely God would be interested in helping out these poor kids. There had to be a solution. "What about fundraising?" he asked, his gaze not quite meeting Emma's.

"Richard has mentioned a bake sale before."

Tyler swallowed a curse. "Is he for real?"

"I know. Sometimes I get the impression he's given up and can't be bothered, and I get so mad but feel so helpless, because how am I to do anything if the board that needs to approve things can't even see the urgency and try?"

"It's wrong," he said, uneasily conscious that so much of this stemmed from his stupid hit on Nick. If he hadn't done that, Leona wouldn't have stolen the money and left them in such a bind.

"I know it's wrong," Emma said, "but what can I do?"

Lacey and Tim looked as downcast as Tyler felt.

God?

An idea sparked. Tyler straightened. "Can you fundraise? Apart from bake sales?"

"I guess so."

"And you need the money to pay contractors, right?"

She nodded.

"What if some are willing to do it for free?"

"At this time of year?" Tim said.

"There must be some who'd be glad for some work, especially if they got some free publicity from it, like from New York's captain."

Lacey nodded. "We could put the word out, couldn't we?"

"And bypass all the board's requirements. They couldn't argue if it was done for free, could they?" Tyler asked Emma.

"I don't see how they could," she admitted.

"So get on the phone to your board and see what they have to say," he advised.

"You think this will work?"

Tyler shrugged. "I think people will be happy to help out, especially knowing it's for such a good cause." He would be, anyway. "Besides, what have you got to lose?"

WHAT DID she have to lose? "Nothing," she admitted.

"So call him. Now," Tyler urged.

Why he seemed to have taken this on as his personal mission she did not know. But what he said made sense. She drew out her phone and called Richard while Lacey and the others took out the platters for afternoon snack time.

"Ah, Emma. What can I do for you?" Richard's gravelly voice met her ear.

"I was just thinking about our conversation the other day."

"Found some quotes already, have you?"

"No. Not yet." She swallowed. "I'm just checking that you were meaning that we can fundraise. Use the money from that to pay for repairs," she clarified.

"I don't know how much a little bake sale might raise, but yes, of course."

"Anything is better than nothing," she countered. "And you'd be happy for me to find companies willing to donate their products, time, and labor, is that right?"

"Of course." He chuckled, like he thought this was a joke.

But it wasn't a joke, she thought fiercely. This was her life, the kids' lives, at stake. This *wasn't* funny. Instead, it was a challenge.

"Very well. Oh, and one last thing. Would I be right in assuming that it's okay to share about this? To let people know that Hopetoun is at risk of closing?"

"Well, we certainly don't want to create the impression that we're in dire straits right now—"

"But isn't that what we are in?" she asked. "My understanding is that if this work is not remedied by Christmas, then the Home will be shut down. So if people are willing to support us, then now is the time for them to know, isn't it?"

"Well, I suppose so."

"Good. Then I assume I have your permission to tell the rest of the staff?" she said, conscious of a guilty sting that perhaps she should have mentioned her concerns to employees like Lorraine and Jacob before mentioning them to Tim and Tyler.

"I'll draft an email today."

"It will need to be sent out today, because I have every intention of doing all I can to save Hopetoun," she warned him.

"Well, in that case, I'll get to it straightaway."

"Thank you. Now excuse me, I have much to do."

She pressed end and exhaled heavily, her mind ticking with the long list of tasks requiring attention. But first things first. She had to thank Lacey, Tim, and Tyler for breathing new confidence into her today.

She went out to the big room to see Tyler listening to Brandon, the little boy's head on Tyler's shoulder as they read a book in the kiddie quiet corner. How sweet.

"He's a good guy, huh?" Lacey murmured.

Maybe. Brandon didn't trust just anyone. "Where's Tim?"

"He's having a look at the furnace with Jacob."

"God bless him."

"Amen," Lacey said. "Then, when he's finished, I think we'll talk strategy."

"What do you mean?"

"You know this is what I feel put on earth to do—to raise awareness of important issues however I can—and I agree with Tyler. I think people will be happy to contribute to such a good cause. And even though people are busy, I think if we emphasize this is the season for giving, then that could be a good draw too."

Perhaps it would. For the first time in days, Emma now felt a measure of hope.

THE NEXT DAYS passed in a welter of visits, phone calls, and more. Between them, Lacey and Tim had spoken to a lawyer and set up a bank account strictly for donations to Hopetoun House, into which they'd deposited twenty thousand dollars already.

Emma had been stunned, but Lacey had said, "You can't get work done if there's no funds, so this gets the ball rolling, doesn't it?"

Such generosity meant she was no longer so heavily concerned about what the results of today's board meeting might be. The board of trustees could pay or not, but with Lacey and others doing what they could to share the plight of the children's home, then Emma would pray that would provide buffer enough to help them through. The other workers had been equally invigorated to stand up for the Home's plight.

"How dare they determine the quality of the care we offer here based on mere numbers?" Lorraine had stormed. "Children are infinitely more precious than that."

Of course they were. But it didn't mean that the lack of dollars wouldn't thwart them. Still, they were doing what they could. Tyler had offered his spare days to repair the porch, and the sound of the nail-gun accompanied most daylight hours. Emma's father had also volunteered his time, and Tim's donation had been partly spent on new timbers to fix the porch. The porch's problems were a good beginning, but some of the other tasks would take much more time. Like the kitchen. But still, they'd take what was offered, and Tyler's offer was wonderful, even if it had led to some awkwardness when he didn't seem to want to speak to her, and tension when Jacob questioned why he was here.

"It's good for him," Lacey had insisted when Emma mentioned some of her concerns. "It gets him out of his head, gets him focused on others. And it's good for me, too. As much as I've appreciated his help around the place, it's like he's a ghost of himself, barely talking, barely smiling. Sometimes I wonder if he would've been better off going to a rehab facility, but Tim says that he's better off with Christians now."

"Because?"

"Because he needs encouragement, not humanistic nothings."

"I don't think all rehabs are like that."

Lacey shrugged. "Tim says if he'd gone to rehab then he would've been sent down to the minors, which would've killed his motivation and sense of purpose. Here he's connecting with Tim and they're talking, and now he's interested in others again."

Interested in everyone except her. It seemed he went out of his way to avoid speaking to her. Not that she'd mention that. "He's great with the kids," she admitted.

"Call me crazy, but I think he'd make a great dad one day," Lacey had said.

Emma now glanced out the window, where Tyler's broad shoulders were hunched over as he placed the new boards and nailed them in. He should be finished today, just in time for the wet weather forecast for this weekend.

She stepped outside, wrapping her thick coat more fully around her. "Tyler?"

He glanced up, then did that thing where he was facing her but not quite meeting her eyes. He'd done that a lot lately. "Am I making too much noise?"

"No, not at all. I just wondered if you'd like a warm drink or something to eat. You've been working so hard."

"I'm fine," he said, head bowing as if he preferred to focus on wood rather than talk to her.

"Okay," she said softly. "Don't get too cold out here."

He nodded, and as she returned inside she heard the *rap rap* of the nail gun again.

"How's Hopetoun House looking?" Tim asked after dinner. He'd been busy with training and team meetings all day.

"The porch is done," Tyler said. "I think the kitchen is the main focus now."

"But they can't really start until after Thanksgiving," Lacey said.

Thanksgiving. A holiday Tyler hadn't celebrated much, although this year he had more to be thankful about than before. But he'd rather spend it by himself—or at least with God —than in the craziness of lots of people demanding his time.

Lacey started collecting plates, and he stood to help, but she pushed him back into his seat. "Sit. You've been working hard all day."

He nodded, not needing a second request, and stretched out his muscles, the past days working at the Home digging pain into places he wasn't used to. Funny how someone could spend a lifetime working on his fitness only to discover he wasn't as fit as he liked to think.

"Hey, after dinner I've got another Zoom call with Mike, Beau, and the guys. Want to join?"

Tyler shook his head. "They're your friends."

Tim studied him. "They could be your friends too."

"Yeah, I don't think so. I know they don't like me."

"They're Christians, not saints, but give them a chance. It might take some time before they're willing to trust you, but the best way to change that is to show them you're a different man from before."

"How?"

"By showing up." Tim grinned. "Don't worry. You won't have to do or say anything. Some of the guys don't say much, but everyone appreciates knowing the others have their back."

Awesome. "What do you do?"

"Pastor Josiah Abrahams—he's a big sports fan from Chicago who started this group with Jai Mullins—he leads it. We usually study some parts of Scripture, discuss how it applies to our life, share about how stuff is going, pray."

It sounded more and more intimidating. "I don't think they'd really want me there."

"You'd be surprised. Mike mentioned that he's been praying for you for years, and just last month, Beau was encouraging us all to not hold that hit against you. I know there might be some who take some time to get over past history—"

"Like Brent."

Tim nodded. "But God is working in his heart as well, so don't hold that against him." He studied Tyler. "I really think you'll find it worthwhile. I've learned that playing pro hockey as a Christian can be a lonely thing, and I really value the encouragement and support of these guys. I think you will too."

"You really think they'll cope?"

"I think they'll need to learn to cope." He smiled. "Come on. I never figured you to be a wimp."

The old indignation flamed, then Tyler recognized the tease. "I might listen in and sit in the background. I don't think they'd want to see me."

Tim studied him a moment, then nodded. "I'll take it."

Tyler exhaled. He had a feeling this would be as hard as this past week spent avoiding alcohol.

A FEW HOURS LATER, Tyler wandered from the guestroom to see Tim on his laptop near the dining room. Tension rose. He braced himself. This was a bad idea.

Tim laughed. "Yeah, we play Washington tomorrow, then Lace and I head to Minnesota to see my mom for Thanksgiving."

Thanksgiving? He'd forgotten it was coming up so soon. Lacey had mentioned something about a soup kitchen, but he had little desire to go back to the big smoke. Not until he felt a little stronger in himself. Maybe there was something nearer he could do.

"Allie's flying in on Wednesday," another voice said. He thought it was Jai, from Chicago. "Gotta admit I'm glad that this time next year we won't be apart."

"The travel gets old quick, doesn't it?" Mike said. Probably the only one who'd be glad to see Tyler. If he dared show his face.

"And the time zones," Jai continued. "Two hours can be a pain."

"Two hours?" He heard a snort. "Try fourteen. Then try figuring out daylight savings changes and seasons. Then you can talk." Brent. He'd married that Australian girl.

"How's Holly doin'?" Beau asked. Tyler would recognize that twang anywhere. "She must be ready to pop soon."

"She's over being pregnant. For a little thing, she looks really huge, but don't tell her I said that."

"I'm pregnant, not deaf," a feminine voice with an Aussie accent called in the background.

Tyler's lips tweaked.

"I meant really beautiful, sweetheart," Brent said, obviously off-screen.

"Sure you did. You know this is all your fault."

"Sure hope so," Brent said, to chuckles from the others.

Huh. The guy had a sense of humor. Who'd have thought?

He knew Brent didn't like him much, had never liked him since Tyler had tried hitting on Holly at Mike's wedding years ago. Little had he known that Brent was interested in her. It wasn't until Tyler had been playing in Calgary—how many teams ago?—that he'd really understood where things stood between them. Brent was a lucky man, snagging a wife with Holly's sass and determination.

"So, how's your houseguest?" another voice—Toronto's Dan Walton?—asked.

Tim turned, saw Tyler, and beckoned him near. "You can ask him yourself."

"Huh?" another voice said. "What's Woletsky doing there?"

"Come on, Chris, keep up," Beau teased.

"No, seriously," Chris said. "You're kidding, right? Isn't he supposed to be in rehab or something? Or a psych ward?"

Whoa. Way to make him feel the Christian love.

"It's not a joke," Tim said, yanking Tyler so he could see the screen. "Say hi to Tyler, everyone."

For a second there was silence. Then a chorus of "heys" accompanied lifted hands and even a few smiles.

"Sit down," Tim commanded.

Tyler sat, and Tim introduced him to everyone on the screen. He knew most of the guys. Some, like Dan and Chris, he'd known for years. Others, like Ryan and Luc, he'd not had much to do with. Then there was the big black pastor dude called Josiah, who greeted him with a grin and a welcome that felt oddly reassuring. Tyler knew his reputation had preceded him when Josiah said something about miracles, but he couldn't argue. The fact he was attending an online Bible study with these guys felt unbelievable to him, too.

"So, Tyler, how are you doing?" Mike asked.

"Okay."

He felt like the elephant in the room, the way everyone seemed to stare at him like they didn't know what to say. That was okay. He didn't know what to say either, especially as he wasn't sure how much Mike and Tim had shared.

"So, um, Tyler, I don't want to put you on the spot or anything, but would you like to share a little bit about what's happened recently?" Tim asked.

Nope. Not to these guys. Not to those who hated him.

"Way to go not making him feel like he's on the spot," Dan said.

"Yeah, I heard you were in the hospital," Chris said. "You tried to top yourself or something. Is that true?"

"Dude." Mike frowned. "Tyler, you don't have to share. It's okay. We're just glad you're here today, aren't we?"

Another second, then, "Yeah."

"Sure."

"Cool."

Tyler ducked his head. He didn't want to have to own his mistakes. But it wasn't like he'd hidden them. His mistakes had littered tabloids for years. The only real surprise was that he was here. Alive. When he could've so easily died. And wasn't confession supposed to be good for the soul?

"I can share. If you want." His voice sounded raspy. "But I

know you have a study or something, and I don't want to take up all your time."

"We've got all the time in the world to hear this, bud," Beau said.

"Yeah." Mike grinned. "I think it's gotta be testimony time tonight, right, Josiah?"

"Speak the truth and shame the devil," Josiah said. "I have a feeling this is something that we're all gonna wanna hear."

Tyler exhaled. Glanced across at Tim, who gave a small nod of encouragement. Then he began to share.

CHAPTER 16

"You're sure about this?" Lacey's voice resounded through Emma's ear.

"Yep," Emma responded, phone tucked under her chin as she corrected the table setting which Lily had set with the forks and knives the wrong way.

"Oh, I'm so glad. I really feel like he needs to be with people, and the kids responded so well, it will be good. So thank you."

"No worries."

Lacey sighed. "I need to go. Tim's mom is an angel, but there's only so much time she puts up with me being on my phone before she gets a little antsy. But I hope you have a good day today."

"And you."

Emma ended the call and slid her phone in her jeans pocket. No, she wasn't going to dress up simply because an NHL player would be here soon. And while the news of his possible encounter with God had scented many of her prayers this past week, she had determined to treat him much the same. Politely. With dignity. Demonstrating the grace that Jesus wanted from her.

Lacey's comment after church on Sunday had drawn compassion. "Tim's mom is expecting us for Thanksgiving, and we haven't been there for nearly a year. I'd really hate to miss it."

"Why would you? Oh, because you're babysitting Tyler."

"Not babysitting, just being a safe space." Lacey's face had fallen as she worried her lip. "Tyler said something about maybe volunteering to serve at the team's soup kitchen event in the city, but I can't help but worry that might not be the best environment for him."

"Because you'll be out of town."

Lacey nodded. "I was thinking it'd be nice if he could maybe volunteer here instead."

Emma's pulse had run a little faster. "Would that be permitted in his condition?"

"He hasn't got a disease, Emma. And it's not like he's on bail. It's just about managing his time and energies so he feels safe and secure. It's not like anyone is going to be taking pictures to post on social media. Some of the things people are saying are really cruel."

She'd seen them. The incident in L.A. had brought out the trolls and seen a procession of photographs from over the years, dating back as far as fifteen years. She shivered. Thank God there were no pictures of what she'd done when she was in her late teens and early twenties.

"It's pretty unfair, isn't it, that people can't leave the past in the past." Lacey sighed. "It's like they don't want to see him succeed, like they always want him to be the snarling agitator they love to hate."

Compassion had twisted again. "That would be tough."

"And while team management is smart enough to look past that, I don't know if some of the fans are, and I worry for him, trying to prove he's different when everybody seems to want him to fail."

"He can come here," Emma had said quietly. "I think the kids would really like to see him again. Who knows? Lily might be able to get him to bust out some more dance moves."

"Yeah, I don't know if he's really in a dancing frame of mind, but stranger things have happened, right?"

Emma had nodded. Miracles could happen. And with all that was happening with TJ—Tyler—maybe there would be another miracle with the Home as well.

The roar of a motorcycle now drew her gaze outside, as it did the children's attention. Jacob shot her a frown, and she gently shook her head. She wouldn't treat Tyler with kid gloves, but neither would she let Jacob continue with his snide comments. Not that she was protective or anything.

A minute later, Tyler was buzzing for entry at the door, and okay, she might've hurried a little to open it. "Hi." She offered a smile.

"Hi." He avoided her gaze, tugging down the sleeves of his button-down as if not wanting his tattoos to be seen.

"Come in. It's good you could come," she added honestly.

He nodded, his lips lifting as Lily screamed, "It's Mr. TJ!" and flung herself at his legs.

"Hey there, Lily." He crouched until they were face to face. "How are you?"

"I'm great! I'm happy to see you. It's been forever!"

"Sure has." His gaze slid up to meet Emma's. "Something smells good."

"So it should. We've had donations galore from a number of different restaurants downtown, and I think they're all trying to outdo each other. Not that we're going to complain."

His lips flickered up, but there was still no smile in his eyes, which hurt her a little inside. She was used to cocky TJ, the arrogant agitator of fearsome reputation, not this man who looked like a shadow of himself. For some reason she wanted to cry.

Blinking back emotion, she motioned to a hall table. "You

can leave your helmet there if you like. You might want to keep your jacket on, though. It's a little cool inside."

"Is the furnace not working?" he asked.

"Tim tried, but it's still proving to be a little temperamental," she admitted.

"Can't you get it fixed?"

"It's complicated."

He eyed her for a moment, then nodded, his features finally lighting as Brandon pushed to his side. "Hey, buddy. How are you?"

Brandon's face shone, something that really did wrench emotion through her. He hadn't looked like that in weeks. Oh, she hoped whoever cared for him would be able to bring that look to his face again.

Tyler glanced at her again. "Is it okay if I hang out with my man Brandon here for a while?"

"I'd love you to," she said.

His eyes flickered, then he nodded and drew Brandon to one side.

"Oh, but I wanted to talk to Mr. TJ," complained Lily.

"Mr. Tyler is busy. I'm sure he'd love to talk to you soon." Tyler looked over at Emma as she said his name, but she pretended not to notice.

Lily's nose screwed up as she tilted her head. "I thought his name is TJ?"

"Maybe the T stands for Tyler."

"What about the J?"

"I don't know," Emma admitted honestly. "Maybe you can ask him, when you talk to him about Barbies," she added loudly enough for the man in the corner to hear.

A quick peek up saw him look away, but she'd seen that small smile. It felt like a win.

"Barbies? Mr. T-yler"—Lily caught herself—"doesn't play with Barbies, does he?"

"I don't know," Emma said. "Maybe he does. You can ask him once he finishes reading with Brandon."

When Lily looked determined to march on over to the corner and demand to know if Tyler played with dolls, Emma quickly steered her to help with folding the napkins instead.

Ten minutes later, the other volunteers were all waiting in line to serve the meal, the main meal being served at lunchtime today. Tonight's meal would consist of leftovers, and others had been rostered on to care for them while Emma was freed to spend the afternoon with her family. She'd always loved Thanksgiving both at Hopetoun and at home, as much for the tradition of speaking thanks aloud here as for her mother's delicious home-cooked meal. She wondered if Lacey had said anything to Tyler about that.

The children were served, Emma scoring the role of dishing up greens, which saw several screwed up noses. "But don't you want to grow up big and strong?" she pleaded with Brandon.

He shook his head, covering his plate.

"I love green vegetables," Tyler said from his mashed potato and gravy station next to her.

Brandon sighed and pushed his plate out. "Not many peas," he warned.

"Just enough," she said, taking care to add a small piece of broccoli too.

"I don't like that," he mumbled, pointing to the broccoli.

"Makes you tough," Tyler said.

"Like you?" Brandon asked.

"Yep."

"See? Look how big and strong you can be if you eat your vegetables," Emma said.

As Brandon moved to where Dolores, one of the volunteer helpers from church, was doling out cranberry sauce, Emma glanced at Tyler and mouthed a thank you.

He shrugged, but she saw the corner of his mouth had ticked up a little.

When they were all seated, Emma took the chance to encourage the children to leave their knives and forks on the table while they prayed. "We usually invite our special guest to say a prayer, but Mr. Tyler may not want to say grace, so perhaps—"

"I'll say it," he said.

"You will?"

He nodded and bowed his head. Catching Jacob's surprised look, Emma quickly bowed her head too. "Thank You, Lord, for this great meal, for these awesome children, and for the chance to be together today. Help us remember Your grace and Your goodness. Amen."

"Amen," she whispered, keeping her head lowered a moment longer to hide the emotion she felt sure must be written on her face. God really seemed to have done something in this man. That hadn't sounded like a rote prayer but one that had come from the heart. Suddenly it didn't matter what pictures were on the Internet, what speculation surrounded him. He was a man whom God was touching, using, the kind of man who could touch her heart.

That last thought flung open her eyes. No. She wasn't going to get carried away. A simple prayer did not a hero make. But the way he paid attention to the children, more so than any attention he paid to the adults, showed a thoughtful consideration that again warmed her. He really seemed to care.

The next minutes passed as people shared around the table what they were thankful for, and again she was surprised when Tyler shared about his gratitude for new friends and second chances. She bit her lip. Second chances, like the one she hadn't wanted to offer him. *Forgive me, Lord.*

Tyler further showed his good natured side when, partway

through the meal, Lily asked him whether he had ever played with Barbies.

A chuckle. The first she'd heard from him today. "You know, I don't think I ever have."

"I loves Barbies," Lily confided.

"Me too," echoed Karinda.

"Can we play Barbies after lunch, Mr. Tyler?"

His gaze met Emma's, and the amusement there drew a new tug of appreciation for his patience. "I'll have to see. If not today, then sure, another time."

"Good." Lily settled back in her seat and calmly focused on her peas, all that remained of her dinner.

Emma barely noticed what she ate—not that it mattered, knowing that in a few hours she'd be sitting down with her family for an Italian-inspired Thanksgiving feast. Good thing she'd had her run earlier this morning. Her mind stayed full of Tyler, something she noticed guiltily when Brandon asked her for another drink and Jacob had to refill his glass.

"You're really distracted," Jacob admonished her.

"Am I? Sorry."

"It's him," he said, nodding to where Tyler was listening to the children discussing the merits of owning a bunny versus a guinea pig. "You can't stop looking at him."

"Really?" She sipped her apple juice, hoping her skin wouldn't decide to blush. "I just think it's remarkable that he seems so soft-hearted."

"You do remember he was fighting in a night club just two weeks ago?"

Ah, that. It seemed so hard to reconcile *that* version of TJ with this praying, patient man. Perhaps it was another good reminder to not get carried away. Still, "It's a good thing people can change, isn't it?"

"Can they? Really?"

"You don't think so?" she asked softly. "What's the point of what we do here if we don't believe that? You know we've brought in children who have experienced terrible things—the loss of families, watching people die. Some of them come here and can't speak. And yet they're able to change, able to find hope and peace when they're in this place where they feel loved. Why don't you think that can happen for adults too?"

"You think he's in love?"

Her heart faltered. "What?" How random. A glance down the table saw Tyler look away.

"There were those pictures," Jacob said thoughtfully.

"What pictures?"

"Pictures of him with some girl. Apparently lots of people heard him say he had a girlfriend."

Oh. Her chest grew tight. She straightened. "I didn't know."

"Well, now you do."

She pressed her lips together and glanced down at her plate. See? This was why she couldn't chase the thoughts Tyler's actions had sparked inside. It was best to put distance between them, no matter what Lacey said. She couldn't afford to care for another man whose history made it obvious he valued flings above commitment.

She drew in a breath. It was best to stay focused on the here and now, not the will-never-bes and the should-never-happens.

"Well." Emma pushed back her chair and rose. "I'm going to clear some plates. I think there are some yummy desserts out there, but before we do that, we'll need to pack up and do a little exercise to make sure we have enough room."

"Exercise?" cried Lily. "Can we do more dancing, Mr. Tyler?"

He looked up, startled. "Um, I hadn't really thought—"

"Maybe after we clean up here you could take the kids for a moment and do some dancing," Emma said. And while he did dancing, she would hand over to the next person, then head over to her parents' and escape Tyler's fluster-inducing presence.

"I, um, wondered about taking a look at the furnace," he said.

"Really?"

"If you like. I don't have to."

"I would like," she admitted. "But it's just that I can't stay too long, as I'm supposed to go to my family's place soon."

He nodded, placed his napkin beside his plate, and glanced at Lily. "You okay if we leave the dancing for another day?"

"Only if you promise to play Barbies as well."

He crossed his heart. "Promise."

"Then okay," Lily said.

Emma pushed to her feet and made a rapid stack of plates, Delores sweeping behind collecting glasses. Once the breakables were out of the way, the kids were then encouraged to come and dump their cutlery in a plastic tub of warm water, put their napkins in the bin, and stack their chairs away. While Dolores started loading the industrial dishwasher, Emma wiped down the bench and listened as Jacob insisted that he'd looked at the furnace just days ago.

"I really don't think you'll be able to do anything," Jacob grumbled. "We need a real repairman to come."

A real repairman they could not afford, according to Richard.

"How long until you go back to playing hockey, anyway?" Jacob asked Tyler.

Tyler shoved his hands in his pockets, his gaze veering from Jacob to Emma and back again. "I have a meeting with team management on Monday." He shrugged. "It's up to them. But seeing I'm here, I'm happy to help."

"Don't you have anywhere else to be?" Jacob asked.

"No," Tyler replied. "Do you?"

Emma bit back a smile and asked Jacob to show Tyler where things were. They could figure that out while she helped organize the children and complete the handover. She glanced at the clock on the wall. She'd need to leave soon.

She had just finished briefing Beth and was preparing to leave, her keys in her hand, when the two men reappeared. Tyler had grease on his hands, and his white shirt wore sooty stains.

"What happened to you?" she asked.

"You were right about the furnace being temperamental," he said. "But hey, I think you'll find it's now working."

He started explaining some technical thing, but all she could do was wonder how he knew so much about such things. "Have you worked as a handyman?"

"From what I hear, he's always liked to work with his hands, huh?" Jacob said, his eyes, his words, holding insinuation and a sneer.

Emma's mouth fell open. "Jacob."

Tyler's face wore a pained look as he shook his head at her, as if begging her not to comment and make things worse. She glared at Jacob. They'd be having words soon.

"Are you leaving?"

"I, um, yes." How awkward. "I'm going to see my family now."

"I hope you have fun," he said politely.

"Thanks."

Her heart twisted. She was off to see her family, leaving the familyless here. Including him. Lacey's concern about protecting Tyler pushed to mind. Emma couldn't abandon him to Jacob's thinly veiled derision nor the attempts of Lily and the like to get him to participate in activities he clearly had no wish to do today. His willingness to overlook Jacob's insult drew fresh warmth, leading her to say, "You don't have to stay if you don't wish to."

He shrugged. "It's been fun."

"But?"

"I might go too."

She nodded and soon called goodbye to the others, grabbing

her bag and glancing behind her to see Jacob watching her as she exited and Tyler grasping his helmet in his hand as he followed.

He'd parked near her car, his shiny bike making the mismatched panels of her vintage Volkswagen look even more dilapidated.

"Nice car," he murmured. "Is it Jacob's?"

His gesture at the sticker that said *Sisters do it for themselves* drew reluctant laughter. "Actually, it may come as a surprise, but it's mine."

"Retro."

"I believe you once called it crappy."

"Sorry."

"It was my grandmother's."

He bent to look in the front. "Is it fun to drive?"

"I love it," she confided. "My sister can only drive an auto, but I love the feeling of changing gears, the way it eats up hills." Sometimes. Well, it had. The motor thingy still needed to be fixed, and the windshield wipers had stopped working this morning.

"Really?"

"What? Don't you believe me?"

"Nope."

"What—that it goes up hills well, or that I like to drive it?"

"Either. You should get a new car."

"Sure. Okay. I'll make sure to do that tomorrow. Right after I talk to the kitchen designer. And my fairy godmother."

He studied her a few seconds. "Are you mad?"

"No. I'm really thankful for your advice. I wouldn't have thought of it myself."

He eyed her, clearly not sure if she was being sarcastic or not. Oh, if only he knew her.

"Anyway, thanks for helping out today," she said, unlocking the car door.

"You sound mad."

"Do I? I'm not. I am starting to run late, though."

He nodded, and she yanked open the car door, which at that moment decided to give an enormous groaning squeak. And promptly fell out and landed on the ground, forcing her to jump back as it dropped into a mud puddle.

Tyler said a word she'd been brought up not to say. It didn't stop her from agreeing with it.

"About that new car," he deadpanned.

"Don't!" She slapped his arm, her emotions teetering between hysterical laughter and outrage. "I can't believe this!"

"Sorry, Emma, but your car is a piece of—"

As he treated her to a pithy description of all of her car's faults—how was she supposed to know if the tire tread was worn too thin?—her feelings roiled from offense to outrage to amusement to reluctant admiration. For all his faults, the man seemed to care a lot about vehicular safety.

"Finished?" she asked.

"Yep."

"Well, I can't deal with this right now. I have to go."

"You can't drive that," he said.

"No. I'm going to lock it up, and—"

"Without its door?"

Oh. Hadn't thought about that.

"Pretty sure nobody is gonna wanna steal it," he said.

"Why not?" she asked, stroking the bonnet. "This girl has been so faithful. My mom drove her too, so she's been part of my family for years."

He nodded, his face blanking, and she suddenly remembered that his family history was fraught. "Anyway, I'll call a cab or an Uber and—"

"I'll take you," he said.

"On that thing?" she said, pointing to the motorcycle. Why were the tires so wide?

"A hot air balloon."

She blinked, images of being in a hot air balloon with Tyler sending shivers down her spine.

"On the bike, Emma, yes. If you want. But you probably don't," he added uncertainly.

It was that note of rejection that decided her. "Um, okay. Thank you. But I don't have a helmet."

"Use mine," he said, holding it out to her. "I promise, I'll keep you safe."

She nodded, her throat suddenly tight at the deep look in his eyes, and whispered, "I trust you."

CHAPTER 17

This was a bad idea. This wasn't in the plan Tyler and Tim had talked about. *Go help the kids*, Tim and Lacey had suggested. They hadn't suggested that Tyler allow his stupid mind to go places it shouldn't.

But that look that had filled Emma's eyes when she said *I trust you* had hit him deep inside, like a grenade splintering all his walls and defenses. He'd tried so hard to stay distant, to stay removed. She had a boyfriend, didn't she? He revved the bike a little harder.

She snuggled closer against his back. Okay, it wasn't exactly a snuggle. She was probably just trying to cling on for dear life. But her nearness lit a fire that this ride was doing nothing to put out. He'd thought it the offer of a gentleman to give her a ride to her parents', but the feelings her nearness provoked were anything but gentlemanly.

He winced. How long would it take before the God stuff really took? Too many years of too many things made him hyperaware of stuff he shouldn't be noticing. Like her curves against his back. Like how good she looked in jeans. Like how his spirits had soared when she'd smiled at him. Like how tall

222

he'd felt when she'd commented on his strength while convincing kids to eat peas.

He was an idiot, craving the pleasure of such things. Craving her smiles. Craving her teasing. She fascinated him with her mix of sass and reserve, and he knew spending time like this with her would only make things worse. He probably should've said no to helping today. He probably should convince the team that he'd be better off playing somewhere else. He probably should do lots of things. But it didn't mean he would. He'd long been a sucker for punishment.

He ground his teeth as he carefully took another bend. Just because he'd been that way in the past didn't mean he couldn't change. God *was* helping him. Even Tim had commented on the change he'd seen. That online Bible study had gone better than Tyler had expected too. People who were rightly justified in hating him had proved to be kind. And that Josiah guy explained things way better than Tyler's own father ever could.

He swallowed another curse word, shame at what he'd said earlier causing his stomach to clench. Yeah, it would take a while before he could fully muzzle his mouth and brain. He knew too many cuss words—"a sign of low intelligence," his father had always said. But he'd never been one for sugar-coating, hence the oversharing of his opinion about Emma's car.

Regret chewed at him, wavering beneath a gloating sense of gladness at the memory of when Emma had gotten on the bike and Tyler had looked up to see Jacob glaring at them from the window. The kid was dreaming. He should be glad that Tyler hadn't said anything more when Jacob had insulted him inside. But was it really an insult when it was true? Tyler *had* always been handsy—there were hundreds of pictures as proof. But he was trying to live a different way, even if he'd need a cold shower after dropping Emma off. Not that he would regret this time with her. He wouldn't really regret anything about coming today. Apart from his mouth. Besides finally seeing Emma, it had been great to see the kids again. Brandon had seemed real happy to see him, while Lily and her talk of dancing and Barbies had perked amusement.

Lily… His smile faded.

Regrets from L.A. faded at a tap on his shoulder, and he saw Emma point and knew she wanted him to turn. He slowed, steering extra carefully and making allowances for the change in weight. Emma might think him lots of things, but her words of trust had fired grit to make sure he'd never let her down. Would never let her fall. Her trust meant everything.

Another tap and he pulled up outside a nondescript home. White garden statues gave the only hint of her Italian heritage. He popped out the kickstand and waited while she got off.

"Thank you."

He dipped his chin. "You're welcome."

"You ride well."

"Thanks. Important cargo."

She smiled, then glanced down, one foot coiled behind the other, before peeking up again, her gaze veering to the bike. "What kind of bike is it?"

"A Harley Davidson FLSTF Fat Boy."

"Fat Boy because it's wide?"

Huh. They were doing small talk on her driveway? "Something like that."

"It sounds cool."

"Yeah." The engine roar was one of the best things about it.

"Well, um…"

She studied him a moment longer, her hands holding his helmet, until he wondered whether he should just grab it. "What?"

"Are you going home?"

"There or Tim's place. It's a bit weird being there by myself but…" He shrugged.

"You're not doing anything with family?"

"Nope." That was a heck of a lot easier than admitting the truth.

"Would you..." She licked her bottom lip.

The sight drew a tug down low that meant it'd be a heck of a lot safer for all concerned for him to get on his bike and leave. Leave and ride far away to someplace safe for his heart and hers. Like Albuquerque, maybe. Dumb mouth wasn't paying attention. "Would I what?"

"Would...would you like to come inside and have Thanksgiving with my family and me?"

THINGS EMMA HAD THOUGHT she'd never do: hug a near-stranger on the back of a Harley; invite that same near-stranger to spend Thanksgiving with her family; not tell her family that she had invited a near-stranger with a mile-wide reputation to join them. Who was she becoming to do such things today?

Of course, there were other things she'd done that others didn't know. Her stomach tensed uneasily. She shifted on her feet, watching the flickering expressions on Tyler's face. Disbelief. Hope. Raw need. Uh oh. This was a dumb idea. She shouldn't have—he would say no—

"Really?"

She nodded. Shrugged. She didn't want to seem eager. But neither was she willing to let him go just yet. She still couldn't explain it, but she couldn't send him away. Not when she sensed that if she did so, he'd get on that bike and keep riding until Miami.

"Why?"

She once again recognized the haunting sadness in the fleeting look before his blue gaze shuttered again. This. *This* was why she'd invited him. The sense he needed this today more than she needed him here. Because she sure didn't need the drama, the questions, the speculation sure to be hers when she entered the house with him.

"Because"—*you need us*—"it'll be fun."

"Do your parents know?"

"Not yet. But they won't mind." Marc might, though. For some reason he'd always held that the traditions of Thanksgiving and Christmas were for family only. Heaven help them should he or Rose finally find a partner.

"I don't—"

"Please?"

Who was she? She barely recognized herself. She wasn't the kind of a girl to beg a man to stay. But his look of hope had dug new resolve to convince her family that this was a good idea.

It *was* a good idea. Maybe she needed to convince herself.

But there'd been something about the look on his face when he'd admitted to not doing anything with family. She suspected there was more healing to be done there, but Rome wasn't built in a day.

"I'm not dressed right."

Oh. He still wore some stains from fixing the furnace. "I'm in jeans. I don't think anyone will care."

"But I do," he said. "I don't want your family judging me any more harshly than they should."

"My family isn't like that," she said. Well, Dad wouldn't be. Neither would her mom. Her siblings, however...

"Would it be okay if I went home and got changed? That way you can find out if they really would cope with meeting me, and if not, then I'm not making things awkward for you."

She opened her mouth to answer when—

"Emma?"

She turned, saw her mom standing on the front porch. She glanced back to Tyler. "That thing about whether they'll cope with meeting you? I guess you're about to find out."

"Your mom?" he muttered.

"Mm-hmm."

"Who is this?" Mom said drawing near. "Hello," she said, holding out a hand. "I'm Antonia Moritello."

"Mom, this is Tyler." They shook hands.

"Tyler?" Her brown-eyed gaze cut from Tyler to Emma and back again. "Are you one of these famous people with just one name? Madonna, Adele, Pele."

"Tyler Woletsky," he said, his voice low, his face tight, like he was bracing for a storm.

"And you drove my daughter here?" she asked, pivoting to Emma. "Where's your car?"

"It's a long story."

"It wasn't roadworthy, Mrs. Moritello," Tyler said. "It wouldn't have been safe."

"And you convinced her not to drive it? Thank you. Why Emma still insists on driving that thing, I don't know. It's been ready to retire for years."

"I like it, Mom," Emma insisted.

"Anyway." Tyler shuffled his feet. "I offered to drop her home. I'm going to go now."

"Wait, were you helping at the kids' home?"

"I was. But now I need to go."

"Oh, but do you have to? It'd be wonderful to have one of Emma's friends join us today. There's enough. And I've made tiramisu."

"I'm not dressed—"

"You're wearing clothes. That's enough. We don't do nudity for meals. Not for Thanksgiving, anyway."

"Mom!"

Tyler laughed, and suddenly Emma didn't mind her mother's complete lack of boundaries. Maybe this would have a chance to work out.

~

THE HOPE that her brother and sister would be understanding faded within thirty seconds of their arrival. Marc had been shocked. Rose had been astounded. Thank goodness for her father who, apart from a lift of his eyebrows that showed his surprise, soon settled back in his chair to watch the football and invited Tyler to sit too. His easy acceptance, and that of her mom, made her glad that she'd listened to that little voice inside. She felt sorry for Tyler, yes, but there was something deeper, too. Something she couldn't quite discern. Maybe it was her own history of being judged before being known.

The football cut to an advertisement, and as Tyler stood to ask her mom if there was anything he could do to help, Rose shot Emma a skeptical look.

Emma shrugged but was secretly proud of him. He was doing more than her own sister or brother had done.

"Thank you, Tyler, that's most considerate, but you can sit down," her mom said, and he obeyed. "People who have helped small children shouldn't be doing more when there are others standing around who could help." She cast a significant look at Rose and Marc.

"What?" Marc protested. "It's women's work."

"You did not just say that," Rose said, glaring at him with slitted eyes.

"Wow," Tyler muttered.

"See? This is why no women want to go out with you. You're a caveman." Emma threw a walnut at Marc, laughing as it bounced off his chest.

She glanced across and saw Tyler's smile, which brought a flush to her cheeks. "Apologies for the crazy family."

"It's okay."

"You sure? I bet this isn't what you expected."

"I wasn't expecting anything, so this is all…" He blinked, and then, as if overcome by emotion, stood rapidly, excused himself, and went outside.

Oh no. After exchanging looks with her siblings, she moved to follow only to see he'd sat on the edge of the deck, looking over the backyard with its bare trees and piles of decaying leaves. Reddy hurried out the dog door, his long auburn tail flapping back and forth as he shifted to sit beside Tyler.

She stood at the window, her brother and sister moving to stand either side of her, like Tyler was the star of their own private show. Reddy nuzzled Tyler's shoulder, and a moment later, Tyler stuck his arm around the dog. Emma's throat tightened. If Reddy, who was as good a discerner of people as Brandon, was willing to put up with being hugged, then maybe this would help convince her siblings that Tyler wasn't as bad a person as everyone thought.

"What is he doing here?" Rose whispered.

"Mom invited him," Emma explained. What a relief that she could pin this on her mom.

"That's right, I did," Mom said, joining them at the window. Heaven forbid Tyler turn around and see he now had an audience of four. "You couldn't expect me to leave one of Emma's friends to go have Thanksgiving dinner alone?"

"*Is* he one of your friends?" Rose asked Emma. "I thought you hated him."

"I didn't hate him," she murmured. She didn't think she had, anyway.

"After what he did to Nick?" Marc asked, not bothering to lower his voice. "How can you invite someone like him here?"

"He's changed."

"Yeah, right. After his drunken orgies two weekends ago in L.A."

"They weren't orgies." Were they?

"Don't tell me," he continued. "You feel sorry for him."

She bit her lip. Maybe she did. But did pity have to be a problem?

~

TYLER CLOSED his eyes and shivered, but not from the cold. There. What he'd suspected but dreaded knowing, finally revealed. He hugged the dog a little harder, emotion balling in his throat. He shouldn't have come. This was a mistake.

But the hope that had penetrated deep inside at Emma's invitation had refused to let him say no. And when her mother had echoed it with a genuineness he hadn't expected, he'd felt his hesitations melt away. Then he'd entered this home and been overwhelmed by the love and sense of family. From everything from the decades-old baby pictures on the wall to the ease with which they teased, he suddenly understood why Emma had chosen to drive her grandmother's car. There was history here. Good memories. Family love unlike any he had known. Unlike any he could ever know. He swallowed.

The dog whined a little, and Tyler released his grip, but it insisted on getting in his space. A bit like Emma did. The woman seemed intent on pushing in—into his face, his business, his heart. Which was ridiculous, because for twenty years he'd not had a heart. Except around her, he kinda felt he did.

He exhaled. Actually, that wasn't true. Last week's re-encounter with God had shown just how battered his heart had been. A limp, bruised organ, barely sustaining life. And then God had touched him. But while he now had a surety of salvation and a faint sense of purpose, there were still too many unknowns, too many questions. And unlike this dog, he knew one of the most important questions wasn't going to be appeased with a solid scratch on the head.

He wanted Emma. He wanted this family. Not just any family, but what they had here at the Moritellos' home. And that knowledge had plunged him into despair as he realized his past meant he would never be good enough, especially in comparison to someone like Nick. Her *boyfriend*.

And now to know she pitied him…

He blew out a breath that escaped in a white puff. They probably didn't know they'd left a window open, that Marc's comments had floated out to strike him in the chest. Yeah. He had to leave.

With a final pat of the head to the dog, he pushed to his feet, dusted off his jeans, and turned. Saw various bodies scatter from the window. Except for Emma, who continued to watch him gravely.

He tried for a smile. Failed. It hurt too much to play pretend. He drew closer to the glass door, the dog scampering at his feet as Emma exited and joined him on the deck.

"You've got a friend," she said, pointing to the dog.

Yeah, not the one he wanted. "I, uh, think I should go."

"What? No, you can't leave."

"I can't stay." He pointed to an angled window that was open. "Especially as I know your brother doesn't want me here. I'll tell your mother thanks for the offer, then go."

"But why?" She rubbed her hands up her arms, like she was cold.

"I told you."

"You're going to let Marc scare you away?"

How to tell a woman it was her pity that had really kicked him in the gut? "I got things to do."

"Like what?" she challenged, hands moving to her hips.

"Stuff."

She blew out a breath, her chest hitching then falling, and he shifted, praying for God to remove the image of her damp T-shirt from Halloween from his mind. He wouldn't demean Emma in that way. She was perfect. Way too perfect for him.

Another tight-throat swallow, then he realized they had their own audience. He lifted a hand to Emma's mom as she joined them outside. "Hey, I think I'll make tracks. Thanks for the invitation, though."

"Please don't leave just because my son was rude," Emma's mom said.

"How did—?"

She pointed to the angled window. "It seems to work both ways."

Apparently.

"I really shouldn't," he said. "Thanks again, though."

Before another female could make him feel worse, he strode around the side of the house and exited out the gate, leaving the dog whining inside. He hurried to his Harley, relieved he'd stuffed the keys in his jeans pocket. The helmet he could do without.

"You can't go," he heard Emma call from behind him.

Yeah? Watch him.

He grasped the handlebars, preparing to steer it so he could start the engine.

Then she placed a hand on his arm. Blinked as if she felt fire too. "Please stay," she whispered.

"Why?" he almost growled.

"Because…" She licked her lips. *Oh, her lips.* "Because it would be kind of humiliating for the first guy I've invited home in ten years to just leave."

Something about the wash of sadness filling her features tore at him. "Emma—"

"And it would be rude, especially since my mom invited you, and let me tell you, you don't want to cross my mom and tick her off."

"She's like you, is she?"

"Worse. She's got relatives from Sicily who she says aren't Mafia, but we've never been too sure."

"Yeah, I think they'd be putting a hit on me to make sure I *didn't* stay, not because I left."

"But you don't want to run that risk, do you?" The blueness of her eyes seemed to shade from tease to pleading to an emotion he couldn't quite decipher but which looked awfully close to tears. Her grasp tightened. "Please stay?"

He studied her, his gaze falling to her hand, then trickling back up again. Why she insisted on getting into his business, he'd never know. It seemed bigger than mere pity, though. He sighed. "Fine."

At her grin, his heart lurched again.

"Come on."

Tyler followed her reluctantly, hating that his exit then re-entrance had been witnessed by her mother. But he'd found himself unable to go, not when he'd seen that moment of sadness sweep Emma's face, that moment when she'd looked like she was going to cry. That'd slayed him. And the fact that she had the power to make him feel like this slayed him again. What was it about her that made him do what he didn't want to do?

He followed obediently through the front door, the dog meeting him with a loud *wuff*.

"Forget something?" her brother asked.

Okay, so maybe Tyler didn't love all of Emma's family. This dude really didn't like him. But Tyler couldn't blame him. Tyler might know that God loved him, but he was still struggling to like himself.

"Oh, good." Her mom again, smiling at him. "You're back, huh?"

"Sorry, Mrs. Moritello." How to explain?

"It's Antonia. Come, sit down," she said, pointing to a chair at the decorated table, murmuring, "If you'd left because of Marc, then you'd really not be the man I thought."

While he really didn't want to know just how badly Emma's mom had thought of him, another part was greedy to know what Emma might have said. She must've spoken about him to some degree. But then the memory of Emma's pity, her boyfriend, doused him in cold water, reminding him to play it cool. "I feel awkward because it's a family day and I'm not family."

"You are today," she said. "Now, sit down."

He cast a look at Emma, whose mouth had hitched up as if she was suppressing a laugh. "You sure you don't mind?" he muttered.

"Who invited you in the first place?"

Only because she pitied him.

He offered to help, but Antonia waved him away, and it wasn't long before the table was groaning with plates of food the likes of which he'd only seen on TV. Emma sat next to him, her mom at the other side at the foot of the table—or maybe it was the head, given she was bossing people around. Rose, Emma's sister, sat opposite, leaving Marc and Tony, Emma's dad, at the other end, which was good because it meant he could mostly avoid Marc's scowls.

Rose kept stealing glances at him, like she wasn't sure what to make of him. Emma wasn't as pretty as her sister, who had a perky Rachel McAdams thing going on. But there was a depth to Emma, something tangible and sure, that held his attention much more than good looks.

Tony prayed a blessing on their meal, something which meant far more to Tyler these days, then they started to eat. "This is really good," Tyler said about the lasagna.

"We don't do the whole turkey thing," Emma admitted.

"Lasagna is good enough for us," her dad said, forking in a huge mouthful.

"It's good because it doesn't have too much sage," her mom said with a wink.

The others laughed—clearly an inside joke—and Emma murmured about a grandmother who had trouble figuring out the right quantities to use.

"My mother was a wonderful woman, but she couldn't cook

to save her life. So I had to learn from a young age," Antonia said.

"Is this the same grandmother who owned your car?" he asked Emma.

She nodded.

"How's that car doing, anyway?" her dad asked.

"I don't know why you keep that thing," Marc said. "It's a piece of crap that's going to die. You should get a new one."

Emma glanced at Tyler, then swallowed her mouthful. "That's exactly what Tyler told me."

"The door fell off," Tyler explained as Marc looked suspiciously at him.

"While you were driving?" Rose asked her sister, wide-eyed.

"No," Emma said. "I was getting in to come here and it fell off. So Tyler brought me."

"And we're very glad he did," Antonia said before offering to refill his glass, which he accepted. "So, Tyler, where are you from?"

"My family"—the word soured on his tongue. What a joke —"is from Nova Scotia."

"Brothers? Sisters?"

"Just me." One was enough, Mom had always said. Turned out one was too much.

"Do you see your folks much?" she asked.

He shook his head. "I don't get on with my dad."

There came a whiffle of sound from the brother, and Tyler bit back a retort. Family was a concept more than a reality in his world. Dad had been too busy with his congregation to notice his wife had fallen out of love with him, then too angry to care when Tyler's hockey skills had seen him drift away.

"Your mom must miss you," Antonia said.

"Yeah, she made her feelings pretty clear when she left when I was fourteen."

There were several gasps.

"I'm so sorry," Emma said, her eyes dark with compassion. "Do you think you'd ever want to be in touch with them again?"

"Nope."

Her look of sympathy nearly undid him, even as his heart felt a ping of protest. Well, maybe he would one day. But not this day. God could work on the earth's-core-deep amount of forgiveness he'd need to find. Right now his insides still felt like a snarled mess. He didn't want to be Emma's pity project, but another part of him was growing greedier for her. Which was bad. He didn't know how to do relationships. He couldn't even do family. His parents had proved that. Heck, even his own birthmother hadn't wanted him.

"This is delicious," he said to change the subject.

Antonia beamed. "You like?"

"I could eat a whole pan," he admitted.

"You can have the leftovers," she said, patting his hand.

"But Mom," Marc protested.

"Uh. I don't want to hear it. You nearly chased this nice boy away with your comment before."

Marc shot Tyler a glare, which made him swallow a sigh with his Bolognese. Maybe it was best to get this out in the open.

"Just to be clear," Tyler said, looking directly at Marc, "there were no drunken orgies two weeks ago in L.A. Yeah, I've been drunk plenty of times, but I've never participated in orgies."

Mike drop.

Emma's dad coughed, her mom laughed, Rose's jaw sagged, and Marc's cheeks burned bright red. Tyler glanced at Emma, who wore her own look of shock. He turned back to the others. "I'm no Saint Margarita, but I am trying to live a different way, and I sure as heck would prefer you to ask me outright rather than whisper stuff behind my back."

"Tyler." Emma placed her hand on his arm, and again that skin-tingling sensation burned.

"I'm sorry if this embarrasses you or if it's not appropriate Thanksgiving conversation." He looked at Antonia. "I had Thanksgiving with the kids earlier, but I haven't done a family meal like this in nearly twenty years." His throat clamped. He cleared it. "And I don't want to spoil things, especially as I know my presence here is a problem, but I can't hide who I've been." He turned back to Marc. "So, ask me anything else. What do you want to know?"

Marc blinked, but kudos to him, he didn't shy away. "So, did you overdose?"

Tyler sipped his water. "I took too many ibuprofen after drinking too much. I collapsed, went to the hospital, they pumped my stomach. It was fun."

"Did you try to kill yourself?" Rose asked.

"Nope. My life has been pretty sucky for a long time, I'm the first to admit that. But it was an accident." He felt, rather than saw, Emma relax. So, she'd wondered that too. His heart wrenched. Good to know.

"Are you going to play for New York again?" Tony asked before taking a sip of wine.

"If they'll have me. I have a meeting with the top brass on Monday. It's up to them. But if not, then I'm prepared to play in Hartford, if they want me."

"And if they don't?" Marc asked, like he thought it inevitable.

"Then I don't know. Maybe retire."

"Around here?" Rose asked.

"Maybe. Don't know. I bought a house in town."

"Where?" Rose asked.

"In Grove Street," he said, knowing his words hurt the woman he sat beside.

"Oh, Emma liked a place on Grove Street, didn't you?"

"Mm-hmm."

"Maybe one day you could be neighbors."

Tyler slid a look at Emma, who returned a wry glance.

Conversation turned to Marc's and Rose's careers, and Tyler was glad for the spotlight to turn from him. A lull soon after brought the realization that he should offer to clear the plates.

"This has been delicious. Thanks so much."

"Oh, but you've still got to try my tiramisu," Antonia said.

"Lacey might've mentioned something about how good it is," he admitted.

"Well, let's clear these plates then, and we'll get onto the next course."

He helped Emma clear, and they were working at stacking the dishwasher when he grew aware she was studying him.

"What would you do if you weren't playing hockey?" Emma asked.

"To be honest, I've never really thought about it." He shrugged. "Maybe study."

"What would you study?"

"I don't know." But looking at her, remembering how it felt to be helping the little kids, maybe that was an option when that day finally came. Retirement came to all players sooner or later. Some, like Nick, were taken out by injury way before their time. Others had personal reasons that saw them give up the game they loved. Some guys transitioned well to life beyond a pro hockey career, some going on to solid media careers or to become successful investment tycoons, others developing property. His skills and savings weren't so great that he could investigate those things. But now he was trying to live God's way, maybe doing something that would help others, maybe even studying social work, might be a plan. Not that he'd want Emma to think he was doing it for her.

"You two ready for dessert?"

An hour later, stuffed to the gills with tiramisu and a few too many of Antonia's delicious cookies, he finally made his departure. He could sense that Marc was a little relieved, and so couldn't help but goad him with a parting comment. "Hopefully I'll get back on the team and maybe see you around."

"What do you mean?" Marc said.

"The team does these hockey hero-for-a-day things, and apparently some are held at some of the city firehouses. Maybe I'll see you there sometime."

"Can't wait," Marc said dryly.

Tyler caught Emma's chuckle of amusement, which deepened when her mother handed him a wrapped pan, to Marc's protest.

"But Mom," Marc complained. "You said I could take the leftovers."

Antonia shot her son a look that made Tyler's lips twitch. Mrs. Moritello was like Emma times two. A boss lady who took no prisoners. He sure wouldn't be getting on her wrong side.

Antonia told him to put it in the fridge until he was ready to warm it gently in the oven. "Do you know how to cook?"

"A little," he admitted. "Thank you, but I probably shouldn't. I rode my motorcycle here, and I don't have any way of carrying this," he apologized, not without regret.

"Oh, Emma can take it for you, then."

"I can't," he protested.

"You can. My son needs to learn to share, and it looks like you could do with a home-cooked meal."

"I could do with a lot more than one," he said without thinking.

Antonia's eyes widened. "Then consider yourself invited anytime."

"I couldn't." And really shouldn't. Being here made him greedy for more, which wasn't wise.

"You can. If Antonia Moritello says so, you can."

"He can what?" Emma asked, joining them.

"Join us for another meal sometime."

Emma blinked. Glanced at him with a look he couldn't interpret, except he was sure it wasn't pleasure. "Uh, sure."

Another lie. He recognized it. But he didn't mind this one.

"Now, Emma, take this tray for the man. He can't fit it on his bike."

"Thank you for having me," he said to Antonia.

"You're welcome. Now, give me a hug."

He bent down, catching the smirk of amusement on Emma's face as the little woman pulled him in for a strong hug, the like of which he hadn't had in years.

"Go. Take that to him," she said to her daughter. "I bet you'll be glad to see what he's done with the place."

What he'd done? What about left undone? Had he done laundry, washed the dishes this week?

"Now go. Put it away before it gets cool."

"Oh, okay. And thank you again."

"Don't thank me. Thank Emma here."

He glanced at Emma, still holding the tray of food. As if noticing his look, her gaze shifted immediately back to her mother.

For a moment it seemed like Emma's mom was pushing him at her. And for a crazy, delusional moment, if he hadn't known that Emma had feelings for the man stuck in bed in upstate New York, he could've suspected she cared. But she didn't. Even if he was so crazy weird as to have felt a spark between them before.

He needed to clarify things. As Emma went back inside to collect the helmet, he shifted to the side and said to Antonia, "I don't want to get in the way of her and Nick."

"Oh, Nick." Her face fell. "It seems so bad to have forgotten him."

"Yeah." He didn't know what that said about the family of Nick's girlfriend if they seemed to have forgotten him.

"I'm sure it doesn't matter." Antonia patted his arm. "You are only Emma's friend, aren't you?"

He nodded. That was all he was. All he ever should be. Saint Margarita needed someone equally pure. Maybe one of Tim's friends—someone like Dan Walton, with his looks and solid faith and good causes like his camp for disadvantaged kids.

"Emma and Nick have known each other since high school," she said.

A strong bond there, then. "So it was really okay for me to be here? It won't upset him, do you think?"

"I don't see how any of us can have a problem if Emma doesn't." She studied him. "Be kind to her, Tyler. She might like to think she's tough, but she has a soft heart."

"I know, and I will. And you don't have to worry about me. There won't ever be anything between us."

CHAPTER 18

There won't ever be anything between us.

Emma's chest tightened, and she swallowed a stupid lump of emotion. There *shouldn't* be anything between them. But as Emma glanced at where Tyler stood with his back to her as he spoke to her mom, there was. Maybe he was in denial, but she couldn't deny the fact he watched her and that she felt a spark too. Once upon a time, if anyone had ever told her she'd feel this strange sense of connection with TJ Woletsky, she would never have believed it. But there *was* a bond, something that roiled deep within and felt a lot like attraction. And as much as she knew she needed to tread carefully to avoid the mistakes of the past, she knew a deeper urge to see where this could go. Which was ridiculous. But also real. Which was why it hurt when he denied any connection on his part.

"Are you ready?" she asked, pleased her voice sounded flat and didn't contain the pain still writhing around inside.

"Uh, sure."

Her mom's brow pleated as she looked between Emma and Tyler.

Tyler drew near, placed the helmet on her head and did up

the strap. From this nearness she could smell his scent, could see the sunset glow on the gingery whiskers of his near-full beard. "Fits okay?"

"Yep."

He hopped on the bike, and Emma shifted to move in behind him, taking care to balance as her mom handed the tray back to her, the tray adding the distance she needed. No way was she going to cuddle up behind him as she'd done on the way over. How humiliating. She must've seemed as desperate as those women she'd seen dancing with him on social media.

"I'll be back asap," she told her mom.

"Take as long as you need."

Yeah, she wouldn't need long. It would take a couple of minutes to ride to his place on Grove. He'd take the tray inside. And then he'd bring her back here. Easy. Ten minutes max. The issue of her car she would leave for another day. The issue with her heart she suspected might take longer.

"Thanks again, Antonia."

"Anytime," Mom said.

No, not anytime, Emma silently protested.

"Ready?" Tyler said.

"Yes," she called.

A kick of the stand and a jerk, then they were roaring away, Tyler riding slow, as before, while she did her best to cope with the tilting moves as the Harley shifted around bends.

But it wasn't to his house he headed, rather Lacey's farmhouse, and he pulled in to punch in the code on the gate.

Her legs were sore from clutching on by the time he pulled in and stopped. A few careful movements and they were both off, and she handed the tray to him.

"Want to come in?"

"No, thanks."

He nodded, like her rejection wasn't unexpected, and hurried the meal inside. Lacey's big dog bounded up to him, slobbering ecstatically like he hadn't seen Tyler in years. It had only been a few hours, but Bilbo was used to Lacey's presence and so was perhaps a little needy.

Emma glanced around, admiring the peaceful setting gilded in the last rays of the sunset. Tim had spent some of his off-seasons sculpting a little lake and some hill-like mounds that now held a grove of small white-trunked birches. It was a beautiful outlook, something that gave peace to her soul. And in the summer, a perfect place for picnics and swimming. Tyler was lucky to have the chance to live here.

"It's a pretty spot, isn't it?"

"Yes." She glanced at him. He wore a different jacket and had finally changed the stained shirt from the Home for something else. "You didn't have to change. It's almost dark. Nobody would've noticed."

"You noticed," he said, his words raspy.

She ducked her head. She couldn't do this. She would not fall for the bad boy again. "Shall we go back?"

"Sure. If you want to," he said. "I just thought—"

She would not ask him. She did not want to know.

She moved to the bike, waiting for him to climb on. When he didn't, she turned. He was studying her. Again.

"Did I say something to upset you?" he asked.

"Why do you think I'm upset?"

"I don't know." He studied the ground, kicked it with his booted foot. "You seemed happy, then not. I'm wondering if it's what I said before."

"Which time?"

"Wow. Which time? I just meant at the table when Marc was looking at me like I was a creep and I mentioned about the drunken orgies—which I really haven't done, honest. But are you saying there was more?"

No way was she about to admit she'd been piqued by his

declaration of non-interest. "Look, I'm tired, it's been a big day. Do you mind taking me home?"

"Back to your folks' place?"

She nodded.

"Sure."

This time she would not wrap her arms around him or lay her cheek against his broad back. Instead, she'd do her best to balance with her hand resting slightly against his torso. The movement of the bike made his hair flutter, and she wondered what those hairdressers in New York City would make of his hair. She bet it was soft, and she didn't think he had enough vanity to have ever dyed it.

He certainly hadn't had much pride in owning his indiscretions before. One question she had yearned to ask, but could not in all good conscience with her family looking on. But she longed to know: in all his relationships with women, did he have any indiscretions that had led to a child?

"You okay back there?" he yelled into the rushing breeze.

"Yep."

"You're tense."

Of course she was. She barely knew who she was. She barely knew who he was either.

Fortunately, the village outskirts arrived, and she could refrain from speaking until he returned her to her mom and dad's. She slipped off the bike, handed the helmet to him, and said goodbye.

"Emma." He grabbed her hand. Again she felt the sizzle between them. "If I said something to upset you, I'm sorry."

"I'm fine, it's fine," she lied, easing her hand from his clasp.

"Why don't I believe you?"

She glanced away. Could she ask him? He'd said her family could ask any questions they liked. If she didn't ask, she'd be worrying the question.

"What is it?" he asked quietly.

No point beating around the bush. She faced him. "You said before you haven't had any orgies. But do you have any children?"

He blinked. Stepped back. Threw a hand through his hair. "Wow. Um, no."

The strain in her chest eased.

"I've done a lot of things I'm not proud of, that I wish I could change. I'm sorry I'm not perfect."

Her throat clamped. "Nobody's perfect," she murmured.

A beat. Then he nodded. "So we're all good?"

"Why wouldn't we be?" She faked a smile. Took a step back.

"Are you going to church on Sunday?" he asked.

"I usually do."

"Lacey and Tim said something about being there. I might try it out, if you think the roof won't cave in."

"I'm sure it won't."

"So I might see you there?"

"Maybe." She gestured to the Harley. "You might need to think about getting a car for the winter. It gets pretty snowy around here."

He nodded. "Maybe we'll have to go car shopping together."

Yeah, that wasn't a good idea. Doing anything together wasn't wise. "Bye, Tyler."

"Bye, Emma."

He offered her a small smile, then put his bike into gear and rode away.

Leaving her heart hurting, a mix of stupid emotions.

She was tired, that must be all it was. Feeling sorry for him. Feeling a rush of relief that he'd agreed to stay for the meal, even though he'd probably just felt sorry for her after she'd foolishly admitted that he was the first guy she'd invited here since Dwayne. She blinked back stupid memory-laden moisture. She couldn't fall for another bad boy. He'd said he'd changed, but everything within her cried caution. Except her foolish heart, which had snagged on his kindness, swelling the pity she'd felt to something deeper and more real.

~

Tyler's intention to make the world's quickest appearance in church today—in after the singing had started, out before the minister had finished the last prayer so he could avoid seeing people's open mouths, like he was a mirage or lost, even though God said he'd now been found—was foiled by Lacey's insistence he travel with them. And when he got to the plain industrial-looking building, he could tell this church would be nothing like what he'd grown up with. There was no steeple, for starters. No pews. The music seemed modern, the people fashionable yet friendly, like they were actually glad to see him. He wondered how many of them recognized him. How many of them would judge him once they knew his story. Tim had said not to worry about that, and Tyler was trying to listen, but it was also hard to remember, especially as the legacy of his father meant appearances were everything to him.

At least Tim had been kind enough to let Tyler dig into his wardrobe to find a shirt to hide his tatts and appear more respectable, like Tim. He'd even gone for a knitted woolen cap to hide his trademark hair. Lacey had noticed and offered to cut it for him, but he'd declined. There was no way to disguise the scars lining his face, so any hockey fans would soon know it was him. Although, maybe it would be a good idea to appear a little more presentable before his interview with New York's management and coach tomorrow.

He hoped Emma would come soon. Not seeing her for two days had left him like a man thirsty for water.

"Lacey."

He turned, saw Emma, and it was like every cell in his body prickled to awareness.

"Oh, it's so good to see you!" she said, giving Lacey a hug, giving Tim a hug, before her gaze fell to him and she nodded.

No hug for the church newbie, then. "Hi, Emma."

"Tyler. Good to see you," she said, her smile polite and not half of what he wanted.

"Isn't it?" Tim said, clapping Tyler on the back. "Who would've thought we'd see this day?"

"Not me," Tyler offered.

Tim grinned, and Tyler's gaze was freed to settle back on Emma. She wore her hair up today, and the warm-looking jacket, jeans, and boots seemed appropriate for the snow-storm that was threatening. Part of the reason for coming out today was to take up Tim's offer of helping him find a car. He needed one. He wasn't averse to riding in the snow, but his Harley could do without it. So he'd promised to take Tim and Lacey out for a nice lunch as a thank you for letting him stay with them these past two weeks, then he'd kidnap Tim for a few hours to take some cars out for a spin. Not that he had a lot of cash to splash—his house purchase meant he would need to be wise—but regardless of what happened at tomorrow's meeting, it would be wise to have an idea about a car option to purchase or lease should everything be okay. If his future was not to be here...well, he didn't want to think about that.

The music started, and he turned his attention to the front. The drums, electric guitars, and singers knew how to play and sing, and he was soon caught up in the music, even if he didn't know the words. But while they weren't hymns, the songs weren't that different from what he remembered from years ago, filled with words of grace, words of life, words of hope.

He felt his spirit stir, and he leaned in, his mind a fraction too slow to know exactly where to sing, but he figured the congregation around him would appreciate not hearing him attempt to hold the tune. He could sing, but he'd always tended to save that for when he was drunk, even if he enjoyed music more than some. A million years ago his dad had sprung for guitar lessons, something that Tyler had occasionally ventured back to, something he might do again one day. He had a guitar waiting in the yellow house on Grove Street.

The minister got up, a man in his mid-forties who had similar dark features to Emma's dad. He gave announcements, eyeing Tyler as he welcomed new people to church, then shared communion before an opportunity for giving was announced. The man seemed friendly, if a little too forceful in his delivery, like he edged his words with power, not grace. But Tyler wouldn't hold that against him. The content still spoke to his soul. He just seemed the type of man who developed strategic friendships and wouldn't be much fun to hang out with at a party.

Maybe Christians didn't do parties here. Although, he knew Lacey and Tim didn't mind a good time. He wondered if Emma did…

He forced his attention back to the front and today's sermon. It seemed Jesus didn't mind a drink, if Jesus was willing to turn water into wine. Surely if God had a problem with drinking alcohol, then Jesus wouldn't have bothered. It had always seemed weird to him, these Christians who got offended over something that the first Christians used for communion.

He bowed his head, listened to the prayer, decided he agreed with it, and said amen.

There. First church service in twenty years that wasn't a wedding or a funeral. Done.

"How you going there?" Tim asked.

"Good."

But he wouldn't mind leaving soon, if the way the minister was zeroing in on him was any indication. He'd hoped he could get away with things and not be recognized, but maybe the Movember whiskers challenge had given the game away.

"Tim!"

Yep, sure enough, the minister was glad-handing Tim, saying hello to Lacey while offering a smile to Emma, and all the while surreptitiously eyeing Tyler like an angler honing in on a prize-winning fish.

"And who do we have here?"

"Tyler."

"Woletsky?"

"Was it the scars that gave it away or the beard?" he asked, shaking the minister's proffered hand.

"Or the fact that you're known to be staying with Tim these days. Welcome, glad you could come."

"Thanks."

"Who'd have thought, huh? TJ Woletsky in our church."

If he didn't shut up about it soon, this might be the one and only time. Tyler kept his mouth shut as the man started on about a bunch of programs Tyler had no interest in. Maybe he could get to the online Bible study thing again, as there was something safe about being with people who lived far away and wouldn't get into his face and business the way this man seemed intent on doing.

Tyler nodded politely, though, agreed to think about it, then caught Lacey's smirk as the minister's attention shifted to Emma, wondering aloud what it would take for her to join the children's ministry team. "We know you have a gift. It would be great to see it used."

Emma pressed her lips together in a manner that Tyler had learned marked reluctance.

It was enough to fire defensiveness on her behalf. "I'd think Emma's gift *is* being used," he said. "Every day at Hopetoun. Wouldn't you agree, Lacey?"

"Definitely," Lacey said promptly. "And I'm sure there are no kids who need it more than those who have felt abandoned. It's wonderful that she's able to bring godly encouragement, even if she's not speaking the name of Jesus to them every day."

"Yes, but—"

"I'd think it a little unfair to expect someone who deals with kids day in, day out to turn around and do it on a Sunday as well," Tyler offered. "But hey, maybe that's just me."

He caught the flash of Emma's smile and the consternation of the minister, who clearly did not want to step back from his idea but didn't want to offend the newbie—and potential giver. Or was that just his inner cynic showing? Regardless, Tyler had encountered this sort of person before. And had no intention of wasting his Sunday playing mind games.

"Well, nice to meet you." Tyler rose, then turned to Lacey and Tim. "We've gotta go."

"Uh, sure."

"Emma?" Lacey said, when the minister had gone away. "Would you like to come and have lunch with us? Tyler's offered to pick up the tab."

"I have family—"

"Come on. Didn't you spend Thursday with them, then yesterday too? You know it's my turn to have you."

"Looks like she's in hot demand, don't you think?" Tim said, turning to Tyler.

"Definitely hot."

Emma flushed as Lacey laughed, and he realized how that had sounded. "I meant hot demand. But you look nice too," he added sincerely.

"Thanks. I think."

Note to self: do not tell a woman you think she looks hot in church, even accidentally. And don't tick off the church minister on your first day. But for years, his filterless existence had meant he'd shot straight from the hip, straight from the lip. He didn't think Jesus was the kind to pussyfoot around either.

A bit more pleading from Lacey finally scored a reluctant agreement from Emma, which scored an internal fist pump from him. Not that he'd show her. She seemed to want to keep things cool, despite all they'd shared at Thanksgiving. He still didn't know what had caused her to retreat, could only put it down to his foolish mouth. But maybe this meal would be the chance to redeem himself.

The meal at a steakhouse saw Lacey share about their time away in Minnesota before Tim shared more about last night's game.

"So, how are you feeling about tomorrow?" Tim asked Tyler.

"It'll be what it'll be."

"So fatalistic," Lacey murmured.

Tyler shrugged. "I'm hoping they'll see I've changed, but there are no guarantees. I've learned that people often see what they want to see."

"Like Derek this morning," Lacey said to Emma. "I still can't believe he keeps asking you about taking on the kids' ministry." She laughed. "His face when Tyler told him off."

"I didn't tell him off," Tyler protested.

"You kind of did," Lacey said. "And it was awesome. He thinks Christians should devote all their time to the church and different church programs, have their kids in Christian schools, etc. It's like he doesn't think Christians who are out working in other environments are able to share the gospel." She sipped her drink. "I love the fact that I get to do what I do because Tim gets to do what he loves to do. It makes me think of that verse about whatever you do, work at it as if you're working for God and not man. So Tim can play hockey and honor God. And I can be myself and connect with other women who may never other-wise have the chance to hear the gospel and be used by God. I think that's awesome."

"I think caring for the kids at Hopetoun is definitely being used by God," Tyler observed.

"Amen," said Lacey. "Oh, that reminds me, hon." She nudged Tim. "Where are we up to now?"

"Donations?" At her nod, he tapped his phone and read the screen. "Looks like we're up to thirty-five grand."

"Is that all?" she asked, her face falling. "We'll have to figure out some more ways to raise money."

"If I make the team tomorrow, I'd be happy to donate a thousand bucks for any goals I score," Tyler offered, refusing to look at Emma. This was for the kids. Not her.

"What a great idea!" Lacey said. "You could see if any others would like to do the same, Tim."

"Sure. I'll mention it tomorrow at training."

"And maybe some of your Bible study crew might be interested."

"Yeah, I know they like to support good causes," Tim said. He smiled at Emma. "And they don't come much better than Hopetoun, right, Emma?"

She nodded.

"How did the trustee meeting go?" Tim asked her.

She fiddled with her water glass. "It was as expected. John, our accounts clerk, is only prepared to release another fifty thousand. They're like that Elina woman, not wanting to throw good money after bad."

"But isn't it their job to be supporting the Home?" Tyler asked.

"You'd think so," Emma said, her glance meeting Tyler's, then sliding away.

"Well, God can do miracles," Lacey said. "So we won't give up hope."

"Whatever you do, do it for God, not for people," Tyler said. "I read something like that this morning in the Bible."

Lacey smiled.

"What? Did I say it wrong?"

"No! It's pretty similar to that. That's the verse I was thinking of before. I'm smiling because I'm just happy to hear you say things like that. Isn't it wonderful?" She nudged Emma.

Emma's face turned to him, her blue eyes slamming into his. "Yes."

His heart kicked. Okay, so he wasn't on this God journey for her, but he sure didn't mind her validation.

Any thoughts of diving into the blue sea that was her eyes faded as Tim's phone buzzed. Tim glanced at it, smiled.

"What is it, honey?" Lacey asked.

He flashed a message. "It's Brent. His wife Holly had their baby girl."

"Aww. Any pictures? Is there a name?" Lacey asked, her face soft.

"Nothing except what he's got here." He showed them the screen.

Mum and bub well.

"She's a mum, not a mom?" Emma said.

"She's an Aussie," Tim explained.

Tyler nodded, not willing to admit he'd met Holly years ago. Maybe that was the other reason Brent had never liked him much.

Lacey bit her lip and stretched her hand to Tim, who took it. Tyler caught the deep look between them, like they wanted a baby too. Maybe they could get on with the baby making if he moved out soon.

He glanced at Emma, who wore her own wistful look, and he wondered whether she, too, would like a family. If so, Nick had better get a move on. His gut tensed.

A waiter came to see if they wanted anything else, which broke the mood. The denials allowed Tyler to request the check.

"So, who's ready to go car hunting?" he asked.

"You're going on a car hunt?" Emma said.

"And we're not scared." Lacey smiled. "Hey, you should join us. You need a new car too."

"I don't—"

"You do," Tyler told her. "Your whole family agrees."

"How do you know that?" Lacey asked him.

"They said so. At Thanksgiving."

"Wait—did you go to Emma's place for Thanksgiving?" Her eyes rounded. "Why did I not know this?"

He shrugged. "You didn't ask."

Lacey turned to Emma. "You should've said."

"Why? So you can make a big deal of it like this?"

"I'm not making a big deal," Lacey protested. "But as your best friend, I think it's very necessary to know important things."

"So now you know."

"Ooh, but I don't know everything," Lacey said. "Why were you there, Tyler?"

"Emma's mom invited me," he admitted.

"Details?"

"I dropped Emma home because her car wouldn't go, and Emma's mom saw me and invited me to stay."

"How did Marc and Rose cope?" Lacey asked Emma.

She wrinkled her nose. "Much as you might expect."

"And they think you need a new car too?" Tim asked her.

"They can think that. It doesn't mean I can afford it. I don't have an NHL salary."

"We're not suggesting you buy a Lamborghini," Lacey said. "Just a car that gets you from A to B."

"Without the door falling off," Tyler murmured.

Emma sighed. "Fine. I'll come."

CHAPTER 19

Okay, maybe there was something to not holding onto the past. Emma steered her new-old Honda around the corner and parked outside Hopetoun, taking a moment to appreciate the features of yesterday's impulse buy. Who knew that cars now came with features like Bluetooth? That she could actually charge her phone within her car? Plenty of people, apparently.

When she'd seen this blueberry-colored number in the yard next to where Tyler had gone to test drive a new black truck, she'd felt the wings of inspiration hit, and Lacey's enthusiasm had overcome her qualms about spending money on a car when the Home was still in dire need of finances.

"You still need a car," Lacey had encouraged.

So she'd gone for her own test drive, decided that she liked it, and when Lacey mentioned that she thought the price a little steep considering it was three years old, the nice sales assistant had knocked two grand off the price. Lacey's next comment—that as the wife of the captain of the New York Rangers she would be making *sure* that people knew about this place and wondered if there were any other bonuses the salesman could offer to help Emma make up her mind—had seen him offer a three-year warranty and a promise that if there were ever any problems, she could speak to him personally.

When the men had returned and checked it out to their shared approval, then mansplained all the things Emma and Lacey had already sorted (prompting Lacey to roll her eyes), Emma had known this car would be hers and had signed on the dotted line in a moment of spontaneity, thanking God her savings were enough she could afford it. Blueberry was her name, and the sleek curves meant she was definitely a her, with none of the ego of the over-large black truck that Tyler had driven. Not that he'd bought it, saying that decision would be pending the outcome of today.

Emma sighed, shot up a prayer that his meeting would go okay, and exited into the cold, next to where her poor bedraggled Beetle sat forlornly, waiting for Dad's tow truck business-owning friend to take it away. It had been pointless to try and rescue it. Some things were beyond rescuing, she had realized. Whereas other things...

It was funny to think she could chide Jacob just last week about his lack of belief in people's ability to change but still be amazed at the difference in Tyler. But his transformation was remarkable. To think that the man who was now reading the Bible and applying that in his life was the same one who had featured in those awful pictures truly blew her mind. God could do miracles. God *did* do miracles. She hoped God had some more. Tyler wasn't the only one with an important interview today.

Her chest tightened. Someone inside needed a miracle, for sure. Brandon's psychologist was due in today, and Brandon's future would be determined either today or tomorrow.

She beeped Blueberry locked—another novel innovation, as far as she was concerned—and moved up the steps.

"Oh, thank goodness you're here," Lorraine said when she entered. "The children are in such a state."

"Why?"

"Lily and Karinda have been fighting, and their hollering is making everyone on edge."

Judging from the sound traveling down the stairs, she could understand why. "Girls?" she called as she hurried up to the girls' bedroom. "Why am I hearing the sound of fighting?"

"I hates her!" Lily screamed, pointing a finger at Karinda.

"We don't talk like that here," Emma said, smoothing a hand down Lily's hair.

"We do when we don't likes someone," Lily insisted.

Apparently so. Emma turned to Karinda. "Would you like to tell me what's going on?"

"No." The little girl's pout and folded arms made that plain.

"She pulled my hair!" Lily yelled.

"Thank you, Lily. I'm not deaf. Perhaps you can tell me why you think Karinda did this. She hasn't done that before, has she?"

Lily copied her former friend with a pout and crossed arms.

"Karinda? Have you got anything to say, or am I sending both of you to the naughty corner?"

Karinda glanced at Lily, then back at Emma. "She called me a name."

"So you pulled her hair?"

It took a few minutes more to sort out exactly what the problem had been. Emma bit back a sigh, the lightheartedness of her weekend fleeing at a million miles an hour.

"Very well. You know the rules. If you can't get on, you'll miss out on play time with the others. No, that's enough," she said, putting up a hand as Lily protested. "I don't want to hear anything more unless it's an apology from both of you."

Lily sent Karinda a scowl, which was reciprocated.

"Okay then. I guess we won't be seeing you for play time, which is a shame, as I was hoping we might have a special treat."

"Is Mr. TJ coming?" Lily demanded.

"Well, I don't think so. But even if he was, you know he won't be seeing little girls who don't know how to apologize."

"I like Mr. TJ," Karinda said.

"Mr. *Ty*-ler," Lily corrected with a smirk. "He's a nice man, isn't he, Miss Emma?"

"Yes." His mix of faith and compassion made him rather nice indeed. "Now, does this mean you're going to say sorry to each other?"

"Sorry, Karinda," Lily said in a singsong voice.

"Sorry, Lily."

"Thank you," Emma said. "And I think you need to say sorry to Mrs. Boardman as well. She does not like little girls yelling or disobeying her when she asks you to stop. Shall we find her and make sure she knows how sorry you are?"

Two appropriate apologies later, Lorraine finally was able to leave.

"I do hope things go well for poor Brandon," Lorraine said. "I hope an appropriate family will be found to take care of him."

"And love him," Emma murmured.

"We want that for all of the children, don't we?"

"A chance to feel wanted, to live in a stable home, to feel loved." Those were some of the most basic needs all people had. Safety, security, somewhere to belong.

Her mind tracked back to Tyler—something it was doing with all too much frequency of late—and she wondered again at his story. How awful it must've been to be a young teenager and have his mother walk out on him. Was it any wonder he felt rejected and had lived a life of little care and shallow relationships? It didn't take a trained psychologist to know he'd acted in ways to protect himself, which meant rejecting first before being rejected.

"You look tired, dear," Lorraine said. "Is everything going okay here?"

"There's still no word on the finances. Richard emailed me to say the board meeting got delayed, so we're back in limbo, waiting for the other shoe to drop."

"I'll cross my fingers for you."

"Thanks."

Jacob appeared, his split shifts matching Emma's for much of this week. She lifted a hand and waved hello as Lorraine continued. "And poor Nick. Has anyone heard from him?"

Nick. She really should make an effort to go see him. Maybe she could with her day off later this week. "Not recently," she admitted.

"Well, let's hope he's recovering."

"That's what I pray."

Lorraine shot her a *you do that, dear* look and made her departure. Emma exhaled.

"You all right?" Jacob asked.

"Yep." Although the knot in her stomach suggested otherwise. "There's just a lot to consider with the interview concerning Brandon today. Speaking of, we might need to check on him to make sure he's doing okay."

They ran through the list of the day's other scheduled activities, which reminded her of the need to get the children to help make cinnamon scrolls for their afternoon break time. An activity like that might be helpful, especially if the interview concerning Brandon didn't go well.

"Miss Emma?"

Emma glanced down to see Lily. "Yes, Lily?"

"I was thinking…"

Emma glanced at Jacob, then back at the little blonde. "It's good to think. What is it you were thinking?"

"Can you please ask Mr. Tyler to visit us?"

Emma coughed.

"I promise we'll be good," Lily said.

"I think he might be busy today." With his interview.

"Oh, but I *wants* him to come. Can you ask him? Puh-leeze?"

Emma fixed on a smile, conscious that Jacob was looking at her intently. "I'll see."

"I hope he brings a bunny. I loves bunnies. And guinea pigs. And fluffy chickens."

"Mr. TJ will do anything Miss Emma says," Jacob muttered.

Emma's eyebrows rose. "Did you have something to say, Mr. Jacob?"

He scowled and shook his head, then walked away—she hoped, to check on Brandon.

But his words still resonated. It wasn't true. Tyler might be her friend, but there was no other intent.

Was there?

Coach Koder and the GM eyed Tyler. He straightened in his chair. Today was all about proving they should keep him. *Lord, help them see I've changed.* He exhaled silently. *But whatever You want for me, God. Your way, not mine.*

He and Tim had talked about it on the trip down to the city, that God's ways could not be confined to what they might immediately assume or want. God could use what others might consider detours to accomplish His plans. And that *was* what Tyler wanted. Living for himself had just led to a whole lot of mess and regret. Following God's directions surely had to mean a better way.

Koder glanced at the sheaf of papers the team doctor had handed him and cleared his throat. "So, the doc has cleared you, but I just want to get a few more things straight. In essence, what you're saying is that you did not overdose deliberately."

"That's correct, sir," Tyler said.

"I don't know what it is about you today, but you certainly seem a lot calmer than I'm used to seeing from you."

"I feel calmer," Tyler acknowledged.

"Care to explain what's happened?"

"Since L.A.?"

Koder nodded.

Tyler shot a look at Tim, who'd been sitting silently. Tim nodded, and Tyler drew himself up. Here went nothing.

Ten minutes later, after a volley of questions and answers that had shocked both Coach and GM and seen them shake their heads, laugh incredulously, and mutter words that Tyler's dad would not approve, Tyler felt maybe he might have a sliver of a chance.

Koder shook his head again. "So, what you're saying is that Woletsky the agitator is gone and we have a soft pushover instead."

Okay, so maybe that chance had fluttered away. Tyler lifted his chin and was going to speak when Tim cleared his throat.

"Coach, are you calling me a pushover?" Tim asked.

"You? No."

"I'm a Christian. I don't think anyone thinks that makes me soft."

"Yes, but you're not someone known for bringing the grit to the fourth line."

"I think I can contribute more than just being a fourth-line goon," Tyler said. "You've seen me play well, you've seen me score goals. I want to contribute here in New York. I've bought a home here, I'm connecting in the community, I've got friends." He pointed to Tim.

"All true," Tim attested. "I've really seen a change in him these past weeks."

"But a couple weeks doesn't mean it's going to last," the GM said. "Then we'll be back here talking about your seventeenth chance, then talking about where you're gonna go next."

Lord, please no. Tyler glanced at the GM. "I want you to know that I've got every reason to live, every reason to prove to you that I'm wanting to succeed here. You saw that I worked well with the guys before. I can do it again. I *will* do it again, if you give me the chance. Sir, I do not want to leave."

The GM's eyes narrowed as he seemed to consider Tyler's words.

"I promise that what has happened in my personal life will only make me stronger. I don't feel the need to fly off the handle because I don't feel that same sense of agitation inside. Yes, I'll continue to play hard, so you don't need to worry that I'll be soft or a pushover on the ice. I'll still bring the same level of grit and intensity people have always wanted from me. But neither will I lose my temper, sir, or get into fights unnecessarily. And I would love the chance to prove that to you."

The room grew silent, hope ticking in Tyler's heart as, outside, car horns and sirens blared.

"You disappointed a lot of people, Woletsky," the GM said.

"None more so than myself," he admitted quietly.

"You know the club would require you to pay fines for your breach of player conduct."

"I understand that. I know the team and fans deserve an apology as well."

"You would have to see our psychologist before we let you play again," Koder added.

Hope lifted within. "I'm prepared to do whatever it takes, sir. I really want this chance to prove myself, more than anything I've wanted before." A face flashed through his mind. Except maybe one thing. He exhaled again. "I understand I've certainly not made things easy, and I can understand if your answer is no. But I would love the opportunity to show you I have changed."

Koder and the GM looked at each other, then back at him.

"You say your dad's a pastor?" At Tyler's nod, Koder shook his head. "I still can't believe that."

"What's he had to say about all this?" the GM asked.

Ah, that. Something Tim had been encouraging him to do. "I plan on talking to him about this soon."

"Do that. You only get one life, and you've been living yours harder than most."

So true.

"Okay." The GM glanced at Koder. "Can you use him?"

Koder leaned back in his chair, his chin dipping. "If the psych clears it, then yeah."

An explosion of joy lit his chest. Tyler grinned. "Thank you, sir. Thank you very much. I promise you won't regret this."

"I better not. Or else it's out of the organization once and for all, and after all the lifelines you've been thrown, I doubt you'd find any other club willing to take you."

"You can trust me, sir. I won't let you down."

AFTER VISITS to the team shrink and media person and a phone call with his agent, Tyler and Tim caught a late lunch before driving back to Tarrytown. Tyler's insides zinged with pinball-like light and excitement.

"I'm so glad. I can't wait. I'm so relieved."

"I kinda get that impression." Tim changed lanes. "So, were you serious about talking to your dad sometime?"

Whoa. Talk about a mood killer. "Yeah. Not that I think he'll be that happy to talk to me."

"How long since you've talked to him?"

"Years." Too many years.

"And your mom?"

"Longer." But he had no wish to see her. She obviously hadn't wanted to be in his life, so he had no fantasy about ever playing happy families with her.

"The GM is right. Nobody lives forever. Maybe that can be a Christmas goal or something."

"I can't believe it's only three and half weeks until Christmas. So much has happened in the past two months."

"Still got plenty of the year left to live." Tim pulled off the highway. "So, you gonna get that truck you saw yesterday?"

"Let's do it."

An hour later, Tyler sat behind the wheel of his brand new vehicle, drinking in the new-car smell and admiring the shiny buttons for features he'd never known existed before. Thank God his team fine hadn't been as huge as he'd imagined. He'd never been a petrol head, but he could now kinda understand the appeal. Tim had laughed about Tyler's little-girl giddiness, but Tyler would be willing to bet the man would be glad to not feel obliged to drive Tyler around. Not that he'd ever really needed to, but it was good to give the man back his space.

Tyler had moved back into Grove Street, and now that things felt more settled with his career, he was ready to get the rest of his life sorted right, too. The psychologist had emphasized the need for structure and order and putting boundaries in place that would help Tyler continue with good decisions. And yeah, he'd needed the past weeks to get his head straight, to feel a sense of structure, to allow the peace of Tim and Lacey's to help him feel strong enough to go forward. And now he'd been given this final chance, he'd do all he could to prove that their time looking after him had not been wasted. Dinner yesterday was the least of it. He owed them big time. He pulled into his drive, wishing he had someone to whom he could show off the vehicle. Well, to share he'd been reinstated. Would she—?

No. She was probably too busy. But he had nothing else to do. And it was always fun to see the kids. And hadn't Lacey said they could always do with more volunteers?

First things first. He sat in his car, pulled up deets about the local florist, and ordered a big bunch of flowers to be sent to

Lacey with a card that said thanks. After their earlier media interviews, he'd taken Tim out for today's fancy lunch—he still owed him a dozen more. He knew the interviews would be airing soon, something he had no intention of watching. The psychologist had recommended deleting all social media for a while, which he'd immediately done. Not everyone would believe his apology, but he'd tried his best all the same. As long as the most important people did. Speaking of…

He glanced at his phone, wondering if he should send a message. Nah. She might appreciate a surprise. He hoped it would be a good surprise.

Five minutes later he was pulling up outside Hopetoun, next to the blue vehicle she'd gotten yesterday. He'd been half tempted to put up the cash for her to get something new, then figured she might have a problem with that and that Nick definitely would.

Nick. Tyler's heart tensed. Where were things at with her and him?

Still, he could go in there and see her as a friend. That was allowed, wasn't it? Guys could be friends with girls. Even if he'd never really mastered that too well. Or at all. But he was all about change these days, and changing for the better. So he'd make this work somehow.

He knocked on the door, which was opened by Jacob. Ah. That expression was one he was coming to know and expect only too well. "Jacob."

"Woletsky." The kid didn't move. "Can I help you?"

"Uh, I wanted to see Emma. Is she free?"

"You know she's working, don't you?"

"I figured. So I'm here to help."

Jacob put a hand on the door frame. "Did you arrange this with her?"

"No."

"Then I don't think she'll want to see you."

"How do you know?" Tyler challenged. "Has she said something?"

"Look, it's been an intense morning, and I really feel—"

"Mr. Tyler!" Lily screamed, rushing at him like a catapult, hugging his knees.

"Hey, Lily. How are you?"

"Are you here to do dancing with me?"

"Um…" He slid a look at Jacob's stony face, bit back a grin. "Maybe."

"Did you bring a bunny?"

"A what?"

"A bunny," she repeated impatiently, like he was an idiot. "I told Miss Emma to call you and ask for you to come and bring a bunny. Did she call you?"

"No."

Jacob's smirk suggested Emma wasn't that stupid.

"Oh. So you don't have one?" Lily looked behind him, as if he'd stashed a bunny basket on the porch.

"Sorry. No bunnies. Just me."

"Oh." Her face fell. Then lit again as she grabbed his hand. "But you can play Barbies with me, right?"

The way he felt now, he'd be willing to learn tap dance. "Sure."

"Come on," Lily said, dragging him through the door, ignoring Jacob's protests.

Tyler's appearance in the big room caused a swell of noise from the children and a wave from a woman he thought was called Bek. But there was no sign of Emma. Not that he wanted to make a big deal of looking for her, especially as there was a bunch of kids here demanding his attention, including Brandon.

"Hey, bud, how you doing?" he said, going to the boy to give him a high five.

Brandon's face lit. "You came."

"Sure did. Had to see my main man. How you doing?"

"My teeth hurt." Brandon pointed to where his front teeth were a jumbled mess of pointy edges and gaps.

"Teeth are weird, aren't they? My teeth do dumb things too. They like to fall out."

"But you're not a kid."

"I know, right? I would've thought my teeth would behave better now, but sometimes stuff happens."

"People make fun of me," Brandon murmured.

"Because of your teeth? That shows how dumb some people can be. Look at this." With a few wriggles, Tyler took out the plate that contained several of his front teeth. "See what I mean? My front teeth all got banged out, so I have to wear something like this, otherwise people think I look weird. But I don't wear it when I'm working, and I don't let that bother me. And you don't need to let it bother you, either. You're a tough kid, aren't you?"

Brandon nodded, and Tyler took a moment to put his plate back in. Sure, he didn't need it when he played—what was the point of potentially damaging thousands of dollars' worth of dental work when he could just wear a mouthguard?—but he had no wish to scare the other kids here. Or to put off Emma.

A glance up saw Jacob still glaring at him. So maybe this wasn't the done thing, but it didn't look like the kids were doing anything too organized, scattered around the room in small groups playing with blocks, cars, and dolls. Speaking of, it looked like Lily was steamrolling her way to him with determination on her face and a couple of Barbies in her hands.

"I think Lily wants me to play Barbies," he muttered to Brandon.

"I don't like dolls. I like cars."

"Yeah, me too. But I kinda promised her, so I'd better keep my promise."

"Yeah."

Twenty surprising minutes later—who knew talking in a

doll's voice could be so fun, especially when explosions and car chases were involved?—he looked up from his game with Lily and Brandon to see Emma still wasn't in the room. Was she away? Sick? In one of those meetings she always seemed to have?

"Where's Miss Emma?" he murmured to Lily.

"She's busy."

"Doing what?"

"She had to make some food."

And it took that long? "I'm just gonna check that she's okay. You keep playing with Brandon and Karinda, okay?"

"Yes, Mr. Tyler," Lily said.

He grinned, drove to his feet, and ignored Jacob as he moved to the kitchen. He pushed open the door but couldn't see her anywhere, although on the counter lay the ingredients for what he hoped might be cinnamon scrolls.

"Emma?" he called.

A thump from the pantry took him to open that door and find Emma picking up a box from the floor. "Emma?"

She hesitated a moment before turning around. "Oh. Hi."

"Hey. I called out."

"What are you doing here?" She moved past him to the counter, washing and drying her hands before plunging them into the dough mixture.

"I, uh, thought I might drop by, tell you my good news."

"Yeah?" Her focus remained on the contents of the mixing bowl.

"They're keeping me on, Em. Isn't that great? God is so good. I'm so relieved. They could've easily kicked me off the team, but thank God for Tim, who I think helped convince them not to do so."

"That's great."

"Yeah." He watched her a little longer, her focus intent on what she was doing. Huh. He'd have thought she might be a little more pleased for him. But then, she was busy. "Is there, um, anything I can do?"

"Were you out playing with the kids?"

"Yeah."

"Then that's probably the best thing you can do."

Oh. She didn't want him around. "You sure? I really don't mind helping, if I can be of help."

She shook her head, gaze still averted, and then her sleeve rolled down. With dough-covered fingers she couldn't push it back up.

"Here." He moved closer, unable not to notice the way she stiffened as he drew near, then unable not to notice the spark as he grasped her woolen sleeve and pushed it up her warm, smooth skin.

His breathing hitched, and he drew in the scent of her hair, noticing the curve of her cheek, the way her lips parted, as if she, too, was affected by the intimacy of how close they stood.

"Tyler," she whispered, "please don't—"

"Woletsky!" Jacob snapped, jerking Tyler's hands away.

"What? Her sleeve fell." Why did he sound so defensive?

"Emma, are you okay?" Jacob asked.

"I'm fine," she said, her gaze finally lifting to dart from Jacob to Tyler then back down to the pastry thing she was making. "I'll be a few more minutes. You can both go, I'm okay here."

Except she wasn't okay. Her nose seemed pink, her eyes red-rimmed. All further inclination to tell her his good news flew out the window. "Emma? What's happened?"

"I'm *fine*," she gritted out.

"No, you're not."

She shook her head. "Jacob, would you mind telling the kids to wash their hands then line up outside until they can come in?"

The kid paused, only moving when she finally said, "*Now* please, Jacob?"

Jacob huffed out a breath and disappeared. Tyler's chest eased. Maybe now they could finally talk. But before he could speak, she was talking again.

"The kids enjoy making cinnamon scrolls. I make the dough but let them sprinkle on the sugar and cinnamon and then roll them up. They really enjoy it."

"I bet they do. Emma, what's going on?"

She shook her head. "The kids are coming."

Judging from the whoops and clamor coming down the stairs, she was right. "I don't know what's going on, but we're not done talking."

"I think we are." Her gaze finally connected with his. "In future, I'd really appreciate a little bit of warning before people just show up. I've had a really busy day, and while it's great you're here to be with the kids, we usually like our visitors to give us some notice. I'm sure you can understand that."

"I wanted to see you."

"I'm working, Tyler. I don't show up unannounced to interrupt your work day, do I?"

Hurt swaddled his chest. Where had easygoing Emma gone? But this moment wasn't about him. "I don't know what's happened, but if there's anything I can do, please let me know."

He found a notepad next to the fridge and wrote his number on it. "Here's my number. Call me. You know I want to be your friend."

She nodded, her gaze averting as he offered to turn on the water so she could wash her hands.

"I'll tell the kids they can come in now, then I'll leave. Okay?"

"Thanks," she murmured.

And he did that, said goodbye, and left.

CHAPTER 20

"I'm just so grateful they've decided to extend another chance to me. And yes, a lot of the stuff that's happened in my career has been from emotions from being competitive and from having a high level of compete for the game. I'm passionate about hockey, and I know I've made some mistakes along the way, obviously, and I've done stuff that I've regretted. Now I just have to prove I'm a changed man to you all. I'm really grateful Coach Koder and Tim and others can see I mean what I say. I told them I'm not going to let them down, and I'm a man of my word. So that's what I plan on doing."

Emma watched Tyler's interview on her computer—the first chance she'd had today to escape the madhouse that was the Home. While the Home remained. Her throat tightened, and she forced herself to focus on what the reporter was saying.

"No, I am not going to comment on the incident in L.A. You may have seen pictures, and while they may say a thousand words, they're not all truthful ones. I prefer to keep those matters private, and I'm grateful to the organization for respecting my privacy regarding this."

She propped her chin in her hands, watching him say the

things he'd obviously come to share with her today—when she'd snubbed him, because she couldn't deal with his concern for her. Not when his concern had drawn so much emotion so she could barely speak. How to explain the board's decision? How to explain about Brandon? She'd felt so overwhelmed that she'd had nothing except a craving for time away from attention, time to get her head together so she could be calm when telling the rest of the staff and kids.

"So, what can you tell the fans about what has changed this time?"

Her gaze snuck back up to the computer as Tyler shoved a hand through his shorn hair. "I guess I've come to realize in recent weeks what really matters. Hockey is awesome, but there are so many more important things. I've been really lucky to have the chance to hang out with some amazing people lately, including some kids at a place near where we train, and I'm grateful to them for reminding me that life is short and we need to make the most of every moment, because we don't know when it will be our last. So, as hard as it may be for some people to believe, I'm determined to make a difference, not just in hockey. but in life as well. I'm still going to play hard and fair, but I want to show those kids and others that being tough doesn't mean losing your cool. I want them, and other important people in my life"—he seemed to look directly at her—"to be proud of me."

Her heart swelled. Maybe she wasn't among the people he considered important, but she *was* proud of him. She was so glad he was back in the team. For his sake and for the team's. And she really should have said something more encouraging in his moment of excitement today. The fact she hadn't shamed her.

"And on that note, I'm announcing that I'll be donating one thousand dollars for every goal I score to Hopetoun House, as part of a special fundraiser to ensure this important community organization continues to serve the children of New York. If you'd like to know more, please check out the special fundraising page organized by Tim and Lacey Carruthers." He went on to give the website address.

She pushed to her feet, glancing around the office that looked marginally better than four weeks ago but which still held the same tinge of chaos that everywhere in Hopetoun did. If it wasn't the cracks in the walls, it was Hopetoun's leaky faucets. If it wasn't the stupid furnace, it was the cupboards and doors that never shut properly. Was this why Richard had said what he had today? She gripped her head. A giant exhalation ripped from her lungs. What was she going to do?

"God, I really need your help right now. I can't even think straight."

The day that had started with girls fighting had gotten worse with the arrival of Veronica, Hopetoun's psychologist, who, after a consult with Brandon, had confirmed that the little boy would be leaving the facility tomorrow.

"But he's doing better," she'd protested. Tyler's presence always seemed to bring Brandon alive.

"He didn't engage with me in a manner that suggested that," Veronica said. "I'm sorry. I know this is distressing, but it seems we have no alternative."

Could she ask Lacey and Tim to be his foster parents? Surely there had to be another option than to see the boy move away. From everything that Veronica had told her about the foster parents, they seemed pleasant enough but not especially equipped to handle a boy with Brandon's issues.

But what if this *was* best for him? Would she be denying Brandon a chance at a better life? It wouldn't be fair to hamstring his opportunities just because of her own love for him. If she could, she'd take all her little charges and adopt them herself.

"God, I don't want to be selfish," she prayed aloud. "I want your best for Brandon and the other kids. But how do I tell him?"

That was always the hardest part. These little lives that entwined around her heart, that made her love them. How could she give them up? But that was her job, a temporary stop as they transitioned into the next stage of their life. But telling kids who didn't want to leave just what awaited them was so hard.

And then there was Richard's bombshell, capped by the awesome fun that was the furnace deciding to pack it in once and for all.

"Oh Lord, help." Was the death of the furnace confirmation that Richard's declaration was right? How could such a decision be the right one?

What was she going to do? Where were they going to go? She'd have to sell her car. Could a car be returned after one day's use?

Panic gripped her. She really needed to calm down. She really needed a vacation. Somewhere far, far away. Maybe the moon had a vacancy.

"God," she continued to pray aloud. "I really don't know what to do. I need your help. Show me."

Her eyes flicked back to the screen, where the interview had ended on a still of Tyler in his New York jersey, his gingery beard scruffy from the past month of not shaving. Her heart hurt. Okay, so maybe once upon a time she'd thought him as ugly inside as his careless appearance suggested, but now she could only see his good qualities. His commitment to God. His willingness to fix the furnace. His mentioning the kids as part of his inspiration to change. The fact he lacked such ego as to play Barbies with the girls. She could've been knocked down by a feather when Lily had told her that as she was reading the kids their bedtime story earlier this evening. But it just went to show the heart of the man —someone whom God had obviously been working on for a long time before the incident in L.A. finally propelled him to his knees. Coupled with all of this was the fact he seemed to care about her. And the fact she now realized she wanted him to.

She shivered, remembering that moment when he'd helped her this afternoon when she'd been making the cinnamon scroll dough—the feel of his skin touching hers as he pulled up her sleeve, his breath stirring her hair, his scent tugging something deep within. She'd frozen, heart dancing with what this could mean, before a rush of memories told her no. Because this was how things had fallen apart years ago. She couldn't afford to let her guard down. She couldn't afford to let him in, to let her emotions lead her astray. For how could she invite him into her heart just for it to be trampled again?

Trampled hearts. She sighed. She needed to tell him about Brandon, their connection such that he'd be hurt if he came and Brandon wasn't here. It still seemed unfair to be asked to keep this to herself, but she couldn't do that to him. Especially not when Tyler had gone out of his way to try to help her today.

She glanced at the post-it note that held Tyler's phone number. No way was she going to call him. But maybe she could text him a little message.

"WELL, THAT WAS GREAT," Josiah said, rubbing his hands. "I guess I'll be seeing you all next time, if you're not playing a game. And congratulations, Brent. I know you'll be a great dad to that precious little baby, because hey, you've got a great role model here on earth with your own and an awesome Father in heaven, too."

"Amen."

Tyler ducked his head from where the guys from the just-completed Bible study—except Mike, at a game—were onscreen. He might have a good Father in heaven, but here on Earth…

"See you, Josiah."

He joined the others in the round of farewells, glad they didn't seem inclined to rush away. After the highs and lows of his day, he now felt antsy, alone in his yellow cottage, his stomach knotting like he was stressed. Which he wasn't. Not really. He should be on top of the world. But since that visit to the Home he'd felt a little…tense.

"Speaking of babies, Lacey wanted me to ask how Holly is doing," Tim said.

"Holly? She was so amazing. She *is* so amazing," Brent gushed, his face soft. "I'm so awed by her. Women are amazing, and Holly, she's just…wow."

Women *were* amazing, Tyler thought. Especially ones with dark hair and blue eyes who cared for broken children. Even when they rejected him, wanting him to leave.

"I didn't know being a dad would feel like this," Brent continued, his voice filled with wonder.

"It's pretty special, huh?" Chris said. "Like you're given this gift from God, this awesome responsibility that you'd do anything to protect your wife and child."

"I didn't know I could love anyone so fiercely," Brent admitted.

Chris was nodding, Tim was smiling, Dan was chewing his lip as if thinking deeply.

Tyler's throat tightened. He knew something about protectiveness, about wanting to help Emma today, but what Brent talked about seemed next level. Tyler liked Emma. But love? But wait, he couldn't love her. She was with Nick. Wasn't she?

"So, the baby," Beau said. "Did you figure out a name?"

"You getting clucky?" jeered Luc.

"Not clucky, but I might have a certain special something to send that might need a certain special little girl's name, so it'd be great if Karlsson could decide on one."

"Okay, okay. It's Violet Grace. Happy?"

"Aww. So sweet!" Beau said.

Tyler bit back a smile at the huge man using a word like *sweet*. He apparently wasn't the only one who found it funny, with Jai and Luc mocking him aloud.

"I don't care a barnacle on a bee's backside what you guys think. It *is* a cute name. Don't you think, TJ?"

Tyler blinked. "Uh, sure. Violet after your grandma, right?"

"You know Granny V?" Brent asked.

"I remember her from Mike and Bree's wedding," he mumbled. A little lady he'd kinda wished could be the grandma he'd never had.

"Huh." Brent eyed him, then nodded. "Well, yeah. Granny V is tickled pink, so she says."

"Sweet, and now tickled pink?" Luc shook his head. "Someone better talk hockey soon or else I'll turn into a girl."

Now probably wasn't the time to tell them he'd played Barbies today.

"No, seriously," Luc said. "That's awesome. Tell Holly congrats again. From me."

"And me," Jai said.

"And me." Chris put up his hand.

"And Lace and me," said Tim.

"And me," Tyler offered.

Brent smiled. "Thanks. That means a lot. And hey, if I have to leave suddenly, it's because I'm trying to figure this dad stuff out. I've already changed a few nappies—"

"Nappies?"

"What Holly calls diapers. Anyway, before I go, just wanted to say congrats TJ, on your news. That's great to hear."

Tyler nodded. Swallowed a small boulder. "Thanks," he rasped.

"Caught the interview," Luc said.

"Yeah, it was good," Chris said.

"Hey, count me in on the fundraiser thing," Beau said.

"The grand-a-goal for Hopetoun House?" Tyler clarified.

"Dude, you're a goalie," Luc laughed. "Tightwad."

"I meant I'd contribute. Man." Beau rolled his eyes.

"Count me in for the grand-a-goal," Jai said.

"Me too," said Dan, echoed by Luc.

"I'm in," said Brent. As one of the top goal scorers in the league, that meant something.

"Appreciate it," Tyler said. "Tim's got the deets on his socials, I think."

"Sure do," Tim chimed in, offering specifics to a round of nods.

"When do you play next?" Beau asked.

"I think Coach said Wednesday night, right, Tim?"

"Two-night road trip north," Tim confirmed.

"Yeah, I think we face you guys on Wednesday," Dan said. "Should be fun."

"It'll be good," Tyler said, recognizing this for the offer of friendship it was. "Maybe we can do dinner."

"You should take him to that place you took me, Dan," Beau said. "That looked like it had awesome seafood."

"Maybe we'll have to all get together sometime after the season," Jai said.

"You're all welcome to join me at my camp," Dan said. "Muskoka is really pretty in summer."

"Sorry, dude. Gonna have to give that a miss," Jai said. "Pretty sure I'll be busy."

"What are you doing?" Luc asked.

"The usual things one might do on a honeymoon."

There was a round of laughter.

"You set a date?" Beau asked.

"Why? You claiming a date in June too?"

"I'd claim tomorrow, but Maggie thinks it's too soon."

"You popped the question?"

"Not yet. But it's good to be prepared, right?"

"I'm gonna have to go. There's way too much girl talk and feelings tonight," Luc complained. "Not that I'm not happy for you guys."

"You just wait until it's your turn," said Chris. "Then you'll understand."

"Come on, TJ. You gotta have something more manly to say. Tell us more about your day," Luc pleaded.

Tyler swallowed a smile. "You mean like buying my new truck, or going to Hopetoun House to play Barbies today?"

There was silence for a second, then a wave of laughter and catcalls. But he didn't take offense, could appreciate them laughing with him as he explained the situation.

"Yeah, Ken never struck me as the macho type," Beau said.

"Barbie probably appreciated the chance to hang out with a real man," Luc mocked.

"You know it," Tyler said to more laughter.

"It's that face fuzz you've got going on," Chris said.

"You knocking this?" Tyler stroked his beard. "I grew it for a good cause, but I'm glad to be saying goodbye to it tonight."

"How much do you want to keep it going another month?" Luc joked.

"Yeah, been there, done that, so no, thanks. I'm trying to help others, but I'm not that committed to the cause." More laughter.

"You were committed to looking like someone from ZZ Top before, hey?" Chris mocked.

"Yeah, you know me. I've always been about looking like a 'Sharp Dressed Man.'"

Tim laughed, catching his reference to the music group's hit song.

Obviously some of the younger dudes here had no clue. Maybe even thought he was really serious about the flowing beard as a style statement. Whatever. "To be honest, I'm kinda glad for the chance to not look like the old me anymore." Even if shaving meant exposing his scars again. "It's time for a change."

There were a few nods and words of affirmation.

"Some looks were supposed to be left in the last century," Chris said. "That beard was one of them."

"Lacey can't wait for me to shave my beard," Tim said, scratching the fluff that barely counted as whiskers.

"Have you been growing one?" Luc said, peering at the screen. "I thought it was just shadow."

Tyler laughed. Okay, so maybe these guys were more fun than he'd thought.

His gaze dropped to his phone, which had lit with a reminder he had an unread message.

Emma: *Your interview today was really good.*

Thanks, he typed back.

Emma: *Sorry about earlier, when you were here.*

Tyler: *You okay?*

He watched the three rippling dots as he waited for her answer to come.

Emma: *Not really.*

Tyler: *Anything I can pray for you about?*

Her reply took a really long time to arrive. Then, when it did, it consisted of one word.

Everything.

His heart thudded.

"TJ, you okay, dude?" Beau called.

"Huh? Oh, sorry. Just something's come up."

"Gotta go change some nappies yourself, huh?" Brent teased.

"What? No. It's something else. And just to be clear, I'm not responsible for any babies or diaper needs anywhere. But hey, congrats to you and Holly again. That's cool."

"And congrats to you too, on getting back in the team," Brent said. "I'm happy for you, Tyler. Really."

He nodded, managed a smile and wave, and shut off his screen. He didn't like leaving early, but this urge to speak to Emma was intensifying. But before he could do anything, his phone started buzzing. Tim.

"You okay, dude?"

"Yeah." He swallowed. "Has Lacey said anything about Emma today?"

"What about her? I don't think she worked there today. Why? What's going on?"

"I'm a little concerned. She didn't seem herself when I was there, and now she's sent me this message that says everything is wrong, and I kinda can't help but feel it is."

There was a pause, then, "I'll get Lacey to call her."

"That'd be good."

He heard Tim ask Lacey to call Emma, then he came back to the phone.

"Thanks," Tyler said.

Another pause, lengthier this time. "Were you going to go visit her?"

"Maybe. I don't know. But there's something wrong. I can feel it."

A sigh came on the other end of the line. "Lacey said she tried to call but there's no answer. So maybe it would be worthwhile driving by Hopetoun and checking everything's okay. But don't stay long. You've got practice tomorrow, which you know you can't be late for, especially with the flight and game on Wednesday."

Tyler sighed. "I'll go, but I promise to be in bed before too long. My bed," he added, just in case Tim got any funny ideas.

"I wouldn't think anything else," Tim said softly.

"'Kay. I'll let you know if there's anything to know."

"Message me."

"Will do. Catch you later."

He ended the call and headed to his truck.

CHAPTER 21

"Want to watch some TV with me?" Jacob asked, his hand on the doorframe.

Emma glanced up from the computer, where the soul-destroying words demanded to be written. "I still have paperwork, sorry."

"Okay then. Well, I'll be upstairs." He was on nighttime duty tonight, checking the kids were asleep.

"Thanks. Have a good sleep."

"You too." He eyed her seriously. "Don't stay up too late. You look like you need a rest."

She couldn't argue. She was exhausted. Why had she sent that stupid message to Tyler? She must've been desperate. Worse, she must've looked desperate. But she couldn't help still wishing there was some way he could have seen Brandon before it was too late. Tomorrow would be too late. And with his training and game tomorrow, she knew Tyler wouldn't have any space in his schedule to see the young boy who idolized him. Which would likely prove so sad, for both of them. *Lord, please let there be a way.*

She bent her head to the task and managed to make some

headway, but sending the final email that would make Brandon's placement official she could leave until tomorrow.

Darkness swelled around her, the night noises fading except for the tap of her fingers on the keys. She would normally have some music playing, but even something as soothing as Heartsong Collective's instrumental albums wasn't going to help this churning inside. She'd never been much of a hard rock girl, but that was kind of what she needed—something loud and hard and relentless that could drown out the sharpness in her guts and bang these conflicted feelings into oblivion. It was a shame Sarah Maguire had never felt led to write those kind of songs.

Her eyelids were getting heavy when a flash of headlights stole her attention outside. A big black vehicle pulled into the drive, like something the CIA might use. Her stomach's tension rushed to every pore. Who was here? At this late hour? It couldn't be anything good. All their regular visitors knew not to come after the doors were locked at eight p.m. She had locked the doors, hadn't she?

But there was no time to check. The man was coming around to the front porch. The security light flashed on, which might halt him in his tracks, but she had to get to the door. She wouldn't risk the kids being woken by the doorbell. Or smashing glass.

A knock. She rushed through the small vestibule and peered through the door's peep-hole. Then flung it open. "What are you doing here? Don't you know what time it is?"

"I came to check you were okay," Tyler said.

The kindness of his words wove inside, and she blinked back tears.

"You're not, are you?" he whispered.

Even though it might be against the rules, she didn't fight when he held out his arms. She leaned into his strength, wishing she could conjure up some of the same. His arms closed around her, and she closed her eyes, drawing in his scent, the softness of his cashmere sweater against her cheek, the thud of his heart against her ear. Here she felt safe and cocooned, like in his arms the troubles of the world would go away. "There's so much going on," she murmured.

"You want to talk?"

No. Yes. "I don't know." She pulled away, sighed.

"When someone says everything is wrong, then I'm gonna get a little concerned. I know what that feels like," he added, his eyes intent on hers.

For a moment she allowed herself to be caught in his gaze, to be the focus of his scrutiny. Did he see weariness and exhaustion too? Or desperation? Her gaze traced the scars her fingers itched to trace.

"Do you mind if I come in? It's cold out here."

Now he had mentioned it, she noticed the coolness eating into her skin. "I, um, shouldn't. Our rules mean we don't let anyone in after-hours unless it's an emergency."

"See, I thought it *was* an emergency, which is why I had to see you. But I'm learning rules are rules, so I'll go. I just want you to know you can count on me for anything, because I'm your friend."

Her friend. She nodded, her gaze lowering as a swell of emotion poured through her chest. See? It was foolish to allow her emotions to get the better of her brain. He'd come to check on her because she'd sounded desperate. He was only interested in being her friend.

"Emma?"

Jacob's voice behind her pulled her farther away from Tyler.

"What's going on? Why is he here?" Jacob asked, eyes narrowing.

"Tyler, um…" She glanced at him, his knit hat pulled down over his red hair, hoping he'd have some way of explaining.

"I was passing and saw the light was on, so I took a chance to speak to Emma as there was something I forgot when I was here earlier today."

"What did you forget?" Jacob asked suspiciously. "We haven't come across any lost property."

"No. It was more something I forgot to do."

That's right. He needed to say goodbye to Brandon. She grabbed his hand. "Come in. It won't take too long, and we don't want to let what little warm air we have inside escape."

Jacob crossed his arms. "I don't like this."

"Could you please go up and get Brandon?"

"He's asleep."

"He's leaving tomorrow."

"What?" Tyler murmured.

"And Tyler needs to say goodbye to him, as he won't get the chance tomorrow."

"But—"

"Just do it, Jacob. Or else I will. But you know as well as I do that Brandon relates better to Tyler than to anyone else, and it would be cruel for him to be taken away tomorrow without the chance for a proper goodbye."

Jacob shot her a look and muttered words she hoped the small kids wouldn't hear, then moved up the stairs. She ushered Tyler inside, waiting as he removed his leather jacket and stuffed his knit hat in the pocket.

"He's leaving?" Tyler asked.

"We only got word today. I'm sorry, I should have told you before, but with everything going on I just felt overwhelmed, and…" She bit her lips as her emotions rose again.

"Hey, it's okay." He placed a hand gently on her arm. "I'm really glad I felt I should come now, then. Does Brandon know?"

"That he's leaving us? The psychologist thought it best not to mention it."

"I'm glad you mentioned it to me. Man, I wish I had something to give him. He's such a sweet kid."

"He is," she murmured.

A stomp of little feet drew their attention to the stairs, which a pajama-clad boy now descended. "Mr. Tyler!"

Brandon threw himself at Tyler's legs, and Tyler bent to hug him, holding him firmly as he lifted him in a long hug, cradling Brandon's head in his large hand. Emma's vision blurred, and a lump grew in her throat.

"Hey, buddy. I wanted to stop by and see you one last time," Tyler murmured.

No, Brandon didn't know, she wanted to remind him. It wasn't Tyler's place to tell him.

"Are you leaving?" Brandon asked.

"Yeah. I've got some more games to play. I've got training stuff all day tomorrow, then I'm going to Toronto, then Ottawa later this week. Do you know where Toronto is?"

The boy shook his head.

"It's in Canada. A bit past Niagara Falls. It's nice there."

"So you won't be back?"

Tyler shot Emma a look as if asking how to answer this question.

"Maybe one day," Emma said, stroking Brandon's hair. "But I think tonight was special just in case he can't see you for a while."

"That's right," Tyler said gruffly. "So, Brandon." He eased the boy down to the floor, then crouched, as if aware that Jacob's crossed arms said he wasn't amused. "I want you to remember three things. You are special, God loves you, and so do I."

Oh. Her heart caught. How wonderful was this man? Were they tears in Tyler's eyes?

Tyler felt in his pockets, pulled out his wallet, and found a laminated card. He glanced up at Emma and muttered, "Got a pen?"

She rushed to get one and handed it to him. He scrawled a few things on the back, then held it up to Brandon. "See this?

This is my picture, and whenever you see it, I want you to remember that I'm praying for you. Okay?"

Brandon nodded.

"So, what are those three things again?"

"Special. God. Loves you and me."

Tyler nodded, his lips compressed, then he exhaled. "That's right." He hugged him again. "Bye, Brandon. I'll be praying for you."

"Love you, Mr. Tyler."

"Love you too, Brandon," Tyler rasped.

"Come on," Jacob said, holding out his hand, which Brandon took while his other hand clutched Tyler's picture as if he would never let go of this treasure.

"You made his day," Emma murmured.

"He's made mine." Tyler exhaled, wiped his eyes. "Wow. I sure didn't expect that when I came here tonight. Playing with Barbies earlier must've turned me into a girl."

The unexpectedness of that comment pulled out muffled laughter. "Lily told me you played Barbies. I couldn't believe it."

"I'm a liberated man, apparently."

"You're a teddy bear," she said softly. "All of this…" She pointed to his tattooed arms—tattoos she'd really like to know the story behind. "It's just for show."

His gaze refocused on her fully. "I wish I was a different man. One without the reputation and scars I always feel like I'm apologizing for."

She placed her hand on his inked arm, felt his corded strength subtly flex, as if he found her touch unnerving. "You don't need to apologize at all, Tyler. You're just right, just the way you are."

"Do you mean that?" he asked, his pitch lower, softer than before.

Something about the intensity in his words, the intensity in his eyes, made her scared heart back away. In the past ten minutes, this man had grown dangerously attractive, and she didn't trust herself enough to handle the heat she could feel waiting to be kindled between them. She swallowed, forced herself to smile. "In fact, you're such a teddy bear, maybe you should consider adopting a kid one day."

"Me? Pretty sure no one would have me. Anyway, don't you have to be married for that kind of thing?"

The idea of Tyler being married wrenched something deep inside. No. *No.*

"What is it?" he asked softly.

Jacob cleared his throat from the top of the stairs. It was getting late.

"I should let you go," she said. "You have a few big days ahead. But thank you for coming."

"Thank you for letting me in. I hope you don't get into trouble."

"So do I. Thanks for coming to check on me."

He nodded and shot Jacob a look, lifted a hand. "See ya, man."

Jacob nodded, his arms still crossed.

"I'll walk him out," Emma said. Not that she needed to explain herself to Jacob. But she didn't want to say goodbye in front of disapproval.

"I'm okay," Tyler protested.

"I'll walk you out. See you off the premises," she added in a louder voice for Jacob.

Tyler's lips flicked up in a swift curve, and once again her heart beat strangely. No. It was silly to make more of this than it was. Maybe it was just that time of the month when her hormones decided to act crazy.

Outside in the vestibule, he pulled on his leather jacket and knit hat, bracing against the cold. "I bet you're glad for your new vehicle," Emma said, motioning to it. "I didn't recognize it before."

"It's a bit warmer than the Harley, that's for sure."

He studied her, the scar over his forehead dipping into silver in the faint light.

She knew an inclination to ask him what he was thinking, but such a question could be dangerous. The night was when dangerous things happened. He needed to leave. For her sake. "Thank you again for coming. Brandon will never forget it. Nor will I," she added honestly.

He dipped his chin, and then, as if unable to help himself, lifted his hand to her cheek.

Fire trickled down her skin, and she closed her eyes, savoring the touch. Her insides clenched, and she felt herself sway toward him. Then felt his hands clasp her upper arms. Her eyes flew open.

"You're tired," he rasped, his eyes glinting in the darkness.

She *was* tired, but his nearness also exhilarated. But no. She should step away. This was how things had started before.

But her feet refused to move as she noticed his gaze fall to her lips, study them. A shiver rippled as she wondered what it would be like to know his kiss.

"Emma." His voice was husky. "I want…I need—but I can't…"

"Oh, but you could," she whispered. If she inched closer, like this, and tilted her head a little more, like so, she might find out…

"I want—" *You,* his eyes seemed to say, his breath fanning her cheek. "But I can't do that to Nick."

"Nick?" What did Nick have to do with anything?

"I couldn't." He stepped back. "Not after what I did. I couldn't hurt him again."

"You wouldn't hurt him." How could one kiss hurt him? "He wouldn't know anyway."

"But you would. Don't you care about that?"

She must be really tired. This conversation was not making

sense any more. All she knew was a sense of shame slithering across her skin, dragon-like as it writhed within. "I have no idea what you're talking about," she said, stepping away, clutching the door.

"Wow." He shook his head, cutting her a scathing look the complete opposite of what he'd offered just moments before. "I can't believe I was so wrong about you."

Wrong about her—how? Why couldn't he want her too? Why did nobody ever want her? She swallowed the ball in her throat, her chest tight. "You should leave."

He nodded, and she shut the door.

She blinked back tears, lifted her chin. What a good reminder to not get swept away. To not let her fickle emotions get hung up on someone who was so very wrong for her. And what a good reminder that after the horror of the next few days, she might need to take some personal leave and escape to visit Nick again.

Toronto's captain slammed Tyler into the boards to cheers and pounding on the plexiglass. He muttered something that didn't sound complimentary about Tyler's ancestry.

God, help me keep it together. The surge of emotion that might normally see his internal thermometer jump into the red dialed back down into calm, and he skated off the ice, his line's shift done.

He waved off the trainer, grabbed a drink, and watched the play. A time-out for the puck that had gone over the glass delayed the game, allowing more time to catch his breath. He might've been training in these past weeks off, but nothing held the intensity quite like playing the game.

One shift more and he'd be done. Jenner's name was called, and they jumped over the boards, skating hard to the puck as it flew by. The Toronto defenseman hadn't timed that shot well. Tyler scooped it up, flicked it forward to Desi, and skated closer to the net. Valesky, Toronto's goalie, was big, but not as big as Beau and unable to cover as much net as Beau could. A flick pass and he yelled for the puck, and was relieved when it missed the stick of Toronto's Jordansen and he could strike it mid-air into the net. Goal!

Amid the helmet pats and fist bumps, some of the tension roiling in his stomach left. New York might not win tonight, but at least he was proving his worth. The fact he was on the fourth line was better than not, and maybe if he could showcase some of his skills, the coaches might see him as worthy of revisiting the second line again, or even the first. That one time he and Tim had played together had been so much better than he'd expected. Goals like this might help the coach remember and want to see some more of that again.

He skated back to center ice, but the horn blared full time to the cheers of the Canadian crowd. That was okay. Toronto could do with the win. The scoreline had been close. And he'd had moments of being close to losing it, but whether that was from the opposition's chirpings, the adrenaline from playing for the first time in nearly three weeks, or from other underlying issues, he didn't know. But he'd survived. He'd conquered his temper, even if it had meant begging God for help several times.

A pat on the helmet for his goal and the sticks banging against the boards made a nice change from yesterday. Yesterday morning's practice session had been raw. He'd barely slept on Monday night, nerves about his upcoming games mingling with regrets about his last game. He'd apologized to his teammates, assured them he was in a fit frame of mind to play and that he wouldn't let them down, but he still felt a certain pressure to perform. Tim had assured him that everyone was pleased to have him back. Tyler wasn't so sure the Hartford player who'd been returned to the minors felt the same, but he'd take it. And after Monday night's mess, he needed to keep busy, to do whatever he could to distract himself from the enormous mistake he'd almost made.

"Good game," Andrei said.

"Nice goal."

Koder eyed him, dipped his chin, which Tyler would take as approval. Maybe he was reverting to being a little kid, looking for validation wherever he could.

"They want you for media," a team assistant said.

He nodded, unsurprised. He'd heard from Tim this morning that yesterday's interview had gone viral, so it was time to face the music again. After a quick upper body workout, followed by the world's quickest shower, he changed and slapped on a New York cap, then joined Tim and Coach Koder at the media table.

After a few questions to the captain and coach, they turned to Tyler. "Congratulations on your goal tonight, TJ. You must be feeling a sense of relief."

"It's nice to feel that I'm contributing."

"Can you talk us through your mental health over the past few weeks?"

His mental health? "I think it's fair to say there's been a dramatic turn around. Where my head was at when I was in L.A. is definitely not the same place I'm in today. I'm extremely thankful to the club, to friends like Tim and others I've had the chance to connect with recently who have really helped me see what's important and make the changes in my life that I've needed to make."

"Can you share more specifically about what some of those changes are?"

How to explain without getting too personal? Something he'd read last week came to mind. "I guess you could say I've been learning a bit about patience, kindness, self-control, those sorts of qualities that are important off the ice as well as on." He caught Tim's smile at his oblique reference to the fruit of the Holy Spirit.

"It seems a bit strange to hear one of hockey's hitmen talk about kindness on the ice."

"I think kindness doesn't have to mean soft. Perhaps it's linked to being less selfish, which is something that is obviously important when you're talking about a team. And to be clear, I don't actually like to consider myself a hitman. I mean, sure, I don't mind finishing a check, but it's never been my policy to deliberately target other players. Some incidents have led to some major injuries, which I'm sorry about. But I'd like to point out that I've been cleared every time by the league, so those hits weren't considered dirty. I hope to prove that just as toughness doesn't have to mean dirty, neither does kindness have to mean weak."

There were a few more questions, then they were released.

Dan met them in the tunnel. "Good goal."

Tyler shook his hand. "Not as good as yours. That slapshot looked like it hurt Desi."

"He was in the way," Dan complained.

"Hate it when that happens," Tim quipped.

"You were right, though, in your interview." Dan glanced at Tyler. "It's not intentional. Just playing hard."

"Like your check on Andrei."

"What can I say? He was in the way."

Tyler chuckled. Dan Walton's hip checks were legendary.

"So, wanna check out this restaurant Beau was raving about?"

"Sure."

The road trip would finish tomorrow in Ottawa, so tonight they'd stay put in Toronto before catching a flight east in the morning. Normally there wasn't an awful lot of time on a road trip to catch up with friends from other teams, so it was nice they could do this tonight. And the fact Tyler had a bunch of guys he was still getting to know but could maybe now consider his friends was even better. Although, he wondered if perhaps the Bible study guys felt more comfortable with him because Tim was paving the way.

Outside, there was a rush of autograph seekers, photos, and the like that Tyler hadn't expected for mild-mannered Dan.

"You got some fans, huh?" he said when he and Tim finally reached Dan's truck, an unpretentious vehicle that didn't scream highly paid NHL player.

"People like hockey here."

"Looks like it."

A little later they were sitting in a restaurant, in a darker corner that would normally mean people might know to stay away. But still they came, meek or bold, asking for photographs, autographs, and more.

"You're like a king," Tyler observed.

"It gets a little old," Dan admitted. "It's not that I don't appreciate it or that I didn't know what I was signing up for when playing here, as I grew up not too far away. But it's all-encompassing, so sometimes I wonder how much of my friendships and stuff are really real."

Friendships, as in… "Relationships?"

Dan's lips tightened, and he glanced away. "I don't date. I don't even know how I'd meet someone who doesn't know what I do." He glanced at Tim. "You were lucky meeting Lacey in college."

"Speaking of," Tim said, glancing at his buzzing phone. "I'm gonna get this because it's Lace."

Dan nodded and turned to Tyler as Tim moved away. "How about you? Anyone on your horizon?"

Admit Emma had been on his horizon since day one of meeting her? "No one that should be."

"Should be?" Dan said before taking a sip of some fancy healthy juice. "Why do you say that?"

Tyler shrugged. "I'm not exactly the clean slate a nice Christian girl would be looking for."

"None of us are as clean as we might like to appear," Dan said.

Huh. Sounded like the dude had his own issues.

"But that doesn't mean that God can't still work things out and surprise us with His mercy."

"Yeah, it might help if she wasn't going out with someone else."

"That complicates things, yeah."

There was silence for a moment, until Tim returned, agitation on his face. "That was Lacey. She's upset. Did you know about the Home?" he asked Tyler.

"What about it?" His chest grew tight.

"They're closing it."

"What? No way. What about the fundraising we're doing?"

"Yeah, apparently the trustees were there today, and the board has confirmed that they'll close down the Home in the new year if we don't get the money." Tim glanced at Dan. "It's a kids' home near where we live, where Lacey works. They look after kids in need of fostering."

"What about the kids?" Tyler asked. Poor Lily. Ben. Karinda…

"They'll be rehomed in the next few weeks."

"Wait, does this mean Emma is out of a job?" No wonder she'd been so weary, so troubled, not thinking straight.

"From what Lacey said, it looks like some of them like Emma will be reassigned as they merge the Home with another organization. But some of the volunteers will be done."

"Man. I didn't know. She didn't say anything the other night." Maybe that's why she'd been acting weird. Maybe he shouldn't have been so hard on her. Of course she'd be looking for some comfort, knowing such things. And that hug, that invitation in her eyes that almost made him kiss her, might've just been because she hadn't been thinking clearly.

"Emma?" Dan asked.

"She's the director," Tyler said. Anything more he couldn't—wouldn't—say.

"She's best friends with Lacey. Really solid Christian. They call her Saint Margarita," Tim said, digging into his clams.

Dan's gaze slid from Tim to Tyler. "I can see what you meant before about clean slates."

Had he been that obvious? Tyler shrugged. "She's involved with Nick Grenier."

"Wow." Dan nodded. "That *is* complicated."

"Huh? Since when are Emma and Nick a thing?" Tim asked.

"Since always. Right?"

"First I've heard of it. I know they're friends, but I didn't know it was anything more."

"For real?" Hope flared in his chest.

"For real." Tim grinned, studying him. "Want me to find out for sure from Lacey?"

"No."

"You sure?" Was that a touch of evil in his grin?

"Do it," Dan advised, his smirk suggesting he was enjoying this way too much. "The dude's gonna be sweating until he knows for sure."

That might be true, but it didn't mean he appreciated it being pointed out. "Man, Luc was right. You guys do talk a lot about relationships."

"Life *is* about relationships," Tim said. "With God, with family, with others. Everything we do flows from how we manage those parts of our lives."

"And I thought I was just coming here for the shrimp," Tyler complained.

"Who knew I'd get a show as well?" Dan said with a laugh. "You should call her. Get things cleared up."

"Do it," Tim urged. "Then maybe you and she could join our team for the team trivia fundraising night on New Year's Eve. You get to dress up fancy, and it's for a good cause. How good are you with music trivia?"

"Not bad," Tyler admitted. He could belt out karaoke better than most and knew a stash of random facts about eighties music.

Tyler glanced at his phone. It was too late now, and tomorrow would be crammed full of travel, team stuff, and the game. "I'll see her Friday," he promised. "But don't go telling Lacey. I can't stand more people knowing that I've gotten things wrong again."

HOPES which Tim had ignited were dashed on Friday morning, their day off, when Tyler went to the Home and discovered Emma was gone. "Where is she?" he asked Lacey, who was deputizing once again.

She looked at him sadly, which made him suspect that Tim had kept his word and hadn't told her. "She's gone to see Nick."

"But I thought—"

"You thought?"

"Nothing."

His chest hurt, and he pasted on a smile while he played with Ben and Lily and tried not to notice the yawning gap where Brandon should be. So much for hoping Emma and Nick weren't a thing.

"Hey, Nick. How are you?"

He motioned Emma inside his apartment. "I'm great."

Nick didn't look great. His clothes hung baggy on a frame she'd always thought lean but strong. His eyes were shadowed, and dark whiskers framed his face. His new place didn't look great either. Dishes and clothes were strewn around the room haphazardly, a bio-hazard waiting to happen.

"So, what's been going on?" she asked, putting the container of Mom's cookies and a fresh batch of her cinnamon scrolls down on the table.

"The usual," he said in that same flat tone.

"Which means?" she prompted.

"Physical therapy. Counselling. More therapy. More counselling."

"Which of your friends have called in?" she asked, suspecting the answer was obvious in the room's disarray.

"You're funny."

"Nobody, then?"

"You're, like, the first person in ages who's bothered."

"I wonder why?" she said aloud, as if to herself.

His eyes narrowed. "I don't know why you've come if it's only to insult me. You can do that on the phone, you know."

"I could, I suppose. If you bothered to pick up." She made her perusal of the room obvious. "The place is a dump, Nick. What's going on?"

"I'm too tired to clean."

"Are you? Or are you too depressed?"

He muttered an unsaintly word under his breath. "Thanks for the encouragement, Em. Feel free to leave."

"Yeah, I haven't driven all this way to leave just yet," she said, taking care with her tone, because she wanted to snap.

"I didn't invite you."

"Because you *are* depressed, aren't you?" Her gaze narrowed in on him, catching the flicker in his eyes. "Is that what the counsellor said?"

He looked away. "I don't want to talk about it."

"You don't want to talk about anything. But you need to. You need to know you do have friends, people who care for you."

"Yeah? The only people who visited me after the first week were you and Aunt Leona. And we all know she won't be visiting anyone anytime soon."

The other fun news of the week: Police had laid charges against Leona, charges she probably wouldn't be able to spend much time fighting, seeing as she was in a mental institution. With all the drama at the Home, was it any wonder the board wanted it closed down? Escaping a few hours north was supposed to be a mind-clearing exercise. Too bad it still hadn't cleared most of the clutter in her heart.

"I'm here. Wanting to talk to you. Wanting you to be real. What can I do for you?"

"You mean apart from fix my back? Make my team want to keep me? Make any team want me? You know Buffalo have stuck me on long-term injured reserve. I'm not gonna play again this season. They don't even know if I'll be able to play next year. And you want to know why none of my teammates visit? It's because I remind them of what they could be."

"I'm really sorry," she said softly.

"Yeah, sorry doesn't go far. I've heard plenty of people saying sorry. It hasn't made an ounce of difference. I'm still the same. But you wouldn't know what it's like to feel worthless, useless, would you, Saint Margarita?"

"Don't say that," she murmured.

"It's true, though, isn't it? You're the perfect person, caring for the weak and lame."

"I'm not perfect. Not by any means."

"Prove it."

It was such a stupid, juvenile challenge. But her frustration was so high that she said the first thing that popped into her head. "I tried to make TJ Woletsky kiss me."

He said another word not blessed by heaven. "Are you kidding me?"

"I know. Dumb, right?"

"I...I don't even know where to begin. You do remember that he's the guy who got me into this mess? The guy who made Leona steal that money?"

"Is he, though? See, I know it's not what you want to hear, but the league never found him guilty for anything more than a fair hit on you. So, as much as I can understand you want to blame him, I don't think it's really his fault. Accidents happen."

He said another word not appropriate for the ears of small children.

"And as for your aunt," she continued, "again, she might've said she needed money, but surely if she needed it for you she wouldn't have been trying to board a flight to Hawaii, now, would she?"

"Aunt Leona's always been a little weird," he mumbled.

"She's had a lot on her plate, with so much tragedy this past year. I hope they'll be lenient with her."

"But you—and Woletsky? I've got no words. How—? I can't even. You're crazy if you think you could ever trust him. Didn't he try to commit suicide a few weeks ago?"

"He overdosed on painkillers after drinking too much last month. It brought him to Jesus, so I'm not too upset by that."

"Are you freakin' kidding? Woletsky is a God-botherer now?"

"Miracles can happen."

Another curse darkened the air.

"Maybe we should pray for a miracle for your mouth as well as your back," she suggested.

"You can shove a miracle right up your—"

"Actually, you're the one needing the miracle. But in your back, right?"

"Go away, Em. I'm tired."

"Would you like me to clean your place?"

"No."

"Oh well. I thought it worth asking. I'm going to do it anyway."

That earned her a small smile and wave of his hand. "Feel free. It's only my place, my life. But hey, ignore me. Join the crowd."

"I find it curious, that concept of a crowd ignoring you," she mused, picking up used glasses and coffee mugs, bowls and plates before heading to the kitchen. "Talk of a crowd suggests there are at least some people paying attention to you."

"Nobody who's as annoying as you right now."

"It's a gift I have," she said, placing the dirty dishes next to the sink. "Did I tell you I've done such a superb job with the Home in Leona's place that I've single-handedly shut it down?"

"What?"

"I know." She did another foray of the room, this time

collecting rubbish, with which she filled an empty cardboard box. "The kids are all being moved into other homes if we don't raise enough money by Christmas. You can't imagine just how good I feel about that."

"You love those kids."

"I know," she whispered, her breath hitching. "I really do. And I'm so sad I haven't done what I thought I could do. You've no idea how humiliating it feels to prove yourself to be way less capable than you thought you were. And now these little lives are going elsewhere, and I feel like such a failure, so I'm sorry you don't want me here, but I'm afraid I need to be here for my sake, because I can't stand being there anymore, feeling like I'm such a disappointment." She released a shaky breath.

"That sucks."

"Yeah. So then, to have the mortification of virtually throwing myself at someone like he-who-shan't-be-named, who then turns around and rejects me, well, it just adds icing to the poo cake of my life."

"Why him?"

Admit it was because she'd seen Tyler's tears and heard his prayers for a little boy? Why not? She had nothing left to lose. She told him.

"Bull."

"No. That was on Monday."

"You're serious?"

"Yes."

"Wow." He shook his head. "Well, Woletsky is an idiot. I mean, we knew that before, but he *really* is now."

"I don't think he actually is. I think he's got some other deal going on."

"Maybe he thinks you're too good for him."

"Please."

"I'm serious. You've always had this thing about you that makes guys think you're too good for them."

"I have not. How can you say that? No one's ever asked me out."

"Because they all thought you were out of their league. Until that tool, Dwayne."

Her stomach tensed. "Let's not talk about him."

"You really were solar systems out of his league, which made it such a shock when you went out with him." Nick commented. "Whatever happened?"

"We were not compatible."

"That's for sure. Which is why I can't buy you and Woletsky. Seriously? Come on."

"You don't need to worry. There is no me and Woletsky. I get to continue my long run of striking out with men. Maybe I should become a nun."

"Or maybe Woletsky needs to know you care and that you're not as perfect as everyone thinks."

"What? How can you say that about me? What happened to Saint Margarita?" she mocked.

He eyed her closely and way too disconcertingly. "I wonder if Saint Margarita might be the biggest fraud of all."

She threw a dishcloth at him, and he laughed.

But maybe he was right. Maybe it was time to show Tyler she wasn't to be put on any pedestal.

SATURDAY DAWNED MILDER than the previous days, allowing Tyler the chance to run. This morning's skate was optional, so he'd opted not to, hoping things went as he prayed. If not, then he'd be there. He jogged the couple of blocks to the house he'd visited just over a week ago, wondering if he'd see—

Yes. The blue car was there. His heartbeat escalated. Okay. She was home. She hadn't stayed. Not that he'd expected her to stay over at her boyfriend's—especially now that he'd begun to question whether Nick had ever been her boyfriend in the first place. But what to do…

A car slowed behind him, and he pulled into a stretch, like that was what he'd been meaning to do. Game plan. He'd prayed, but he needed to prepare. Plan out the potential conversation, play by play. Confess he'd been an idiot, admit he wanted more than just to be friends—

"Tyler?"

He jumped. Spun to face Mrs. Moritello, sitting in her car, her window powered down. "Um, hi."

"You here to see Emma?"

"Is she in?" Maybe she'd flown to see Nick. His spirits sank. She probably had—

"She's in. Got in late last night, so she's probably still asleep. But you can come in, have a coffee, some pastries. You liked my cookies, didn't you, last time you were here?"

"I couldn't," he said. "Thank you, but I'm not dressed—"

"You look dressed enough for me. Come on. You haven't come all this way not to talk to her, am I right?"

"Yeah. But whether she'll want to talk to me, especially here at her home…"

"You a man or a mouse? Get in there." She pointed to the door.

Okay, so Antonia Moritello had some intensity he kinda admired. But he still wasn't going to go barging through the front door by himself. Who knew what he might find? A shotgun in his face? Marc's fist? Or worse, Emma's look of disappointment?

He waited until Mrs. Moritello exited the car, collecting her groceries while she fussed at him, admiring the haircut he'd splashed out on yesterday when his plan to see Emma at the Home had taken a detour. He'd also done a few more things to his house but was amazed at how long the hours dragged without people to talk to. He'd even investigated a local pet store, wondering if that might spread some cheer in these last few weeks before the Home disbanded.

"Okay, let's see if that daughter of mine is awake." Antonia went through the door, gesturing him to follow. "Come on. Don't be shy. We don't do shy around here."

Not something he'd been accused of for a while. His entry was met with joyful drooling from the dog. "Hey, Reddy."

"Emma!" she called down the hall. "Are you up? You have a visitor!"

"Mrs. Moritello—"

"It's Antonia, okay?" she said, gesturing him to put the bags on the counter. "No more of this Mrs. Moritello business. That's my mother-in-law, and boy, she was scary."

He chuckled, following her lead as she gestured for him to put away the cold items in the fridge.

"I, on the other hand, would make a great mother-in-law, don't ya think?"

"The best," he declared. "Honestly."

"Right? Huh. I even believe you mean it. I keep telling my kids they need to bring someone home, so I like your style in coming here yourself."

"I really didn't mean—"

"Tyler?"

He turned, his mouth drying, as he placed the carton of milk back on the counter and closed the fridge door. "Hi."

Emma wore purple flannel pajamas with clouds on them, her hair was out and mussed, her glasses off, and she was squinting at him. "What are you doing here?"

"What does it look like he's doing here?" her mom said. "He's helping me with the groceries."

"What?"

"Hurry up. Put some real clothes on, then come and help me with the scrolls. You like cinnamon scrolls, don't you, Tyler?"

"Emma made some on Monday, but I never got to try any."

"Oh, see what you've done to the boy, Emma? You're breaking his heart. Hurry up. Get changed. Then you two can talk and eat my scrolls. Which might be almost as good as Emma's," she added with a wink. "Now, how do you have your coffee?"

"Black."

"Good man. What's the point in hiding the flavor with syrups and stuff?"

"I agree."

"I knew I liked you. Now, tell me about your tattoos while you help me make these scrolls."

He'd just finished mixing the dough when he noticed Emma reappear. She eyed him, then eyed her mom, then looked at the pastry sitting on the blue plastic pastry sheet. "It looks good," she said.

"Tell you what's good is this picture of a lion. Have you seen it?" Antonia called her daughter over. "Go on, Tyler. Lift up your sleeve and show Emma your lion."

"I, uh, can't exactly…" He waggled pastry-encrusted fingers.

"Oh. Well, maybe Emma can help you with your sleeve."

"Mom, he doesn't want to," Emma protested.

"How do you know? Maybe Tyler wants to share about lots of things."

"Maybe he is, but he's not likely to with you around."

Should he point out he was still in the room?

"Am I in the way here?" Antonia demanded of Tyler. "You let me know. I'd love to know I'm bugging my daughter enough that she finally does something about a young man."

"Mom!"

He laughed, then as two pairs of eyes turned his way, had to apologize. "Sorry."

"You should be," said Emma.

"I am. I really didn't mean—"

"Tyler, I'm real sorry, but I'm just gonna have to interrupt you there. If you've got something to say to my daughter, then you need to get the scrolls finished so you can eat them, drink your coffee, and apologize properly. Okay?"

"Yes, ma'am."

"Oh, I do like this one," Antonia said, pinching his cheek. "He's a keeper, Emma, don't ya think?"

He heard Emma sigh and knew her patience was wearing thin. "So, what do we do next?"

Ten minutes later, scrolls were baking in the oven, and he was cleaning his hands next to Emma at the kitchen sink. He noticed her looking at the ink on his arms and wondered if she was as intrigued as her mother seemed to be. Maybe she was repelled and that was why she'd avoided following her mother's instructions earlier.

"Would you like another coffee?" Emma murmured, drying her hands on a kitchen terry towel with a snowflake design.

"Please."

"I'll have a coffee too, thanks, Em," her father said, coming into the room.

"Tony." Tyler dried his hands and shook the man's hand. "How are you doing?"

"I see the girls have roped you in, huh? Don't you have practice or somethin'? You got a game tonight, right?"

"Optional practice, but necessary game." Should he? "I can get tickets if you like." He hoped he could at this late stage, anyway.

"Yeah? Maybe that'd be good. What d'ya reckon, Antonia? Feel like a night on the town?"

Emma shot Tyler another raised eyebrows look. "Are you serious?" she murmured.

"What?"

"Are you trying to charm my parents?"

"Actually, I'm hoping to charm you," he admitted.

"That looks like our cue to leave," said Antonia. "Or at least for you two to leave. Or at least go to the living room while these scrolls finish baking."

"Or maybe go somewhere else," he muttered to Emma.

"Like Timbuktu?" she murmured.

"I'm happy to go there if that's where you'll be."

Her smile flashed. "The living room should do."

He inhaled, then released his breath. And prayed she'd finally hear his heart.

CHAPTER 23

"Thanks, Mom," Emma said as her mother placed on the coffee table a plate of delectably scented pastries dusted with cinnamon sugar.

"Now, don't you mind your father and me. We're going to go out. I suddenly remembered that I haven't gone out with him for breakfast for months—or is it years? Anyway, we won't be here to disturb you, okay?"

Could her mom be any more embarrassing—or any more sweet?

"These look great, Antonia," Tyler said, gesturing to the plate.

"I think so. Must be the help I had in the kitchen, huh?"

"Goodbye, Mom," Emma said, catching the twitch of Tyler's lips, as if he found her mother entertaining. Or maybe he was amused by their family dynamics.

Finally her mom and dad left, and Emma and Tyler were joined by Reddy, who sat at Tyler's feet, patiently eyeing him as if pleading for a crumb of pastry that he might be weak enough to give. She sipped her coffee. "Well, this isn't weird."

"Not at all." Tyler glanced at her and smiled, his amusement provoking her into a reluctant laugh.

"I'm sorry."

"Why are you sorry? You've got nothing to apologize for. This is actually great. Good coffee, good pastries, great company."

Her heart fluttered at the look in his eye.

He took one of the scrolls, his expression melting as he took a bite and ate the pastry with a little moan. "This is good."

"Mine are better," she murmured.

"You might have to prove that to me one day."

"Maybe. One day."

Twinky strolled in, eyed them, eyed Reddy, then leaped onto the opposite lounge chair, her green eyes studying them balefully before she turned to lick herself.

"I don't think that cat likes me," Tyler muttered.

"Twinky doesn't like anyone very much. Except Mom. Good thing Reddy is a fan."

"It is." He settled back onto the sofa. "I gotta say, this is certainly not what I expected when I came running today."

"What did you expect?"

He sighed, put the rest of the pastry down, wiped the sugar from his mouth, and turned to face her more fully.

Oh. So it was going to be one of *those* conversations. She braced internally.

"I went to see you yesterday, but when I got there Lacey told me you were seeing Nick, and it got me all agitated. See, when I went to visit him in the hospital all those weeks ago, I saw you holding his hand, and someone said you were his girlfriend. It took me a while before I connected that girl with you, but by then I thought you were with him, and so I didn't want to get close to you and in the way of you and him."

Her heart flickered. Did this mean he'd held back from kissing her because he'd misunderstood?

"Is there a you and him?" he persisted.

"No. There never has been, there never will be," she assured. "Nick was only ever my friend. I used to tutor him when we were at high school together, and he was my boss's nephew, so we hung out a few times. He's only ever been a friend, that's all."

Tyler exhaled, as if her revelation had taken a great weight from his shoulders. "I've been an idiot, then."

"Or maybe you were being honorable."

Another sigh. "I wish I was. I wish I was the clean man that you deserve, without the stains and scars. Maybe it's dumb to say, but you know I don't do well with filters. I say it as I see it, so I'm just gonna say it." He took in a breath. Released it. Eyed her seriously.

Her heart tensed, her nerves pattering faster, anticipation rising, ready to soar.

"I like you, Emma. I like you, Margarita Anastacia Moritello. But that's the thing. You deserve Prince Charming, and I will never be him."

Hopes that had fluttered high flapped a little slower. "What are you saying?"

"You know who I am, who I've been, and I can't hide that, even though I swear to you I'm not like that anymore."

She nodded. She could see that. God had changed him. *Was* changing him. "None of us are perfect," she whispered.

"But I can't pretend it didn't happen." He took off his sweat-shirt, showed her the ink tattooed on his arms. "This lion your mom likes? I got it when I got drafted first round. I'd promised myself when my family fell apart that I would do that and prove myself brave. This one?" He pointed to a mountain etched on his left bicep. "This one I got to represent that I'm strong. My mom, when she was leaving to start her new life with her new boyfriend, told me"—he swallowed—"told me I was adopted. So my dad isn't really my dad, and I really don't know who I am at all."

"Oh, Tyler." She placed her hand on his arm, her heart aching for him.

"Don't pity me," he growled. "I can't stand your pity."

"Is it pity to say I wish your life hadn't been so hard?"

He exhaled, shrugged. "It can't be changed. It's made me who I am. And though I've been weak in lots of ways, I've survived, and God has been reminding me that I'm stronger than I thought I was. So yeah, this." He gestured to his tattoos. "These show who I am."

"Someone who's strong and courageous."

"Huh. Well, trying to be. But I'm not pretty, Emma. I mean, I know that's no surprise, but this"—he pointed to his forehead —"and this"—then his mouth. "No amount of plastic surgery will make that go away."

He watched her closely as she gently traced the scar on his forehead. She heard his breath hitch as her wayward fingers slipped to the scar above his mouth. "What happened here?"

"Puck to the face. Knocked out several teeth. See?" A minute later he held a plate of false teeth in his hand, and the man she'd seen on TV weeks ago with the gap in his teeth stared at her.

But this man was not that cocky, arrogant person. This was someone who seemed to be doing his best to try to show her why he wasn't right for her. What could she do to convince him that he was?

"Why do you wear it?"

"Because I don't like to scare people," he admitted. "I see their looks of disgust. I see the way people judge me. I'm not going to invite that any more than I have to."

"You don't disgust me," she said softly.

"I should. I'm not right for you. You're too good for me."

"Tyler—"

"I'm not a virgin," he said hoarsely.

She blinked. That was no surprise. "Why do you need to tell me that?" she asked softly.

"Because you deserve the best. And that's not me."

Should she tell him? But how could she let him make a statement like that without sharing some of her secrets too?

He drew back, and she rushed to fill the space where coolness was settling in, the churning inside refusing silence anymore. "I'm not as good as you might think. I'm no saint. I…" She swallowed, licked her dry lips, noticed his gaze fall to her mouth, then lift. "I broke up with my college boyfriend Dwayne because…because he pressured me to have sex with him."

His eyes rounded. "He raped you?" he rasped, eyes ablaze.

"No. I wanted it too. At least, I thought I did. We were at college and he wanted me to prove I loved him, and…and it happened. I got pregnant, and I"—she swallowed—"I had an abortion."

He inched back, and it was plain in that moment that she had lost him. He was disgusted by her. Ironic, considering his background, but men often seemed to hold women to different standards.

"I…I don't know what to say."

"I'm no Saint Margarita, despite what everyone says."

His eyes filled with something that looked a lot like pity. She shrugged, hurt writhing under his sympathy. Then realized this was what she'd done to him. Shame shut her eyes. She could never explain all the ins and outs of what had happened with Dwayne. The heady excitement of his kisses that led to intimacy she'd promised God she would keep for her husband. The horror when she'd realized the consequences. Her desperation to deal with the consequences. She thought she'd dealt with these feelings long ago. God *had* forgiven her. But just the telling of her secret shame seemed to have opened an aching land within. One stupid moment of weakness had stolen so much—her confidence, her trust, her style. Rose was right. She had been different.

Emotion soared, a tangle of feelings—shame, relief, sorrow, confusion—and she inched away. "I should go."

He drew near again, touched her upper arm, wrapped his fingers around her skin. "Is that why you do so much to help others?" he asked softly. "Do you ever feel like you need to make it up to God?"

Her eyes stung, and a boulder filled her throat. She nodded.

"I know I can never make it up to God for all the stuff I've done," he said, his voice raspy. "But as Tim reminds me, isn't that the point of grace?"

Grace. God's goodness, undeserved. She'd always known she hadn't been able to earn her salvation, but had somehow forgotten that friendship with God didn't require her perfection either. She took off her glasses and leaned forward, put her hands over her face, closed her eyes. *Lord, I'm so sorry.*

"I know I'm new at this," he continued, "but something I read yesterday made me think. I don't think God wants us running around driving ourselves into the ground trying to prove to Him or to others or ourselves that we're good enough. God knows we aren't good enough, but we've been made good enough because of Jesus, and surely that should take the pressure off."

What would her life look like if she took off the pressure to perform? If the saint mirage were to finally crumble and fall? Not that she had any intention of living like a sinner, but maybe God's grace was bigger than she'd thought.

"Lacey mentioned the stuff with the kids and the Home. Even there, Em, God's in charge. He loves those kids even more than you do," he assured her. "You might be responsible, but ultimately God is large and in charge. We do what we can, but ultimately we have to trust them to His care."

She nodded, startling as she felt his hand on her back.

A moment passed, and she felt like he must be praying for her, for there was a peace and warmth unconnected to anything she'd experienced with him before that flowed from her back and right through her.

Somehow she managed to pray through the jagged parts of her heart, the clashing thoughts, until there was a sense of rightness with God, and she knew, *really* knew, that the stains of her past need not dictate her future any more. She exhaled. Swiped at tears. Grabbed a tissue when the box bumped her knees. "Thank you."

"Em, I know there are people who could say this so much better than me, but you are special. God thinks you're special. I know, your family knows, the kids know, you *are* special."

Another deep breath. She sat back, her gaze slowly lifting to his.

"And you should be with a man who recognizes how special you are—a man who loves you, who doesn't need you to prove it to him, who is willing to wait. I wish, I *wish* I could be that man."

"Tyler—"

"I wish I'd never done half the things I've done and could be that man instead of being the kind like your ex—selfish, using women. I wish I could be someone who could stand before you now and say I haven't done any of that stuff, but I still choose you."

Her eyes filled.

His fingers lifted to whisk away a tear trickling down her cheek, and she had to fight not to lean into his hand. His touch electrified, and she forced herself to sit very still as his fingers traced her skin down to her chin. "You deserve to be treated as wonderful and special, because you are."

Her heart—her foolish, untrustworthy heart—leaped at his words, at the hope in his eyes. But she'd been proved wrong before.

"I'm not pretty, I'm no catch," he said softly, "but if you'll take a chance on me, then you'll know that I'm yours, only yours, forever."

His words touched her deep inside. Could this humble man really be the one God had for her after all? *Lord?*

Tyler grasped her hand, his fingers drifting over the thin, delicate skin on the back of her hand.

She looked at their fingers twining together. Maybe this could work. Neither perfect. But both living with God's grace, wanting His purpose for their lives.

"Emma?"

Her gaze lifted to his blue eyes, and she could see the hope there. She lifted a hand to his face, and once more traced the scars. He closed his eyes, and she saw his lashes burnished with gold.

"What do you say?" he asked hoarsely.

"I say"—she swallowed—"yes."

"Really?"

She nodded, her heart leaping as sunshine beamed from his grin.

"We'll take this slow," he promised. "You set the pace. No kissing or anything until you're ready. And if that's years, well, that's okay. We'll do dates when we can—oh, that reminds me. Are you free on New Year's Eve? Tim mentioned there's a fundraiser event in the city. Maybe we could go as our first real date."

"We have to wait until then?"

"You want to go out earlier?" He tucked a wayward curl behind her ear.

"What are you doing after tonight's game?"

His lips twitched. "Well, apparently I'm going to be seeing your parents, so maybe we could do dinner together afterward."

"With them?"

"Or without. Up to you."

"I vote without," she murmured.

"So New Year's Eve is a yes?"

"Yes." Maybe Rose could help her to shine like she used to.

"Awesome." His smile lit his face, like a glowing choir boy. "I promise, I'll go as slow as you need. Like, it can be only smiling at each other for the first six months, if that's what you want."

She glanced down at their hands. "I'm okay with this."

"You sure? I don't want to presume—"

"And the occasional hug, too."

"Really?"

She nodded, shifting so she was forced to release his hand as she drew closer and once more stroked his face. His breath hitched, and her chest filled with a hammering like a dozen pixies belting out a tune. "And maybe one day—"

A noise startled her attention to the door.

A second later, Marc appeared, his grin fading as his attention shifted from her to the man she'd been about to kiss. "Woletsky?" He looked at Emma. "Are you for real?"

"Hi, Marc," she said, shifting closer to Tyler so he was forced to put his arm around her. She reached up to grip his hand.

"Marc," Tyler said, gently squeezing her fingers.

"Are you serious about him?" Marc asked her.

She nodded.

Marc's eyes widened, then he turned to Tyler. "Are you serious about her?"

"One thousand percent."

Marc said a word that caused Twinky to hiss. "Wow. Well, you'd better be. You'd better not hurt her, else I'll come find you and hurt you."

"Marc, stop," Emma protested.

"I mean it. We all remember how cut up you were when that loser Dwayne and you broke up years ago. If he does anything to hurt you, I will come and hunt him down." This was said with a stabbed finger at Tyler. Then his brow creased. "Wait, you'd better not be sleeping with her. If you do, I know people with shotguns who aren't afraid to use them."

"Marc, go away," Emma said. "There'll be no sleeping together. Now, go away."

"Is it okay if I sleep with her after we're married?" Tyler said.

Emma gasped as Marc's eyes rounded. "Are you engaged?"

"No!" Emma protested. Tyler wasn't serious. Was he?

"But one day I hope we will be," Tyler said coolly. "If that's going to be a problem, then you need to say so. I won't come between Emma and her family."

"I, uh—" Marc glanced at Emma. "Is he for real?"

Emma cut a look at Tyler, whose face wore the calmness she was coming to love. "I think so."

"Wow." Marc whistled. "Well, as long as you don't hurt her, then I guess I'm okay."

"Good," Tyler said.

"Good," Marc said.

"Great," Emma murmured, smiling at her brother as she snuggled into Tyler's side.

"I LOVE what you've done with the place," Emma said, surveying the inside of Tyler's cottage with a smirk.

He laughed, enjoying her sass. "I like to think of it as minimalist."

"You got that right," she said, glancing around the space, near-empty save for a sofa and a basic coffee table and big-screen TV.

Her smile tugged at his heart, begging him to kiss her, but true to his word, he wasn't going to touch her unless she initiated it. So far their going out had consisted of meeting up twice after games in the city and holding hands while snuggling on the couch at the Home after a big day.

"Look, it's not like I've had time or motivation to do much decorating anyway."

"I wonder what would motivate you?" she asked, moving to the window to gaze over the near-bare yard.

"Well, you know me. Anything for a worthy cause." Like marriage to her. One day. He hadn't been kidding with Marc last week. There was little point being in a relationship if it didn't lead somewhere permanent. And he wanted permanent. He wanted a family. A dog. Kids. Marriage. Her. But there was no point in saying anything more or freaking anyone else out— not until they settled into learning what relating in this relationship meant.

But life was pretty busy for too much in the way of dates, December being filled with games, occasional goals, visits to the Home to do what he could to raise its profile and funds. The grand-a-goal idea was catching on, with a number of other players from New York and other teams matching him and Tim. Each day the funds raised rose a little higher, but Christmas Eve was drawing closer, and the shortfall still seemed too wide.

He'd continued to help out as he could, cutting costs on the kitchen remodel by volunteering with Tim, Andrei, and Desi to rip out the old cabinetry and clean things up so the new kitchen could be installed by the professionals. The brand new kitchen —one of many donations that had poured in—had been destined for a luxury apartment in the city before the owner changed their mind, and a slice and dice of cabinets meant it could be refitted into the space at Hopetoun House. So things were coming together, but he couldn't help wonder if they'd meet the target.

He was there every spare hour, helping Emma and the others, wishing he could do more. Her focus was on the kids, and he didn't regret it one bit, knowing that the lack of closeness was only good for him. Besides, when she smiled at him, his heart filled with such anticipation he was really happy to keep this relationship low-key until she finally wanted more. But spending time getting to know her, talking on the phone and messaging, was something he'd never really done with a woman before. And he loved getting to know Emma, this compassionate woman with a heart of gold who had guts and strength and spoke straight and bold. She might not be a saint, but she was perfect to him. Beautiful, too.

"You doing okay?" he asked softly. He shifted closer. Not as close as he'd like, but he was trying—with God's help—to practice self-control, and just as he was managing his temper, he was managing to harness other passions also. "You've been so busy lately."

She sighed, her hand reaching for his. He threaded her fingers with his own. "I know it's still a week or so until Christmas, but it feels like we'll never reach our target. Last I heard from Lacey, we're still nearly eighty thousand short."

He rubbed the back of her hand with his thumb. "Don't give up. God's in control."

"You're good to remind me." She turned, inched closer. "I've been giving some thought to what you said about what I would do if I wasn't working at the Home."

"And?"

"And I still don't know. Maybe I'm stubborn, but I refuse to believe that all of this is for nothing. What you've done, what Tim and the rest of the team have done, what the guys from that Bible study group of yours are doing, it's amazing."

"God is good, huh?"

"Really good," she said, glancing down at their joined hands. "Hey, Mom wants to know what you're doing for Christmas this year."

"I hope that's an invitation," he dared.

She grinned. "Maybe."

"Only maybe?" He clutched his chest. "You're breaking my heart here."

She laughed. "I think she wanted to make sure you weren't doing anything with your family."

Ah. His family.

"I'm going to guess from that expression that the answer is no, you're not."

"I hadn't planned on it."

"Not even to give them a call?" she said, drawing closer.

"I have zero desire to speak to my mom."

"What about your dad? Doesn't he miss you?"

"Emma, please don't push."

She placed a hand on his arm. "I don't mean to. One day you'll talk, when you're ready. If he's still around to talk to."

He groaned. "Really? Lay the guilt on me, why don't you?"

"I'm sorry," she whispered, wrapping her arms around him.

"I forgive you," he murmured, his words husky as he spoke into her hair.

How much did God want from him? For she was right. Nobody lived forever. And just as she'd convicted him about connecting with his father, her words had seeded another challenge. Maybe it was time to take ownership of his broken past and use it for a greater good.

CHAPTER 24

Monday night before Christmas held a kind of bittersweetness. Quite possibly the last Monday they'd be here at the Home, the shortfall of fifty thousand not impossible but increasingly unlikely as the deadline inched closer. Emma's conversation with Richard earlier that day made it fairly certain that would prove to be the case.

But for now, with the kitchen newly installed and the paint drying, it was enough to enjoy the relative peace of kids in bed, workmen gone, and the chance to watch tonight's hockey game with Lacey and Jacob.

The commercials ended and Emma unmuted the TV.

"And we're back," the announcer said. "Gotta say, there's nothing like competitive athletes with a good cause to ensure a high-scoring game. I'm sure there are lots of fans out there who are really pleased to see this initiative of Tim Carruthers and TJ Woletsky with their grand-a-goal plan to save Hopetoun Children's Home."

"Woohoo! That's us," yelled Lacey, waving her scarf, her shift tonight preventing her from attending the game.

"I don't think I've seen such a high-scoring game between

New York and Detroit in years. It's my understanding that Brent Karlsson has also signed up for this challenge."

"Good thing he's one of the highest paid stars in the league, considering he's scored three goals tonight."

"And here they come back onto the ice now. Hold onto your hats, people. We've still got a wild ride ahead of us."

And a wild ride it was, with shots on goal at both ends getting the commentators and the crowd as excited as Emma and Lacey were. It was fun to get caught up in the emotions, to put aside some of the Home's troubles for a little while at least. Tim scooped up the puck and raced toward Detroit's goalie, flicking the puck through the air to Tyler in a saucer pass. Emma's fingers clenched as he cushioned it then passed it back in a tic-tac-toe sequence that saw Tim shoot at the net. Detroit's goalkeeper blocked it, but the puck went free, allowing Tyler to scoop it up and shoot again. Score!

Emma cheered as the lights flashed and horn blared, and Lacey high-fived her. "That was awesome!" She glanced at Jacob. "Don't you think that was awesome, Jacob?"

"Yeah."

His disgruntled tone drew a roll of the eyes from Lacey, who shoved a chip in her mouth. "I love this chicken flavor."

"Thank the supermarket in White Plains who donated boxloads of them. There was no way we were going to eat them before their use-by date on Friday." Christmas Eve. Her heart tensed.

The game continued, but even while she cheered, another part of her sorrowed at what this would mean. She was trying to have faith, to trust God for her future beyond the Home, but every time she prayed, it still felt like any answers were shrouded in fog. But Lacey was right. God could do miracles, like the fact Brandon had settled in with his new family well. Emma needed to trust God and take each day as it came. One day at a time.

The game finished, with Detroit's Lehtonen scoring one more goal in the closing seconds to break the deadlock and win the game for the Red Wings.

"Huh. Well, if it had to be anyone, it's good it was someone who's part of the grand-a-goal scheme," Lacey said.

"Doug Lehtonen is?" Jacob asked.

"He's one of Karlsson's friends," Lacey said. "So that now makes five thousand more tonight, just from Detroit."

"Plus another four from New York," Emma said. "I hope they all know to deposit it in time," she added.

"I'll send reminders. Every dollar counts."

The TV commentators continued for a while longer, then the camera switched to a reporter beside the ice. "And look, we're lucky enough now to speak to one of tonight's goal-scorers. TJ Woletsky, you must be pleased with your efforts tonight. One goal and an assist?"

"The team put in a really solid effort," Tyler said to the camera. "I'm really pleased to be contributing any way I can, especially scoring goals at this time."

"That's right," the interviewer said. "Tell us a little more about this grand-a-goal initiative."

"Tim Carruthers and I thought this could be a good challenge, a fun motivator to score goals while raising money for Hopetoun House, a kids' home just north of New York City that cares for kids in need. It's had some challenges recently, so we're doing what we can to help keep it open to serve the community."

"You're passionate about keeping this kids' home open, aren't you?"

He nodded, sweat gleaming on his forehead. "Hopetoun House is really close to my heart. Most of you don't know that I was adopted, left on the doorstep of a neighbor's home by my birthmother when I was a baby. I was adopted by a family who gave me the life and opportunities I would never have had otherwise, which ultimately led me to playing in the NHL." He wiped his brow. "These kids might have been betrayed and let down by life, but now they have the opportunity to feel a part of a family at Hopetoun House. I know what it's like to have been rejected, to feel like I'm on the outer and I'll never fit in, and I'm sure there are many watching who have felt that way too. I'm really glad to have partnered with this program and to support them in all kinds of ways. They can really do with our support. Every dollar counts."

He smiled, and Emma's heart caught. This was a good man. How could she ever have misjudged him?

"He's adopted?" Jacob asked.

"Yes."

The commentators continued, their surprise at Tyler's revelation as great as Jacob's own. Tyler nodded. "I really appreciate the opportunity to talk about this. Oh, and because the final decision date is this Friday, I've decided to put my Harley up for auction, with all proceeds going to Hopetoun House."

Emma gasped.

"Did you know about that?" Lacey asked.

"No. He never mentioned a thing." Her eyes watered. What a *good* man.

"Wow," one of the commentators said. "I might even put a bid on that."

"Visit the Hopetoun House fundraiser site set up by Tim and Lacey Carruthers to find out more." He gave the website details. "And hey, I just want to give a shout out to my man Brandon, wherever you are. Miss you, bud. And thanks again everyone for your support." Tyler grinned, saluted the camera, and the screen shifted back to the studio.

Her heart felt like it might explode. What a good, *good* man.

"Emma," Lacey said, staring at her phone.

"What is it?"

"It's trending."

"What is?"

"Hopetoun House is trending on social media." Lacey tapped the screen, then gasped.

"What now?" Emma asked.

"The fundraiser. It's going crazy." Lacey showed Emma her phone. The number was ticking up, by twenty dollars, fifty, one hundred. Then it jumped by one thousand, two thousand, three.

Breath hitched. Maybe they would make it. "Do you think it's Tyler's talk?"

"I'm sure it is," Lacey said. She hugged Emma. "I think we're going to make it."

"Please, God," Emma murmured.

"Amen," Jacob said.

"He's a good guy, isn't he, Jacob?" Lacey teased.

Jacob grunted, slid Emma a look, and sighed. "He's not terrible, I suppose."

"He's amazing," Emma said. An amazing man, open, honest, vulnerable. A Christian man, kind, generous, compassionate. An imperfect man, just as she was an imperfect woman, but one who was growing in God just like she was. Tyler Woletsky was a man she could love.

"Name this song."

Tyler grinned at the look of excitement filling Emma's face. What a whirlwind this past week had been. From the nail-biting rush of meeting the goal and raising the money to having Christmas with the Moritello family, during which he had been strongly encouraged by his girlfriend to call his father. Which he had. And it hadn't sucked as much as he'd thought it would. Then a quick away trip, then two games at home before tonight's New Year's Eve game followed by their charity fundraiser, which involved music trivia here in the Big Apple.

They'd had to squeeze their dates in around their work commitments, which meant plenty of hand holding and even a few of those hugs, even as his body screamed for more. Which was fine. He'd learn patience. Self-control.

"What do you think, Tyler?" she asked him now.

About? Oh, this song. "Sorry, I missed it."

"You've been off in fairyland all night."

"I can't help it. You turned up dressed like that." Her dress revealed curves his body hungered for. But after praying, he'd actually felt a calmness settle on him, even as another part of him delighted in the looks on the faces of the guys. Yeah, he knew he'd punched way above his weight with Emma.

"Guys, we missed it," Lacey complained. "Come on. Focus."

Tyler squeezed Emma's hand, unable to prevent his focus from stealing to her. Tonight had proved fun. Who knew she was so good at music trivia? Between them and Tim and Lacey, they'd had plenty of laughs guessing songs from two-second music samples, finishing the lines, even busting out some karaoke. He'd especially loved it when certain song titles meant he'd had the chance to subtly—or not so subtly—tell Emma more of his feelings.

"Okay," the emcee called. "Who can guess this one?"

Two seconds and Lacey's hand shot in the air. "'*Baby*' by Justin Bieber."

"Well done!"

"Very well done," Tim said, touching his wife's stomach.

"Shh," she said, her glance meeting Tim's, then veering to an open-mouthed Emma.

"Are you saying what I think you are?" Emma whispered.

"I'm not saying anything, not until twelve weeks," Lacey murmured.

"Congrats," Tyler murmured, giving Tim a fist bump under the table. "That's awesome."

He missed what the emcee said next, but couldn't miss the

definitive guitar of the next song. "*'Livin' on a Prayer,'* Bon Jovi," he called out.

"Correct!"

"That's me," Tyler said. "Praying all the time." Praying for patience, praying for grace and self-control. Praying for Emma, the kids, Tim and Lacey. And now he'd be praying for Tim and Lacey's new baby.

"Our next one might prove a little trickier. Let's see who knows this one." The emcee pointed to the sound guy, and there came a techno-dance beat followed by a woman's voice singing, "La, la, la."

"Ooh!" Emma waved. "*'Can't Get You Out of My Head'* by Kylie Minogue."

"Who?" Tyler muttered.

"You," she said, smirking.

"Is that so?" he murmured.

"Correct!" The emcee looked at his cards. "And for our next one, let's listen carefully."

This was a more mellow sound, but it wasn't long before Lacey yelled, "*'Kiss Me!'*"

"Okay." Tim swooped in and obliged, to everyone's laughter.

"By who?" the emcee asked.

"Sixpence None the Richer," Lacey said, fanning herself.

"I like that song," Emma said.

"Yeah?" Tyler murmured. "I think I could like it too."

"Is that so?" she asked, her eyes holding his.

"Mm-hmm. One day. In the meantime, I guess I have to go with some classic U2."

She pivoted to face him more fully. "Such as?"

He slid a hand down her cheek. "*'All I Want Is You.'*"

"Is that so?" she whispered.

"That is very so," he murmured, that soft look in her eyes making him suddenly wish they were alone right now.

"Not '*Take on Me*'?" she queried, her lips pulling up in a half-smile.

"That too. Most definitely."

"Excuse me? Are you two playing anymore?" Lacey asked.

"I'm not playing," Tyler rasped, tugging at his collar.

"Neither am I," Emma said. "In fact, I think I need some air."

"Me too. Weird."

"Very strange." Emma exhaled before turning to Lacey and Tim. "Excuse me for a moment while I, um, go powder my nose."

"Okay. Want company?" Lacey offered.

"Um, no."

"Yeah, I think I'm needing a little break too," Tyler offered.

"Yeah, I bet I know what kind of break you need," Tim said.

"Can't help these things," Tyler said, palms up, grabbing his jacket as he followed Emma from the room.

"Hey, Em. Wait up."

She stopped just outside the ballroom, pivoting on her elegant high heels to face him. "Fancy meeting you here."

"Fancy."

She tugged him to a small alcove, where a window overlooked the gleaming lights of New York, then slid her hands up the sleeves of his white dress shirt. Even through fabric her touch did him in. "Very fancy," he rasped.

"Is it too much?" she whispered.

"No."

Heart hammering, he slid his hands down the sides of the soft fabric of her dress to her waist as she nestled closer, lifting her hands behind his neck.

"I feel like there's something you're trying to say, Miss Emma."

"What do you think I might be saying?"

He bent closer, lowering his head until the plumpness of her lips was just a breath away. He liked to dream about her lips at night when he couldn't sleep, wondering, hoping, dreaming…

"I think you might be saying something like the title of that song."

"Really? Well, maybe I am."

"You might be, or you are?" he murmured.

"Kiss me," she whispered.

"You sure?"

"I love you, Tyler Woletsky," she murmured.

"Really?" His heart filled with golden heat as she nodded. "I love you too."

She smiled, lifting her head so all he needed to do was dust her lips with his for one beautiful, precious second. Then he pulled back.

Her eyes were still shut, her smile sending sparklers through his heart. "Another, please."

This time, he took a little more time to explore her lips, to determine the softness and taste as she reveled in kissing him too. But he wouldn't push too far. He would never let her down. She was far too precious a gift—a gift of most undeserved mercy.

"I never dreamed I'd meet somebody like you," he murmured.

"Are we still playing?" she murmured.

"I'm not." He pulled back, gently cupping her face in his hands. "I love you, Margarita Anastacia Moritello. You are beautiful and perfect to me."

She traced a hand down his face. "You're so sweet."

He grinned. "That's not a word I've heard describe me very often."

"You'd better get used to it," she murmured.

"I still can't understand how someone as wonderful as you could like someone like me. I know I've made plenty of mistakes—"

"Haven't we all?"

"—so I know I'll never be the catch some may think, but I will be yours. Forever. I'm happy to take this slow and one day at a time. But I'm yours. Only yours. And God's, of course."

"Of course," she whispered.

"I love you," he said, bending to kiss her again.

"And I love you, Tyler James Woletsky," she murmured against his lips before sinking into his embrace in a way that suggested there'd be many more to come.

EPILOGUE

May
New York

"And lastly, it's my privilege as the general manager of this wonderful organization to hand out a new award, the Help from the Heart award as initiated by Tim and Lacey Carruthers, to honor a team member who has gone above and beyond during this hockey season. I'm sure many of you, like me, had some reservations about this young man when he first joined our team last year, but you, like me, would also be amazed at the turnaround we have seen in him. His generosity and commitment to charitable organizations has been most remarkable, most notably toward Hopetoun House, which we're all pleased to see is thriving under the leadership of Ms. Emma Moritello, who is here with us tonight."

Emma smiled and waved and squeezed Tyler's hand under the ballroom's table.

"Not only has he made regular visits to Hopetoun House, but

he has also proved to be a hit with a number of fire houses in Manhattan and served at the recent Mother's Day function in the city. In short, his commitment and personal sacrifice has gone far above the usual expectations of our team members. It should therefore come as no surprise that the inaugural winner of the Help from the Heart award is Tyler Woletsky. Tyler, please, come on down."

Tyler grinned, leaned across and kissed Emma, then made his way to the stage as applause from his teammates, sponsors, media, and others filled the auditorium.

He stood there, dressed in a dark blue tuxedo, hair neatly trimmed, the playoff beard all gone. Humble, soft-hearted, battle-scarred, but handsome. Emma's heart swelled with pride.

"As many of you may know, giving of his time isn't the only way in which Tyler has shown his generosity and commitment to those in need, but I suspect he was not aware of our policy to match the donations of players to particular charities. As Hopetoun House has been affiliated with our charitable arm for a number of years now, when this young man auctioned off his beloved motorcycle, we, as an organization, matched that donation, and the amount raised put his donation far above the threshold of what was required. So it is my solemn duty, young man," the general manager said, turning to usher Tyler forward, "to inform you that your motorcycle has now been redeemed and awaits you at the back of the auditorium."

Tyler's dropped jaw as he stared toward the back drew heads around to see what he was looking at. Sure enough, his Harley gleamed there.

"Did you know about this?" Emma asked a very pregnant Lacey. She was due in two months' time.

"No."

"Did you?" she asked Tim.

He shook his head in reply, smiling.

She glanced at Tyler's father but was pretty sure his acceptance of Tyler's invitation tonight didn't equate to having had a hand in redeeming his son's Harley.

"I don't know what to say," Tyler said. "Except thank you." He moved to the microphone. Cleared his throat. "And thank you to the organization for taking a chance on me. I know it was a risk, and I'm really thankful that people like Tim and Coach Koder were patient and worked with me and helped me over a few rocky moments. I'm so very grateful that you persisted." He looked out into the audience, his blue gaze finding Emma's. "And for others, like Emma, I'm truly grateful for your friendship and your willingness to see past the exterior and to love the broken things of this world. You do it with those children every day, and you do it with me. I know I'm never going to be perfect, but I'm so grateful that you love me anyway. And speaking of gratitude, I'm really thankful for my heavenly Father, and the fact that my earthly father is here with us tonight too. Thanks, everyone." He held up the small gold pyramid-shaped trophy. "You've blessed me."

"Wow," Tyler's father said, misty-eyed. "I never thought he'd acknowledge me."

"He loves you," Emma reassured him.

"And he loves you," he said, his lips quirking like Tyler's wry smiles in a way that may not be hereditary but she recognized as inherited all the same.

Later, there was dancing, and the sweet bubble of contentment Emma found with Tyler brought further ease to her heart. So much had happened in the past seven months. And now, with Tyler's time more free and talk of Bible study guys' weddings and the like, she couldn't wait to see where this relationship would go.

Day by day, Tyler was becoming a closer friend, someone she could share with, be honest with, be herself with. Tyler made things real.

"Did you have any idea they'd nominate you for the NHL's

community service award?" she asked him, her hands around his neck as Spandau Ballet's *"True"* floated in the background.

"No." He shook his head, chuckled. "Never would I have imagined that in a million years."

"God is good, huh?"

"So good." His eyes darkened as his smile grew tender. "Never would I have imagined doing this either."

"Waltzing around a room, being lauded by all and sundry?"

"That—even if I don't know what all of that means exactly—but more specifically, you. You're such a huge blessing in my life."

Her heart trembled. To hear this man talk about blessings made her want to cry.

His head lowered, the scar above his mouth glinting in the ballroom's chandelier. "What's wrong?"

"Nothing. Everything is so right. I'm just amazed at how God has changed you."

"Nothing is too hard for God, right?"

"No one is too hard for God." She placed a hand on his chest, and he covered it with his own.

"No heart is too hard, either."

"How perfectly perfect is that?"

And he smiled and lowered his lips to hers, his kiss holding every promise for the future.

THE END

Check out Muskoka Blue, the next book in the Original Six contemporary romance series

Thank you for reading *Big Apple Atonement,* the fifth book in my new contemporary romance series, which combines my love of ice hockey with appreciation for the cities that comprised the NHL's original six teams.

Please make sure you check out the other books in the Original Six hockey romance series, a sweet & swoony, slightly sporty Christian contemporary romance series.

The Breakup Project
Love on Ice
Checked Impressions
Hearts and Goals
Big Apple Atonement
Muskoka Blue

Reviews help other readers find new-to-them authors, so if you can spare a moment to write a quick review at Goodreads / your place of purchase, I'd be very grateful.

I'd love for you to check out my other books and to sign up

for my newsletter at www.carolynmillerauthor.com where you can be the first to learn all my book and contest news, and discover more behind-the-book details and photos.

A huge thank you to the following people for their encouragement and eagle eyes: Brittany, Rebekah, Jana, Bea, Kaye & Becky - I appreciate you all so much! Big thanks to the ladies in my Facebook group, Carolyn's Books & Friends, for all your support in helping promote my books.

Please turn the page for a peek at *Muskoka Blue*, the next in the Original Six hockey romance series.

MUSKOKA BLUE

It was the perfect time to be brave. The sun shone, bouncing brightness off the smooth blue glass of Lake Muskoka. *Musk-oh-ka.* She rolled the word around in her mouth as she drank in the postcard-like scene. Tall, deep-green pines leaned over the shore, watching expectantly, guardians of this beautiful sapphire two hours north of Toronto.

Sarah glanced around. Nobody was here to talk her out of it. Nobody was here to say, "Sarah, are you sure?" and start the second-guessing that was all too familiar now. Nobody was here to see the scars that marked her side and look at her with pity or, worse, ask those questions for which she didn't have answers.

She stepped off the small patch of sand into the water.

"Ah!" She screeched as the icy water bit her skin, pressing her lips together to stop another groan. Of course Canadian summers would differ to those back home—but surely the water should be warmer than this!

Be brave.

Memories flashed: moving to a new country. Singing in front of thousands. Learning to walk again. She lifted her chin.

Took another step. Sun-warmed air made the cold shock all the more, but she plowed on regardless. Things were never as they seemed. Superficial calm could hide pain so deep—

No. *Don't think about it.*

She took another step. Gritted her teeth. Then plunged in headfirst.

The water slapped her face, her chest, her skin tingling in a million pinpricks. She gasped, heaved air past the rocks in her lungs, and sliced her arms through the water. *Stroke. Stroke. Stroke.* Movement eased the chill, bringing a modicum of warmth. Once the icy fire in her lungs abated she could see the red-and-white buoy in the lake and, over on the lake's far shore, small fir and spruce sheltering under the arms of larger trees. Kicking with her good leg, she pivoted to study Aunt Angela and Uncle John's small, homey cottage. It huddled under a pair of poplars cathedral-high.

She glanced across at the three-story mansion next door, all gleaming windows and big fancy deck. It even boasted its own hot tub, little jetty, and cute red boathouse. She made a face at it and turned toward the buoy, forcing her left leg to kick like her physical therapist back home had taught her and slowly carving her way closer.

Her hip felt better today. Maybe those sadistic exercises over the past two years were working. Her hip hadn't seized up for… almost four days. Not since that ultra-embarrassing episode on the plane when she'd started cramping halfway through the sixteen-hour flight from Sydney to Vancouver, needing sedation to stop her gasps and whimpers from scaring the other passengers. Her skin crawled at the memory. Cowering in the aisle. People staring, probably thinking she was deranged. Bile rose—

No. She sucked in a breath. *Don't think about it.*

She scooped her way closer to the buoy bobbing happily in the lake. Fifteen meters. Ten. Five. And touch. She began treading water as a smile threatened to escape. Yes. She'd done it. Victory.

She flipped over onto her back and gazed at the blue bowl of sky, cloudless, open to the heavens. "See, God? See what I can do without You?"

No answer, but that wasn't surprising. God had stopped answering her prayers eighteen months ago. He certainly wasn't going to start talking now.

Sarah closed her eyes. The splash of water played against her ear as she floated, drifting like a broken stick on the sea. It would be so easy to stop trying, to cease this struggle to stay afloat, to just let go and sink to the bottom of a foreign lake…

She frowned. Except if she did, her parents and sister would be devastated. And her aunt and uncle would never forgive themselves for going into town today. And anyway, she'd already spent way too long at the bottom.

Be brave.

She opened her eyes—and stared straight up into a pair of deep brown ones.

Bump. Her head hit something hard. Then water filled her nose and she was underwater, long strands of red hair swirling in front of her. Her heart hammered: *Can't breathe! Can't breathe!* Hands grabbed her upper arms. She clawed at them. The pressure released. Her head broke the surface and she spat out water. Gulped in precious air. Saw the brown eyes again. Kicked away.

Her hip cramped, the spasms shuddering up her left side. "Ow!"

"Hey!" The man stretched a scratched hand toward her. "Want a hand?"

She shook her head and tried to swim away. Dumb move. Her hip was on fire, her left leg a dead weight. Drowning wasn't on the agenda today. *Oh God, please help me!*

"It's at least a hundred meters to shore. Can you make it that far?"

Cramps continued ratcheting up her side. Sarah bit back a moan to study the shoreline. She gulped. Glanced back.

The man leaned over the boat's side, dark eyes concerned. "Do you need help?"

No. She was sick of people needing to help her all the time, sick of being pathetic, sick of being sick. But something in his face suggested kindness. And hopefully he'd be like all those plane passengers and she'd never see him again either. "Yes."

Sarah inched her way to the side of the boat. The man reached down, grasped her right hand, and hauled her up like she was a feather. Her knees scraped against the metal rim, then she landed with a grunt in the bottom of a sleek, modern runabout. She eased into the seat he gestured to, pressing deep into her side as she glanced about. Fishing rods were propped into narrow slots, their lines stretching taut into the water. The smell of bait penetrated her nostrils, threatening to send her insides out. She fought the nausea and studied her rescuer.

Brown hair, unshaven jaw, tanned skin, dressed in a scruffy beige T-shirt and khaki shorts—he looked very…brown, like an advertisement for Mr. Wilderness. Judging from the muscled arms he'd used to haul in her not-so-dainty self, he probably wrangled bears in his spare time while off camping somewhere hundreds of miles from civilization—and a decent coffee shop. She drew up her knees and wrapped one arm around them, grasping the side for balance as the boat gently rocked.

"I'm Dan." He smiled.

Her heart fizzed. Good-looking guys always made her feel tongue-tied, like she was still the pale ugly duckling she'd been years ago in high school. "Uh…" She swallowed against the squeakiness. "I'm sorry."

His mouth curled up one side. "Well, hello, Sorry."

She blinked. "I meant I'm sorry for scratching you." She

motioned to his gouged hands. "I didn't know what was happening."

He shrugged, his gaze dropping to study her knees. "You're bleeding."

"I'll be right."

"As long as the sharks don't get a whiff of it, we'll be okay."

"Sharks?" Her eyes widened. "There aren't any sharks around here." Were there?

"Hey, I need an excuse for the lack of bites today. Not everyone will believe a mermaid chased them all away." He turned to reel in a line.

Her cheeks heated. There was a limit to how much apologizing one person should do per lifetime. "I was just trying to get to the buoy."

"Did you say boy? What boy?" He frowned and moved closer to the front of the boat, stripping off his shirt as he scanned the water. "Why didn't you say so?"

She blinked. The man's torso screamed muscle definition.

"Hey!"

Her eyes snapped back up to his face—his frowning face.

"Where'd you see him?"

"Who?"

He muttered something under his breath and shook his head. "The boy!"

"What boy? I meant that buoy!" She pointed to the red-and-white floating structure.

"Huh?" He blinked. "You mean the boo-ey?"

She nodded.

He stared for a moment, then cracked up, his laughter echoing around her.

She stiffened, his mirth layering new ice around her heart. Laughing off teasing was like worship leading—she couldn't do either anymore. She studied the lake's far shore until a huge shiver betrayed her self-control.

"Hey."

She looked back, and he gently lobbed a blue towel at her. "Get dry, then you can show me where you belong."

Sarah wrapped the towel around her shoulders, huddling into its soft warmth as his words pierced her soul. Where she belonged? How about back home in Sydney, or maybe in PNG? Better yet, next to Stephen—that was where she really belonged. Grasping the ring on her left finger, she blinked away the hot sting in her eyes.

Be brave.

Dan started the engine, then glanced at her, amusement still sketched on his face. "Now, where shall I take you?"

Throat clogged, she pointed to the jetty belonging to the big house next door.

He raised an eyebrow. "Really?"

She tilted her chin at his odd look, then nodded before glancing away.

The boat's motor throbbed as it quietly cruised the short distance to the dock. He pulled up, killed the engine, tossed a rope around a pole. The boat rocked as he hoisted himself out onto the dock, then he turned back to her, a hand outstretched. "M'lady."

Was he still making fun of her? She stood, carefully folded the towel, and left it on the spare padded seat in the back, moving gingerly as the boat dipped and swayed.

"Here, take my hand."

She grasped his hand and clambered onto the dock, wincing as her hip protested the sharp movement.

He glanced down at her leg, eyes widening as he saw her scars.

Humiliation flowed, lava-hot. Why hadn't she worn board shorts today? She backed away, turning to hide her degradation. "Thank you."

"You're welcome." His smile made her heart quiver.

Stop. She had no right to find another man attractive. She forced herself to walk slowly away and not scamper like she wanted. *Don't look back, don't look back—*

"See you around."

She glanced back to where he stood, hands on hips, mouth still tilted on one side. "I doubt it." She tossed her hair and veered off onto a stone-strewn path that led to the cottage. And tripped.

Scrambling to her feet, she swiped hair from her hot cheeks, ignoring his yelled, "You okay?"

She picked up pace, heedless of the small bushes slapping her legs.

Forget trying to be brave.

Now was the perfect time to run away.

###

"Look who I found!"

Dan swallowed a smile as the woman in the hammock jerked, blinking, her eyes widening as she peered from her aunt to him. Yep. He'd felt much the same when Angela had called earlier—his melted muscles protesting, brain rebooting too slowly after his nap to make sense of her invitation at first.

"Dan, this is my niece, Sarah Maguire." Ange's fine features melded into a slight frown. "Sarah, you remember me telling you about Daniel Walton, don't you?"

"Um, no." Sarah's gaze flicked from her aunt to him. "Hi."

"Hey." He dipped his chin. "So, you're not 'Sorry' after all."

Her lips twitched, then her gaze skimmed away, back to her book.

He turned to her aunt. "We met yesterday and had a slight miscommunication over boys and buoys."

Ange's eyebrows rose, and she stared at Sarah, blue eyes wide.

Sarah shrugged. "I didn't think it worth mentioning."

She didn't, huh? His lips notched up another degree. "Ange invited me to dinner."

Ange nodded, the June sun bouncing off her wavy auburn hair. "Dan is staying next door. No doubt you'll come across each other occasionally."

"Next door?" Sarah squeaked.

He nodded. *That's right, Princess. Trying to bluff your way onto my dock, saying that's where you belong.* He knew a moment's satisfaction to see her so disconcerted, followed by a ping of relief that she wasn't some crazed stalker fan, as some of his teammates had occasionally dealt with. Muskoka was for relaxing, not wondering about who might be out to find him.

He rolled his eyes at himself. Please. Like he was any real celebrity.

Movement behind him signaled John's arrival. "Dan. Good to see you, my friend."

"Hey, John." He gripped the pastor's hand. He'd first met John and Ange McPherson when he'd started attending their Toronto church, then they'd moved here five years ago. His living here over summer meant they were still his pastors more than anyone else. It was often hard to get to church once the season's schedule released. "How are you doing?"

"Can't complain. You?"

Dan shrugged. "Can anyone complain when they wake up to that view each day?"

"God's country."

"For sure." He glanced back to where Sarah was gingerly sitting up in the hammock. "So, is it true?"

"Pardon?"

"'I'd rather be reading…'" He quoted the phrase emblazoned on her T-shirt.

She nodded, clutching her book to her chest as the hammock began a wild swing. Then, before he could blink, she'd rocketed from the hammock only to stumble at his feet like a beggar.

"You okay?" He offered a hand to help her upright.

"I'm fine," she muttered, ignoring it.

"Falling for me, eh?" he teased.

She stiffened, startled green eyes shooting to meet his before she ducked to collect her book. "Excuse me." She slid open the glass door and slipped inside.

He turned to John and Ange, eyebrows raised.

"You must forgive her. Sarah has…well, let's just say things haven't been easy for her." Ange eked out a smile. "She may be a little prickly at times, but she used to be one of the warmest, loveliest girls you could ever hope to meet."

"Uh huh." Uh oh. He appreciated his pastors, but not Ange's hopeful look, nor where this conversation seemed to be going. Better change the subject. He nodded to John. "We'll have to go fishing soon." The fish seemed to like John, almost leaping onto his line whenever he was out.

John's expression lightened. "That'd be good."

Fishing consumed most of the conversation for the next half hour as the sun began its slow descent through the pines. An aroma of garlic and onions tickled his senses, digging anticipation for when they finally sat down at the dining table.

Dan gestured to the vase of pink and red roses Ange slid to the table's end. "They're pretty." And looked expensive.

"Sarah gave them to me for my birthday yesterday. And a voucher for the Muskoka Shores spa, too."

He nodded. "Did you enjoy your day?"

"How could I not? We had a lovely meal at Muskoka Shores, thank you." She patted his hand. "You and Sarah are both so sweet and thoughtful."

"Glad you enjoyed."

Sarah plunked a steaming dish of lasagna onto a heat pad in

the middle of the teak table, then slipped into the vacant seat, opposite Dan. She didn't look at him.

"That smells fantastic," Dan said. "Is this another secret family recipe, Ange?"

"Ask Sarah. She made this."

He eyed the cook. Nope. Still not playing.

"Let's give thanks." John reached across the table to hold his wife's hand.

Dan reached across to grasp Sarah's hand, her soft fingers barely holding his as her uncle prayed a blessing on their food. As soon as John finished, she dropped his hand like a hot tong. The action lowered his defenses a fraction more. Yeah. Definitely not like some of those other women.

The next minute was a frenzy of plate passing as they loaded up with garden salad, garlic bread, and the baked pasta dish.

He forked it in. Nearly moaned. "This is really delicious. Sure beats whatever I would've had to throw together."

Sarah seemed surprised, then pleased. Well, she didn't smile exactly, but her features eased a little.

He took a sip of water. "So, do good cooks run in your family?"

A glimmer of amusement touched Sarah's face before she replied solemnly, "I don't think Ange runs, and I prefer swimming."

"I meant—oh, right."

Huh. A flash of humor.

The meal progressed amid polite nothings about the weather, the tourists, and what had changed in past weeks. Sarah seemed to be relaxing, peeking at him every so often like she wasn't sure what to make of him. That made two of them. He wasn't used to women so aloof they could be mistaken for an ice princess.

He took a sip of water and eyed her. "So, Sarah, your accent tells me you're not from around here."

"No."

He swallowed a smile along with his mouthful. "Where did you grow up?"

The green eyes met his warily. What had her so withdrawn?

"You don't have to answer if it's too personal."

"It's not that," she finally said, glancing at Ange. "It's not easy to condense into a sound bite."

"Try me."

She studied him a moment longer, then gave the tiniest nod. "Papua New Guinea."

"Seriously?"

"Yes."

"Wow." He leaned back in his chair. "I don't think I've ever met anyone who's been there."

"I was a missionary kid." She sipped her water, eyeing him over her glass. "My dad is from the US, Mum is from Australia. We left PNG when I was twelve and moved to Sydney, where Dad pastors a church."

"So that accounts for the accent."

She shrugged. "Growing up between various cultures always marked me as somewhat strange."

"Oh, Sarah, you don't still believe that, do you?" Ange protested.

Another shrug.

He studied her. He didn't think her strange. Intriguing, maybe, despite the prickles and frost.

John motioned to Dan's nearly empty plate. "Help yourself, Dan. There's plenty more."

"Thanks." Dan served himself another portion of lasagna, then glanced at Sarah again. "You're pretty lucky having family in different parts of the world."

"I think it's important to encourage family members to live in places one would like to visit, if at all possible."

He nodded. "Amen."

The rest of the meal continued with conversation with Ange and John, Sarah answering the occasional question in monosyllables. What was her deal? Was she shy? Proud? No, the self-deprecating humor suggested otherwise. He stole another look. She was pretty, with that milky skin and glowing hair, but seemed pretty cold, too. Glacial, even.

He was still puzzling it over when Sarah excused herself to go wash dishes.

"I'll help you," he offered, pushing back his chair.

"Thanks, but I don't need help."

You sure about that? He bit back his response, instead passing his empty plate across as she requested. Light flashed from a ring on her left hand. She was engaged.

Later, after Sarah had pleaded a headache and said goodnight, Dan joined Ange and John for coffee on the deck. He slouched into his seat, the pungent scent of Ange's homemade anti-bug lotion tickling his nose. Distant lights twinkled from across the lake as the breeze sighed through the pines. He rolled his shoulders, trying to release the tension.

"So, Dan." John placed his mug on the table. "How long will you stay in Muskoka?"

"I've got two months before duty calls me back. How about you? Do you get much of a break this year?"

John's graying head nodded slowly. "A few weeks."

"You deserve it."

John gave a tired smile. "For once, I think maybe we do."

The night sounds grew louder—the hum and whirr of crickets and cicadas, the lake's gentle wash, the slap as a mosquito found a patch of unprotected skin. John and Ange sat at the table, the porch light revealing the strain of the past few years in the fine lines around Ange's eyes.

John reached over to hold her hand. "At least Sarah's here."

"I didn't realize how hard she was still—" Ange bit her lip and glanced over at Dan.

"God can work things out for good," John murmured.

"I know." Her eyes sheened as she nodded. "We keep believing."

Dan chewed his lip. The past two years had been tough for them as they'd struggled through church issues, the funerals of friends, and some family drama for which Ange had gone away for several weeks. He'd spent many hours praying for them, had upped his weekly offering and sent them anonymous gifts and donations for their own needs. John and Ange were good people and a blessing to so many. They really needed a break.

Dan stretched out his legs. "So, what's her deal?"

His pastors glanced at each other. So, there really *was* a deal. He'd found it oddly amusing, the bedraggled kitten with the big green eyes and claws that he'd plucked from the lake who then turned her nose in the air and her personality down to frozen. But the earlier glimpses of humor and generosity had signaled Sarah's personality might be more like her aunt's than the initial ice princess act had suggested. So, what had happened?

John steepled his fingers. "Sarah was…hurt a while back."

Oh. Remorse bit as he remembered her scars. And judging from the tension he sensed, any explanation was likely complicated. Still, she was engaged, so life couldn't be all bad. The knowledge she was engaged eased a knot of concern. He must've misread Ange's look earlier.

"Have you heard of Heartsong Collective?" Ange asked.

"The music ministry with all those albums, right?"

"Sarah was involved with them for a few years. She was one of their best…" Ange's voice faded as she glanced at him, then offered a wobbly smile. "Excuse me for a moment."

She left, leaving Dan to exchange glances with John, who murmured, "She's okay."

"You sure?"

Apprehension lifted at John's nod. Dan took another sip of coffee, then plunked his mug on the table. Change of subject time. "So, John, are you free to go catch some walleye later this week?"

"Just tell me when."

They discussed details, and Dan gave a small smile of satisfaction. Yeah, even with an ice princess around, this summer would be good. Water, sun, fish...what could be better?

Purchase your copy of Muskoka Blue today!

ABOUT THE AUTHOR

Carolyn Miller lives in the beautiful Southern Highlands of New South Wales, Australia, with her husband and four children. A long-time lover of romance, especially that of Jane Austen, Georgette Heyer and LM Montgomery, Carolyn loves to write contemporary and historical romance that draws readers into fictional worlds that show the truth of God's grace in our lives.

To find out more about Carolyn's books, and to subscribe to her newsletter, please visit www.carolynmillerauthor.com

You can also connect with her at

<u>Regency Brides: Promise of Hope</u>

Winning Miss Winthrop

Miss Serena's Secret

The Making of Mrs Hale

<u>Regency Brides: Daughters of Aynsley</u>

A Hero for Miss Hatherleigh

Underestimating Miss Cecilia

Misleading Miss Verity

'Heaven and Nature Sing' from the Joy to the World Christmas
novella collection